Commit To Memory

Second Edition published 2026

Cover design by Morgan Warju

ISBN: 978-0-9890153-0-1 (Paperback Edition)

ISBN: 978-0-9890153-1-8 (Digital Edition)

Acknowledgments:

Thank you to every English teacher I've ever had, who encouraged me.

To Mary Jane, Mom and Dad for the edits.

To my family and friends for all the support. To Dave and my children, whom I love most of all.

To anyone reading this book. This means the world to me, and I am thankful to have people appreciate it.

And to those in my life who never got to see this dream realized, I love you and miss you every day.

Commit to memory:

My name is Jackie Dawes and I have amnesia. I'm probably reading this right now, so if I am, that means I've had another episode and I can't remember anything. Should this journal find its way into hands that aren't my own, it is vital that I get it back. My current address is written in the cover, as is a phone number.

I live in New York, or at least, that's the city I keep waking up in. I live with two amazing people, Archie and Maxine. Archie has an appreciation for the 1980's, and mostly communicates through a small note pad, however, once in a while you'll hear him spout lyrics. Strictly 80's, of course. Maxine is transsexual, but she's like a mother to me, and since I don't know who my real mother is, she's the best thing I've got.

I woke up yesterday morning on the subway with no memory. Maxine was sitting next to me, but I had no idea it was her, and I escaped from her, running through the city, before I fell on some steps and scraped up my arm. Maxine told me we were going home from the hospital where I had just had an MRI and my doctor, Dr. Karish, can't find any damage to my brain. However, I've forgotten my past, and my new memories don't stick, so there has to be something wrong. He suggested I see a therapist to talk about my condition, which I did today. Her name is Karen Novak. She told me to start a journal in an effort to help me remember things when I have what Maxine refers to as an episode. I must record every fact about myself, every thought I have and every experience, regardless of whether it's good or bad, doctor's orders. I need to know who I am. It is important that I write this down because there's no telling if I'll remember it tomorrow.

1

"Don't you want me baby?"

The man's questioning voice startled me. My head snapped up from where it had been resting against my chest. I looked up and judging by the crick in my neck, I'd been sleeping for a while. How long exactly, I wasn't sure. I suddenly noticed I was sitting in a padded office chair facing a computer screen that was showing an almost completely blank document. I squinted and leaned forward to read it: *Commit to memory.*

I felt my face scrunch. Commit what to memory? There was nothing else there. Why did I type that, assuming I typed it? I had no idea what needed to be remembered, so how could I have typed it? The words seemed so strange to me. I heard that voice again that reminded me I wasn't alone.

"Girl you know it's true. I love you."

I turned around to see who was talking. In the distance of this spacious room, in a kitchen area was a man talking on the phone. I felt a sigh of relief because I had been hoping he wasn't talking to me. I stared at him; he was wearing a dark purple silk jacket with the sleeves pushed up and the collar popped. His hair was tidy and gelled and there was a pair of sunglasses on his head. He was pacing back and forth, indicating his phone conversation was not going well.

He set the phone down and walked back into the large room I was in. He sat on the couch, put up his feet, smiled at me and turned on the TV. I turned back around in my chair, listening to the noise of the TV, and looked back at the computer screen. *"Commit to memory"*. I wondered if this –all this: the computer, the guy, this living space –made any sense to me, before I had fallen asleep.

I sat quietly and tried to assess the situation: I was in some sort of apartment or loft that I supposedly knew, with a guy I also supposedly knew, and I had absolutely no recollection of any of it.

My body was ready to panic, but I reasoned myself out of it. I deduced that this was either my apartment or a friend's place, possibly that stranger on the couch, and if this was indeed a place I was supposed to be familiar with, it was probably in my best interest if I at least pretended. In keeping cool, I decided to start thinking about the basics: my name, my age, my location.

My name.

Name.

I didn't know my own name. I didn't know any of the basics. I tried to think hard of any sort of memory of anything or anyone at all.

Nothing.

I slowly started hyperventilating. Should I ask that guy? Would he just laugh at me?

I decided to memorize the room while I worked up the courage to ask this "stranger" who I was. I guessed it was a newly inhabited environment, as there wasn't much in it: only a few books on the shelf, a lone plant resting on the windowsill and a few picture frames here and there. The desk I was sitting at seemed like the most popular spot in the apartment. There were empty cups and candy wrappers about and a few papers, but I noticed they, like my mind, were blank. I stared at everything. Nothing looked familiar at all. I turned to face the guy on the couch. The couch was modern-looking with a low back and an ocean of cushions protruding from it. He looked like he was floating among them. He looked at me as I opened my mouth to speak.

Thankfully, I heard the door open before I could say anything embarrassing. Both our eyes shifted from each other to the door. He didn't look as concerned as I did. He knew who was coming, while I peeked over the chair, nervously excited to meet someone else.

"Ugh! Sorry I'm late. Lee's took forever! But I've got sushi!"

The voice began before the door opened, and in stepped a woman in a sequined tube top and tight red leather pants. She wore a printed vest and her long brown curls were pulled tightly into a ponytail on the top of her head. Her face was painted thick, and as if she wasn't already a good six feet tall, she towered in a pair of platform heels. The paper bag I guessed was full of sushi looked tiny in her giant hand. She unloaded a huge purse from her shoulder and began distributing the food, starting at the couch.

"Here you go, sweetie." I suddenly perceived her strangely deep voice. It didn't seem to match the person.

"Domo Arigato, Mr. Roboto."

I distorted my face. I'd heard that phrase before. Wasn't that a song lyric? Come to think of it, what he said earlier on the phone sounded like lyrics I'd heard somewhere. I pondered each phrase. I wasn't positive, but I was sure those were Eighties songs. Well, now this was strange. How was it that I couldn't remember anything about myself, yet I could recognize songs from the Eighties?

I decided now would be a good time for a mental inventory. Things I did know, and things I didn't. I knew the date. I knew what year it was. I knew basic skills like math and proper grammar, I apparently even had an extensive memory of song lyrics, but I couldn't place my own name. I had been so much in my own head, I hadn't even noticed the box of sushi at my face and the woman talking to me.

"Hello? Anybody in there?"

I blinked back to reality and smiled a bit. If she only knew.

"Take your sushi, Jackie," she demanded.

Jackie! Was that my name? She certainly seemed to be talking to me. I wondered why it wasn't ringing any bells at all.

I took the box and opened it. I couldn't remember if I liked sushi, but I assumed since she brought it to me, I must. However, the smell alone was enough to churn my insides. Quickly, I picked up a piece and popped it into my mouth. I noticed she was still staring at me, watching me chew that repulsive, papery sludge.

"What the hell, Jackie? You act like you've never eaten sushi before." I couldn't even mask my disgust as I continued chewing.

"Is this paper?" I asked, pulling a strand of black waxy seaweed from my mouth. She stared daggers into me, while simultaneously grunting in laughter.

"Jesus, Jackie. What's with you?"

I laughed to recover quickly. "Just kidding," I smiled, shoving another piece in. It was just as gross the second time, but I had to keep the façade. She wasn't buying it at all.

"Are you okay?"

I nodded. She looked away. I decided to be more involved in my lie. I clicked an "X" in the corner of the computer document and it asked me if I wanted to save what had been written. It was only four words, so I saw no point, but it was an unusual phrase, so I thought for a moment. Glancing down, I found a notebook, which I opened with the intent of writing it down. Amazingly, the words were already there, on the front page of the notebook. I imagined I must have written it down earlier, but every curve of every letter was completely unrecognizable. I supposed someone else could have written it, but who would? I shut down the computer–surprised that I did know basic computer skills-closed the notebook and joined the other two on the couch.

"So, Arch, how did it go with Thea?" the woman asked. The guy shook his head.

"Oh, I'm sorry, honey. It's okay. You'll meet someone better."

I tried to focus on what we were watching, but my mind was stuck on "Jackie". I just found it so odd that hearing my name didn't sound familiar. I couldn't even remember someone ever calling me that before.

I jumped slightly when I heard the other two burst with laughter. Something funny had just happened on TV. I laughed too late, only to notice her eyes on me.

"Jackie, are you sure you're okay?"

I nodded again, but I knew she didn't believe me. *I should just fess up*, I thought, *but it's just too embarrassing*. I got up off the couch and started for the kitchen, but she grabbed my arm and pulled me into another room. She seemed to understand my need for discretion, shutting the door behind her.

"Okay, what's up? Don't lie to me, Jackie. Something's bothering you. You're acting like you don't remember me." I looked into her eyes when she said that. Her eyes bulged. "Oh my God, you *don't* remember me?"

I shook my head, so mortified, my eyes welled up. She wrapped her arms around my head, pushing me close to her chest.

"It's alright, honey. Just tell me what happened."

"I don't know."

"Well, did you hit your head or something?" She touched my head, feeling for lumps.

"I don't know."

"Does anything hurt?"

"Just my neck a little from sleeping in that chair."

"Then why don't you remember me?"

I straightened up, wiping my eyes and taking a deep breath. "It's not just you; I don't remember anything. I woke up at the computer; apparently, I'd been writing and fell asleep. I found a few words typed, and that guy was talking on the phone. I have no idea where I am, who I am or who either of you are."

"Maxine," she said pointing to herself. "Archie." She pointed to the door.

"So, you seriously don't remember anything about yourself at all?" She seemed more intrigued than anything. I shook my head and she nodded. "Okay," she began. "Let's see… your name is Jackie Dawes, you don't have a driver's license because we live in New York, or at least, I've never seen you with one. I don't know where you came from, but you never talked about your past, so I never asked. You do have a cute little t-shirt that says "Florida" on it, so I suppose you could have come from there.

Um, you work at Brandisham's Boutique, you *used* to like sushi, and we like to hang out at The Corner Nook a lot, which is a little café not far from here."

She folded her hands in her lap, but I wasn't entirely satisfied.

"That's it? That's all you know about me?"

"More or less," she answered. "But Jackie, you've only lived with us for three weeks. We don't know if you've been here in New York very long, but you just showed up here one day with our ad circled in the newspaper. Archie and I haven't had much time to know you, but that's the long and short of it."

"And you just let me stay, no questions asked?" I started to cry, because now I was just scared.

"Who are we to judge anyone else?" Maxine continued comforting me, and after a long while she advised me to walk around the bedroom, hers apparently, so I could regain my composure, and mull things over. So, now I had a name, but no identification, a job, and I had a place to live and a couple of roommates, neither of whom knew anything about me past the last three weeks. Maxine did seem to think I'd hailed from Florida. I wasn't so sure; hot weather didn't sound appealing. I may have come from Florida, but I certainly wasn't from there. Then again, I supposedly also liked sushi before.

"So, this is your room?" I asked, trying to calm down. She nodded and smiled proudly.

I stood up and looked around. The walls were a light shade of lavender with a couple of huge posters pasted to the walls. They were old-fashioned advertisements for nightclubs. The bed was enormous, taking up most of the floor, and the room was lined with dressers, all different sizes and shapes, all the same deep - almost black- purple. Each one had on top a mannequin head or two, decorated with colorful wigs and scarves, and picture frames to fill in the spaces. There was a closet in the corner with no door, but rather, a red silk embroidered curtain. Directly next to it was a large vanity desk packed with various supplies and a great mirror outlined in round bulbs. I imagined her sitting there every day, looking and feeling like a glamorous movie star. She pulled me around the room to each dresser, showing me the pictures.

"See this one? This is me and Archie at Halloween last year. I was Tina Turner and he was Prince. And this one here is my mama and sister Penny. And this one is of my girls at the club: Serena, Angel, Carmelina and Sasha. Oh! And here's one of you. You were helping me pick out an outfit for a date, and my camera ran out of film and you put in a new roll and as you handed it to me, it snapped and took this great shot of you!"

I looked at the photo. It was almost completely blurred with streaks from the mirror lights, but then, in the middle in clearer blurriness was my face, looking downward. I did notice that there was a small indent under my ear in the photo, so I held it close to my face, and then touched my ear, feeling for it.

"Your scar?" Maxine asked.

"Yeah. How did I get it? Is it really noticeable?"

"It's not terribly noticeable. I don't know how you got it, you never said."

I held the picture away and looked at the face as a whole. I knew it was me because she said it was, but I didn't recognize me at all; I had even forgotten what I looked like. I had to admit I was slightly disappointed. I wasn't ugly, I just wasn't very stunning. I was average.

Maxine kept going. "Here's one of you, me and Archie on the first night you moved in. We were celebrating. And this one is of you and Archie sitting on the couch. I wanted to use up the roll so I could get it developed." Even a clear shot of me looked average. Again, more disappointment crept in. I think she could tell, so she distracted me with more photos.

"This one is of my sister and me about ten years ago." This photo caught my attention. I had expected to see two girls in the picture, but I saw a chocolate-haired girl and next to her was a boy with no hair and piercings in his nose and eyebrow. His face looked familiar. I looked at her.

"Is that you?" I asked.

"Yeah, silly," she smiled. "That was before."

My eyes bulged. "You're transsexual?"

"Yeah, Jackie. I completed my last surgery over a year ago, so I prefer to just be considered a woman now, but Jesus, couldn't you tell? You knew before, but good Lord, the voice should have given it away."

At first, I was shocked, but the evidence of her slightly masculine features and voice became obvious, and although I had been surprised, I felt relaxed and cool, like hanging out with transsexual seemed completely normal. I liked that she was comfortable about the whole thing, not just explaining about herself with good humor, but also about me not remembering anything. *Who am I to judge?*

"Don't worry, Jackie. I'll help you figure this whole thing out, I promise. We both will," she said, patting my head as she looked toward the door. My eyebrows perked as she looked back at me.

"Oh, don't worry, we can tell Archie. He's been my best friend for five or six years now. He helped me through a little identity crisis of my own. I'd trust him with my life. Besides, he will figure it out eventually; you're not exactly the best actress ever."

"So, what should we do? How can we find out information about me?" I asked.

She thought for a moment. "Okay, well, first, we need to get you to a doctor. Since you didn't hit your head, I imagine this could be some sort of brain tumor or something, and we need to know before it gets dangerous. We'll wait until tomorrow; you seem fine right now. And we should go tell Archie."

We went back out to the couch to explain the whole situation to Archie. He stared at me intently, nodding his head while we talked. Then, I asked if he knew anything about me, and he got out a small notepad and began to scribble some pieces of information. Unfortunately, it was all the same as what she told me before. I was confused as to why he was writing things down, and not speaking, but she answered before I could ask.

"I don't know if you noticed, but when he talks, it's usually song lyrics. Eighties song lyrics."

"Yeah, why is that?" I asked, looking at the both of them.

"I don't know," Maxine replied. Archie shrugged.

"Wait, you don't know? Either of you?"

"Well, if he has some sort of reason behind it, he's never told me. That's how he was when I met him, and that's how he still is. If he can't say it in a lyric, he writes it down. That's just him. He never asked why I was turning myself into a female, so I never asked why he talked like that. All I know is he takes care of me and I take care of him, and that's all that's important. And we're going to take good care of you too."

"I'm sorry, but I'm just thinking of the right words to say. I know they don't sound the way I planned them to be," he said and the three of us laughed.

"When in Rome?" I asked.

As he nodded, Maxine grinned. "Hey, you got it!"

I chuckled and looked at him. "That is so weird. I love it."

For the first time since I'd woken up, I noticed how incredibly at ease I was around these people, how even my own name didn't feel like me, but being with these two people felt right. I felt like I really belonged there, on that couch, with the two of them.

2

I woke up the next morning, excited by the fact that I remembered the day before. I remembered my roommates, my name –Jackie Dawes- and everything. I lay in bed for a few minutes, familiarizing myself with my room; it looked different in sunlight than it had the night before. It was pretty bland, mostly because I'd only been there for three weeks. I wasn't sure if I had been into a minimalist style of decorating before yesterday, but I knew today, I didn't like it. Especially after scoping out Maxine's room last night, I wanted colors, and pictures and furniture. I had no desk or mirror at all. My walls were blindingly white. I had one dresser, two nightstands pinching my bed and a doorless closet, which I could see from the bed, was practically empty. At the window, there was a tiny little plant, a cactus, the only spot of color in the room. It was ridiculously sparse. I didn't even have a blanket, just white sheets. It bothered me enough that I noted after I figure out who I am, my next priority was definitely going to be this room; I needed to paint this room. It struck me as odd that I felt so strongly about changing my bedroom, but the walls were as white and blank as my memory; my bedroom needed to find its identity as much as I did.

I got up and opened the dresser to peek at my wardrobe: jeans and t-shirts, mostly, and a few pieces of office attire. Looking at the blouses and skirts reminded me that I did have a job. Maxine said it was Brandisham's Boutique, and that I talked about sorting clothes a lot. I wondered what my actual title was.

As I pondered this, the phone rang in the other room. I went out to answer it.

"Hello?" I asked, as Maxine peeked out of her bedroom and Archie peeked out of the bathroom.

"Yes, Jackie?"

"Yeah."

"This is Portia. Were you planning on coming in to work today?" The voice on the other end sounded angry and even a little snooty.

I panicked. "Oh my God, yes, I'm sorry. I'll be there as soon as I possibly can. I'm so sorry!" I heard a sigh, and then a click, as I almost dropped the phone. Maxine came running out of her room dressed in woman's pajamas that emphasized her fresh, new woman's physique. She grabbed my arm and led me back into my room, into my closet, throwing a blouse and a skirt at me. I dressed as she tugged at my hair and face.

"Shit, I forgot you had to go to work today. Let me call the hospital and see if I can get you an appointment with a doctor for later. Do you think you'll be alright for now?"

I took a deep breath and bobbed my head.

"Now," she continued. "I am nowhere near presentable for the streets, but Archie will walk with you. Your store is on the way to the bank where he works."

I nodded like a spy being briefed for a mission. Maxine was quick, and glancing in the bathroom mirror, I didn't look half bad. Archie was at the door, waiting for me. He threw his arm around my shoulder, handed me a purse and rushed me out the door, down the steps and out into New York City. He rushed me in so many directions; I honestly couldn't pay any attention to where we were going. I was guessing we were pretty close, because he took out his notepad and scribbled furiously. We stopped in front of a skinny, white concrete building wedged in between two darker buildings with huge, wide windows dressed with mannequins wearing barely-there clothing. I could see inside both windows, which I discovered were both part of the same store, which meant that the skinny space in the center also went with them. Archie ripped the page out of his book and handed it to me.

This is Brandisham's Boutique. I don't know anything about what your job title is, but you work here four days a week until five. I will be back to get you then.

He waited until I had finished reading, before waving at me and walking away. I watched him turn the corner, and then I took a deep breath and went inside.

"Oh my God, Jackie. There you are! Did you forget what day it was?" I didn't look to who was speaking; I was busy memorizing the place.

"Something like that," I smiled.

"Well, are you going to stand there all day or are you going to get to work?" I turned to see this beautiful girl standing at the front desk, armed with a microphone earpiece and radio pack. She had reddish brown hair pulled back into a tight ponytail with her bangs pinned back in a bubble, like she had a tumor on the top of her head. She was dressed in all black, thinning out her already small frame, with a single white lining on the low-cut neck. I just stood there looking at her. This must be Portia.

"Well, are you going or what?" Her eyes looked angry.

I suddenly realized I was staring. "Oh, sorry. Um, I'm a little bit out of it today. Where do you want me to go?"

"Oh my God, Jackie," she rolled her eyes. "You go to the basement, where you've gone everyday for the past three weeks. What the hell is wrong with you? Are you hung over or something?" I smiled and walked past. I had a feeling I hadn't liked her before my awakening.

The place was blank enough that it was easy to see a black railing in the back against the wall. I headed down the stairs, completely unsure of what I was going to find.

The basement was chocked-full of racks filled with various articles of clothing. From the stairs, I could see the clothes moving.

"Hello?" I called.

The movement stopped. A small, mousy blonde head attached to blue, thick-rimmed glasses bobbed up in between two racks. As soon as the eyes met mine, they were gone. I continued down the stairs in search of the strange face I'd seen.

To my surprise, I ended up at the end of the racks, in a small corner with two small desks pushed up against the wall.

"Hi."

I jumped and turned to see that strange head I was looking for. It was attached to a tall, lanky body dressed in huge tan pants and a baggy white shirt. I smiled and to my surprise, her eyes grew large and she laughed.

"You are different today, Jackie." Her words shook me for a moment. I was not sure how to respond, or if I should even respond at all. "Why do you seem so strange today?"

"I don't know," I answered, wondering if it had been a rhetorical question.

"Well, judging by your enlarged eyes and the way you are looking at me and this basement, not to mention your apprehension about continuing down those stairs, I'd say you feel like you're in unfamiliar territory. Like you don't remember this."

I was shocked. "How did you know?"

"My name is Chrissy," she continued. "We work down here in the stock room, or as we like to call it, 'the dungeon'. Just you and me."

"You and me? Just us? Down here? Do we ever go up there?"

She shook her head. "We go up there to bring them outfits. Otherwise, no. They leave the sales to those other girls. Margot Brandisham has the idea that those modelesque looks will sell more clothes, so she stuck us down here. Me, because she thinks I might be crazy, and you because you just started. I think she sees potential in you, but because you don't look like them, she wants to see you prove yourself." She walked over to her desk and sat down, so I headed to what I assumed was mine. "I'm so glad you're down here," she continued. "Because I used to get so lonely, even though I don't think it's right."

"What's not right?"

"Mrs. Brandisham not giving you a chance because you don't look like them." My stomach suddenly dropped. I had been so absorbed in my own disappointing perception of myself that I hadn't thought about other people being disappointed in how I looked too.

"I don't care what anybody says, I wouldn't buy anything from them. They're not pretty to me, and they're all so fake. You, on the other hand, are very pretty. You have classic beauty, like a Victorian painting. You look like a real person."

I understood what she meant, and was flattered, even if it sounded a little bizarre. "Thanks," I said, blushing slightly. "You as well." I thought I sounded stupid, saying that, but Chrissy knew what I meant.

I decided that I really liked Chrissy. She was sort of talking nonsense about me being pretty, but the strangest part was that I actually believed her. She seemed so perceptive about everything else that I was overwhelmed with the feeling that anything she said was the truth. And of course, I couldn't get over the fact that she knew I couldn't remember anything.

"So, what exactly do we do down here?"

"Well, we keep track of the inventory on the computers," she adjusted her glasses. "We deal with shipments and we sort through the clothes, we keep the racks organized and mostly, we wait for the upstairs people to radio us, looking for specifics and we deliver. We're basically warehouse rats. Don't worry, I'll help you with everything. They won't figure it out." I sighed, relieved.

"Speaking of, how did you know?" I asked.

Chrissy looked deep into my eyes and smiled. "I don't exactly know, but I could just tell you were different today, and the look on your face when I said hello just told me you didn't know me."

"Don't you want to know what happened?"

"Only if you want to tell me," she answered nonchalantly.

"I fell asleep at my desk at home and when I woke up, I didn't remember anything."

"Anything at all?"

"Anything at all."

"Fascinating."

Again, I made a mental list of yet another reason why I liked Chrissy. She readily accepted me as I was, amnesia and all, no questions asked. How many people in this world would have ever done that without even the slightest hint of curiosity?

The next hour or so went by well. Chrissy took over the orders from upstairs –the very few that we had- while I wandered through the racks, absorbing the clothes, and fiddling with the computer's inventory system. I still couldn't believe my brain had retained any knowledge of computers, as I sat right down to use it without any hesitation.

Soon enough, the noise from upstairs increased, obviously some sort of busy period. "It's mostly older ladies and socialites," Chrissy said, as I listened to the shuffling feet above. "They act like they own the place, which is true, I suppose, since nobody else can afford to shop here."

Over the radio, a voice chirped for Chrissy to find a satin, strapless, floor-length gown in a dark color. She took off down an aisle, humming. Shortly after she disappeared, the radio chirped again.

"Jackie, Kat Pendleton is here."

"Who?"

"Funny. Could you please bring her selected pieces from the Crimson collection to try on please?"

My heart leapt. What were her selected pieces? I stood up, craning my neck, hoping Chrissy would appear, and when she didn't, I moved down the aisle, trying to remember where the Crimson collection was.

When I did find the rack, I hoped to find a list of some sort or tags on particular dresses, but of course, I found nothing. At this point, I was furiously searching for Chrissy to tell me who Kat Pendleton even was.

"Jackie, Ms. Pendleton would like to try on her pieces to-*day*!"

Nervously, I shuffled through the pieces, grabbing three of the most elegant gowns I could find.

Reaching the top of the stairs, I could see Chrissy's legs poking out from underneath a pile of satin, like she was some sort of dump bin, while the salesgirl showed one dress at a time to an older woman dressed in peach and a permanent frown.

"Jackie!"

I turned to see a girl, not all that dissimilar to Portia, except her hair was gold. Standing next to her was a girl with jet black hair, choppy all over. She was wearing a short black dress and a red leather jacket. Her wrists were plastered with gold bangles and on her feet were what I could only imagine Maxine classifying as "hooker boots". She was smacking gum and heatedly typing on her phone. I also noticed she was still wearing her gigantic sunglasses indoors. This had to be Kat Pendleton, and therefore, I immediately regretted my choices, wishing feverishly I had seen her before she saw me, so I could have rethought the dresses.

Ashamed, I walked over to the two of them, the salesgirl, whose name tag read "Chantal," almost ripped the garments from my hands. Kat looked up from her phone, and even with her sunglasses on, I could tell she wasn't pleased.

"Those are not my clothes," she said blankly. Chantal glared at me, as my nerves began to work in hyper-drive.

"I, I'm so s-sorry. I s-seem to have forgotten -your cho –" I stuttered, trailing off.

Kat's eyebrows peeked over her sunglasses. Chantal's face turned bright red.

"You forgot my choices? How dare you! What the hell kind of service is this?" Kat asked crossly. I stared at her, trying to explain something, anything, but everyone in the store was now staring at us.

Just then, I felt Chrissy grab my arm.

"I'm sorry, Ms. Pendleton. She meant that she had forgotten your file. She misplaced it, is all. We'll be right back."

I thought Chrissy would be mad, but of course, Chrissy knew my secret, and at the bottom of the stairs, she apologized to me.

"I'm terribly sorry. I tried to get those dresses taken care of as soon as possible, but Victoria tends to keep me up there. I had forgotten Kat was coming today. Anyway, Kat Pendleton is one of our biggest clients, who always views our collections before we put them out, and we make notes and keep a record of her picks. She gets photographed a lot, so we like to keep her picks on file so when we're selling a piece, we can mention her name."

By this time, she had printed off the list of dresses and had taken me back to the rack and handed me three of the pieces. They were all short, jewel encrusted and very revealing. I was disappointed that this is what passed for fashion these days. I suddenly felt ridiculously old, even though I didn't know how old I actually was.

Chrissy and I went back upstairs, still being followed by all eyes in the store, and placed the dresses on a changing room rack. We both frantically apologized to Kat, who at this point looked like she'd completely forgotten what happened, more concerned with the problem unfolding in her text message universe and then we descended back to the dungeon. We nestled back into our chairs, as Chrissy told me all about Kat Pendleton.

"Her father was a movie producer in Hollywood, and when she was about five, he died of a heart attack in the middle of a meeting for a movie he wanted Kat to be in. It was a musical or something. Other people wanted her to still do the movie as a tribute to her dad, but her mother wouldn't hear of it. She immediately moved the two of them to New York and she remarried a wealthy man. Kat spent the next ten years of her life in some private boarding school in Switzerland, completely out of the public eye, and then about three years ago, some photographer recognized her at a fashion show with her mother and took her picture. All of a sudden, there was this nostalgic media frenzy. Everyone wanted pictures of this little heiress grown up, and it's been nonstop ever since, especially due to her behavior. She's always yelling or screaming or fighting with somebody and she goes out to places she's not even old enough to be in, and people just eat that stuff up because she has 'daddy issues'." Chrissy took her hands and made air quotes at that last remark.

I strangely found that after hearing that, I actually felt a little bad for Kat. I could only guess how difficult it would be to grow up undetected and suddenly thrust in the spotlight at still a young age, being known only as "the girl whose famous dad died." Not that I had any idea, I guess. Or maybe I did?

We changed the subject, but not before Chantal came stomping down the stairs, flanked by Portia and Victoria. This could have been for intimidation purposes, but it could also have been that they were frightened of the dungeon.

"What the hell was that, Jackie? Do you think you're funny or something? Why would you do that?"

"I'm sorry, I got mixed up," I sputtered.

"Sorry doesn't cut it. Kat was pissed and she just walked out of the store without trying on any of her pieces. She said she wasn't feeling them anymore. She wasn't feeling them because you made her wait! Everyone knows she's an impulse buyer!"

Portia took over speaking; obviously, she didn't want Chantal to have the complete satisfaction of yelling at me. "There were paparazzi outside, Jackie. They saw everything, they probably even heard Kat. This will be in *The Star* tomorrow, and not in a good way. You are in so much trouble, Jackie. When Mrs. Brandisham hears about this, your ass is going to be fired."

The three of them stomped back up the stairs, Victoria still silent. I wondered if she had joined them not because she wanted to yell at me, but perhaps because of some comedic rule of three or something.

I feared for my job, even though I thought it was a stupid incident to get fired over. The notion that this incident would reach the ears of Margot Brandisham, the owner of the store and famous in her own right, who's too busy for petty issues involving the far less famous people working at her little boutique, frightened me horribly.

My hands began shaking and I sweated nervously. Chrissy patted my shoulder. "It's okay, really. Mrs. Brandisham won't be too mad."

I didn't want to, but I started to cry and couldn't stop. "How could she not be mad? Didn't I just lose our biggest client?"

"We might just have to tell her the truth."

"I don't think I can do that. It's too embarrassing. Oh! And this is going to be in *The Star*, too! Oh, I'm so embarrassed!"

"Don't worry. Ever heard the phrase, 'There's no such thing as bad publicity'?"

"No, I haven't."

"Oh, right. Well, you probably have, but you don't remember." She chuckled. I started to laugh myself. I was suddenly so sure this whole thing was just blown out of proportion and would be alright. Chrissy was so good at making me feel calm.

As I began drying my eyes, the radio chirped.

"Jackie, could we see you upstairs please?" It was a voice I didn't recognize, but Chrissy did.

"Brandisham," she whispered, fear washing over her face.

3

I stood up, and walked through the racks, up the stairs, like a prisoner walking the Green Mile to their death. Chrissy walked next to me for moral support.

The store was completely empty, except for the three salesgirls, and another one, I'd come to know later as "Tascha," huddled around a tall, slender figure in a flowing zebra print dress. This woman's face was old and wrinkled, but still very youthful, and her light gray hair bounced on her shoulders.

"I understand there was some sort of problem," she said flatly. I couldn't look at her, but I could feel her intense stare.

"Yes, ma'am. I'm extremely sorry. I-I'm just not feeling very well today, and I made a mistake and I apologize. It's all my fault. I'm sorry." My hands were shaky, and my face was sweaty.

"You know I don't like problems."

"Yes, ma'am. I am sorry-"

"You have cost me a lot of business today."

"Oh," I said quietly. Tears started streaming down my face.

Mrs. Brandisham pinched my chin with her fingers and raised my face to meet hers. Her eyes narrowed, and then softened, and I saw her whole demeanor change.

"You don't look well, my dear. Maybe you should go home."

Chrissy took me back downstairs to gather my purse and she bid me goodbye. As I headed for the door, I passed the glares of all of the salesgirls. Mrs. Brandisham was at the door.

"Get some rest, Jackie. Feel better," she said calmly. "If you're ever sick again, it might be best if you don't come in. Perhaps that way, these things can be avoided."

I knew she was serious about me doing less damage just not showing up, but I swore that I detected the slightest humor in her voice.

I was at the street corner, lost in my own thoughts, before I realized that I had no idea how to get home. I decided to walk around, to clear my head a little bit, and then perhaps, I'd go back to the store and wait for Archie.

I dug a pen out of my purse and seeing I was out of paper, I wrote the street names on my hand, connecting each one with a small arrow. This place was amazing, and terrifying at the same time. I figured it probably also conjured the same feelings in someone who had all of their memories in tow. I looked in all the shop windows, wincing slightly at each clothing store, but finding some little places that looked enjoyable.

I was trying to clear my head, but I found that rather difficult, as every sense was in overload, trying to make myself aware of my surroundings. I had been hounded for some time by a wonderful smell coming from a busy little café on the corner of the street. I could no longer resist, and following my nose, I stepped in and sat at a table tucked out of the way.

I slumped into a seat, slamming my purse on the table. Something in the bag made a ting, and I realized that I hadn't looked in my purse all day. There could be "clues" in there. I opened the bag, to find practically nothing but a cell phone and a wallet.

"Can I help you?"

Out of the corner of my eye, I saw a man in an apron standing at my table. I looked up. The waiter's eyebrows rose suddenly.

"Hey." His mouth made a sideways grin and he scratched the stubble on his cheek. "Would you like your usual?"

I stared at him. "Excuse me?"

"I asked if you wanted me to bring you your usual."

"Do you know me?"

"Uh, yeah, sort of." His eyes squinted as he watched my face curiously. "I see you in here a lot. You and your friends are regulars."

"My friends?"

"Yeah, a guy who looks like he time traveled from the Eighties, and some woman, who looks kind of like a man. Uh, that is, I mean, um, she has a masculine face?" He tried to recover but was failing miserably. His eyes continued to stare; he was puzzled. "I'm sorry. I think, maybe I confused you with someone else?"

"No," I sighed. "That's me. Um, yeah, bring me my usual. Wait, it isn't sushi, is it?"

The waiter scrunched his face a bit and chuckled, walking away. He went to the kitchen, pulling up his sagging pants every couple of strides.

I turned my attention back to my purse. I took out the wallet, hoping I had money in it to pay for my "usual." Luckily, there was some cash. There was a laminated card with that unfamiliar name –my name – on it and an account number. In the corner was a symbol for the Eastern Mutual Bank. Behind that was a temporary identification card with my name on it. I remembered Maxine saying I didn't have a license because we live in New York, so I figured the temporary identification card was probably to get the bank account. Then, I wondered how much money I had in the bank. Grabbing a napkin from the holder on the table, I jotted down the bank, as a reminder to check my account later.

After rifling through the wallet, I moved on to the phone. Of course, it only had four phone numbers in it: Archie, Brandisham's, the apartment, and Maxine. I contemplated calling someone because it was only two o'clock. I was going to sit there for three more hours. Archie was at work, and I wasn't exactly sure where Maxine was. As I debated what to do, the phone suddenly vibrated and a small icon of an envelope appeared on the screen. I opened the phone and found a message from Maxine.

"I couldn't get an appointment today, but we definitely have one for tomorrow. Try to get the day off work."

The waiter came back with my food, a turkey sandwich on a baguette and a soda. I looked at it, relieved it wasn't sushi.

"Is there something wrong?" he asked.

"Oh, no. I'm okay."

"Actually, I meant with the food," he smiled. His eyes seemed to look at me differently, less confused and more concerned. "But are you sure you're okay? Maybe you should see a doctor or something. You don't look well."

"Thank you," I said curtly, and he walked away.

I ate the sandwich furiously. I hadn't really eaten anything since the sushi last night, and I was starving. It was amazing. I was so glad this was my usual. When it was finished, I decided I should probably call somebody to come get me.

I called Maxine, because she had promised to take me to the doctor today, so I hoped she wasn't working. She answered right away.

"Jackie? Everything alright?"

"Um, not really. I had a bad day at work. I, uh, seem to have found The Corner Nook, and I don't know how to get home."

"Okay, Jackie. I'm on my way."

I sat in the café, looking like some friendless bum, staring out the window and wishing I had another sandwich. Twice, I caught the waiter staring at me, looking away quickly as we made eye contact.

"Jackie?" Maxine snuck up behind me. She sat down and I told her all about work and everything that happened. I told her about each girl on the sales floor, about Chrissy and Kat Pendleton, trying not to leave out anything.

"Don't you worry, honey. Margot Brandisham didn't fire you, so you're good. Besides, that Kat Pendleton is a bitch, so she needs a little dose of reality once in a while." For the first time in hours, I smiled.

"Should we get going then?"

I nodded as we stood up. I paid my bill and we left.

Archie was waiting for us when we got back to the apartment. "Hey little sister, what have you done?"

"Oh, sorry Arch! I forgot to call you," Maxine said.

"Did you go to Brandisham's?" I asked. He nodded.

"Did they tell you what happened?" He nodded again. I took a deep, aggravated breath and dropped my purse, walking to my bedroom.

4

"Hi, Portia, it's Jackie. I'm afraid I won't be able to come in today. I'm feeling very sick."

"Fine," she huffed and hung up.

I woke up in a better state. My memory of the past two days was still intact, and I didn't have to face another embarrassing faux pas at Brandisham's because today, Maxine and I were going to meet with a doctor about my condition.

I dressed in a pair of jeans, a T-shirt and a jacket, and then went to the kitchen to rifle through the cupboards. Eventually, I found a loaf of bread, so I popped two slices in the toaster. Then I found some peanut butter and slathered it on my toast. I offered a piece to Maxine as she came out of her room, but she declined.

"No thanks," she said, slipping her feet into a pair of size twelve high heeled boots. "I usually just grab a yogurt for breakfast." I was slightly jealous at her healthy choices, and yet I pitied her for missing out on this delicious peanut buttered toast.

"Now, are you ready to go? Our appointment is at ten."

I nodded and gathered my purse. Maxine checked herself out in the full-length mirror by the door.

"How do I look?"

"Great," I answered. She amazed me that she took so much time and effort to dress up. Even on a day when she wasn't going to either of her jobs at El Mercado or the Sunset Club, she was in a skirt and heels, in silks and furs, like a fashion model.

We went out on the street and I started to hail a cab, but Maxine pulled me back. "We're taking the subway today, dear," she instructed. "We don't have time for a cab."

I followed closely, fearing I would get lost, and in fifteen minutes time, we were at the station, heading down the steps. Maxine paid for the two of us, and I followed her through the turnstiles, down more steps to the landing. In almost no time at all, I could hear the train approaching. I leaned over the ledge, like a child, fascinated by facing the train head on, but Maxine pulled me back.

"It's just a train, honey. It's not special," she scolded, motherly.

"Max, you forget, this is my first time. Or at least, the first time I can remember," I reasoned.

"Right, and how old are we now?" She joked. "Perhaps you are a lot younger than I thought. But how on Earth could a twelve-year-old possibly make it to the big city all by herself?"

"Ha ha. Your sarcasm astounds me," I replied.

When the train stopped, we got in and sat down. As the train started to move again, I looked around at the people in our car. They all were busy reading papers, or books; one lady sat with a pair of knitting needles furiously working through some yarn. Everyone seemed so tied up in their own little lives, completely unaware of anyone else's. Even Maxine had her own subway riding activity, as she got out a tiny sketch pad and began drawing.

I didn't even realize I was leaning over her shoulder until she looked at me.

"You gonna put your head in my lap?"

"Sorry. I was just watching you draw," I replied sheepishly. Her drawing was beautiful. It was a scene of a waterfall surrounded by trees and rock formations, interspersed with grasses and vines. Every plant was so detailed I could clearly recognize them: ferns, lilies, ivies and moss.

"Wow, that's amazing," I marveled.

"Oh, thanks. It's nothing. It's just a little doodle I've been working on to keep me busy lately."

I was surprised to hear Maxine sound so embarrassed. These past two days, I had come to know her as an unshakably confident, bold, almost intimidating pillar of a woman. Now, here we were and I was seeing her being bashful, her confidence easily shaken by an honest compliment. I realized there was much more to Maxine than I or anyone else had ever known. I felt like I wanted to learn everything about her. She was my hero. My hero, the transsexual.

"You should pursue your drawing, Max. I'm serious. You're very talented."

"Thanks. I'd love to, but I don't have that kind of money. The supermarket and The Sunset Club don't pay that well, and I've got rent and things. My savings doesn't exactly grow exponentially after each check."

The train began to slow; Maxine said it was our stop and we were off the train, onto the landing, up the steps and back out into New York City again.

The hospital was visible from the subway. It was six stories tall, with long, skinny windows cut out of the bricks. A large illuminated sign came into focus as we got closer that read "Saint Teresa General Hospital" in blue letters.

Inside, the activity was fairly mellow. For some reason, I had expected a frenzy of rushing doctors and bleeding patients, but all I found was a waiting room full of older people and a couple of sprained appendages. I sat down as Maxine checked in at the front desk. She joined me with a clipboard of papers to fill out. She handed me the clipboard, and I stared at it, like it was written in Japanese.

"What's this?" I asked. Maxine leaned over and examined the paper.

"These are standard information forms. They won't see you unless they have your information."

"I don't know any of this stuff. Insurance? I don't even think I have insurance."

"Fill out what you can. I'll do the rest."

I put my name and our address, impressed that I remembered it, before handing it back over to Maxine. She began to fill in boxes, and I leaned over to see what she was writing.

"I'm filling out that you're in seemingly perfect health. Your family history is not available. Don't worry about insurance. I've got that covered."

"What do you mean?"

"Just don't worry about it."

She returned the clipboard and we continued to sit and wait. Maxine immersed herself back into her drawing, and I gazed around the waiting room, watching all of the people, before resting my eyes on the TV in the corner. It was showing a movie about a girl who was transported by a tornado to a magical land where she met a village of little people. The villagers were celebrating when all of a sudden, an evil witch appeared. I suddenly realized that I recognized the movie. I remembered that scene; I remembered the characters, too: that poor girl was Dorothy, and her dog Toto, and that evil woman was the Wicked Witch of the West.

"Max!" I whispered excitedly, tapping her shoulder. "Max, look at the TV."

"Yeah, it's *The Wizard of Oz*. Why?"

"I remember this movie, Max. I remember it. This isn't something we've watched in the past three days, but I know this movie. I know what happens. Dorothy goes to Oz and then she wakes up." Maxine seemed nonplussed at first and continued drawing, but then her eyes bulged and she looked up at me.

"Oh my God, Jackie! You remembered something from your past! Your memory is coming back!" She hugged my shoulders, just as thrilled as I was at the possibility of getting my memory back.

A nurse in pink patterned scrubs came out from behind the desk and called my name. Maxine and I followed the woman, who reeked of cigarettes, to a small examination room, where I sat on the bed and Maxine sat in a chair. The nurse began to take my blood pressure and ask me questions.

"Jackie, how are you today?"

"I'm okay," I answered, feeling the arm band tighten.

"Good. Now, what are you here for?"

"I'm here because I seem to have amnesia."

She looked at me funny when I said that and began asking me questions.

"Are you experiencing dizziness, nausea, or severe headaches?"

"No."

"Any pains in your body?"

"No."

"Are you having problems functioning, like walking or anything?"

"No. I have no symptoms. I just can't remember things."

She squinted her eyes and leaned into my face.

"Do you have a problem with alcohol? Does your amnesia come after a night of heavy drinking?"

"No! I'm not drunk! I just can't remember anything." I was getting irritated and she could tell. She wrote some things down in a folder and left the room.

The Doctor came in shortly after that. "Hello, my name is Doctor Karish." He opened my folder and hummed as he read it.

"Okay, Miss Dawes. What can I do for you today?"

"I think I have amnesia," I answered. I then proceeded to tell him how I had woken up three days ago sitting at my computer and had no idea where I was or anything."

"I see. Now, did you not remember *anything* at all?"

"Well, actually, I couldn't remember my name, or where I was or who my roommates were, but I knew simple stuff, like using a computer, and using a toaster. It's like everything is here," I pointed to my head and then massaged it for a moment. "Everything but my life. I don't know who *I* am. But, I did remember something today, though. Something not from the past three days."

"Oh yeah? What was that?"

"I recognized *The Wizard of Oz* on TV in the waiting room."

"Hmm," Doctor Karish smiled. "That is a great movie." He did a bit of writing in the file, then, he finally said, "Jackie, this is very interesting that you can remember certain things and not others. It seems to me that you have combined types of amnesia. You can't recall the past, you can't remember the present. I would like to do a physical exam right now, if we could, so I can get an estimate on your health."

He opened a drawer and pulled out a drab, olive colored, backless gown, and stepped out while I stripped and put it on. Then, he re-entered and began his exam. He had me do some stretches, touching my toes and some jumping jacks in rapid succession. He waited until I was breathing heavily before he asked me to stop. Then, he asked me to sit back on the exam table. He turned on a flashlight and shined it into my eyes. Then, he wrapped his hands around my neck, and began lightly pinching, and turning my head.

"Any idea how you got this scar?" he asked.

"Nope."

"Okay. That, I suppose, could be a factor." He felt around the scar, tracing its length with his finger, and pressing on it.

"Does this hurt?"

"No."

Once he had finished examining my head, he asked me to lie on my back.

"Does this hurt?" he asked, pressing on my stomach.

I shook my head as he pressed harder. Still, it didn't hurt.

"Good, good," he mumbled, helping me sit up. He took a small silver hammer out of his coat pocket. "Now, I'm going to test your reflexes. It will just be a light tap on the knee." He positioned his hammer and quickly struck the cap of my knee. My leg wiggled slightly, but unexpectedly, I started to giggle.

"I'm sorry," I said, holding my mouth to stop.

"It's okay," Doctor Karish replied. "Sometimes people are amused by this. I'm going to do it one more time."

He struck my knee and my giggle, which had hardly stifled, exploded into a howl of laughter. The doctor watched me curiously, waiting for me to finish. "I'm so sorry. I have no idea why I'm doing this. I really apologize."

He made a few notes on my file. "Miss Dawes, I would like to schedule an MRI for you, if we could. That scar on your head leads me to believe that this might be a case of head trauma, and I would like to check for any noticeable brain damage. Your burst of excessive laughter is also revealing that perhaps you have some nerves and senses that have been rerouted. Once we can diagnose your condition, we'll know how to treat it. As far as finding personal information, you could maybe try going to the police station."

"And do what?"

"They could take your fingerprints and maybe look through a missing person's database. If you're opposed to that idea, you might even be able to go the library and search for birth records or family histories."

He wrote something on a paper and sent us out to the desk to make another appointment. Maxine talked to the woman at the desk, making all of the arrangements, and then we left. She began telling me all about what an MRI was, and how I should prepare for it, but I was only half listening. It sounded so complicated, and I was still thinking about Dorothy and Toto.

5

We walked down the street, and I noticed Maxine strolled right by the subway station.

"Where are we going?"

"I thought since we were in the area, we could go visit Archie. We'll tell him what the doctor said and see if he's interested in grabbing some lunch or something."

I followed Maxine through the streets, which were so crowded, I grabbed her arm, afraid of being separated. She pulled me through, like a fish being reeled through water, and into a large, old building. We went in a small door on the side and down a few steps into a large hall.

"This is the Bank of New York. Archie's dad is the executive president. He wants Archie to be an executive like he is, but because of what he considers to be Archie's 'problem', he's been reduced to working down here. He's fabulous with numbers, but that goes unnoticed because he speaks in lyrics. They can't get past it. Did you know that he has two college degrees?" I shook my head, as I obviously didn't know anything about Archie. "He's a financial wizard, and he works in the deepest depths of this bank because his father is embarrassed of him. Nobody takes him seriously; it's a damn shame."

The already large hallway opened up to an even larger room. At the back of the room was a vault that went from the floor to the ceiling. I stared in amazement at the grandness of it all. The vault was protected from us by an entire wall of glass, and I could see Archie sitting at a desk behind the glass too. Maxine tapped the glass, and Archie came out, pressing a code into a little metal box by the glass door.

"Hello, is it me you're looking for?"

"Lionel Ritchie," Maxine and I said to each other simultaneously.

"You're so good at this game!" she laughed.

I grinned, trying not to chuckle. As enjoyable as it was, I did still need to get used to it.

"Hey Archie. We just thought we'd stop and say hi. Jackie and I went to the hospital today and she needs an MRI. We made her an appointment and we're going to go to the police station, and maybe the library –"

"Can I help you, Miss?"

Maxine stopped talking and she and I both turned to see a man in a suit standing next to us. I had no idea who he was, but judging by his clothes, and the look of fear on Maxine's face, he was important.

"Hello, Mr. Van Holm. It's me, Maxine Perlita, and Jackie Dawes. We just wanted to say hi to Archie while we were here in the area."

The man's eyes tightened. As he silently gave us the stare of death, I felt a chill down my spine.

"Jackie sprained her wrist, so we went to the hospital."

Mr. Van Holm peeked over Maxine's shoulder and looked at me. I quickly grabbed my wrist and held it tightly.

"Turns out," Maxine continued. "It wasn't sprained at all; she just pinched a nerve, so she's fine."

Mr. Van Holm looked back at Maxine and then to Archie and said, "Well, I'm glad to see everything is in order, but I must insist that you leave right now. Archie is much too busy, what with *working* and all, and I don't know who showed you our basement entrance, but you really shouldn't be down here. This basement is reserved for banking staff. I'll show you ladies to the door- the *right* door."

We waved to Archie, who waved back, less lively this time, and Mr. Van Holm rushed us out the front revolving door of the bank. It felt like we were trashy teenagers being kicked out of some fancy restaurant. Again, I was surprised by Maxine's rolling over.

"What was that about?" I asked.

"That's Mr. Van Holm. He's Archie's dad," Maxine huffed. "He doesn't like me at all. He thinks I'm responsible for Archie's 'condition,' which I'm not. Plus, he's a very strict, conservative man who doesn't approve of people like me because I'm different. He's well aware that I used to be a man, and so he's very disgusted by me."

A wave of sympathy swept over me. I understood what Maxine was talking about. I remembered Chrissy at Brandisham's telling me that she and I weren't allowed to be salesgirls because of the way we looked. It wasn't fair, the way people were treating my friends - or me. I couldn't believe there were people that were this prejudiced in the world.

On our way to the police station, Maxine stopped at a street vendor and bought a map that she stuck in my purse. "To guide you if you get lost," she snickered.

The station was a square building that looked like a school, only there were squad cars that filled the front lot. Inside, the office was buzzing. People were scurrying everywhere. We sat in the empty waiting area, watching officer after officer walk in, see us, ask what they could do for us and then leave. At least an hour went by before anyone actually came to attend to our needs.

"What can I do for you, ladies?" The officer asked, walking us to his desk.

"We need to find some information on this beautiful girl here," Maxine said, showing me off.

"What do you mean?"

"She has no memory of anything before yesterday, and we only met a few weeks ago, and I don't know anything about her, so we were hoping we could dig up information as to who she is."

"We don't do that here. I guess we could search the Missing Person Files, and do a fingerprinting, and see if you have a criminal background." The Officer spoke flatly, but he was staring at both of us like we were crazy.

I had never thought about having a criminal background before. To be honest, at that point, I was so desperate for my life back, I would have gladly taken a criminal past.

The officer took us to a small room where another officer wiped my fingers with oil and pressed each one onto a greased piece of glass. I watched in amazement as my fingerprints appeared on a computer screen next to it. When he finished, we had to wait thirty minutes while he searched the database for matching prints. My chest felt tight, like I was awaiting test results for some disease.

Thirty-three minutes passed, as I watched the clock, and then the officer appeared in the doorway clutching a folder. Excitement began to build when I saw the folder. This was it; this was my past in that folder.

"Sorry, Ms. Dawes. Your fingerprints and background check were clean." He tapped the folder on his hand a couple of times and I looked down at my hands, as Maxine squeezed my shoulder.

"We'll check our Missing Persons Reports and stay in touch. Now, I have to ask, are you staying somewhere safe? Do you have someone looking after you?"

"This is my roommate," I said, pointing to Maxine.

The officer nodded. "Okay. We'll do what we can to help you." Maxine and I both thanked him for his help and were on our way.

I wasn't exactly sure why I put so much expectation on the police being able to identify me right away, but having no criminal record, I actually felt crushed. I wanted to cry as soon as Maxine and I left the station. Instead, I sulked, folding my arms, and stomping my feet down the steps.

"It's okay, Jackie. So the police didn't help. So what? We'll go to the library and see if we can find any newspaper birth announcements or something."

"I don't think it'll work, Max," I sighed. "I'm not from around here, remember?"

She thought for a moment. "Actually, I just assumed you came from Florida, but that doesn't mean that you couldn't have been born here." I still didn't see much hope in her suggestions, but I was desperate, so we headed off to the library.

Maxine hailed us a cab, and during the drive to the library, I watched the city, wishing that something would become familiar, even though I knew nothing would.

We climbed the steps to the library. Maxine was catching her breath because she was in heels, I was catching my breath in awe at the majesty of the library's architecture. There were four massive columns in front, with a grand entrance seeping out in between two of them, everything was the same cream-colored marble, and even the littlest corners had immaculate detail. Inside was just as lavish. I was overwhelmed that this was just a library.

Maxine pulled me to the newspaper archives. "Okay, let's look for birth announcements."

"How old am I?" I asked. Maxine stared at me, like she had forgotten I had no memory.

"Well, when you moved in, you said you were twenty-five. I seriously doubt you are, but you could be. I think we should just start at 1980 and work our way up."

We spent the better part of two hours looking through newspapers from 1980 on up to 1990. Of course, there were no results. It was after five, and Maxine sent Archie a text, asking him to meet us there. He showed up a few minutes later. He didn't seem sad or upset, which I thought he would, after getting in trouble with his dad. Instead, he approached us, grinning, and whispered, "Everybody Wang Chung tonight." There was nothing to do but laugh around Archie. He was just funny, especially since I was beginning to think that maybe he couldn't control what he was doing. If that was the case, I wished that was my problem; I'd give anything to quote Wang Chung all the time if it meant I could remember things.

Maxine filled him in on the birth records, and the Dawes family tree which we traced at great length. He went to a computer and started typing my name into various search engines.

"Here's a woman on the cover of a business magazine named Jackie Dawes. She's obviously not you, though, she's like sixty." I watched as Archie searched my name followed by every state, and still the only match we had was an elderly businesswoman.

As we left the library, I resumed sulking. All I wanted to do was cry. Maxine didn't say anything. She put her hand on my back and gently patted it. "I'm really sorry that we can't find anything, I just feel terrible. I want you to know that we are committed to helping you, okay? So don't give up yet."

The three of us got back on the subway headed home. I was in between the two of them, Maxine back to drawing, and Archie staring straight ahead at the opposite window of the train. On this return trip, I didn't pay so much attention to the people around me, but rather to myself. I sat in the seat, slouching over, my feet inverted like a ventriloquist's dummy. Maxine sat so still and pristine with her legs crossed, and I looked like a bum. I turned my eyes to the other passengers, but not the way I had before. Now, I was wondering who was watching me, judging me by how I looked. I suddenly became paranoid about everyone, trying to figure out who was condemning us; condemning Maxine for being transsexual, condemning Archie and me for being associated with her. But Maxine, she was just as classy as anyone, so who cared that she was really once a man?

When we arrived home, I flopped onto my bed, crying as quietly as I could. I wasn't even sad anymore, I was more angry than anything. I couldn't believe that there wasn't a trace of me anywhere.

Crying made my head hurt, and I started yawning. I must have dozed off, because I was startled by a knock at my door. Maxine came in and sat on the bed at my feet.

"You okay?"

"Not really. I just wish I could find something out about me. Anything."

"We'll keep searching."

She convinced me to come out of my room, and the three of us made some pasta before Maxine had to rush off to work at the club. I tried to take my mind off my problems, so when she left, I started to tell Archie about Maxine's drawing. I wanted to show him, but she had taken it with her. He didn't need to see it though, as he pulled me up and took me into her bedroom. He crouched down and reached under her bed, unearthing a long box. He opened it, and inside, there were hundreds of drawings of various places, each one more beautiful than the next. She had drawn pictures of mountains, rivers, and landmarks; she truly had a gift.

"These are amazing," I said, marveling at a picture of the Eiffel Tower. "Archie, has she ever gone to art school or anything?"

Archie shook his head.

"She should," I said. He took out his notepad and scribbled:

I've been trying to save up some money or borrow some from my dad so she could go to art school, but it's just too expensive. My dad certainly won't budge.

I had almost completely forgotten about Mr. Van Holm. Being reminded of him made me sad, and I wrapped my arms around Archie. He hesitated for a moment, unsure of what I was doing, before he hugged back.

"I'm sorry about the way some people treat you, Archie, especially your dad. He should love you just the way you are, no matter what. Just like Maxine and I do." I wasn't sure why I said it, but I felt like it had to be said. I felt him hug me tighter.

"Thank you babe, for being a friend."

"And shinin' your light in my life," I answered. His eyebrows rose, as did mine, surprised I knew that song.

"'Cause ooh, I need you," we sang together.

We both laughed and continued to look at Maxine's drawings. Eventually, we noticed it was late and we both grew tired. I put on my pajamas and washed up and brushed my teeth, then crawled into my bed, where I sat for a while, just appreciating Archie and Maxine, thinking how lucky I was to know them.

6

There were horns beeping. I opened my eyes, still hearing horns, that I guessed were coming from out of the window I was facing. I wondered where I was. I was in a white bed, with white sheets, in a room with white walls. I sat up. Was I in some sort of hospital? I decided not, as the bed and other furniture seemed too nice for a hospital, plus, I was wearing pajamas with elephants on them.

Suddenly, the alarm clock next to me went off. I pressed a button to stop it, but it didn't stop. I pressed another, and still, the alarm sounded. Frustrated, I hit the whole clock, but it didn't stop. Clutching the whole clock in my hand, I threw it across the room. It hit the wall with a bang, leaving a small indentation, and fell to the floor, turning itself off.

Two people leaned their heads in through the doorway, looking for the source of the loud bang. Then they looked at me.

"You alright, Jackie?"

Jackie? Who was that?

"Who?"

"Oh, Jesus, she's forgotten again," the taller of the two said. The other one just looked back and forth between us. Then the taller one motioned for the other to come in the room, and help me out of bed.

"Come on, Jackie, come with us," the tall one said. I hesitated a bit, unsure of what was going on, but I was reassured that it was okay to follow. I was led to another bedroom that looked like some sort of movie star lived in it. They sat me on the bed, and the tall one went into an explanation, while handing me various pictures to look at.

"Okay, I'm Maxine. I'm transsexual. This is Archie, he only says Eighties lyrics when he talks, otherwise, he's silent. I don't know why he's like that; he just is. Your name is Jackie Dawes; we live together here in New York City…" She continued to explain everything to me, about how I had lost my memory four days ago, about the police station and the bank and the hospital, and an unfortunate incident I had at my job. Then she told me about my job at Brandisham's Boutique.

The other person, Archie, began to write some things down in a notepad for me. Unfortunately, none of these things were at all familiar. I had to admit, I was fairly scared by having no memory of any of this information. Maxine then left the room, saying something about calling a doctor, and I watched Archie write down another piece of information:

The doctor wants you to have an MRI so he can figure out why you're forgetting things.

Maxine returned to her room moments later and started putting on a short skirt and make-up. "Doctor Karish said to just try and tell you everything we remember and hope something rings a bell." I watched her in the mirror as her eyes enlarged, and she turned back to me. "Oh my God, Jackie! Do you remember *The Wizard of Oz*?" I thought for a moment. Something sounded familiar about that, but I wasn't sure.

"Dorothy and Toto?" she asked.

I did remember. "The yellow brick road, the Wicked Witch of the West, right?"

"Yes, yes, yes," Maxine smiled. "Okay, good, so we're getting somewhere. Um, today is Thursday, so you are scheduled to work today. Do you want to call in sick or do you want to go in?"

"You said I called off yesterday, right? I should probably go in then." I went back into what I guessed was my room and searched through a dresser until I found a nice pair of pants and a blouse.

"You can't wear that," she said, as I came out of my room.

"What? Why?"

"You wore that on Tuesday."

"Oh." I stood there, looking at my outfit, debating whether or not I should change. I figured since I didn't remember, maybe no one at work would notice.

"Here, let me get your clothes out." She followed me back into the room and started rifling through the drawers. "You can't wear the same thing twice in a week, and you certainly can't wear the same clothes twice in a row. We'll have to start writing down what you're wearing every day."

Then I sat down in front of her lighted mirror while she put make-up on me.

"I work at El Mercado in the morning, but Archie will walk you to work again," she said, swiping a bushy brush across my face. She was preparing me for my day, but I was still stuck on something else.

"Hey, Maxine? Why is it that I can remember *The Wizard of Oz* but I can't remember you or Archie or even myself?"

"I don't know, honey," she replied, putting the brush down and looking me square in the face. "But I do know that after witnessing the frustration this whole thing has put you through, if you can remember anything at all, hold on to that. Don't let it go because it's the best memory you've got."

Archie knocked on the door, and Maxine and I left the bedroom. Archie handed me my purse, and as we walked out of the apartment, Maxine called after me. "Don't forget to request off next Wednesday. You have to get your MRI that day. Please don't forget. No, I better write it down. Archie, remind her again, okay?"

Archie walked me to work, pointing at the street signs, which I took to mean he was showing me how to get to the store. He dropped me off at the entrance and gave me the note telling me to request next Wednesday off, and I took a breath, reminding myself to act like I knew what to do. According to Maxine, I worked in the basement at the back of the store, so all I had to do was slip inside and down the stairs without any suspicion. Maxine said something about a girl named Chrissy down in the basement who would help me get through the day.

I walked in, passed the desk, where a girl was sitting, glaring at me. I tried not to even make eye contact; I was focused on the back wall, and the stairs. I made it with no trouble, and I went halfway down the stairs, before I called out to Chrissy.

"I'm back here," she called back, and I followed her voice to two desks in the back.

"Hi," she smiled.

"Hi, Chrissy."

"How are you doing today? Are you feeling better?"

"Yeah, I'm alright. Actually, Chrissy, I'm not okay. I've lost my memory. Again, apparently. I just spent the better part of my morning listening to a recap of the past few days. I hope this isn't going to be difficult for you today. I really am sorry about the other day."

"No you're not," she said, "You don't even remember it, so don't worry about it. Everything will be just fine. You know, you should write things down so you don't forget them."

"Yeah, I meant to, but you know, I forgot."

Chrissy and I both laughed and she began to explain things to me about the computers and the clothes to get me back up to speed. She sent me up and down the racks to familiarize, or I guess re-familiarize myself with the merchandise.

The day went by fairly quickly. Chrissy did most of the work, letting me make a few notes on the clothes, using the computer and who the other girls were. At lunchtime, Chrissy pulled out a small pink lunchbox and began unwrapping a sandwich. I watched and suddenly realized I didn't bring anything to eat myself. Upon realizing I had no food, I suddenly felt hungry, and my stomach growled. Chrissy looked at me when my stomach growled and smiled.

"Here, you can have some of my sandwich," she said, extending a half.

"Oh, no. I don't want to eat your food. I'm fine," I said, staring at the sandwich. My stomach disagreed with me, growling again, longer and louder.

"Why don't you run out and get something?"

"Would that be okay?"

"Oh, sure. We're allowed to go out for our lunches. I just happen to bring mine with me. You used to too, sometimes."

"Oh, okay. I don't know where to go," I said, grabbing my purse, feeling something rectangular in it. I opened it up and found a map. I wondered how I got a map in my purse, but I figured it must have been from the last time I had an amnesic "spell."

"I know of a little place that's close by," Chrissy said, taking my map and opening it up. She made little crosses with her pen to show me where I was and where I had to go. Once I traced the path a couple of times with my finger, I felt like I was up to facing the city alone and I climbed the stairs and slipped out of the store, seemingly unnoticed.

I clutched my map, following it exactly the way I traced the path. The place was a few streets over on a corner. It looked quaint on the outside, like the kind of café that would be on a side street in Paris. As I walked inside, I read the sign swinging over the door: *The Corner Nook.*

Inside, it was a fairly busy atmosphere. I was in a hurry to get back to the store, so I stood in line at the register, reading the menu above. I still hadn't decided when it was my turn at the register. The guy behind the counter looked at me.

"Hi," he smiled.

"Hi," I answered.

"Are you feeling any better today?"

"Um, yes. I'm fine." I shot him a suspicious look.

I looked back up at the menu. There was a chicken salad sandwich that sounded pretty appetizing, so I ordered one to go.

"Okay. No usual today? That's cool. Trying something different."

"What? What do you mean?"

The waiter cocked his head sideways. "Uh, you almost always order the same thing when you come in here. It's the turkey sandwich. You don't remember us having this conversation a few days ago? Are you sure you're okay?"

"Just get me my order please," I said tersely, digging through my purse for money. My face heated, but soon I felt bad, because I didn't mean to be rude. I wasn't angry at all; I was just confused and annoyed. I was not adapting to this forgetful thing. It felt strange to be recognized by people I didn't know. The whole situation was frustrating.

My sandwich came and I left, still holding my map in one hand, I made my way back to Brandisham's. I was so proud of myself when I saw the skinny white building ahead of me.

I walked back in the store. The girl at the desk, Portia, I think was what Chrissy called her, stood up and looked at me.

"Where'd you go?" she asked confrontationally.

"Out for some lunch. Is that a crime?"

"No, but why would you go to lunch during our busy time?"

I glanced around Portia's shoulder. The store was as empty as it was when I came in at nine o'clock that morning.

"Portia, there's nobody here."

"But we could have had a rush, you never know," she said, putting her hands on her hips. I could see now that she was just looking for a fight. She was in luck, because in my frustration, I happened to be in a fighting mood.

"A rush for what? Thousand-dollar prom dresses? Pant suits? This is a high-end fashion boutique; there's no such thing as a 'rush.' This store is run by appointment only." I started to walk by, but she stood in my way.

"If you don't like this place that much, then why don't you quit? Believe me, after what you did the other day, you'd be doing us all a favor."

"I didn't complain about my job. My job down in the basement is just fine. Now please, get out of my way." I stepped around her again and headed to the basement.

"Jackie," she called after me.

"Go take some diet pills or something. Some of us have work to do," I shouted. The other salesgirls, who were standing around talking, stopped and stared at me. I saw their jaws drop. I was even surprised at myself. Why would I talk like that to anyone?

Chrissy was waiting for me at the bottom of the stairs laughing hysterically.

"You made it back," she giggled. "And you brought some attitude with you."

"Yeah," I smiled. "And a sandwich." We went back to the desks and I started to eat. The chicken salad wasn't as great as it sounded, but it was still edible. Chrissy watched me eat with admiration, every once in a while, she laughed and said, "'Go take some diet pills.' Ha! It's priceless, priceless! Where did that come from?"

"I don't know."

The rest of the day was fairly tame after that. Chrissy said that Mrs. Brandisham was out of town for a couple of days, otherwise, Portia would have tried to get me in trouble for what I said. Deep down, I was extremely glad Mrs. Brandisham was gone. I was terrified of what would happen to me, especially after what I heard about the Kat Pendleton fiasco.

Five o'clock rolled around, and Chrissy and I began to clean up our spaces to go home. We walked up the stairs together, and the other girls walked by us, gathering their things and leaving, giving both of us even more of a cold shoulder than I imagined they used to. Portia had already left; I swore I heard another girl on her phone say she went home after lunchtime.

Archie was leaning against the wall outside. I had forgotten he was coming back for me.

"Hey, Jack! What's happenin'?" I laughed because I knew it was a lyric, but I'd never heard it. I reminded myself to find that song sometime. For now, I was too excited to dwell on a lyric; I had to tell Archie about what happened at lunch.

When I finished, he laughed loudly, clapping his hands in enjoyment, as we walked home. We stopped at a crowded corner, waiting to cross the street. Archie turned his head and began scanning the crowd.

"What?" I asked. He pointed at a girl adjacent to us. It was one of the girls from the store. I tried to remember what her name was, I think it was Tascha. I grunted.

"Ugh. That's one of the girls from Brandisham's," I said.

Archie nodded and kept staring.

"What? Do you like her?" Archie looked at me and smiled. "You do like her!" My voice unintentionally carried, and out of my periphery, I saw Tascha turn her head. Archie's face turned red.

Could you talk to her for me, please? He wrote.

"Archie, come on. You could do so much better than that." He suddenly stopped smiling and looked away and I felt a little bad for disapproving of his crush. "That being said," I continued. "If you would like me to talk to her, I will." He looked at my face and smiled wide. Then he added to his note: *If you remember.*

7

The next few days were pretty low key. I didn't have to work again until Monday, so I hung around the house, making lists, and little fact cards which I posted in various places around the apartment. Maxine and Archie didn't mind, in fact, they kept remembering more things for me to post. Archie brought home a giant calendar on Friday and hung it up in our living space by the phone. On it, he wrote when he was at work, Maxine's schedule and the four days I worked as well. He also wrote down important things, like the MRI appointment, which was helpful because I had forgotten about it.

The truth was, for as quirky as the whole thing was beginning to be, I was glad to have some reminders around the place, because I was never sure if or when I was going to have another one of my spells. Every time night rolled around, I'd become terrified, because I had no idea what was going to happen in the morning. Every time Maxine or Archie left for work, they hugged me ferociously and every goodbye hinted at "so long forever." It was sad the way they treated me like they would never see me again, but I understood. I may always be here, in the apartment, but I could always be a different Jackie, and I wouldn't even know it.

In order for all of that to not happen, I took full advantage of reading every post I made every time I crossed one to ensure a complete memory, or at least some familiarity if I ever woke up unknowing again. I got out the map I found in my purse and spent the better part of Saturday studying it. I wanted to know exactly where everything in New York City was. I made a small dot with a marker where the apartment was, Brandisham's, the bank where Archie worked, and even the supermarket and night club where Maxine worked. Archie took my marker and made a dot over-top an already marked spot. I realized it was The Corner Nook, and I remembered the post by the refrigerator door that said, *"We frequently go to The Corner Nook Café and eat or just hang out and have coffee. It's 'our place'."*

I decided to impress Archie with my studying skills and offered to go to the café and get us some food. He thought it was a marvelous idea, but insisted that he follow close behind me, just in case.

We left and headed down the block and around corners; I felt a wave of independence, walking by myself, yet still comforted, knowing Archie was right behind.

I was ecstatic when I turned a corner and found the Corner Nook. I didn't have any trouble getting there at all. I stopped in front of the door, and Archie put his arm around my shoulder.

"Yeah baby, she's got it," he chuckled. I laughed heartily.

Inside, I moved toward a small table in the center of the floor, but Archie pulled me off to the side, to a table against the wall. This table had cloth bench seating that looked far more comfortable than the regular chairs. Archie's notepad explained that we always sit at that table, the three of us huddled on the bench, so we can see the whole café, and outside as well. It was like we were some cool clique in high school, sitting at the popular table, scoping out the other, less popular kids.

A waiter walked by and said hello. He looked at Archie, who raised two fingers and the waiter replied with, "The usual, then? And you as well?" I nodded. I remembered the gross chicken salad from the other day and decided since I did have a usual, it was probably my usual for a reason, and so I should probably try it. Archie and I sat quiet, watching out the window at the people passing.

A different waiter stopped and dropped off our food. I recognized him as the same waiter from the line the other day. He pursed his lips and looked at both of us as we thanked him but said nothing. When his eyes met mine, he quickly looked down and hurried off. Obviously, he still remembered the other day. Fortunately, I did too, and I scooted Archie out of the booth so I could get out and I followed him as he went back behind the counter and headed into the kitchen.

"Hey," I said loudly, as he was opening the kitchen door. He paused and turned around.

"Can I get you something?" he asked shyly.

"No, I just wanted to apologize for yelling at you the other day. I was just having a bad day and I wasn't mad at you or anything. Just frustrated. So, I'm sorry."

"Oh, okay," he replied, grinning slightly. "Um, apology accepted."

"Great," I smiled and headed back to the table. Archie was still standing next to the booth, watching me. I could tell by the look on his face that he was curious as to what I was doing. As I slid back into the booth, I explained that I had freaked out on him for no reason.

We ate our food silently, entranced by watching the people outside, like it was a TV show. Archie kept elbowing me and motioning his head toward the kitchen. Every time I looked, but I wasn't sure what I was looking at or for.

That waiter keeps looking over here, his notepad told me. I looked up, and sure enough, his eyes quickly averted. Archie was grinning idiotically, and his smirking and head motions made me smile, but then I just started giggling. Still laughing, I looked again at the waiter, who didn't take his eyes off me so quickly this time, but when he finally did, putting his head down, filling a glass for someone, I could see the hint of a smile on his lips. We played eye-tag with one another for a long while, but I realized I was distracting him, as a few of the line cooks had to call his name, "Reece", a few times to get his attention.

Archie paid for our food, and we left, but not before I got one more glimpse of the waiter. Outside, Archie handed me the map and let me get us back home. I found the apartment with only one incident where I started to turn left and heard Archie whistle, so I promptly turned right.

Back home, I went to throw on some lounge pants, and I noticed how bare my room was. It was a little more colorful these days with my little notes everywhere, but not much. I decided what I really needed more than anything was a nice color for the walls. I didn't really need any furniture, because I didn't seem to spend much time there, but it needed a personal touch; something that felt like "me." The only problem was I wasn't exactly sure what "me" felt like.

"Hey Arch, I was thinking about painting my room. It seems so bland, and maybe if my room had some personality, it would help me if I ever forget again. What do you think?" I said, walking into the living area and joining him on the couch.

He nodded, still looking at the TV.

"How about tomorrow? Are you free to help me tomorrow?" I glanced at the giant calendar by the phone and saw that Maxine wasn't working until late either. "Oh, and Max can help too! Now I'm excited," I said, mostly to myself. I curled myself into the arm of the couch and rested my head on a pillow. I tried focusing on what was on TV, but my mind was racing with color choices for my room. *What color suits me?* I wondered. I had visions of my room in every color I could think of. I grabbed a post-it note off the coffee table and wrote: *You're painting your bedroom tomorrow.* I wanted to remember I was doing this, so my room wouldn't continue being so empty and bland.

8

I woke up early Sunday. I wanted to get to a hardware store and pick out a color for my bedroom, and I wanted to do it all by myself. I needed to prove that I didn't have to depend on Archie and Maxine all the time. I left them a note on my door, promising to call them if I get lost, but I knew as long as I had my map, I was okay.

I walked down the street and stopped at a small vendor on the corner, who showed me on my map how to get to the closest paint store. It wasn't terribly close, but it was in walking distance. I studied my map and found the store with no trouble; the city was becoming easier to navigate.

The store was huge; it took up most of a building, which took up most of a block. I suddenly grew nervous being alone in such a massive store. I wasn't exactly sure where to begin; I apparently had never shopped for paint in my life because it was a skill my brain didn't know how to do. I found a woman wearing a red apron standing by a counter, so I approached her.

"Excuse me, I would like some help. I want to paint my bedroom, but I'm not sure what color I want or how to go about acquiring paint." I felt so embarrassed after I said it. I sounded like an idiot.

"Sure, I'd be glad to help," she said softly, not noticing, or at least pretending not to notice my embarrassment. "First, let's go over to the paint chip wall and pick out a color. Did you have one in mind?"

I stared at the wall she was pointing to and blankly shook my head.

"Okay, that's fine. I usually tell people to walk down the wall and back and grab any chip that holds your attention. Most people say they find a color that evokes some emotion out of them. Usually, the right color is the one your eyes keep going back to."

She started me at one end and slowly, we walked together, my eyes scanning up and down the colors that were sorted from dark red to light purple. It was a lot to take in. My eyes homed in on a greenish blue, but I kept walking. As I walked, I turned my head back to the greenish blue. The woman urged me to at least walk the whole length of the wall once, before going back. I did, but my mind had made itself up. I wanted that blue. I went back and picked the chip and handed it to the woman. The paint chip had the blue color on the top and matching accent colors on the bottom. I picked a lighter pale blue as my accent and the woman set off to mix my paint. As I waited, I scanned the wall again, looking to see if any other colors stood out to me or made me feel a certain way. I found a lot of colors that I thought were pretty, but nothing that evoked any feelings. Except when I got to that blue. When I saw it for the second time, my mind visualized a serene beach, where the sky and the ocean were indistinguishable at the horizon. My whole body felt suddenly relaxed and happy.

"Breathe Easy Blue," she read, cheerfully. "That one is so nice."

The woman came back shortly with two cans of paint. I wasn't sure how much they were going to cost, and I had yet to go to a bank or ATM and take out some money, but luckily, I had a hundred dollar bill that Archie gave me for the paint yesterday. I paid for the paint, I thanked the woman for being so helpful and was off, headed for the apartment.

It was difficult to carry two heavy cans of paint and still hold my map, so I was forced to stick it back in my purse, and go the course blindly, which I thought I could handle. I was absolutely sure that I had the path correct until I suddenly found myself walking down a street I didn't recognize. There were no signs or stores or even any windows, only doors that blended in with the cement walls. Above my head I saw some fire escapes that would be of no use to anyone if a fire ever occurred; they were rusted to the core and seemed to be dangling for dear life on the side of the buildings. I realized I was not where I was supposed to be and set my cans down to view my map. I realized I had turned right instead of left, so I turned around and headed back to the main street again.

As I turned the corner, I bumped into a man, who was hurrying down that windowless street. I stumbled backward a bit; the already heavy cans in my hands stretched my muscles even more as I attempted to balance.

"Sorry," he said, rushing past.

"It's okay," I answered. He stopped. He spun around, his eyes staring at my face. He took three large steps at me, his eyes never blinking. A grin stretched across his face.

"Why hello, Mara. Long time, no see." He spoke with a deep, devious sound.

"I'm sorry, who? That's not me. You have me confused with someone else," I mumbled, terrified. I had no idea who he was or who Mara was, but the ferocity with which he seemed to recognize me was frightening. I turned my back to him, but he grabbed my arm.

"No, no, no," He whispered, still smiling. "I would never forget you, Mara. I couldn't. No matter what color you change your hair to, I'll still know you."

"I'm sorry. My name isn't Mara. My name is Jackie. You have me confused with someone else. I'm not Mara." I tried not to show it, but I was panicking on the inside.

He could apparently tell, because he never stopped smiling, all the while, he was inching closer to me, as I kept backing away.

"Oh, so it's Jackie now, is it? Of course. You certainly would have to change your name along with your hair color. That's how one forms a new identity, isn't it? And clever too, going into hiding without ever leaving the city. New York certainly is big enough. You were always much more clever than I gave you credit for."

"What are you talking about? I've never seen you before in my life." My voice quivered.

"Come on, Mara. You were my right hand; always the one to stick to the deal. In, then out, no exceptions. You followed the plan to a tee. I never expected you to disappear like you did. But here you are, still in New York City, of all places. You are very good at hiding."

"I don't even know what's going on. What deals? You've got the wrong girl. I'm not Mara," I was starting to sound less frightened but more angry.

"Mara, oh, I'm sorry, it's Jackie now. Jackie, you remember. You were my number two runner. When Kane dealt the stuff, you took the cash, it was a simple operation. And you were good at it. Until you disappeared on me." He started to sound just as frustrated, as I continued to stare blankly. "I wish you would drop this act you have going on. The jig is up. I found you. Now, tell me where the money is."

"What money?"

"Jackie, don't toy with me. You know what I'm talking about."

"No, I don't. What money?"

"Jackie, it's me, it's Razi. All I want is for you to tell me where the money is, and I'll leave you alone. You can go on pretending to be something you're not, and you'll never see me again, I swear. Just tell me where the money went."

"I don't know where the money went. I don't know anything about any money at all. I don't even know you!" I shouted. He slammed his hand against the wall; it came within inches of my face and I jumped.

"Dammit, Mara! Stop lying to me! You've cost me a lot, as it is. Because of your little stunt, Kane got pinched and is in prison for the next three years." His teeth were clenched while he spoke. "So then, I wasn't only short a runner, but now, I'm short a dealer as well. I think the least you could do for me now is let me have my goddamn money!" His voice carried and I wondered why nobody passing by this corner stopped to see what the commotion was about.

"I don't have your money anymore," I lied. "I spent it." I hoped that sounded convincing.

"How did you spend seventy-five thousand dollars in six weeks? You didn't spend that much money. Now where is it?"

"I spent it on lots of things. I bought clothes and hotel rooms and I took some trips and put a little in various bank accounts around the country. But I swear to you, I don't have it anymore." I was actually impressed by my improvisation. He was not.

"You have my money. Since you don't seem to remember how much I hate being messed with, I'm going to remind you," he threatened, grabbing my hand, paint can and all, and pulling a knife from his pocket.

"This paint will be so hard to carry home without any fingers, won't it?"

As the knife touched my knuckles, I screamed. Then, without even thinking, my other hand swung up and struck his face with the paint can. He dropped his knife, and fell to the ground, yelling.

"I will find you, you bitch!"

I turned around the corner and ran as fast as I could. I bumped into more people than I could count, but I didn't care; I was just trying to get the hell away from Razi. Eventually, I had to stop, first, because I was out of breath and my lungs were starting to burn, and second, because I had no idea where I was. I saw a sign for a bookstore and ducked in.

I walked to the back of the store, stood behind a bookshelf and set my paint cans down. Then, I slowly slunk down to the floor, my heart pounding wildly, my breathing, so loud that other people were staring at me. I sat there for a moment, frozen, trying to calm myself down. I was scared, but I didn't even have time to think about that. I needed to get back to the apartment before I could dissect what just happened.

I got out my map and realized I didn't know where I was. I saw a man standing at the end of the aisle where I sat, so I called him over. He told me where I was and was even kind enough to show me on my map. He appeared concerned at how shaken I seemed, and walked me out of the store, hailing me a cab to take me home.

9

I shuffled slowly into the apartment. Archie and Maxine were both awake, sitting on the couch, waiting for me.

"There you are. We were getting worried," Maxine said. "I see you found the paint store all by yourself. Did you have any trouble getting there or back?"

I shook my head, intending to keep silent, but I knew I couldn't. "Not getting there," I said, my voice choking. "But on the way back."

Maxine's face fell and she stared at me. Archie stood up from the couch, staring at me also. I started to cry, and he grabbed my shoulders and moved me to the couch. Then, he grabbed the cans out of my hands and set them down. I cried hard, as Maxine hugged me and stroked my hair.

"It's okay, Jackie. Tell me what happened."

I straightened up, wiping the tears away. Archie handed me a tissue, and after a few deep breaths, I proceeded to tell them about this Razi person, and how he recognized me, kept calling me "Mara". I detailed the drug deals, and how someone named Kane got arrested when I disappeared. I told them how I hit him in the head with a can of paint and ran away.

Archie turned on the computer and did an internet search through the *New York Times* archives for a drug bust with a dealer named Kane. He found it in no time at all, as it was a fairly recent event. The three of us hovered over the screen, reading.

ARRESTS MADE IN HIGH-END DRUG DEAL
A drug deal was busted Wednesday, after an anonymous phone call lead cops to the home of Hector Guerez, a fine art dealer and multi-millionaire. The cops found Guerez in the basement of his Manhattan townhouse, conversing with a gentleman identified as Leonard Kanterelli, known in the drug community as "Kane". Both

men were arrested when police uncovered a secret room full of cocaine behind a wine rack twenty feet from where the men sat. While the drugs had been found and both men detained, police are still looking for a believed third party, who possibly has the money Guerez allegedly paid for the drugs.

We stood there, silent, no one sure of what to even say. I was afraid of what Maxine and Archie were going to think, if they thought I had anything to do with it or not.

Finally, Maxine broke the silence. "Jackie, are you involved in this?"

"I don't know, Max. I don't remember. This Razi seems to think so."

"Do you have a bank account?" Maxine asked.

I remembered my bank card, and dug it out of my purse, handing it to Archie, who drew up the account online. "It says there's seventy thousand dollars in my account," I said, slowly building panic. "Razi said I stole seventy-five thousand, but I obviously spent some. That means I'm an accomplice to a crime! What am I going to do?"

"It's not that I don't believe you, because I've witnessed your memory loss, but Jackie, this is serious. Did you have anything to do with this? Do you remember any of this at all?"

"No. Maxine, I swear to you that I don't remember any of this. I wouldn't even suspect myself if that money wasn't so close to the amount missing. I could have been involved I guess, because I honestly don't remember anything, but I'm not that kind of a person. You have to believe that I would never be involved in a crime like that now. I swear."

Maxine's eyes looked at me intensely. She searched my face for a long time before she relaxed and said, "You're right. I do believe that you wouldn't do anything like that now. If you did do this, though, then we have to do something, don't we?"

I nodded but cried hard again. "Just don't let me go to jail. Please, don't send me to jail."

"Oh, no, no, no, honey. Archie and I are not going to let you go to jail. We'll figure something out."

Archie snapped his fingers and started writing in his notepad.

What if we just turn in what's left of the money anonymously? We can transfer it and tip off the police but leave it at that. As long as they get the money, do they need the accomplice?

Maxine thought for a moment. "That could work, Arch. We could just find a way to either take out the money or put it in a different bank account or something and then notify the police. Now, if we do this, we have to be very careful, and we have to figure out how to get the money out of the bank without anyone suspecting anything."

The plan sounded solid. My brain relaxed, but my body was still tense. I felt a little sick, still in shock that I may or may not have been involved in a crime. I read over the article one more time while it was on the screen. *There was an anonymous call, which could very easily have come from someone involved in the crime. Maybe I was the anonymous phone call,* I reasoned.

The sickness had yet to subside, so I told Maxine and Archie I was going to lay down. I covered up with my sheet and went to sleep. For the first time, I begged myself to have another amnesic spell while I was asleep. I wished that in a couple hours, all of this would be forgotten. I would have no idea about Razi, or Kane, or any of it.

Three hours later, Maxine woke me up to see if I was hungry. I opened my eyes, recognized her and knew that my troubles were not gone. I sighed loudly and hid my face in my pillow. She came and sat by me.

"How are you feeling?"

"I feel horrible. I wish this would all go away. Why can't I forget things when I need to?"

Maxine smiled. "Honestly, I was hoping you would forget too."

"Are you guys mad at me? Are you going to turn me in?"

"Absolutely not, Jackie. We would never rat you out, especially since I firmly believe you're not the same person you were when you did that -*if* you did that."

"I don't even know what kind of a person I was. I mean, I tried telling myself that maybe I didn't know what I was getting in to, or maybe I was in need of shelter and money at the time or something. I keep trying to justify myself."

"Which is why I believe you're a different person. If you had been involved in that drug ring, and you knew it was wrong and did it anyway, you wouldn't be defending yourself now. Even after you lost your memory, if you were truly a bad person, you'd still be a bad person, and you're not." I wiped another tear from my eye and she leaned over me. "Don't you worry, Jackie. Archie and I are here to help you. We're in this together, and we're not going to leave you behind. I promise." We both smiled, and I knew everything would be okay.

Maxine left my room, and once she was gone, I realized she had never confirmed whether or not I was hungry -which I was. I debated getting out of bed to get something, but I just didn't feel like getting up. Luckily, Maxine came back with a plate of food for me; she knew me too well, I had to admit. I sat up and she sat with me as I ate the chicken and mashed potatoes. It was delicious. I felt like such a pig, sucking down all that food so fast.

"Are you up for painting?" Maxine asked when I finished my food.

I shook my head. "Not really. I feel like junk right now. I probably shouldn't have eaten that food."

"Oh, it's okay. You're just upset. You'll be fine."

"No, I'm serious, Max. My stomach really hurts now. I thought it was just nerves earlier, but now it's really painful." I flung the sheets off and jumped up, sprinting to the bathroom. I slunk down to the toilet.

I spent the better part of the rest of the day lying in the bathroom, throwing up that wonderful food Maxine had cooked. I felt awful. Maxine and Archie took turns guarding the door, checking up on me, which added to my misery, taking away a day of their relaxation.

"You know, Jackie, it's probably nothing. You have just experienced a traumatic episode, and I probably shouldn't have fed you. I'm so sorry." Maxine was apologizing up and down, but it wasn't her fault at all.

"No, Max. It's my fault; I ate too fast. I'll be okay. Just let me lay here for a while," I said, resting my head on my arm. The vomiting had worn me out, and I soon fell asleep.

When I woke up again, it was dark. I realized I was now back in my bed. The clock said ten o'clock. I didn't hear any noise from out in the other room, so I figured Archie and Maxine were in their rooms. I stood up, stretched my arms and walked into the bathroom. I ran the tap and washed my face with some cold water. I watched my reflection in the mirror as the water rolled off in large drops. I was in a trance; my eyes would not look away.

I kept thinking about Razi, the way he looked at me. He truly did recognize my face, and I knew it. I could tell by the flare in his eyes and the grin on his face. I knew as soon as I read the article online that I was involved. It had to be me; I didn't exactly look like everyone else. I was confident now that that was the reason everyone seemed to know me in this big city; millions of people, and I get recognized by two or three strangers every day. My stomach ached again, this time, with fear. I suddenly realized that Razi knew I was here in the city, and he now knew my name, therefore it was only a matter of time before he found me again.

I tensed up again. What if he found Maxine and Archie too? What if he hurt them to get to me? I didn't want that to happen. My hands began to shake; I was terrified. What was I going to do?

I had to leave. That was the only thing I could do. I would take some money out of my account and leave New York. I would have to change my name –again, apparently. My brain made a list of plans, as I headed back for my room. The floorboards squeaked underneath me, no matter how quiet I tried to be.

"Jackie, are you alright?"

I turned around and found Maxine standing outside her door.

I nodded, and went to my room, and started taking the clothes out of my drawers. The door suddenly opened and Maxine looked at me.

"What are you doing, honey?"

"I can't stay here," I whispered. "Razi knows I'm here and he also knows my name, so it's only a matter of time before he finds me, and I can't risk you or Archie getting hurt because of me. So, I've got some money, and I'm just going to get on a bus and go somewhere and try to hide."

She stepped in front of me and grabbed both of my arms by the wrists. "Now you listen here, Jackie." Her voice was quiet but stern. "You are not going to run off somewhere by yourself. You could get hurt or you could have another episode or something, and then what would you do? I'm not afraid of this Razi guy, and Archie isn't either. We can take care of ourselves. Right now, our priority is making sure that you're okay. So put all of your clothes away and go back to bed. You're staying put."

And that was that. I put everything neatly back in the dresser and crawled into bed. She waited for a moment before returning to her room, and I closed my eyes and fell asleep.

In the morning, I dressed for work, ate and left with Archie. Maxine never mentioned last night and neither did I. I realized she was right. I couldn't take care of myself, especially in my condition. Then I thought how terrible it would be if I had left and then had one of my spells. I would have completely forgotten Archie and Maxine, and I would be alone, with no idea what to do with myself.

Work seemed to go by alright. I had some notes that I went over, and Chrissy helped remind me of things which I appreciated. Twice, I volunteered to be the person to bring outfits upstairs. I wanted to prove that I was capable of remembering where the clothes were. Chrissy was so proud both times, clapping her hands when I came downstairs with a victorious strut. I had to admit I was feeling pretty good about my job.

It was nice to feel good about something. I hadn't slept very well the night before, still worrying about Razi. Even now, I was afraid he would just show up at Brandisham's. Focusing on the work helped push that thought to the back of my mind. *It will be impossible for him to find you,* I reasoned. *There are millions of people in this city, and you had been here for six weeks before he ran into you.*

The day ended quickly, and I saw Archie standing outside and Chrissy and I left. As soon as I was outside, Archie nudged me. I asked what and he glared at me. I suddenly remembered I was supposed to talk to Tascha for him.

"Oh, right. Sorry Arch. I forgot to talk to her today. I'll do it tomorrow, I promise."

It wasn't until we got home that I realized my note was still pinned to my purse. I decided to write myself another little note to remember my other note. I stuck it on my dresser.

Again, that night, I couldn't sleep. I tried closing my eyes, but every time, I could see Razi's face. When I couldn't do it on my own, I decided to watch TV until I fell asleep. I figured the mindless noise would help.

I took the sheet off my bed and curled up in it on the couch. I turned the TV on and started to watch an infomercial, but when they introduced the product as the "Bullet Slicer" I changed the channel. Eventually, I settled on reruns of *Seinfeld*. I was so engaged in the show that when I felt my eyelids drooping, I was tempted to get up and put cold water on my face. Laziness won, however, and I did end up falling asleep.

10

In the morning, the TV was still on, and Maxine and Archie were in the kitchen eating. I got up and dressed for work, and Archie and I left. Maxine had pinned a reminder about the MRI this week to my purse, so I wouldn't forget, like I was six years old. Archie nudged me before he left me at Brandisham's door, and I nodded. Whether I wanted to talk to Tascha or not, I owed it to him.

I found Tascha standing at the desk, talking to Portia. I immediately walked by. I wasn't going to talk with Portia around. She seemed to have an influence on people, just being in the near vicinity. I had made a brief pause at the desk, then continued walking, however, I remembered the note on my purse and returned to the desk to tell Portia I couldn't come in the next day. She huffed and puffed and snarled and glared at me, so I was forced to tell her it was for "medical reasons."

"Well, Jackie, this is ridiculous. You should have requested this day off last week. I don't know if I can give you the day off."

"Aw, come on, Portia. I meant to request it off before, but it kept slipping my mind. I need tomorrow off. Chrissy can handle the stock without me. This is important to my health," I begged.

Portia looked me up and down and made a sour face. "Well God, Jackie. Do you have some sort of disease or something? I mean, you look gross."

"I don't want to talk about it," I muttered, my face reddening.

"Fine, you can have your day off. Now don't wipe any of your germs on anything. If I get sick, Jackie, I swear to God…" She didn't finish her sentence, and I was already walking away.

I sank into my chair at my desk and took a deep breath. Chrissy looked up from her computer.

"You okay?"

"No. I have to ask Tascha if she would be interested in going out with Archie."

"Oh. That's all? I meant that you look like you're about to keel over and die. *Is* something wrong?"

"I just can't sleep these days. I keep having these nightmares." I knew Chrissy wouldn't ask about them, and I was glad she was that way because I didn't want to tell her I may have been involved in a drug ring.

"Ugh! Why did he have to be interested in her?" I tried to turn the subject back to Archie and Tascha after a brief silence.

"Well," Chrissy said matter-of-factly. "While I sympathize with you, I really do, Tascha is no Portia, that's for sure. So just be thankful it wasn't her."

Chrissy was right; at least Archie wasn't interested in Portia. I wouldn't have cared how much I owed him, if he had liked her, he would have been out of luck. I mentioned my almost-approach upstairs, and how awkward it was when I noticed Portia standing there.

"I just don't know when or how to do this, you know? I mean, I definitely don't want to say anything in front of Portia, but I've never seen Tascha without her somewhere in the wings. And what do I say?"

Chrissy straightened her glasses. "Just ask for a moment alone and say you have a friend who was wondering if she would like to go out sometime. You could point him out at the end of the day when he comes back to get you."

I dropped the subject, and unfortunately for me, the day went by incredibly fast. Before I knew it, Chrissy was gathering her stuff and waiting for me to get mine.

"Are you ready to talk to her?"

"I guess," I said, defeated.

As we walked up the stairs, I mentioned my MRI to Chrissy. She wished me good luck with everything and hugged me. It was sort of strange, like I wasn't going to make it back alive. Then, I noticed the other girls all rushed out the door, Tascha behind them, looking for something in her purse. I took a deep breath, readying myself and Chrissy patted my shoulder and headed out.

"Hey, Tascha?"

She looked up. Her face looked far less threatening than I had expected. "What?"

"Um, can I talk to you for a minute?"

She stopped walking and put her purse down.

"Um, I have this friend. He's my roommate, and, uh, he wanted me to ask you, um, if, uh, if you'd be interested in going out with him sometime."

She scrunched up her face, so I kept talking, really trying to sell him. "He's really nice, and he's got a good job. He works at the Bank of New York. Um, he's just a really swell guy."

"A swell guy?" She asked, snickering at my adjective. "What are we in, the Fifties?"

"Come on, you know what I mean. He's just really great."

"Is he that one who waits for you every day?" Her tone didn't sound excited, but she certainly wasn't being rude.

"Yeah, he's right out there," I said, pointing at Archie's back through the window.

"He likes to dress like he's from the Eighties or something."

"Yeah, I know. And he does have a tendency to talk in song lyrics."

"Why does he do that?"

"I don't exactly know, but-"

"You don't know why he talks like that? Have you ever asked?"

"Yes, but he never answers, but it's just a little quirk; he's not a freak or anything, I swear. Half the time, I can't even tell he's talking in lyrics. But he has a good heart."

Tascha looked out the window for a minute, chewing a piece of gum. "You know, that's really weird, about the lyric thing. But he's kind of cute. I guess we could go out once. Yeah, Jackie, okay. Tell him I'm interested in a date. He can meet me here Friday night around seven and he can take me out to dinner."

I wasn't trying to, but I smiled. "Great. I will tell him. Friday night, meet you here around seven. Thanks, Tascha. I really appreciate you doing this."

I stood there, waiting for her to leave first, but I forgot she had the keys to lock up, so I skipped out. Archie was dying for news. I couldn't hide my smile from him.

"You have a date Friday at seven. You meet her here and you can take her anywhere you want for dinner."

Archie wrapped his arms around my head and squeezed so tight, I became lightheaded for a moment. Next, he hugged my shoulders, and then he hugged me normally. His face was illuminated, and he practically ran us home.

I was feeling fatigued from all of the sleep I wasn't getting, and decided to nap for a bit, but I had a dream about Razi sitting outside my window, and I couldn't go back to sleep, or even be in my bedroom after that.

I went out into the living space, but Archie wasn't there. I knocked on his bedroom door. No answer. I opened it and went inside.

I had never been in his room before, and I had to admit I was curious. The walls were the faintest gray color, and his bed was pushed up to the wall, covered in a dark gray comforter. There was a dresser like mine, and a desk next to the bed. On the desk was a gigantic boom box. I wondered why I'd never heard Archie playing it, but then I saw a pair of headphones attached to it. Between the desk and his closet were two tall bookshelves full of CDs, tapes and records. My eyes searched the room and fell upon the record player in the corner. I walked in and sat on the bed. The fabric of the comforter was the softest thing I'd ever felt. I ran my hands across it a number of times, before I bent down and pressed my face to it. I closed my eyes, imagining hanging out in here with Archie, him playing some obscure Eighties band on the boom box.

Suddenly, I worried Archie would find me in his bedroom. Embarrassed, I hopped up and out of the room. I was overreacting, I kept telling myself, because I didn't even know where he was. He definitely wasn't home. My brain froze. What if Archie was taken? By Razi? What if he stepped out for a minute, but never made it back? My heart started beating hard. I ran to the window to watch for him. It was getting dark outside, and every person who passed below scared me more and more.

I was practically hanging out of the window, searching for him when he turned the corner. I was so happy to see him in one piece, I almost squealed. I watched him, unblinking, all the way to the building, and once he was inside, I stood up and ran to the door. I met him in the hallway, because I couldn't wait for him to come in.

"Archie! There you are! I was so worried!"

He gave me a funny look and continued into the apartment.

"Where did you go? I woke up and you weren't here!"

He went into the kitchen and set down a bag I suddenly noticed he was carrying. He pulled out three boxes of Chinese food, before turning around and grabbing a note posted on the wall, and handing it to me.

"Went to get us some Chinese Food. I'll be right back."

My face burned with embarrassment. "I'm sorry, Arch. But you have to understand, I'm getting paranoid about you and Maxine being away from me, because I'm afraid of Razi finding you. So please, forgive me for freaking out."

Archie smiled and hugged me. "It's okay, I understand. This ain't no never-never land."

I couldn't even contain my laughter.

11

Maxine came home early from the supermarket and had enough time to make a little dessert for us, but I wasn't hungry. I was really tired. Even though it was only six o'clock, I changed into pajamas and crawled into bed. I was freezing cold in my bed, which I thought was unusual because it was August, but eventually, I got so cold, I had to put on a sweatshirt and long fleece pants. I kept muttering to myself that I needed to buy an actual blanket sometime soon; these sheets just weren't cutting it.

I was woken by Maxine sitting at my side, brushing my hair with her hand. "Jackie," she whispered in her deep voice. "It's time to get up. We need to get to the hospital."

I got up, showered, and put on a comfortable pair of jeans and a t-shirt. Because it was still early, it was a tiny bit chilly outside, so I put on a sweatshirt. Maxine was already dressed to perfection in a pair of pinstriped pants and a chic blouse and tall heels, cooking a quick batch of eggs for us in the kitchen. I joined her, getting out plates and pouring out two cups of juice, hoping the food would wake me up, watching her cook. She looked so professional; I did a double take at the calendar by the phone, because I was certain she had taken the whole day off to come with me.

"What?" she asked, turning to see me watching her.

"Nothing," I responded, sleepily. "Max, why do you always look so well dressed? You're always in an amazing skirt or professional outfit of one kind or another. Don't you ever wear jeans and t-shirts? Or pajamas?"

"Pajamas in public? Ew, gross. Jackie, no one should ever wear their pajamas in public. I dress up every day, even when I don't work because I have a look to maintain. If anyone ever saw me not looking incredible one day, then why should I bother looking good any other day? I mean, people would have seen what I transform from, so the transformation would seem unnecessary. Do you follow me?" She was smiling like she was joking, but I could tell she'd thought this out.

"I guess so," I answered, rubbing the sleep out of my eye. "Geeze, you trannies are so weird."

She laughed hard. "Well, weirdness aside, Jackie, I was never much of a jeans person before, anyway." She silenced me with a plate of eggs that were so deliciously warm they heated my insides, thawing me out.

"I'm so glad these eggs are hot. I needed something hot to eat after my sleep last night. It was freezing."

"Oh, yeah. I forgot your bedroom is the only bedroom with a window. Archie's and mine butt up to the neighboring apartment. You're going to get a little cold at night these days. We should really get you a blanket."

"I want one like Archie's. It's so soft and comfortable." She laughed again and we finished our eggs and headed out.

I followed her to the subway, and during the ride, she told me all about our last trip to the hospital. I felt bad that none of this information sounded familiar to me, especially since it sounded exciting when she got to the part about me recognizing *The Wizard of Oz*. She showed me a drawing that she had been working on the last time. It was beautiful; I wished I could have remembered watching her draw that. I asked her why she wasn't in art school, and she laughed and told me we'd discussed that before.

At the hospital, we sat in the waiting room for about ten minutes. We had a scheduled appointment, so they took us right in. The doctor was in a room waiting for us, I remembered Maxine told me his name was Doctor Karish. Maxine made sure to tell him that I had had another spell after my last appointment, to which he "uh-huh"ed and "hmm"ed, taking some notes. He had me dress in a drab, gray gown that tied in the back, and then we left Maxine to wait with my clothes while he took me down the hall into a room with a giant machine that was shaped like a donut. There were other people in the room wearing green outfits and lab coats. The doctor introduced them as the technicians who would be conducting the MRI.

"Lay down right here, Jackie. This little bed is going to go inside that ring and take pictures of your brain. Now, I want you to put on these headphones, they will help you relax. You will hear some soothing music, and then when we get you situated, I am going to be in that room over there, and I just want you to stay calm and we're going to take pictures of your brain."

I lay down on the bed. There was the slightest breeze coming from somewhere and my body broke out into goose bumps. I shivered a little bit, but put on the headphones, trying to ignore it. The headphones were already playing soft flute music. I closed my eyes, trying to relax. The bed started to move slowly. I was still shivering, and my eyes opened, unintentionally and I watched the donut pass over me, like I was being placed in an ultramodern coffin. I looked all around me; the closeness was disturbing. I started breathing heavily, even though I didn't think I was claustrophobic. I guess I could have been; I didn't remember.

The music grew louder, and I shut my eyes tighter, thinking about slower breathing, hoping my lungs would slacken. It worked, as I soon found myself comfortable in the cramped space.

The bed started to move again, and I opened my eyes to watch the donut uncover me again. I lay still until the doctor came to help me up.

I was led back into the little room where Maxine was waiting, and I changed back into my clothes. She and I were sent home and asked to come back in the morning for my results.

We went home and I called off the next day at work before the day's end. Portia was difficult as usual, but when I reminded her it was one more day she didn't have to see my face, she was more lenient about letting me have the day off. "As long as you keep your germs away from me, you can take the day," she said.

Again, in the morning, I was awakened by Maxine and I mindlessly washed up and dressed and we again took the subway to the hospital. When we arrived, we were asked to wait in the lobby. It was still fairly early in the morning, and my lack of sleep was wearing on me, so I curled up in my chair and nestled my head into Maxine's shoulder.

I was in a heavy sleep when Maxine woke me up. I glanced at my watch; we had been in the lobby for almost an hour. Finally, my name was called and Maxine and I were taken to another little exam room, where Doctor Karish had just stepped in, and I rubbed my eyes, trying to focus on him.

"How are you feeling Jackie?"

"I'm tired, Doctor Karish. Did you find out what's wrong with me?"

"Well, as I assumed before, you do seem to have amnesia. Now, we often classify amnesiacs as having one of two types. The first type is when you can't remember the past, and the second type is when you can't make new memories. Now, it seems like you can make new memories, but for some reason, they delete themselves after a time. Looking at your MRI results, I see no clear damage to your brain."

"I guess I don't understand. What does this mean?"

"Well Jackie, your brain seems fine. You just can't retain your memories."

"So, is it fixable?"

"I don't know. It might be, but I'm not entirely sure. We've never 'fixed' someone's amnesia before. Most people end up remembering on their own; they snap out of it."

I bit my lip, trying hard to resist, but I started to tear up.

"What's the matter?"

"Well, you said that my new memories aren't sticking, so that means when I have another episode, all of my new memories will be gone again. I won't even be able to remember Maxine's name. I don't want Maxine to have to explain who she is to me every day."

Maxine, who had been silent for a while, finally interrupted. "Excuse me, doctor, but were you able to figure out what causes her episodes?"

Doctor Karish shook his head. "Unfortunately, no. But I will venture to guess that it's probably brought on by stress or trauma. Of course, it could also just happen. I would suggest trying not to get worked up or stressed out and see if that makes any difference."

"Oh, of course, I won't get stressed, what, with not being able to remember anything about my life," I mocked.

"I do have a suggestion," he went on, ignoring me. "I think you should consider seeing a psychiatrist. A therapist could be beneficial to you in your condition, teach your brain exercises to help your memory. Let me give you some contacts." He wrote down a couple names and numbers and handed them to Maxine.

"Please, Jackie, give these doctors a chance, okay?" He released us to the front desk, where Maxine took care of payments or paperwork or insurance or something; I wasn't exactly paying attention.

We got back on the subway and headed home. I sat in my seat, staring straight ahead, lost in thought. I decided I was hopeless. It apparently didn't matter what happened because I was just going to forget things anyway. I began to grow overwhelmingly sad at the prospect of never ever being able to remember Maxine or Archie. As worried as I was about forgetting them all the time, I also imagined how annoying it would be to have to look after me twenty-four hours a day. Maxine often told me that they would never turn their backs on me, no matter what, but I could only wonder how time might change things.

I could feel Maxine's eyes on me. She was concerned, no doubt. I knew that taking care of me wasn't easy, and it was hard for her to know what I was experiencing. I leaned forward and buried my face in my hands. She rested her hand on my back. As worried as she was over me, I honestly felt worse for her; only being able to sympathize, never to completely understand.

"Jackie, I'm going to call one of these doctors for you when we get home, okay?"

"It doesn't matter, Maxine, it won't work," I answered, my head still buried.

"Don't talk like that, honey. You have to be hopeful."

I closed my eyes and tried to rest my mind. I was just so tired; I couldn't even stand it anymore. Slowly, I drifted off, my head sinking from my hands down onto my knees.

12

I felt a jolt. Opening my eyes, I realized my head was buried in my knees. It was quite an uncomfortable position. I slowly tried to sit up; my back was aching. Another jolt sent me upright. I looked around. I was on the subway. What was I doing here?

As I looked around, something on my back started moving up and down. I leaned against my seat and pressed hard.

"Ouch! Oh my God, Jackie, what's your problem?"

I looked at the woman next to me. Did she know who I was? I thought she had just called me "Jackie." Was that my name? It didn't sound familiar. I looked at her strangely. If she knew me, then why didn't I know her?

My heart froze. I determined that she was pretending to know me. She was probably going to mug me or murder me or something. I had a plan, though. I wasn't going to let anything happen to myself.

I leaned forward and freed her hand. Then, I sat, motionless, moving only my eyes around the train. I could tell the woman was watching me, which was going to make my getaway difficult.

I felt another jolt from the train, and soon, it began to slow. My plan was going to work faster than I had anticipated. The train stopped, the doors opened and I watched as people got off and on. Quickly, I stood up.

"What are you doing?" The woman asked. "This isn't our stop."

As the door started closing, I darted out. The door opened back up, when it sensed me exiting; long enough for the strange woman to exit as well. *Damn,* I thought. *This isn't going to work.*

I started running as fast as I could through the people and up the stairs. I could hear her behind me yelling.

"Jackie! Slow down! Where are you going?"

I just kept running. I had no idea where I was or where I was going, but I needed to get away from that woman. What did she want from me?

The streets were crowded. I had to shift my body to get by. Looking ahead, I saw a large building that I recognized. It was the Chrysler Building. I was in New York City!

Wait, what am I doing here? I thought. My mind started to race with all kinds of questions. It was getting difficult to concentrate on running. Soon, my lungs started to burn. I wanted to stop, but I didn't.

When I couldn't take it any longer, when my lungs were on the verge of bursting, I slowed down, intending to stop, when I tripped. There was a large marble courtyard with tall concrete steps in front of me. My foot didn't raise high enough, and I lost my balance. I hit the next step with my forearm, followed by my other hand and my knees close behind. I rolled over and sat up, clutching my arm in agony. Tears streamed down my face, as I watched the blood flow down my arm. I looked up at all of the passing people; not one person acknowledged my injury.

I couldn't move. My arm hurt too much. I felt like such a baby, sitting on the steps crying. Trying to focus away from the pain, I started asking myself questions, like what my name was and how old I was and what I was doing in New York. I concluded my name could be Jackie, but I wasn't positive. I had no idea how old I was or why I was in New York. Even more curious was that my brain seemed to assume that I had just appeared here, out of nowhere, like there was no possibility that I had grown up here. My mind was a flurry of questions that I had no answers to, and suddenly, I was terrified. What was I going to do?

"Jesus Christ, Jackie. There you are! What the hell were you doing? Why did you run away from me? You know I can't run in heels!"

I looked up and saw the woman standing over me, panting as hard as I was. She bent down, clutching her side. I didn't move. She sat down next to me.

"What's going on? Did you have another one of your episodes?"

I had no idea what she was talking about. I stayed silent. She was still panting and holding her side. Leaning toward me, she looked at my face, then her eyes shifted to my bleeding arm.

"Holy hell, Jackie! Are you okay? Oh my God, we need to get you back to the hospital." She stood up, but I stayed still.

"Come on, Jackie. Look, there's a pharmacy right across the street. Let's at least get you some gauze or something." She pulled on my other arm, and even though I was still hurting, I went with her. I didn't trust her, but I didn't know anyone else in this city, so my need for kinship won over my pain.

"Who are you?" I asked as she hoisted me to my feet.

"Ugh! Not again," she muttered. "I'm Maxine. I'm transsexual. We're roommates with a guy named Archie who dresses like he's from the eighties and he speaks in lyrics. Nobody knows why he does that, he just does. I'll explain everything when we get home, but good Lord, can we at least get you home in one piece?"

We crossed the street and went into the pharmacy. Maxine dragged me up to the counter where the clerk's eyes bulged at the sight of my arm.

"Okay," Maxine said. "I need alcohol, some Band-Aids, salve and a couple rolls of gauze, please. Oh, and do you have a bathroom?"

The clerk said nothing, backed away slowly from the counter and returned with the items and pointed us toward the restrooms. Maxine pulled me like a dog on a leash into the bathroom and shoved my arm under the faucet. Next came the alcohol, which stung worse than the actual wound itself. Once clean, I could see that it wasn't a very large cut, but deep; it wouldn't stop bleeding. The actual pain was coming from under the cut, where my arm was harvesting a large bruise and bump already. The clerk had brought us a box of gigantic Band-Aids, one of which, after the application of alcohol and salve, was stuck over the cut and bruise. The pain increased with the pressure of the Band-Aid, and again after Maxine wrapped a roll of gauze around the bandage.

When I thought we were done, she grabbed my other hand and flipped it palm side up. There was a minor scrape, but she cleaned it anyway and wrapped another swatch of gauze around it. We left the bathroom and went back to the counter where Maxine paid for our medical supplies and we left.

Back on the subway, I finally spoke. "What were we doing?"

"What?"

"What were we doing before all that running?"

"We were at the hospital. You were getting your results from an MRI you had yesterday. Doctor Karish said you've got a mixture of two types of amnesia." She continued to tell me about my procedure and about my previous attacks, which led to me creating hundreds of reminders for myself. The whole thing scared me, to know that this had happened before, but I did take a bit of solace in the fact that there would be tons of little notes waiting for me at home.

"The doctor gave me these numbers for psychiatrists. I think it would be a good idea for you." I agreed and allowed her to make me an appointment when we got home. I stayed silent the rest of the journey, listening to her talk about me, my body aching.

Our apartment was lovely. The living space was very modern with wood floors and brick walls and huge, boxy low-backed furniture. As expected, little yellow notes sprinkled the entire apartment, kitchen and bathroom included.

Maxine set out to make us some lunch, while I set to reading all the notes. It was sort of thrilling, reading about me; the trouble was it didn't feel like it was me. I felt as though I was learning about someone else. But I kept reading, hoping something would stick.

I moved around the apartment like I was on a scavenger hunt, frantically reading each note for a clue to my past. I ended up in a plain, white room, which the note on the door told me was my room. It looked empty and drab, but as I walked around, I tripped over two cans of paint sitting on the floor.

You are going to paint your room sometime, if you don't forget first. This room needs personality, said the note on one can.

I looked around the room. It was really plain. There was a small plant sitting on the windowsill. It was a cactus, which was probably good, because if I was going to be forgetting things all the time, at least I wouldn't have to worry about forgetting to water the plant.

I sat on the bed and continued to look around. I shot a glance back to the paint cans. I wondered what colors they were. I tried to think of a color that would suit me, but nothing came to mind. I wanted to open one can, just to see, but the searing pain in my arm and hand reminded me that I probably didn't have the strength right now to pry open a can of paint.

My fall from earlier was catching up to me; my knees were starting to ache, as was my back. I wanted to lay down, but I worried if I did, I wouldn't get back up again, so I forced myself to my feet and shuffled back out into the living area.

I slowly sat on the couch and turned on the TV. In the background, I could hear Maxine walking around in the kitchen, talking on the phone. I wasn't sure what she was cooking, but it smelled delicious. I heard her say "goodbye" and listened to the floor creak as she left the kitchen to hang up the phone.

"Everything alright?" she asked, jotting something down on a giant calendar.

"I'm starting to feel that fall."

"Ah, I see," She smiled. "I just got off the phone with a doctor's office. They had a cancellation for tomorrow, so I got you a spot. Sound good?"

I nodded, and she went back to the food. In minutes, there was a plate in front of my face loaded with a noodle and meat combination.

"It's stroganoff. I hope you like it. You're tastes change all the time, and I never know."

I took a bite. "It's amazing," I smiled.

"Well, I can think of one good thing that arises when you have one of your spells: every meal I make you think is the greatest meal ever," she chuckled.

We both ate, while channel surfing, looking for anything good to watch. I wasn't paying much attention to the screen, until I saw Maxine pass a channel with a flash of gold and red.

"Wait, go back," I shouted. She turned it back and the picture became a clear image of golden bricks, and sparkling red shoes dancing.

"I know what this is," I surmised.

"Oh yeah! I forgot! This is *The Wizard of Oz,* and for some reason, you remember this even when you forget everything else."

A smile crept onto my face. I was so excited about remembering something. Maxine left the movie on, and we watched it as we continued eating. I found myself singing some of the songs, and Maxine would laugh, and soon I found myself laughing too. Eventually, we settled down and finished the movie and our food.

Maxine washed our dishes while I dried them. She then noticed I had bled through my bandages and changed them for me, like she was my personal nurse. Once I was re-bandaged, I laid back down on the couch and fell asleep. I was feeling fatigued, like I hadn't slept in days. I wondered if I really *hadn't* slept in days. I decided to ask Maxine if she had any idea why I was so sleepy, but I was just going to take a little nap first…

I woke up to Maxine's voice coming from the kitchen. She was quiet, almost whispering, having a conversation with herself. I didn't remember her well enough to refute the questioning of her sanity, but I figured she must be talking on the phone. I wasn't going to listen, but the fact that she was whispering intrigued me.

"I swear. She has no idea." I wondered who had "no idea" about what. I tried to listen closely, perhaps to hear the voice on the other end of the phone line, but I could still only hear Maxine's voice. "I was just thinking, maybe we could just not tell her about it. She won't worry about him if she doesn't know about him, right? This worrying can't be good for her. You've seen how tired she looks lately." I wondered now if she was talking about me. What was she not telling me? Should I even trust her if she's keeping secrets from me?

"Then she could keep the money, and we don't have to turn it in or anything. I know, I know, it would be the right thing to do but think about it. We're the only two people who know where that money came from; she doesn't even know. And we can't even confirm that the money was Razi's to begin with. She seemed to think it was, but we don't even know for sure, right? So technically, we could just say that she's always had that money."

"Hush, keep it down now, voices carry." I figured that must be Archie. There was a long pause and now I could faintly hear some scribbling. Then Maxine spoke again.

"You're right. I know. I just want her to be okay. I guess I was just being selfish, like it was my money, but it's not. We'll tell her and we'll get rid of the money."

I waited until there was absolute silence, before I opened my eyes and sat up. I didn't want them to think I was eavesdropping. My mind was racing with what I had just heard. I wondered who Razi was and what money Maxine was talking about. I couldn't help but think about it, even though I didn't want to. I knew they would tell me when the time was right. Unless they were assuming I would forget again. I suddenly became paranoid that they were plotting against me, exactly what, I had no idea, because I had no clue what they were even talking about.

When I sat up, they saw me from the kitchen and came out to the couch, smiling. They joined me, Maxine on one side, Archie on the other, and Archie formally introduced himself by handing me a piece of paper with a mini story about him on it.

"Maxine said you don't talk unless it's in a lyric," I said, realizing that I wasn't exactly going anywhere with that.

"You got the right stuff, baby."

"That's awesome," I laughed, and he smiled. Then, his eyes magnetically moved to my arm. He picked it up and examined the bandage.

"Oh! I forgot to tell you, Arch! When she ran away from me today, she fell," Maxine said, almost proudly. "Jackie, tell him what happened."

I tried to describe in as much detail for both of them how I woke up on the subway, feeling Maxine's hand on my back, and how I ran until my lungs burned, before tripping on the concrete steps. Archie laughed and smiled and raised his eyebrows very animatedly as I spoke, and I noticed even Maxine, who experienced the events, was listening intently. I yawned a couple of times when I first started, but as the story went on, the number of yawns increased, until finally, I finished my story and decided that I needed to go to bed.

"I'm sorry, guys," I said. "I don't know what's wrong with me. I'm just so tired all of a sudden."

"Maybe it's from all of that running you did today," Maxine suggested innocently. I nodded in agreement, unable to shake the feeling that there was more to this fatigue than she was letting on.

13

Both Maxine and Archie had to work in the morning, so Maxine hired a friend of hers to take me where I needed to go. This friend, Carmelina, was a bartender at the club where Maxine worked at night. Her instructions were clear: Carmelina was supposed to walk me to the doctor's appointment and walk me home. Maxine made me promise her four times that I wasn't going to run off on her. I said I wouldn't but reminded her I couldn't promise anything with my amnesia.

Archie was already gone, and Maxine was practically outside, antsy for Carmelina to arrive so she could leave. "I should have told her to be here earlier. She's always on her own time," she was muttering, standing in the hallway, outside the door. She put me on guard at the window, but I had no idea who I was looking for.

"You'll know her when you see her," Maxine kept saying. "She has blue hair." I didn't want to alarm Maxine, but I saw three people walk right by our building with hair that was one shade of blue or another; two of them were a pair of teenagers dressed in black leather and chains, and the other was a tiny old lady on a motorized chair.

Eventually, I saw a woman turn the corner in heels higher than even Maxine's. She wore a zebra print fur coat, even though it was August, and bright red hot pants. A pair of big, rimmed sunglasses rested on her pale face, and sure enough, her head was topped with a straight mushroom-like bob that was dark blue -almost black- with streaks of a lighter blue framing her face.

"Uh, Max, I think I see her," I said. I felt positive it was her. Maxine ran to the window and smiled.

"Yeah, that's her. Good eye, Jackie!" A short minute later, Carmelina was walking through our doorway, and Maxine was passing her on her way out.

"Carmelina, Jackie. Jackie, Carmelina. Jackie: behave. Actually, you behave too, Lina. Remember the deal. There and back. No running off, Jackie!" Her voice grew faint as she was walking away, and then she was gone. Carmelina and I stood still, staring at each other; she still had on her sunglasses. The door to the apartment was still wide open.

I wanted to say something, but I had no idea what to say. Finally, she spoke. "So, therapy, huh? What's that about? Are you crazy?"

"No, well, I don't know. Maybe. I can't remember things and Max says my doctor suggested I see a therapist to teach me brain exercises. Or so I'm told. I actually had a spell right after the appointment."

"Oh yeah," she smiled. "Max told me on the phone. Is that your souvenir?" She pointed to the bandage on my arm.

"Yeah, I guess," I smiled back.

It was silent for another moment, and she walked over to the calendar on the wall and skimmed it, then pulled a piece of paper out of her coat pocket and compared the two. Then she turned back to me and smiled again.

"Shall we go?"

We left the building and walked down the street. Immediately, she had a cigarette hanging from the side of her mouth. She never pulled it from her lips, it just hung there, while smoke seeped from her mouth and nose.

I tried to stay slightly behind her to follow, but she intertwined her arm in mine, so we were side-by-side.

"Don't worry. I won't let you get lost." She reminded me of Maxine, but I couldn't figure out why. Her voice was gruff like Maxine's, but much higher pitched. She seemed pretty nice, but definitely not in a motherly way like Maxine. Watching her out of the corner of my eye, I noticed she was walking with her back straight, one foot in front of the other, like she was on a catwalk. I suddenly realized it was her demeanor. She exuded the same sort of poise as Maxine, as if they were meant to be worshiped, like they were movie stars.

"So, are you transsexual too?" My face turned red immediately after I stopped talking. I knew it was terribly inappropriate, but I couldn't help myself from saying it for some reason.

She didn't take too much offense to it, I guessed, because she laughed heartily and looked at me. "No, silly. I'm one hundred percent female."

"Sorry," I muttered.

"No, it's okay. People assume things like that all the time when I'm hanging out with Maxine and Angel." We were walking by a building of windows and she watched herself as we walked. "I guess I do dress like some sort of tranny, now, don't I?" She giggled, finally taking the cigarette in her fingers. I laughed too and suddenly felt a little more relaxed.

Five more blocks and another cigarette later, we arrived at a small building with small, curtained windows and one door leading inside. A long hallway stretched from the entrance to the exit straight back. Branching off the hallway were eight doors, all of them offices. Carmelina scanned the directory on the wall and then led me down the hall.

The plain brown door numbered 207 opened up into a small waiting area with little green padded chairs lining the walls, which were a dark colored wood. A little window in the corner opened into a reception desk. Carmelina dragged me up to the window.

"Hi, this is Jackie, she has an appointment."

The receptionist scanned a book in front of her and nodded. "Have a seat," she said. "The doctor will be with you shortly."

We sat down and perused the magazines on the little coffee table in the middle of the floor. Only a few minutes passed, before the door opened and a woman stepped out.

"Jackie?" She looked at Carmelina.

"Yes, that's me," I said standing up. She looked at me and raised her eyebrows.

"Oh, okay, come with me, please."

I followed her past the reception desk and into her office. The office was no bigger than the waiting room, but instead of green chairs, the walls were lined with bookshelves. There was a couch against one wall, and a grand desk in the center. She sat behind the desk, so I sat in the corresponding chair.

"Hello, Jackie. My name is Doctor Novak. If you would feel more comfortable, you can call me Karen. Now, what brings you to me today?" She spoke in a soothing tone, but her eyes never left my face, which rendered me uncomfortable.

"Um," I stuttered, unsure of how to explain. "Well, I have this problem where I keep waking up and not remembering things. I was told that I was at the hospital yesterday getting results from an MRI, and my doctor said I have a mixture of two kinds of amnesia, but I don't remember what Maxine said."

"Okay," Doctor Novak said slowly. "Now, you said someone told you that you went to the hospital. Do you not remember that?"

From there, I explained to the doctor everything I remembered, starting with waking up on the subway. She only moved her eyes from my face once to glance at the bandages on my arm. Then I told her about Maxine and Archie and about the notes I found all over the apartment. She asked about the notes, so I tried to tell her everything I remembered off of them, but it was bits and pieces.

I was surprised at how good it felt to just talk and have her listen. I was so relaxed, I almost talked about the whispering from last night. I stopped myself, but I don't know why. She looked at me intently, taking it all in, and when I finished, she scribbled a few notes on a paper before saying, "Jackie, you mentioned that you wrote little notes for yourself, or that you assume you wrote these notes. I would like you to think about expanding on that."

"How?"

"Start a journal. Keep a log of what you do or things that interest you every day, and if you wake up with no memory again, you'll be able to read your journal and maybe things will become familiar. You could even use your journal to incorporate all of your little notes. I'm sure that would be easier on you if all of your notes were in one spot, instead of spread around your apartment. That will be your assignment for the next couple weeks, and we'll talk about the journaling and see if you're progressing then, okay?"

She walked me out of the office, and the receptionist set me up with another appointment. She asked if I wanted to pay my bill right now, but I didn't have much money on me, so she said she would mail it to me. The doctor wrote the appointment down, wrote down for me to start journaling, and that the bill would be mailed, and handed me the paper.

"Keep this in your purse and show it to your roommates. It's important that they stay involved in helping you, okay?"

I nodded and went into the waiting room, where Carmelina immediately threw down her magazine and we left. Before we had even left the building, she was shuffling through her purse, producing a cigarette and a lighter.

"What time is it?" she asked, taking a long drag.

I looked at my watch. "Noon," I answered.

"You hungry?"

I didn't want to say yes; my brain was fashioning this strict rationale that we were supposed to stick to the plan: there and back. She still seemed intimidating to me, and I worried that straying from the course would do something bad, like incite another spell, or fill me with food so I become sluggish and an easy target for predators.

"I'm starving," I heard my mouth say. *No! What are you doing?* I thought.

Carmelina smiled and squeezed our interlinked arms tighter and toted us down a side street. I watched as our course disappeared from view.

"I know this fantastic Chinese place. You like Chinese?"

"I don't know. I don't remember ever having it."

"Really? Wow. I'm sure you've eaten Chinese food before, everyone has. But this will be a treat then."

14

She took us through so many tiny streets and around so many corners, I doubted we'd ever return to our original course. Just when I thought these streets couldn't get any smaller, Carmelina shoved me down an alley. I worried it was going to get smaller and smaller until I couldn't fit any further. But, as soon as I thought I was going to get stuck, the alley ended, and Carmelina pushed me out into a nice, wide, open street.

There were little paper lanterns strung across balcony railings that crisscrossed over the street. The shops around had little makeshift stands and carts outside their doors with merchandise to lure in customers. I, myself, was tempted to peruse the merchandise, but Carmelina, stomping out cigarette number two, still had hold of my arm, and led me onward.

She pulled me into this quaint little restaurant. The smell from the street was intoxicating enough; she didn't need to pull me. The restaurant was small, with little red booths and more paper lanterns, which appeared to be the only light sources. We walked to an empty table and sat down. There were already menus tucked behind a bottle of soy sauce, which Carmelina took, sliding one to me across the table.

I read the menu twice through and had no idea what I wanted. Nothing had a description. Carmelina watched my face.

"Don't know what you want?"

"I don't know what any of this stuff is."

"Okay. Let's see. If you're a beginner Chinese eater, you probably want to start with basic fried rice. Now, you need a meat. You like meat, right? Chicken? How about chicken? Okay, so we'll get you some fried rice and chicken. Oh, and we'll throw in an eggroll for good measure." I chuckled at the way she ordered my food like it was some kind of science.

The waitress came and Carmelina gave her our orders, while I sat there, looking and feeling like a child, having my "guardian" do things for me. The two of us quieted for a moment, before Carmelina leaned back in her seat, staring at me.

"Can I ask you a question? What's it like?"

"What's what like?"

"Amnesia. How does it feel when you can't remember things?"

"Um, I don't know," I replied, giving her a strange look. "I mean, it's terrifying when you wake up and you don't know where you are or who you're with. It's also frustrating to not be able to recall what you did yesterday or what you were like as a kid, or even what your parents look like. But, every time I forget, I forget everything, so it's not like I *miss* remembering my life."

"So, you don't even know your family or where they are or even if your parents are still alive?"

"Nope. I don't remember anything past yesterday."

"Wow. You scared?"

"I'm terrified," I answered casually.

She stopped talking but continued to stare at me, which began to make me uncomfortable, until our food came. She smiled when my plate was set down, waiting for me to take a bite.

I gulped and slowly raised my fork full of rice to my mouth. It was delicious. I smiled while I chewed and Carmelina clapped her hands and laughed. "You do have to admit though; one good thing about having no memory is that you get to experience things over and over again."

We ate in mostly silence, peppered with an occasional question from Carmelina. When I finished, I went to use the bathroom, only after promising Carmelina that I was capable of leaving the table for a minute without getting lost or forgetting.

The bathroom was across the restaurant, so I had to snake my way through the tables to get to it. Getting there, I paid no attention to any of the other people in the restaurant, as I was focused solely on the restroom. But leaving, I found myself looking at each person at each table I walked by. Most of the people were actually Chinese, but a few tables were occupied by other nationalities. One table I noticed was full of guys talking and laughing, one of whom looked directly at my gaze and smiled. Nervously, I quickly grinned back and almost ran back to my table. Carmelina and I began chatting lightly, while I noticed she kept looking off to the side.

"What's the matter?" I asked after about the fifth side glance.

"Do you know that guy?"

"What guy?"

"The one who is staring at you over there. He keeps glancing over here, and when I look, he looks away, but I can see him out of the corner of my eye right now, and he's staring at you."

I looked, and sure enough, my stare caught his, before he quickly looked away. "No," I said. "I've never seen him before."

"Huh, too bad. He's kinda cute."

We were quiet again, before I started asking Carmelina questions about herself, like how she knew Maxine and where she grew up, anything I could think of. She answered most of my questions but still seemed distracted.

"Seriously, Jackie," she almost laughed. "You have no idea who that guy is?"

I jerked my head to the side and openly looked at him. He again looked down, and then at his friends. Then, ever so slightly, his eyes turned back to me. I looked back at Carmelina.

"No. I swear. I have no idea who that guy is."

"Maybe you used to know him, you know, like, before you had your last amnesia-thing."

"Or maybe he's just some weird guy," I answered, slightly frustrated by all of the back-and-forth staring.

"He's cute, though," she said, openly looking over to his table. "You should go talk to him."

"Um, no. That's okay."

"What? Why not? You're not shy, are you?"

"I don't know?"

"You can't be shy with a condition like the one you have. You can make a complete ass of yourself all the time, and never be bothered with it, because you're just going to forget anyway, right? So why don't you go over there and talk to him?"

"I just can't. Can we go now, please?"

"Okay, whatever. Let's get out of here."

She paid our bill and back into the street we went. Carmelina smoked two more cigarettes on our way back to the apartment. Surprisingly, she got us back on our original path much quicker than when we first strayed.

When we got to the apartment, she was nice enough to walk me all the way inside. I asked her if she wanted to stay until someone came back, but she had errands to run before she went to work at the club later. I thanked her for looking after me today, and also for the food.

"No problem," she smiled. "It was actually fun. I'd love to babysit you anytime."

She left, and I watched her walk down the street from the window, and then I was alone again. I looked around at the apartment, trying to think of something to do to keep me occupied until Archie and Maxine came home. I turned on the TV and sat on the couch. My purse was sitting on the table, and I remembered I had doctor's instructions in there. I got them out and went to stick them by the calendar, when I read the note about starting a journal. I decided that was what I was going to do.

I sat down at the computer and turned it on. As the screen loaded, I saw a green notebook underneath a pile of paper. It looked brand new, so I opened it, and found on the front page a single phrase: *Commit to memory*. I wondered if that was mine; if I had started writing that some time ago.

The computer was ready and I found myself in a predicament: to type my journal, or to write? I placed my hands on the keyboard, looking at all the letters. There was something so stilted about them, they seemed so impersonal. I didn't want my memories to feel any less like my own. I quickly shut down the machine and picked up a pen.

I read over those four words, and then set my pen to the page, but nothing happened. I couldn't decide how to start. I sat there, staring at the paper for fifteen minutes.

Whatever I write, it has to be important things I need to remember, I thought. *Also, it should be details about things. Oh, and I should probably write down situations that happen so I can recall them later. So basically, I should write down everything.*

Once I had the topic settled, I needed a place to start. What information would I want to read first?

My name is Jackie Dawes and I have amnesia. I'm probably reading this right now, so if I am, that means I've had another episode and I can't remember anything. Should this journal find its way into hands that aren't my own, it is vital that I get it back. My current address is written in the cover, as is a phone number.

I live in New York, or at least, that's the city I keep waking up in. I live with two amazing people, Archie and Maxine. Archie has an appreciation for the 1980's, and mostly communicates through a small note pad, however, once in a while you'll hear him spout lyrics. Strictly 80's, of course. Maxine is transsexual, but she's like a mother to me, and since I don't know who my real mother is, she's the best thing I've got.

I woke up yesterday morning on the subway with no memory. Maxine was sitting next to me, but I had no idea it was her, and I escaped from her, running through the city, before I fell on some steps and scraped up my arm. Maxine told me we were going home from the hospital where I had just had an MRI and my doctor, Dr. Karish, can't find any damage to my brain. However, I've forgotten my past, and my new memories don't stick, so there has to be something wrong. He suggested I see a therapist to talk about my condition, which I did today. Her name is Karen Novak. She told me to start a journal in an effort to help me remember things when I have what Maxine refers to as an episode. I must record every fact about myself, every thought I have and every experience, regardless of whether it's good or bad, doctor's orders. I need to know who I am. It is important that I write this down because there's no telling if I'll remember it tomorrow.

I began to describe everything in detail about the past two days, trying not to forget anything at all, in case it might be important to me later. When I had finished, I was still in the mood to write. I looked around and noticed all the little yellow notes everywhere.

These are some facts about me that I found around my apartment:

I wrote every word of every note down, numbering them as I went along, and soon enough, I had ten pages written. Finally, I reached the end of the notes, and I set my pen and notebook down and gathered all the notes and threw them away. Now that they were compiled, I didn't need them spread about the apartment. Archie and Maxine would be happy about that.

I felt like I had actually accomplished something. I also felt like the memories would stick better now, that they were logged. I decided to reward myself with some cookies I found in a jar in the kitchen. Then, I sat at the window and watched the sky darken.

Archie was the first to come home, I saw him coming from the window, but he gave me a brief, "Hey Jack, what's happenin'?" and went to his room. I wondered if he was going to come out soon, but then I heard him move to the bathroom and the shower turn on. I resumed my watch at the window.

Maxine appeared shortly thereafter and rushed to the kitchen to fix dinner. I followed her to help, but she motioned for me to sit on the other side of the counter, out of her way as she fluttered about the kitchen.

"Where's Arch?"

"He's in the shower. Well, not now. I guess he's in his room now."

"Why's he in the shower?"

I shrugged my shoulders.

Archie came out of his room, dressed in a navy suit coat with the sleeves pushed up, and matching suit pants. Under the coat was a white t-shirt and on his feet were blindingly white shoes and no socks. He strutted out into the living area, twirling, like a model. Maxine and I just stared at him, confused.

"Where are you going?" Maxine asked.

Archie groaned and walked over to the calendar and picked it up. Shoving it in our faces, he pointed to Friday, where he had written "Date with Tascha." I sat there, blankly, but Maxine understood.

"Oh, yeah, sorry, honey, I forgot."

"Who's Tascha?" I asked.

"She's a girl that works with you. You got Archie a date with her."

"I did?"

Archie nodded and hugged me. "You know you're something special and you look like you're the best."

I smiled, trying to recall setting up Archie's date, then laughed when I realized he had quoted Duran Duran. He left soon after, and Maxine and I ate before she had to get ready for work at the club.

"Did you have a nice meeting with the doctor?" She called from her bedroom, while I sat on the couch.

"Yeah."

"Well, what did she say?"

"She told me to start a journal."

"Okay. Did you?"

"Yes. I put all my notes in it."

Her head peered out of her door and she gazed around the room. Smiling she said, "Wow, no more yellow notes. Look at how empty our place looks now."

I told her all about the meeting, and about Carmelina taking me to a Chinese restaurant. Her head peeked out of her room again when I mentioned that and she looked concerned, but I reassured her that she asked me and I said yes, so it's my fault.

"But I made it back in one remembering piece, so I'm okay. No harm done," I explained.

She came out of her room looking glamorous as always. Her club clothes sparkled a lot more than what she wore to the supermarket. Imitating Archie, she twirled and modeled, this time though, I clapped and she laughed. But then she left, and again, I was alone.

15

Eventually, I fell asleep and was awakened some time later by the door opening. I looked up and saw Archie. I looked at the clock; it was only about ten.

"What are you doing home, Archie?"

He looked downtrodden. He slumped onto the couch and wrote me a little message:

Tascha never showed up. I waited outside Brandisham's for two hours.

I was livid. I couldn't even remember who Tascha was, but I knew that when I went back to work on Monday, I was going to let her have it. I called her a few choice names, but Archie shushed me, and I apologized.

"I'm sorry. I'm just mad is all. She just doesn't know what she's missing," I said, hugging him tightly.

He smiled a bit and said, "Boys don't cry," before heading off to bed.

I turned on the television, eagerly waiting for Maxine to come home. I was so mad about this whole Tascha thing, that I couldn't wait to tell her. Deep down, I knew the real reason I was mad was because I apparently set them up.

I fell asleep again and woke up as Maxine was walking through the door. She didn't even have time to set down her purse, before I was in front of her telling her what happened.

"No way!" she shouted, before using a few of the same choice words I had earlier, and then she went into Archie's bedroom. I wanted to follow, but I just sat back down, letting the two of them have a chat. Maxine came out of his room a short while later.

"He's okay," she said reassuringly. "He's just bummed out a little bit because he was really looking forward to the whole date, but he'll be fine. He'll bounce back; he always does." She went to her bedroom, and I decided I should go to mine.

In the morning, Maxine was at work before I had gotten up. I found Archie sitting on the couch, eating a bowl of cereal, so I joined him. He smiled when I sat next to him but said nothing. He seemed like he was okay, much better than last night, anyway.

"Archie, do you want to do something today?" I wanted him to feel completely better. I also wanted to get out of the apartment for a change.

"I'll do what you want me to do."

"I thought we could go sightseeing. I know you're familiar with the city, but I'm not. Why don't we go do something that's ridiculously touristy?"

He smiled wide and nodded before hopping up to get ready. I did the same, going to my room and dressing in plain jeans and a t-shirt. I grabbed my journal from my bedside and stuffed it into my purse. As we walked out the door, he handed me a little digital camera to document our day. I slid it into my bag, alongside my journal.

Archie wanted to surprise me with all of our ventures. *Follow me, no questions*, he wrote. We walked to the subway and rode for a bit, getting off at the Times Square station.

The street was overwhelming: people everywhere, colorful signs, and shops galore.

The first order of business was a double-decker bus tour. He made sure we secured a seat on the top. There was a cool breeze outside, but nothing compared to the wind generated on the top level of the bus. My arms took turns holding my camera with one hand while the other was crammed inside my shirt.

Once the tour ended, we walked up and down the street, Archie pointing out things we had seen, and writing me notes about them. It was much easier to take it all in, off the bus. I snapped pictures of everything he pointed at, hoping later I would remember why I had a photo of McDonalds.

After the excitement and chaos of Times Square, he took me to the demure setting of the Museum of Modern Art. As soon as we entered, I noticed people parked in front of paintings, conversing or just staring at the art, like it might move at any second. I found myself, however, rushing through each gallery, nonplused; I was looking, but nothing stood out to me as anything but a simple portrait or still life. Finally, a painting captured my attention, and I stopped to admire the beautiful blue and green brushstrokes swirling across the canvas. I leaned to the wall to read the inscription.

"*The Starry Night,* Vincent Van Gough," I read. "It's beautiful."

Have you ever seen it before?

"No. Should I have?"

Archie shook his head and scribbled furiously. *It's one of the most famous paintings in the world. You don't recognize it at all?*

"Nope," I said, handing back his notepad. "It doesn't ring any bells."

Apparently, my unfamiliarity with the painting caused him great distress, as he grabbed my hand and pulled me through more galleries, stopping at certain paintings that everyone on the planet was supposed to know.

I was ready to go when we stopped at a picture of melted clocks. "*The Persistence of Memory,*" I read, before turning around for the exit. "Very funny, Archie."

I asked if we could go see the Chrysler building, telling him that I had recognized that building when I was running from Maxine. The building was huge and intimidating. I remembered the architecture from before: the stacked horizons on the top. I wished I knew how it was that I recognized this building by name. Suddenly, it occurred to me that I knew more New York monuments like Central Park and the Statue of Liberty also. I deduced that it was because these were things ingrained in my conscious, like the way I remember how to speak, or read, or the way I can recognize Archie's Eighties lyrics. These were not my life, these were not life experiences, and for some reason, my brain clung to them. I wished it would cling to things that were important to me.

Archie and I walked down the famous shopping streets. We went into a grand toy shop. The main floor had a large room full of video games, and another room full of board games, and various newer toys. We rode the escalator up to the second floor where we found an entire pink floor devoted to one doll. The amount of pink was really overwhelming.

"What's with this doll?"

You don't know who Barbie is?

I shook my head no; he laughed and pulled me into the Barbie store. There were Barbie dolls for every single thing I could imagine. She was a pilot, a teacher, a ballerina, a doctor, and then my eyes fell on one Barbie in particular. She was far less pink than the others.

"Archie, look, it's Dorothy," I said, picking up the box and showing him the doll with her blue checkered dress and ruby slippers. Archie smiled and motioned for us to continue looking through the store. I put the doll down, but Archie picked it back up and put it back in my hands.

We moved on to a bluish room that I guessed was for boys, since it was full of building blocks and miniature cars. Archie showed me some of the toys he played with when he was little. There was one remote controlled car he was particularly fond of. He wrote that he had one when he was twelve.

"Do you still have it? At your parent's house or something?" I asked.

He shook his head no. *My parents didn't keep any of my things from when I was little. My dad actually threw this car away because I left it out and he tripped over it once.*

"Oh, Arch, that's horrible." I got out the camera and took a picture of him looking at the car. When he noticed, he put the car on the floor and sat down, pretending to play with it, while I took another one.

Archie took the Dorothy doll up to a register. "No, you don't need to do that, Archie," I said, but he just shook his head. Once he had paid and we left the store, he wrote me a note saying: *It's something tangible for you to keep remembering.*

It was far past lunchtime, and my stomach was reminding me that I hadn't eaten since breakfast. Archie suggested that we go to our usual place, because I didn't remember it again. Our excursion came to an end, as we wound up at The Corner Nook. He showed me our usual booth, and when he got up to use the restroom and order our food, I dug out my journal and began to write about the things we saw. Archie rejoined me at the table and watched me journal. A waiter brought out our food, and he smiled at me.

"So, Chinatown yesterday, huh? What brought you over there?" he said, setting our food down.

"What?" I looked directly at him and realized I recognized him. He was the guy from the Chinese restaurant that kept staring at me. He was slightly different today; there was a pair of thick black rimmed glasses hiding his blue eyes. His tousled brown hair was also hidden under a knitted hat. Carmelina was right: he was kind of attractive. I looked at his nametag: *Reece.*

"I'm sorry. I saw you at Chen's restaurant yesterday. At least, I thought it was you."

"Oh, now I remember. I didn't recognize you with your glasses on. Yeah, that was me. I, uh, had an appointment over there." His smile widened when I spoke. Then he jumped, a little startled, when I reached across the table for my plate.

"Whoa. What happened to your arm?"

"Oh," I said, bashfully. "I fell the other day. On some steps."

"Ouch, are you okay?"

I started to answer, only to be interrupted by a booming voice from the kitchen.

"Order up!"

He looked toward the voice, and then looked back at us both, smiling again, before walking away.

A little while later, he walked out of the kitchen, his apron traded for a simple black hooded jacket. He smiled at us and waved as he walked out. I smiled back, and Archie snickered.

"What? He waved at us."

He waved at you.

"Oh, come on, Arch. Don't be ridiculous. You said yourself that we're regulars here. He was definitely waving at both of us."

Archie shrugged but kept smiling and chuckling. I grew so embarrassed, my face burned, and I demanded that we go home.

16

When Monday rolled around, I found that I was looking forward to going to work. It had nothing to do with the job, of course, but I had been practicing all weekend what I was going to say to Tascha.

Archie walked me to work, which I told him he didn't have to; I was afraid he would catch a glimpse of her and become upset again. He insisted in writing, however, that he always walks me to work on his way to the bank. "You're a hard habit to break," he said.

"That reminds me," I said, walking to the door of Brandisham's. "I found this bank card in my purse. Would it be possible for us to stop at my bank later? I'm a little low on cash."

Archie made a funny face, but then smiled, nervously and nodded. Then, he was gone. I turned back to the door.

"Hey Jackie! How did your MRI go?"

I twisted my head to see a tall mousy looking girl walking toward me. I got out my journal to see if I could guess who she was.

"Let me see," I said, paging through the journal. "Are you Chrissy?"

She nodded and smiled. "You've forgotten again?"

We walked inside together, and I began telling her about my weekend. Through the store and down to the basement, I told her about running away from Maxine, and going to the therapist, and the journal. She was intrigued by the whole tale. I then rolled up the sleeve of my blouse to show her my bandages, and she gasped in awe at the size of the bandage but looked even more horrified when I quickly peeled the bandage back, revealing the blood of the gash mixed with the salve.

After my adventure was told, I then mentioned the part about Tascha.

"That's horrible!" She exclaimed, her mouth agape.

"I know. The worst part is I don't even remember setting them up or any of that, and now I feel like it's my fault."

"That's not true, Jackie. You only set them up because Archie asked you to. I remember us talking about this. It's not your fault. Tascha is just a horrible person."

"I'm aware of what kind of person she is, and I don't even remember her!"

I knew I would have to approach her, but now that I was at work, I was afraid to. I needed to work up my nerve. In the meantime, Chrissy and I kept discussing my amnesia; she interjected little stories for me to write down. I told her everything I could think of to tell her. I wasn't sure why, but it seemed to me that the more times I told these things, they started to become part of me. I even mentioned the guy in the Chinese restaurant who I discovered also worked at The Corner Nook.

"I don't know what it is about that guy, but everybody keeps teasing me that he likes me or something, and it's really embarrassing, especially since I don't remember him before Friday. Have I ever talked about this waiter before?" I asked, suddenly picturing his unshaven face in my mind, smiling at me, wearing his black glasses and floppy hat. I sort of smiled myself, just thinking about him.

"No," Chrissy giggled, and I knew she could see me day dreaming, so I promptly stopped, but not before my face reddened slightly.

I managed to avoid going upstairs all day, instead, getting re-acquainted with everything in the basement. Even though I couldn't remember, I had the feeling I had done this before, and I suspected it was just as daunting then, too, trying to remember all of the merchandise and the computer inventory.

It was five o'clock and I knew Archie would be waiting for me. He was going to have to wait, as I had a plan to chat with Tascha. Chrissy and I were leaving the store when she pointed out Tascha to me; she was leaving as well.

"Should I leave?" Chrissy asked.

"You can stay if you want. I'm not going to hurt her or anything."

Tascha began to open the door, but not before I pushed it closed.

"How was your date on Friday?" I asked flatly, blocking the door completely.

She jumped. "Oh, it went okay, but I, uh, I just didn't feel a connection."

"Huh, that's funny."

"Why is that funny?"

"Oh, I don't know, probably because your date was here at Brandisham's waiting for you for three hours," I exaggerated, hoping it would make her feel bad.

"Look, um, I'm sorry, but I'm just not interested in that guy."

"Archie. His name is Archie. And if you weren't interested, all you had to do was say that in the first place. It wouldn't have gotten his hopes up and crushed him so badly when you stood him up."

Then, Tascha did something that completely bowled me over. She started laughing. I thought I was making her feel guilty, and here I was just making a fool of Archie and myself.

"What the hell is so funny?" I asked, getting angrier now.

"Oh please, Jackie. That was the funniest thing I've ever heard. I can't believe he was "crushed". It's like he ever thought he would possibly have a chance with me. That's priceless."

Without even thinking, I grabbed her by the shoulders, swung her around, and pushed her up against the window. She was so much skinnier than I was that it was fairly easy. I was surprised I didn't break the window, as hard as I pushed her.

She gasped, with a look of terror on her face. "Listen here," I growled. "You are one mistaken little girl, if you think you're better than anybody else. Look at yourself. No wonder you're alone. You think you're such hot shit, but as far as I'm concerned, you're nothing more than scum on a flea, and you don't deserve someone like him. You disgust me."

I felt compelled to go on, but Archie, rushed in, shouting, "hey, hey, hey," and grabbed me, prying us apart. Chrissy had been right at my side the whole time, and once Archie pulled me away, she leaned in, whispered to Tascha, and was suddenly back at my side again.

Tasha straightened up, horrified. She brushed her clothes with her hands and looked around, like she was missing limbs or something. Her eyes were still bulged, and she was still breathing heavily as she looked back and forth between me, Chrissy and Archie.

Her eyes rested on Archie quickly, as she muttered, "Thanks," and ran to the bathroom. Archie, still holding my waist, hauled me outside, and Chrissy followed. I knew he was angry, but I didn't care. Tascha got was she deserved; less, actually.

Chrissy smiled at me. "We'll talk tomorrow," she said, before she skipped off. Archie eventually let me go, and started walking, far ahead of me. I ran after him, tugging at my blouse to straighten it.

"Archie!" I called, but he didn't respond. "Archie, please stop and listen to me." Still, he kept walking. "Dammit, Archie, stop right now!" I screamed at the top of my lungs. This stopped him, and everyone else on the street.

I grabbed his arm and spun him around, facing me. "Please, let me explain what happened. I know you're mad and I'm sorry, but if you had only heard what she said." Archie leaned, resting his weight on one foot and crossed his arms, which I took to mean he was allowing me to explain, so I did. I told him everything I said, and everything she responded with. Twice, I apologized for approaching her while I was angry but noted that it wouldn't really have made a difference if I was mad or even mildly peeved.

"I mean, she laughed, Archie. She laughed at you. And then she had the nerve to tell me that you never had a chance with her, and I know I shouldn't have, but I just lost it. And I meant everything I said to her. I wouldn't take any of it back, because you do deserve better than that and she does disgust me because she thinks leading people on is a game. So, I'm sorry if you're mad at me, but I'm not sorry about what I did."

He stared at me for a long time, silently reading my face. I was wearing a look of anguish, because I didn't want him to be angry with me. When I didn't think I could take his silence anymore, he grinned and then wrapped his arms around me. I hugged him back, thrilled at the gesture. Then, with one arm still around me, he took out his notepad and scribbled me a note:

I was mad at you, but this isn't your fault. I guess I should be mad at her.

"Are we cool, then?" I asked. He thought for a moment too long, so, growing impatient, I elbowed him and he laughed and then nodded.

Now that we were square, I decided to ask if he would take me to the bank. He stopped again and looked around. Then he reached in his pocket and handed me a folded pile of cash.

"Thanks, Archie, but I need my own money."

No, this is fine. You can have some of mine.

"Archie," I said sternly, taking my eyes off the notepad. "Why won't you take me to the bank? I need to get my own money out of my own bank account. Please."

Very reluctantly, Archie sighed, and we turned around and headed in another direction. It was a tiny little bank, not like the one I read about in my notes that Archie worked at. The floors were carpeted brown, and there were only three tellers. I filled out a little sheet and gave it to the teller, who took my card also, and pressed some buttons on the keyboard until some bills popped out of the machine next to her. She counted them out to me.

"Would you like a balance of your account, ma'am?" she asked nicely.

"Yes, I would, thanks."

She printed it out, and handed it to me, not looking at the amount. I looked at the paper and was shocked at the number.

"Everything alright?" she asked.

"Oh, yes. Everything is fine. Thank you!" I turned to leave, and Archie followed me out. I wasn't sure if I wanted to tell Archie or not; I was remembering back to last week when I heard Maxine tell him about my spell.

"We're the only two people who know where that money came from; she doesn't even know."

"Hey, Archie, look at this. Look at how much money is in my bank account," I said, handing him the paper. He glanced quickly, and handed it back, saying nothing.

"That sure is a lot of money," I continued. "I wonder how I got so much money. Did I ever tell you how I got so much money?" I was trying to sound confused, but I could tell it wasn't working. I was a horrible actress.

Archie was pretty bad himself. He sighed, and looked around, shifting his eyes, going, "uh-uh, uh-uh." His nerves were showing badly.

I wanted to interrogate him right there, but I decided to hold off for a while; I felt like I needed more evidence to accuse him and Maxine of hiding something. But now, I was going to be doubly aware of their actions.

17

The next day at work, I was prepared to walk into a room full of stares from all the girls; no doubt Tascha had told them what I'd done. To my surprise, the girl at the desk I noted as Portia didn't even acknowledge I had come in. Neither did any of the other girls for that matter. I went straight to my desk in the basement. Chrissy wasn't far behind me, and when she got to her desk, she was beaming.

"You'll never guess what I just heard upstairs."

"Nope, I probably won't."

"Tascha called off work today. She didn't go into any detail with anybody, she just claimed she was feeling sick."

I was happy I wouldn't be dealing with her today, but I must have seemed nonplussed by the whole thing because Chrissy felt compelled to explain.

"Jackie, Tascha has never called off work a single day in the past four years that she's worked here. She never gets sick and she never has emergencies. This is big news upstairs that she's gone today."

I changed my expression so that I looked impressed with myself. I was, but in a way, I did sort of, maybe a little tiny bit, feel bad. I had wanted to make her feel guilty, not afraid of me. All the same, she was very cruel in the way she cast Archie off like that, so I pushed all of my guilt aside.

"Honestly, Jackie, yesterday was amazing. You were so brilliant! I'm pretty good at reading people, and I never imagined you had that kind of ferocity in you," she gloated.

I smiled, flattered, but now I was starting to think strange thoughts about myself. Where *did* that ferocity come from? Was I really a violent person? Is that what happened with that Razi guy? Did I do something violent to him and steal his money?

My thoughts were fairly cloudy, making it hard to concentrate on my work. Chrissy didn't even seem to mind; she helped me with everything, not once did she complain that I should be retaining some of this work by now.

"So, Jackie, I was thinking. I had an idea on how we could get back at Tascha."

"No, Chrissy, I don't want to do anything to her. I made Archie pretty mad, I mean, for whatever reason, he still seems to like her."

"Then this is perfect," Chrissy continued, pushing up her glasses. "What we could do, is steal Tascha's organizer. Every appointment, every customer's name, and every single piece of clothing they try on is listed; it's basically all of the information we keep down here. The girls upstairs live by those things, if we were to maybe lift hers for a few days, she'll be put in a tight spot with a client, which will force her to need our help accessing the client database."

"At which point I could offer to help her in exchange for a date with Archie," I finished. Then we both smiled at each other. I liked Chrissy's thinking. This was a perfect chance for me to make Tascha give Archie a chance and hopefully see that he's not a bad guy at all.

"That's genius. Let's do it," I said, thinking how great it was working with Chrissy. She was my partner in crime. A flash of yesterday popped into my head; I remembered Archie pulling me away from Tascha and Chrissy stepping up.

"Hey, Chrissy, what did you say to Tascha when Archie pulled me away?"

Chrissy's face turned red and she giggled a bit. "It was stupid. I'm not nearly as clever as you."

"What did you say?"

"I told her: 'You'll get what's coming to you.'"

I had to laugh. That was probably more terrifying to Tascha than I was.

Chrissy and I spent a good portion of the day scheming about how to get Tascha's organizer. Chrissy explained that upstairs, next to the bathroom, there was another staircase that led to the second floor. This floor was where Margot Brandisham's office was, as well as her workspace. The office and workspace occupied the right side of the building, and half of the left. The other half was a break room for the girls to store personal items and eat lunch. I asked if we had ever eaten up there. She shook her head and I wondered why.

"I don't know, actually. I mean, I've never eaten up there in all the years I've worked here. I pretty much stay in the basement, and when you started, you stayed with me. It's not like we're not allowed up there, because we are. I guess because those girls hate us so much, it's just been better that we eat down here or go out."

"Well, let's change that," I said indignantly. "Let's eat up there today. And we'll get Tascha's organizer."

We plotted about where exactly the book might be kept. Since I'd never been up there and Chrissy hadn't been up there in years, we couldn't thoroughly plan, but we had a couple half-hatched schemes in the works.

At lunch time, Chrissy grabbed her lunch and peeked at the sales floor from the basement steps, looking to see if it was busy. She motioned for me to follow, which meant that there weren't enough customers that we would have to take turns eating lunch.

Slowly, eyeing everybody, we made our way back to the bathroom, and we climbed the stairs. I was confident no one saw us; according to Chrissy and my journal, they tended to ignore us most of the time. We thought our plan was going flawlessly, until we walked into the break room.

Portia's eyes bulged when she saw us. "What are you guys doing up here?"

"We're eating our lunch, what does it look like we're doing?" I retorted.

"You don't eat up here."

"We can if we want to." This was starting to sound childish.

"You never have before."

"Well, we never wanted to before," I said, pulling out two chairs from the small table and plopping myself down in one. "But now, we do."

Her mouth hung open, like she was searching for a remark, but she was finding it rather impossible. Chrissy smiled at me and we opened our lunches and began to eat.

"Hey Chrissy, did you get those dresses for Tascha? I was supposed to do that for her today, but she never called me on the radio, so I assumed maybe you did it instead. Did you?"

"No," Chrissy said, biting her lip to avoid smiling. "Come to think of it, I don't remember seeing her on the floor when I came in this morning."

"Well, I'm sure she's here. Didn't you tell me that she has had perfect attendance since she started working here?"

"I did tell you that, so you're right. She must be here."

I saw Portia squirm a little out of the corner of my eye. "Hey Portia, have you seen Tascha today?"

"No," Portia mumbled. "She called off."

"What?" Chrissy asked.

"She called off today." She announced.

"Oh, wow," I said, raising my hand to my mouth. "What's wrong? Is she sick?"

"She never gets sick," Chrissy answered.

"She just said she wasn't feeling well. She didn't go into specifics," Portia replied, watching both of our faces carefully. I hoped she wasn't suspicious of us.

We ate in silence for a few moments, and I could tell Portia was still looking at us. I set my sandwich down and openly glared back at her, saying nothing. Her eyes quickly averted back to her food, but I kept staring, watching her squirm. She was growing increasingly uncomfortable, until finally, she threw her trash away and got up.

As she left, I said loudly to Chrissy, "Boy, I sure hope Tascha feels better. I hope it's nothing that's going around." Portia paused briefly but then continued down the stairs. Chrissy and I giggled quietly, and finished our lunches, while we perused the room, looking for the organizer.

The room was pale pink, and the furniture, which consisted of a table surrounded by chairs and a couch against one wall, was a dark brown. There was a tiny microwave that sat on top of a tiny refrigerator, and next to the appliances, was a curtained doorway, where I could see hung coats and purses inside.

"Maybe the book is in there," I said, getting up from the table and lifting the curtain a bit, as I stepped inside. The room was lined with hooks, and in the corner, I found a table, with cubby holes stacked on top. Each cubby hole had a name on it, and they were all empty but one. I checked that it had Tascha's name on it, just to be sure, and pulled the book out of it.

"I got it," I said, stepping back into the break room. I stopped in my tracks, as I saw Chrissy's face in shock. I looked up next to her and saw someone else standing there, staring at me. The girl drew her hands up to her hips, and her eyebrows lifted. I half expected her to start tapping her foot any moment and demand an explanation.

My brain went blank. I was trying to think of something to say. Suddenly, my mouth just started talking. "I forgot what dresses I needed to gather for Tascha today, and my computer's been acting up." *Impressive,* I thought.

The girl continued to glare at me. "Tascha's not here today."

"Oh, I heard, but I would like to get these dresses gathered for her so she has them when her appointment is rescheduled." I set the book down on the table, and Chrissy pulled a piece of paper out of her pocket and an ink pen. We paged through the book, finding the right day, and then Chrissy pointed to a section with a list of items which I copied.

The girl watched for a few seconds, before losing interest and sitting down to the table and eating her own lunch. When I had finished writing, I closed the book and took it back into the other room. Scrambling, I looked around for something to hide the book in. How was I going to get it out of there now without being caught? Panicking, I stuck the book under my blouse. My blouse was a smidge tighter than usual, and the appointment book was fairly large, and I could tell it just looked ridiculously obvious.

"Hey, Chrissy, is there a light in here? I've lost my contact lens. Could you help me find it?" I couldn't get over how fast these lies were flowing when I was in a panic. Chrissy lifted the curtain and stepped inside. We had to be silent, so I motioned to the book and mouthed, "What are we going to do?"

Chrissy did exactly what I had done, looking about the room. I then noticed her shirt was fairly baggy, as were her pants. I stepped behind her and lifted her shirt, covering the book with it. She froze at first but then realized what I was doing and she reached back and finished tucking the book into the back of her pants. Then, she straightened her posture, trying to hide any weird shapes in her clothes. I never realized how tall she was; she slouched most of the time.

I gave her thumbs up and then slapped my hand over one of my eyes, and we stepped out of the room. The girl looked up from her food. She glanced at the unusually rigid Chrissy, and then back at me.

"Thanks, for your help, Chrissy. I need to get this back in my eye."

I pushed Chrissy out of the room; she walked like she was in armor. We walked down the stairs and as quickly as possible, headed for the basement.

As soon as we reached the bottom of the stairs, Chrissy pulled the book from her shirt. We ran to our desks, laughing silently. She sat the book on my desk, and we stared at it for a moment.

"Now what?" I asked.

"Um, I guess we hide it," she shrugged.

"Where? Like in the desk?"

"No," Chrissy shook her head. "We have to put it somewhere where nobody else could possibly find it." She looked around the basement and then snapped her fingers. “I know! Let’s hide it over here.”

I followed her down an aisle to the other side of the basement, where she took a couple pieces of clothing off the rack and handed them to me. She moved the rack forward a few inches, and I saw that it was resting on a broken tile. She peeled back the tile, and set the book there, and then moved the rack back. The tile, she set off to the side, and I handed the clothes back to her.

We laughed and high-fived each other as we walked back to our desks. As soon as I sat down, I got my journal out of my purse and wrote down what had just happened, including where we hid the book, afraid I would have another spell, and wouldn’t be able to find it again.

18

To our surprise, Tascha was absent from work again the next day. When she returned the following day, Chrissy and I spent as much time on the floor as possible, trying to see if Tascha would crack under the pressure of not having her organizer.

Even more to our surprise, she acted as though nothing was out of place at all. She seemed to have everything together, despite not knowing what clients were coming in. I had to admit, I was actually a little impressed at the way she worked, pretending to remember the client's picks.

On Thursday, Chrissy and I took our lunch break later than usual. Nobody was eating in the break room, but I heard some noises coming from the coat room. It was a little groan, followed by a couple curse words, then, Tascha stepped out from behind the curtain. She looked frustrated, but her expression changed when she saw us.

"What are you guys doing up here?" She asked in a tone less defensive than Portia's.

"We've started eating up here," I answered flatly.

"Oh," she remarked and she rushed out.

Chrissy and I sat down, and waited until we knew she was gone, before we started to giggle. I suddenly wondered why no one approached us yet about the book.

"Tascha probably hasn't told anyone it's missing. I've overheard the other girls talking plenty of times about how she's too perfect an employee and makes everyone look bad. I'm sure she knows they don't like her because she doesn't tend to associate with them unless it's necessary. If they knew her book was missing, they would never let her hear the end of it. She would just as soon suspect one of them before us."

I wished Chrissy wouldn't tell me things like that; I was starting to feel bad for Tascha. Lately, I had to constantly keep telling myself that she deserved this, and it was necessary in order for her to give Archie a chance. It was for the greater good.

After work, Archie and I headed to the Corner Nook to meet Maxine for dinner. I invited Chrissy, who gleefully accepted. We sat down at our usual table by the window and waited for Maxine. She came in not long after we did, and I introduced her to Chrissy and we ordered our food.

The waiter came over to our table, and I suddenly felt my heart drop. It wasn't the same guy, Reece, if I remembered correctly what his nametag said. I wasn't sure why I was so disappointed that he wasn't here. It wasn't like I had some silly crush on him or anything. Or maybe I did.

Our food came out and the four of us ate and talked, Chrissy told Maxine all about my encounter with Tascha, and Maxine stared at me with her mouth open. My face reddened as she spoke; I was a little embarrassed having Maxine aware. But when she finished, Maxine pursed her lips together, before saying, "Well, Jackie, that was quite a spectacle. And I don't think it was appropriate," her lips melted into a grin. "All the same, she did have it coming, didn't she? Laughing like that."

I didn't sleep well that night. For some reason, I was still thinking about the waiter, wondering where he was. I knew he must have had the day off, but then I started to wonder if maybe something had happened to him, like maybe he was sick or injured. Then my mind fashioned a couple crazy scenarios in which he had been mugged or left for dead in an alleyway. My lungs tightened, as I started to panic.

I got out of bed and went to the kitchen for a glass of water, to calm me down. I sat on the couch and turned on the TV; I had to get Reece out of my mind. My worrying was stupid, I realized, I hardly knew him.

Maxine stepped out of her room in a long, fuzzy robe. "Jackie? You alright?"

"Yeah, I'm just having a little trouble sleeping is all."

"Again? You want me to join you?"

"Sure," I said as she sat down next to me. "Maxine? What did you mean when you said 'again?' Have I not been sleeping well?"

"I didn't say that," she answered quickly.

"Yes you did. You said, 'Again? You want me to join you?'"

"Oh, well, that was a slip of the tongue. I mean, I guess you had a few rough nights sleeping a few weeks ago, but it was no big deal."

"Do you know why?"

"No. I think you had an episode around that time, so it was probably from that." Her eyes never left the screen as she spoke. I instantly knew she was lying, but I dropped the subject.

They were probably never going to tell me what was going on. I then told myself that since they were keeping a secret from me, and nothing bad had happened to me, maybe it was for the best that I just let it go.

I woke up in my bed the next morning. Maxine and Archie had both gone to work, so I stayed in bed. My journal was on my nightstand, so I opened it up and wrote a bit. I revealed my disappointment about the waiter and how I couldn't sleep, thinking about him.

When I finished, I realized my journal only had one page left. I decided that whenever I chose to get up, I would go out, by myself, and buy a new one. I put the used journal in the drawer of my nightstand, but then changed my mind, reasoning that if I ever had another one of my spells in public, I would need my journal on hand to read. Finally, I rolled out of bed and walked to the entryway, where I stuffed the journal in my purse. My purse was fairly large, and since it held nothing but a phone and a wallet, I figured a used notebook wouldn't add too much weight.

After a toasted waffle and a shower, I dressed and attempted to re-bandage my arm. I was finding it extremely difficult, so I decided to leave the bandage off, but when I caught a glimpse of my arm, a week after my fall, it still looked disgusting. The cut was now just a long scab, but the bump and bruise were completely black, with a yellow ring around them. It grossed me out to look at, so instead of a bandage, I searched the bathroom cupboard where I found a flesh-colored cloth roll. I wrapped that around my arm and used the little metal wedge to fasten it.

Once my wound was addressed, I sat on the couch and pulled a map from my purse. I was surprised to find that there were little markings all over it already, but I felt good seeing the apartment was marked, so I could always find my way back.

I returned with a journal in tow, rather quickly. Since it was my first venture out into the city by myself, I didn't want to get carried away; I had to take baby steps. I put my new journal in my purse with my old one, as I didn't have anything to write about now.

I sighed, and looked around the apartment, looking for something to do. I didn't feel like watching TV anymore, and in case of a future amnesic spell, I didn't think it would be in my best interest to read a book. I found the computer in the corner, and decided to turn it on, and maybe play a game or something on the internet.

When I clicked the icon for the internet, I decided that I should research amnesia, to maybe understand my condition, especially since, now that I'd forgotten my doctor's appointment, the only information came second-hand from Maxine.

Maxine found me at the computer when she came home around six o'clock. I was so engrossed in what I was reading; I had no idea of the time. I didn't even hear her come in. She didn't want to disturb me, so she peered over my shoulder for a minute, and then went to the kitchen to start cooking something for dinner.

"I went to the store today. All by myself," I announced, as the three of us sat down to eat our dinner. Archie looked at me proudly, but Maxine glared at me.

"Jackie, I wish you wouldn't do things like that. If you want to go out somewhere, just wait until one of us can go with you. Or Carmelina. I'll give you her number, and you can call her anytime you want to go gallivanting through New York. Just don't go off by yourself, please."

"Why not? I need to be independent, Maxine. I can't rely on you forever. I need to be able to function on my own," I said, defiantly.

"I know, Jackie, but the problem is I'm terrified that you're going to forget while you're out there, and you won't come back."

"No, see, I've used up my first journal, which I'm keeping in my purse, so if I do forget, I can read it."

"Okay, well, what if you get mugged and your purse is stolen, and then you forget?" She was sounding crazy, like an over-protective mother. I didn't want to be insubordinate, but her reasoning was insane.

"Maxine, I won't get mugged. I'll be fine, I swear. Besides, I just took one little trip outside. To the store and back, that was it. I was gone for maybe a half hour."

"It took you all of five minutes to have an attack on the subway last week."

She wasn't going to listen to my reasoning, so I continued to eat in silence, as Archie had this whole time. When I was finished, I went to the desk and grabbed my new journal and took it to my room. A while later, there was a knock at my door, and Maxine came in, dressed for a night at the club.

"Jackie, can I talk to you?"

"I guess," I said coldly.

"I know you think I'm being crazy, but I just want you to be safe. I never would have been like this, if you hadn't fallen asleep on that subway and run off on me. Witnessing that made me realize that you are capable of anything, and I don't want you to run away from us again."

"Fair enough."

"No, Jackie, you can't be mad at me for wanting you to be safe. That's not fair."

"Well, you can't babysit me all the time. I'm an adult, I think. I need to be able to be on my own at some point."

"Okay, I understand that. But do you understand me?"

"Yeah, I guess."

"So, let's compromise then. I don't want you going out on any long excursions unless you're with somebody, I don't care who."

"And if it's a short trip, like to the store and back?"

"If it's a short trip, I want to know before you go, so call me, or something, and I want a follow-up call as soon as you make it home."

"Deal." She sat down on the bed next to me and hugged me. She whispered something that I couldn't quite make out, but I thought for sure she said, "thank you."

An entire week went by with my memory still intact. I wrote down everything, just for reassurance, but so far, my memory was working well. I had already completed my second journal and started my third. Archie brought me home three medium sized brass rings that he said were for me to bind my used journals together. I wrote a little number on them, marking their order, and kept them all bound together in my purse, unless I was writing.

Things were looking up for me; at work, I was competent with the merchandise and the computer system. Tascha had gone with Margot Brandisham to Paris for two weeks, as her personal assistant during Mrs. Brandisham's fashion shows, so Chrissy's and my plan was on the back burner for a while.

When I wasn't at work, I was at the apartment, or the café, journaling or reading my map. Archie, who had been much more lenient with me, was letting me walk ahead of him to the apartment or the café from work, and sometimes, he would send me to the corner for a newspaper or something small, while he watched me from our apartment window.

I was completely happy with my memory, and my journaling, and couldn't wait to see my therapist in a week. She was going to be so impressed with my progress.

I didn't see much of Reece, the waiter; most of the week, we ate at home, but a couple of times Archie and I did go to the Corner Nook, I was overjoyed to see he was there. Overjoyed, of course because that meant he hadn't been murdered or he wasn't sick anymore. The café was suddenly a busy place; it was getting colder, so people were going inside to eat. Because of the influx of business, he didn't have any time to stop and chat with us at our table, which depressed me a little, but he always made sure we made eye contact at some point, and would smile and wave, which made me feel better.

While Archie and Maxine were at work, I hung out and cleaned the apartment. I dusted and swept floors; I even did a couple loads of laundry. While the clothes were washing, I took a break to watch some TV, and while I was sitting there, my stomach began to growl. I ate a Pop Tart, but a few hours later, the hunger was back. I ransacked the kitchen, looking for something larger to eat, but everything required massive amounts of cooking. *Leave it to Maxine to only buy foods that were meant for long hours of preparation,* I thought.

With the growling now continuous, I had the brilliant idea to go to the Corner Nook. I looked at the clock and realized Maxine and Archie would be home in a couple hours, so my idea expanded to include them. *Why not have them meet you there?* I thought. *They'd be really impressed if you walked there all by yourself.*

I called Archie and left him a message on his phone, and when I reached Maxine, she seemed reluctant, but I kept telling her that I was calling her to let her know where I was going, and she was going to meet me there, and eventually, she budged. She told me she had to stay a bit later at the supermarket, but she'd still have time to eat before taking off for the club. I knew Archie was going to stay late, because his text message mentioned he was going to start doing some extra work for his father.

A little before seven o'clock, I dressed and grabbed my purse and a jacket and headed out for the Corner Nook. I glanced at my map once and then stuck it back in my purse. The sun was slowly going down, but I was still able to see, and successfully managed to make it to the café, with no trouble at all. I clapped to myself and went in and sat at our booth by the window. The café had a few people inside, but not as many as there had been for the past week. I guessed it was probably because the café closed at eight, which was just long enough for us to at least eat something. I wasn't sure how long I would have to wait for either of them, but I got out my journal and started to write.

"Hey, where're your friends?"

I looked up and saw Reece standing there, in his baggy clothes and glasses, but no floppy hat today.

"They're coming. I walked here all by myself," I said proudly. He gave me a funny look and then a smile and I suddenly reddened with embarrassment, realizing that he had no idea about my amnesia.

"Uh, I have a tendency to get lost," I muttered.

"Oh, okay," he laughed. He was about to say something, but the door opened and two new customers walked in. "Excuse me," he said, walking away.

I turned my attention back to my journal, when suddenly, someone pounded on the window. I looked up, but it was completely dark now, and I couldn't see anyone at all. As I stared into the darkness, the door opened again, and two men walked in, one was eying me intensely and grinning.

They started in my direction; the one man was big all around, like some sort of bodyguard. He looked like he didn't say much, and he stared straight ahead. The other man continued to look right at me, his eyes widening as they grew closer. I noticed a large, scabbed scar on the side of his face.

The big man stopped at the opposite side of my booth, while the smiling man sat down. I straightened up, uncomfortably, as he leaned forward and whispered, "Why, hello again, Mara."

19

"Who is Mara? Who are you? What do you want?"

"Oh, we're going to play this game again, are we?"

"What game? What are you talking about?"

"You know exactly what I'm talking about, Mara. You've got my money, and I want it back. This time, I've brought reinforcement."

"This time? Have we met before?" I started to slide my hands back, readying myself to make a mad dash for the door. His hands flew out from under the table, gripping mine, and pulling me toward him.

"Oh, you don't remember? We go way back. You stole my money and ran off. I couldn't find you for six weeks, and low and behold, who should I run into a few weeks ago, but you, Mara. You don't remember this?" He tilted his head to the side, exposing his injury under the light.

I just stared at him, unable to say anything, but he continued. "Yes, yes, this was you. You remember? You hit me in the head with a paint can," A mental image appeared in my head of the cans of paint on my floor, and the small dent in the one. "I have a concussion thanks to you. But now, there is no escape, not with Dolph here. So why don't you tell me where the money is."

"I don't know what you're talking about, or who you are, and I don't have your goddamn money, now let me go!" I yelled, as people in the café started staring.

"You think you're so funny, trying to cause a scene. You see what Dolph has under his jacket?" I looked as Dolph opened his coat flap slightly. "He's got a gun. And if you cause a scene, you're going to get a bullet in the back of your head. Now let's go." He tightened his grip on my hands, and he slid out of the booth, pulling me, forcing me to follow.

"Hey, what's going on here?"

Both men turned around. I peered over the scarred man's shoulder. It was Reece. He looked back and forth between the two men, and a couple of times at me. The scarred man pulled at my arms, which propelled me closer to him.

"Nothing of your concern, man. Now, why don't you go back to your business and leave us to ours, eh?"

Reece took a deep breath and then took off his glasses and rolled up his sleeves. "Well, as a matter of fact, she is my customer and that makes her my business," he said, his voice slightly faltering. His whole demeanor was like he was the underdog hero in a movie.

"You think you're going to attack me or something?"

"I will if you don't let her go."

"Hit me. Come on, tough guy. Hit me. Save the girl."

Reece stepped forward, the scarred man directly in his sight, but suddenly lunged sideways and smacked Dolph in the face. Dolph didn't move, he just blinked, unshaken. But in a matter of seconds, Reece was on Dolph's back, his hands over Dolph's face, poking his eyes, and smacking his cheek. Dolph, panicked, swinging his body back and forth, trying to fling Reece off, while his big arms flopped uncontrollably.

Unsure of why he went for Dolph instead of my oppressor, I tried to pull myself away while he watched his bodyguard, but his grip was pretty solid. Once more, I used all of my strength to pull away, which drew him forward, and me to the floor. He was starting to fall on top of me, when he was smacked in the face by Dolph, sending him falling in the other direction. He let go of my hands, and I quickly crawled under the table. I watched him squirm on the floor and then I looked at Reece.

"Run. Get out of here!" He shouted, and I didn't have to question whether that was directed at me. I grabbed my purse, crawled up the booth seat, and jumped over the other side. I stood there for a second, with the other onlookers, waiting to see if Reece would be okay. Suddenly, another man watching jumped right in, pinning the scarred man down on the floor. I couldn't look away, but then a hand grabbed my shoulder.

"Jackie? Oh my God, what happened?"

Maxine was staring at the scene in horror. I opened my mouth, trying to speak, but still, I had no words. Again, Reece, hanging off Dolph's back, looked at me and mouthed, "go."

"Come on, let's go." Maxine pulled me out of the café. As soon as we walked out, Maxine was on her phone.

"Archie? Go right home, okay?" she said, promptly hanging up. We walked fast, I felt like we were near running. I was amazed at how Maxine could walk so fast in heels. At the end of the street, I was relieved to see a police car with two cops inside. Maxine rushed up to the car and tapped on the window.

"Excuse me, officer, there are two men at the Corner Nook café who are attacking a waiter. I think they're drug dealers or something," she said, making her voice sound as soft and feminine as possible. The cops got out of their car and started running down the street. My mind quickly eased, knowing they would be able to help Reece.

Maxine and I continued to walk, she got out her phone again and this time she was talking to someone I didn't know.

"I have a little situation. Can I meet with you right now?"

We quickly changed directions, and headed down an alley, coming out to another street, which never seemed to end, as we headed north. After a few minutes, my side started to hurt, from the fast walking. Luckily, we soon stopped. Maxine dragged me inside a brick building with dark windows and no sign out front. The first door on the left did have a sign that I quickly read: *Law Offices of Manuel Cavantes*. There was a man waiting for us inside, who rushed us back into his office.

Maxine let me go and I sat down, while she hugged the man and kissed his check, murmuring something in Spanish. Then the two of them sat down too.

"Now, what can I do for you, Maxie?" The man asked, with a heavy accent.

"Uncle Manny, we have a problem. We're sort of accidentally involved in something, where we've acquired a large sum of money which we have no idea how we got it, but we suspect it had to do with something illegal. Now, there is this guy named Razi, who I think might be a drug dealer, who thinks the money we have belongs to him. So first of all, I want to know what to do about the money. Can we get rid of it anonymously? Or do we have to admit involvement?"

The man sat back in his seat and rubbed his moustache, thinking. "How much money is it?"

"Seventy thousand dollars."

"And is all the money there?"

"No, but most of it is. She only spent some on necessities." Manuel looked at me, and I knew he could tell I was the person Maxine was referring to when she said "we". He also nodded, like he knew exactly where the money came from.

"Is the money in a bank account?"

Maxine nodded.

"Turning in the money will prove to be difficult, so we will have to leave it in the bank and tip the police off to the account. Now, what we will have to do is change the name on the account."

"But the people at the bank will have my information, they can tell the police who I am," I blurted out.

"Archie!" Maxine cried. "Your bank is a smaller extension of the bank his father owns. He can get into their system and change the information."

It seemed too simple. I feared Archie would get caught, or he wouldn't get all of the information.

"You haven't made a ton of transactions there. You made one huge deposit, and then, you've probably only made one or two withdrawals and that's it. Nobody's keeping a ton of information on you. Your paychecks don't even go directly to the bank."

I sighed, and looked around the room, having nothing else to say. Maxine patted my shoulder, comfortingly, and then turned back to her uncle.

"Now, Uncle Manny, what are we going to do about this Razi?"

Manuel asked for a description, which I provided, making sure to give him every detail, including the lump on his face. Manuel wrote down everything I told him and when I finished, he said, "Okay. My boys will take care of Razi. Don't worry about him."

Maxine smiled and thanked him, and the two of them hugged, and we got up to leave. Manuel shook my hand and escorted us out.

We were halfway down the street when I finally asked, "What the hell was that about?"

"Uncle Manny is a lawyer for Oscar Bettino, who is a leader of the biggest Mexican gang in New York, so he deals in pretty shady business, sometimes. Manny's like Oscar's right-hand man. He'll get all the information he can on Razi, and Oscar Bettino's gang will get him."

"I don't want him killed. I just want him in prison or something."

"They won't kill him. They'll just scare him a bit; maybe make him go into hiding. If Razi knows that you're associated with the Bettinos, he won't so much as think about you ever again."

I was silent the rest of the walk, my mind racing with images of Razi's smiling face, Reece on Dolph's back, and the Bettinos tracking Razi down. I asked Maxine to please explain, if she could, why I had Razi's money and she told me all about the day I went out to buy paint all by myself when I ran into him. She recalled me hitting him and running away, and then she told me about the article they found on the internet, which detailed a drug bust and a missing seventy thousand dollars. A wave of nausea swept over me, and once we were inside the apartment, I rushed past Archie, straight to the bathroom and vomited.

I used my jacket as a makeshift pillow for my head on the bathroom floor, and I reached for my purse. Realizing how light it was, I began to panic.

My journals were gone.

My mind was a flurry, thinking of all of the possibilities of my missing journals being in the wrong hands. Razi could find me. Anyone could find me. It had every piece of information about me in it. I hoped maybe the police would have broken up the fight and taken Razi and Dolph into custody and maybe one of the officers had it. Or maybe, it stayed in the booth, and nobody took it. I decided I needed to call the café -now. I started to stand, with the intention of finding the phone number, but standing only made me queasier, so I sat back down.

Maxine knocked on the door and asked if I needed anything. "Some paper, please. And a pen," I said. She didn't ask why, but brought me the paper, and in between fits of vomiting, I wrote down everything that had just happened. There was absolutely no way I was going to forget any of that.

20

I opened my eyes to find myself lying on the floor of a bathroom. Whose bathroom, I wasn't sure. My head was resting on a jacket that was wadded up. I was on my right side, my left arm was bandaged and clutching a glass of water, my right hand clutching some pieces of paper that were slightly wrinkled. I thought I might have been laying on them. Rolling over onto my back, I came within centimeters of a bathtub.

I held the papers up to read them. It was the strangest story. The narrator was involved in some crazy fight with a drug dealer who had a lump on his head, and a cute waiter who tried to help her. Then, the narrator went to visit a mafia lawyer with a person named Maxine. I didn't understand what I was reading, but somehow, I knew I must have written it.

There was a knock on the bathroom door, and I heard a deep voice. "Jackie, are you up? How are you feeling? Can I use the bathroom?"

I sat up. He was obviously talking to me, so that must mean my name is Jackie. I grabbed my jacket and the glass and the story and stood up. I opened the door to find a tall, masculine-looking woman standing by the door.

"Oh," I said, surprised. "I thought I heard someone else ask for the bathroom."

"Uh, no, it was me. Are you okay?" She asked with that same deep voice.

"Yeah, I'm fine," I lied, still looking at her, trying to recognize her face.

"Jackie? Did you have another episode? Do you remember me?" I shook my head and she grabbed my hand and took a few large breaths, then she led me to the couch.

"Okay, here's what happened: you have a rare form of amnesia where every so often you have a little attack, and you forget everything about yourself. Your name is Jackie Dawes, my name is Maxine. Our other roommate is Archie. You've been keeping a diary; it's in your purse. I'll go get it."

I watched her get up and walk to the door. She brought back a medium sized bag, which I opened and found nothing but a cell phone, a map, and a wallet.

"Oh no, your journals are gone!" She sat on the couch, staring at my empty purse. "Those journals had everything in them. Everything you knew about yourself or everything we could fill you in on. I suppose you don't remember where you left it, do you?"

I shook my head. "I didn't know I'd written anything until you just said I did. Well, I knew I wrote this." I held up the wrinkled papers. Maxine took them and looked them over.

"This is from last night. So, if you didn't have your journals last night, you must have left them at the café," she continued talking, I broke her off.

"Wait, this is true? This happened last night?"

"Well, yeah, Jackie. You were meeting Archie and me at the café, and you had gone there all by yourself, and when I walked in, you were under a table, watching that waiter fight with those guys. Now, since you've already read this, you know all about this Razi guy. You might have been involved in a drug deal of his awhile back, and you have a large sum of money that might be his, that's how all this started. We went to my uncle Manny to see what we could do about the situation."

"Hmm, so I've read," I said flatly.

"Look, I've got to get ready for work, but Archie will be here and maybe the two of you can go to the café and see if your journals are there." She stood up and peeked her head into another room and then went into the bathroom and closed the door.

I read the story over again, and then saw a man come out of the door Maxine looked into. That was Archie, I concluded. He was in a pair of boxer shorts and a t-shirt. He went into the kitchen, and soon joined me on the couch, handing me a toasted waffle.

"Oh, what's this?" I asked, smiling at the gesture.

"Open up your mouth and feed it," he replied. I scrunched my face. That sounded familiar to me.

"What did you say?"

"Open up your mouth and feed it."

"Where have I heard that before?"

"It's a song lyric. From the Eighties. Weird Al, I think," I heard Maxine say from the other room. I shrugged and ate my waffle.

Maxine left and Archie and I sat on the couch, watching some cartoons. After a few cartoons, we both got up, Archie showed me to my room, and I got dressed. I unwound the bandage from my arm to see what it was hiding and gasped at what I found. It was a disgusting cut and bruise. I touched it, not believing it was real, but the pain that followed told me it was. I went back out to the couch and waited for Archie. When he came out of his room, he found me examining my bruise. He went into my room and came back with my flesh-colored bandage. He sat down next to me, scribbled something down on a small notepad and handed it to me. I read it as he put the bandage back on.

You had a spell of amnesia on the subway, and you ran away from Maxine and tripped on some stairs.

"Really?" I asked, putting the note down.

Archie nodded.

When I was bandaged again, we got up and he led me out of the apartment, headed for the cafe from my wrinkled story.

The café was a quaint looking place from the outside. Inside, it was crowded with people. Archie left my side, which startled me a little, but he returned before I had time to panic and pulled me into the corner to the only empty table in the café. He wrote me a note pointing out our usual table, which was occupied at the moment. He wrote that he checked for any journals but didn't see any over there. I didn't seem too upset about these journals, which was probably because I didn't remember writing them. So, we set that aside and ordered some food.

A waiter stopped at our table, and Archie gave him a little hand gesture. The waiter nodded and looked at me. "And for you?"

I wasn't sure what to get, so I just answered, "The same," completely unsure of what I had just ordered. When he walked away, I remembered my story said something about a waiter who tried to help me. I got the paper out of my purse and read it over.

"Archie, do you know who this guy is? This Reece person?"

Archie glanced at my paper and then sat back, thinking for a moment. *He's one of the waiters here. I only remember the name because he gets in trouble for talking to you. He likes you.*

I blushed, reading his note. He laughed.

"Is he here?" I asked.

Archie craned his neck, looking around, then gestured to me to hold on, and left the table. He returned in a moment, and shook his head no.

Our waiter came back with our food and then gave me a funny look. "Aren't you that girl who caused the fight last night?"

"I, uh, well, I don't think I caused it, but I guess I was here," I answered defensively.

"No, I remember now. You were in that booth, and those guys were with you. You got Reece into a lot of trouble, you know. He spent the night in jail."

I suddenly felt incredibly guilty. Archie nudged the guy and shook his head, indicating to him to stop, but I wanted more information. "He went to *jail*? What about those other guys?"

"Well, they went to jail too, but they were probably released this morning like Reece was. The cops came and busted it up before it got too ugly."

"Is he okay?"

"Who? Oh, Reece? Dunno. I think today was his day off anyway, but I can't say for sure."

The rest of my day was met with distraction. Archie didn't know where else to look for my journals, and I could offer no suggestions myself. We gave up and went back to the apartment where I occupied myself in front of the TV, trying to think about things, wishing I could remember anything about my life prior to the story I found from yesterday.

Archie seemed uncomfortable with my lifelessness. He sat down with me, only to get up a few minutes later to go to his room. I noticed his uneasiness but was trying too hard to dig up any memories, even just faces for the names in the story: Reece, Razi, Dolph. I had none; my mind felt completely blank.

After a couple hours, Archie came out into the living area with a doll, which he handed to me. I could see it from across the room, and the blue checkered dress and red shoes registered with me.

"Is that Dorothy?"

Archie smiled and handed me the doll. I looked her over and smiled back, realizing that my mind did recognize something. It wasn't blank after all.

21

I barely managed four days of work at Brandisham's, having no idea what I was doing. I was able to hide from the salesgirls as much as possible, while my fellow basement dweller, Chrissy, did the work of both of us.

She knew when I walked in that I didn't remember her, and when I acted impressed, she shrugged it off and proceeded to tell me about the last two times I showed up with no memory, which she also guessed right off the bat. "Even the very first time," she said. "Before you were diagnosed with amnesia, I knew you didn't remember me. Now, if you want to be impressed by something, be impressed by that."

She walked me through the merchandise and the computer and then gave me a stapled packet that explained all of the same information over again. "I typed this the last time, because I figured it might come in handy to you. There's a copy in your desk drawer, and you can keep that copy with you."

"Thank you," I said, truly appreciative. "I know this probably gets annoying, having to re-explain everything to me all the time. You're very patient with me and I appreciate all your help."

Chrissy smiled and pushed up her glasses. "I don't mind. Besides, it's not like you can help it."

During the week, while I hid in the basement, reading my manual and walking through the racks of clothes, Chrissy would tell me things about myself and girls in the store. She told me about this Tascha, who I set up Archie with, and who stood him up. I was appalled when she told me I had roughed up this girl, but Chrissy insisted she deserved it.

"We stole her appointment book," she continued, "and we were holding it ransom until she agreed to go out with Archie, but she's been gone with Mrs. Brandisham to Paris, for the past week, so that's kind of been on hold. She'll be back next week though."

I kept begging Archie to stop at the Corner Nook on our way home every day when he came to get me from work, but he thought we should stay away for a while, especially if Razi was still on the loose.

He might be hanging around the café, or he might have some guys hanging around there or something. We should wait at least until I'm able to access your account, because when we turn over the money, we can turn over his name too. Then, we'll be safer, knowing the police are after him.

I agreed with his note. It was probably best to steer clear until we could get rid of the money. But still, part of me wanted so desperately to find this Reece guy and thank him for helping me or at least apologize for getting him arrested.

On Thursday, I studied my map at work and decided I would take a little trip to the café on my lunch break. When I got there, it was crowded, and I looked at every waiter, none of whom looked familiar to me at all, and I left, discouraged. I couldn't even remember what Reece looked like, so I wasn't sure how I was going to find him. I guess I hoped he would find me.

"Jackie, don't forget you have an appointment with Doctor Novak tomorrow." Maxine said that night, as we were getting ready for bed. "Now, my friend Carmelina will stop by here and take you to the appointment. She took you last time, remember?" I started to say no, but Maxine kept talking. "I've told her about Razi, so she'll be on the look-out. And if you want, I can ask her to stay with you afterward."

"No!" I shouted, suddenly. "I mean, that's okay. I'll be fine here alone."

Maxine gave me a funny look. "Uh, okay."

Friday morning, I woke up to an empty apartment. Archie and Maxine had both gone to work, so I dressed, made myself a bowl of cereal, and waited for this Carmelina.

I heard footsteps in the hall outside our apartment, and I assumed it was her, but I thought I would wait for a knock.

"Jackie, it's Carmelina. Let me in," she said, without knocking.

I opened the door and surprised myself with how unsurprised I was at what Carmelina looked like. Her hair was bleached blonde, with tinges of blue everywhere, especially the roots. These seemingly newly blonde locks were pulled up into little pig tail buns. She was wearing long black leather pants, platform heels, and a zebra fur coat. I recalled Maxine saying something about the fur coat the night before, when she described her to me.

"How are you today? Do you remember me?"

"I'm sorry, I don't," I said, a little ashamed.

Carmelina smiled, an unlit cigarette hanging from her mouth. "Huh. What a shame, eh?"

I grabbed my jacket and we headed out. She linked arms with me and led the way to the doctor's office. We walked in silence most of the way, but every once in a while, Carmelina would ask me a question, which I couldn't answer, having had an episode since the last time I saw her.

As soon as we arrived, the receptionist sent me to the doctor's office.

"Have a seat, Jackie," the doctor said as I entered. "How have you been this past two weeks? Everything alright?"

"No," I answered flatly.

"What happened?"

I started with the first thing I remembered, which was waking up on the bathroom floor. I told her about the story I wrote, which turned out to be true; I even showed her the wrinkled pages, which I had been keeping in my purse. She read the story and then asked for me to continue with what I could remember.

"That's pretty much it," I said. "The rest of this week, I've been hiding out, avoiding working, because I can't remember how to do anything."

"Now, what about the journaling I told you to do last visit. Did you do that?"

"Yes. I mean, I guess I did, but I lost it. My roommates said I did, but after I woke up, Maxine went to get my journal, and it was gone."

The doctor was silent for a moment, writing some notes in her little booklet. "I guess what you might have to do is start your journaling over again. A notebook is great to carry with you, but maybe, to prevent losing it again, what you could do is write in a notebook and then transfer your entries to a computer. The repetition will help your memory. You could even post your journal on the internet. That way, you always have a back-up, and no matter where you are, if you are without your journals, and you have access to the internet, you can find your journals there."

"Why would I do that?"

"Well," Doctor Novak replied. "Some people find that when you post your thoughts or feelings somewhere where everyone can read them, you might discover people with similar plights who can relate to you. Blogs and online communities are very popular right now, because everyone is looking to find someone to whom they can relate."

"I don't think anyone can relate to me."

"But you don't know that for sure, now, do you?"

"I guess not. But even if this journaling thing works out, it still doesn't help me remember things. I mean, you saw that I clearly wrote about that incident the night before my spell, and I still don't recall it. It's like I'm reading something about somebody else. It's like it's not even real."

"I understand, but repetition is the key to recovering from a condition like yours. You just have to give it some time, and it might not work right away, but eventually, you'll start to recover certain things that are important. You told me last week that you remembered scenes from *The Wizard of Oz*, even though you hadn't watched the movie recently. That proves that your brain can retain information, and since it seems to be that you remember that and nothing else, that proves that your brain was possibly exposed to the movie a number of times in your life, causing it to stick. Now, I deal with patients all the time who have lost their memories or have suffered head injuries, so believe me when I say that writing down your experiences is a good idea, even if you don't remember them, because there is always a chance you will just snap out of it."

"Snap out of it? Are you crazy?"

"Jackie, most people suffering from amnesia have their memories restored on their own. Often, it is helped with doctor visits and brain exercises, but even without any of that, the chances are likely that one's mind will just put itself back together again. One day, their brains turn back on again and they suddenly remember everything."

"Well, what if that doesn't work for me?"

"It takes time, but if you're certain that it won't ever come back, then I suggest that you give the repetition a try; repetition of your journals, of people's names and faces, of your surroundings, all that kind of stuff. Make connections with people."

"I have connections. I have Archie and Maxine and Chrissy and Carmelina."

"You need to make deep connections with these people. You need to go out and do things with these people, get to know them better, write their stories down, too. It sounds to me like you're only scratching the surface of each relationship. Dig deeper. Can you do that? Can you stop being just a spectator?"

"I guess," I answered. What she said made sense, so I decided I'd give it a try.

"Would you like to get some Chinese food, like last time?" Carmelina asked, lighting a cigarette, as we stepped out of the doctor's office.

I hesitated, wanting to get right home so I could go to the café after she left, but then she said, "Maybe we'll run into that cute guy that was checking you out last time."

My brain wondered if that was possibly Reece, so I smiled and nodded.

Unfortunately, the restaurant was nearly empty, and I was a little let down. The food almost made up for it, however, as the meal Carmelina ordered for me was exquisite.

"This is so much fun, watching you 'try Chinese for the first time' even though this is probably the hundredth time you've eaten it," she marveled, while we ate. "I'm sure I've told you this before, but you know what's cool? Everything is new again with you. Nothing has time to suck, because you forget it. Every person in the world would kill to be you."

"They can be me if they want. I'd trade lives any day."

It wasn't that I didn't like her, because I did, very much. She fascinated me, I guess in the same way I fascinated her. But I was anxious to escape my babysitter, so I could go to the café and see if I could find Reece to apologize.

Linking arms again, we walked from the restaurant in Chinatown, back to my apartment. I was afraid I would have to come up with some excuses to shake Carmelina, but as we approached the building, her phone rang, and she had to leave immediately. I stood outside the building and watched her walk away. When she was around the corner, I immediately started in the other direction. I was impressed that I found the café without looking at my map, but didn't dwell on it, as I had other business to take care of.

22

The café was less crowded than it had been the day before, but it was still fairly busy. This time, I was going to wait and make sure that I found him. I grabbed an open seat at the counter and waited. I closely watched every waiter that walked by, trying to figure out which one was Reece. Finally, I saw a waiter I did recognize. I knew it wasn't Reece, but it was the waiter from the last time Archie and I had been in.

"Hey," he said, politely, standing at the counter in front of me. "What can I get you?"

"Oh, nothing. I was just wondering if Reece was here today."

"Geeze, you don't give up on that guy, do you?"

"I want to apologize to him. And when I set my mind to doing something, I follow through," I answered, and then quickly muttered, "I think."

The waiter eyed me suspiciously. "I guess you do owe him a pretty big apology, getting him in all that trouble. He was here this morning. He did our breakfast shift, but he left over an hour ago."

My face fell and I stared at the counter.

"Sorry," he said. "But I think he comes in tomorrow afternoon. If you want, I'll tell him you were looking for him."

"I'll be back tomorrow then, I guess." I got up from the seat and started to walk away. "Thank you," I said, turning back to him. He nodded and I walked out.

I stood outside the door for a moment, thinking about what to do next. I told myself to just go home, but I didn't feel like being cooped up there all afternoon. I decided that I could maybe go for a little walk, so long as my map was in my hand. I opened the map, to see where I wanted to walk to, when out of the corner of my eye, I saw a man in the distance, standing completely still as people walked past. He was facing me, his eyes covered with sunglasses, so I couldn't tell if he was looking at me or not. A wave of paranoia passed through me, and I became suspicious, so I turned my back, and walked away from him. I stopped and pressed myself against the wall, held my map up again, and using my peripheral vision, I could see that he was stopped also, but closer to me now than before. I looked around at everyone walking by, and across the street, I saw another guy, standing stationary by a lamp post. He too, had on sunglasses, and was facing me.

I started to walk again, and this time, I watched the man across the street start walking in sync with me. I turned around to find the first man following me too. I quickened my pace, and they too, quickened theirs. Then, in panic, I broke out into a run. I tried to be careful not to run into anybody on the sidewalk, or trip. I was hoping to slip inside a building to lose them, but with one watching me from behind, and the other watching from across the street, I knew they would find me. And I wasn't sure exactly how many more men were following me.

As I ran, two younger men in blue jackets appeared. Staring straight at me, one of them had his arm extended, to stop me. I ran into his arm, before I could stop, and they pulled me over to the wall.

"Don't be afraid of us. Uncle Manny sent us," the one not holding me said.

I remembered Uncle Manny from the story in my purse, so I stopped fidgeting and relaxed. The two of them stood next to me like we were in a line-up, and both men crossed their arms, freezing like statues. I watched as the men tailing me caught up to where I was and then stopped suddenly. The one from behind me looked to the one across the street, who shook his head and started walking away. Then, he too turned around and headed in the opposite direction.

"Those were Razi's guys," said the guy who caught me. "They've seen you with us, so they know now that you're with us. They won't be following you that closely anymore."

"Thanks," I said. "Are you guys following me too?"

"No," he said. "We don't need to. We've got our brothers everywhere in this city. We'll be able to find you anywhere you go. You'll recognize the blue jackets. Don't worry though; we're only here to protect you, Uncle Manny's orders. Do you want us to walk you home?"

"No, but thank you again. I'll be alright. I appreciate your help." I left the two men still leaning against the wall and headed around the corner. I started walking quickly, but I soon realized that I had no idea where I was now. I got out my map and started to read it, walking at the same time, and when I turned another corner, I walked right into somebody, and I fell backward, and hit the ground.

"Oh my God, I'm so sorry, are you okay?"

"Yeah, I'm fine. I'm sorry I ran into you," I said, taking the hand that was extended to me, and standing up.

"I'm not," he said. "Hi." I looked up at his face; he was grinning.

"Okay," I mumbled, wiggling my hand out of his grasp. He looked down at my hand and quickly let go.

"It's Jackie, right?"

I looked back at his face. "Uh, yeah. Do I know you?"

He narrowed his eyes, still grinning a bit. "Yes. I mean, well, sort of. The Corner Nook?"

I stared at him blankly. I tried to remember seeing him in the café.

"Oh, wait. I usually have my glasses on. Maybe that's why you don't recognize me."

I shrugged, but I was still confused.

"Um, I caused the fight last week?"

My eyes widened. Was this Razi? I looked around, planning an escape, as he kept talking.

"My name is Reece."

I perked up at the sound of the name, taking a deep breath, relieved it wasn't Razi. I looked down, shyly, as he was more handsome than I pictured he would be.

"I have your journals."

"What?" I was shocked.

"I found your journals on the table that night."

"Oh, wow!" I laughed. My shyness disappeared for the moment and was replaced by excitement. "This is great! I thought I was going to have to start all over again! You have saved me!" His grin turned into a nervous smile when I said that. "Where are they?"

"Oh, um, they're back at my apartment. I'd been carrying them with me, but I never saw you. I found your address and phone number in the cover, so I thought about calling you, but I was too nervous, I guess. Then, I was going to mail them to you. I held off on it though. I hoped maybe if I had them it would be an excuse for you to come see me. Would you like to come with me to get them? My apartment's not far from here."

"If you don't mind," I said, growing sheepish again.

He turned around and started walking as I followed alongside. As we were crossing the street, a rush of people surrounded us and another stream of people heading in the opposite direction flowed through our crowd. I was worried I would lose him in this sea of people, and without even thinking, I grabbed the arm of his jacket tightly. He jumped and then looked at me.

"Sorry," I muttered, turning red. "I have a tendency to get lost. Do you mind?"

He laughed, then grabbed my hand and linked our arms. "Not at all."

We walked for a bit before I noticed we were in familiar territory. "Are we in Chinatown?"

"Yeah."

"I was just here earlier today."

"Did you eat at Chen's restaurant?"

I nodded.

"You know, I saw you at Chen's once. A few weeks ago. Do you remember?"

"No, I don't actually," I responded.

We were both awkwardly quiet for a moment. As we passed Chen's Restaurant, he spoke again. "So, did you come all the way to Chinatown just to eat?"

"I had a doctor's appointment near here."

"Oh, with Doctor Novak?"

"Yes. Wait, how did you know that?"

He didn't answer. We stopped in front of a building and went inside. The hallway was too narrow for the two of us to walk side by side, so I slid behind him, still holding his arm. We walked up a couple flights of thin stairs and then to his door.

Reece's apartment was small, much smaller than mine, but it was quaint. The walls were plain, but there were bookshelves everywhere and they were full of all kinds of things. As for furniture, he had a tiny loveseat-sized couch, and a reclining chair, not much else.

"You can have a seat if you want," he said. I sat down on the couch. It was more comfortable than the couch at my apartment. He stepped into one of the rooms on the side, which I took for his bedroom, and immediately stepped back out.

"Here it is. You'll have to forgive me, but I started reading it. I only meant to look at the first page, just to find out your name, but I couldn't help myself. I'm sorry," he said, joining me on the couch.

"Oh, it's okay. I think. I mean, I don't even know what's in it. I've forgotten since last Friday."

"Well, that would explain why you don't remember me ever. I honestly kept thinking, 'Is she really so stuck up that she doesn't even remember talking to a petty waiter like me?' But thankfully, that's not the case at all. You have amnesia."

"Did you really think that I was stuck up?"

"I didn't know what to think. I mean, one day, you'd be talking to me, or you'd smile or wave and then the next day, you would act all funny around me like you didn't recognize me."

"It's alright. You didn't know what was wrong with me. I keep forgetting that not everyone knows."

I opened the journal marked with a number one and started to read a little bit. After a few pages, I noticed Reece was peering over my shoulder, so I started reading it aloud. I started with the details of the day I started the journal, which was the day of my last appointment. I read about Carmelina and her taking me to get Chinese food, even though we weren't supposed to go anywhere but to the doctor and home.

"There was a table of guys in the restaurant, and one of the guys kept staring at Carmelina and me. She claimed he was staring at just me, and she asked if I knew him, but I didn't. "Too bad. He's kind of cute," she said. I said he was weird, but secretly, I agreed."

Reece chuckled when I read that. I put the journal down and looked at him. "What's so funny?"

"Huh? Oh, nothing. It's just, um, well, that's me, you're talking about."

"You?"

"Yeah. That was the day I saw you at Chen's. I asked you outside if you remembered that. That was me. I was there with some of my friends, and I saw you come in, but I wasn't sure if it was you because of the girl you were with. I'd never seen her before and usually I always saw you with those other two. Archie and Maxine, I think you said."

I blushed ever so slightly, as it wasn't an outright admittance, but I had basically just read aloud that I had an interest in him. I should have stopped right there, but I kept reading. I started reading the listed things that my journal said were from notes. I mentioned something about yelling at Portia at work, and then I read the next number down which said I had apparently yelled at a waiter that same day and apologized the next time I saw him.

"That was also me," Reece interjected.

I read on, and every once in a while, I mentioned a nameless waiter, and how I was teased because he was looking at me or waving at me. Reece's face reddened a bit when I got to those parts.

"We went to the café today, and I found that I was gravely disappointed when our waiter turned out not to be our usual waiter. Reece, I think I heard someone call him once. Then, that night, I couldn't sleep because..." I trailed off and put the book down. Reece stared at me.

"What? Couldn't sleep because why?"

"Nothing. It's stupid. Never mind." My whole face was burning with embarrassment.

"What? I want to know."

"No, you don't. This is my private journal. I don't have to tell you what I wrote." I started to stand up, but he grabbed the journal out of my hand. I turned to snatch it back, but he was already up off the couch, and walking to the kitchen, smiling.

I followed after him, and tried to grab the book, but he turned his back to me. I tried reaching around him, but he extended his arm. Then, he jumped up onto the counter and stood so his head touched the ceiling. With that distance between us, he thumbed to the page and started reading silently. I stopped fighting because I knew it would do me no good.

I was mortified; I thought he was going to laugh at me, but what he did surprised me. He stopped smiling and sank so he was just sitting on the counter now. He put the journal down to his side and looked me square in the face.

"You couldn't sleep because you were worried about me?"

"Yeah, I guess."

"Aw," he said, grinning. "I just had the day off. Actually, I was visiting my grandmother that day."

"Oh. Can I have my journal back, please?"

He hesitated for a moment, so I opened my purse and got out the folded, wrinkled pages. "I need to copy this down."

"What's that?"

"It's about last week, I think. About the fight. I wrote it down as soon as I got home, so I wouldn't forget and it's a good thing I did that."

"Can I read it?"

"You don't need to. You were there."

"Yeah, but," he paused.

"But what?"

He laughed and said, "I'd like to know how you saw it. How you saw me."

I started to shake my head, but he pleaded. "Come on Jackie, I've already read all the embarrassing things, so why not?"

I rolled my eyes. "Fine. But let me write it down first."

I sat back down on the couch and began to copy my story down in the journal marked with a number three. Each time I finished with a wrinkled page, I set it off to the side, where it was quickly snatched up by Reece. When I was finished, I sat back and watched Reece's face as he continued to read. He seemed thoroughly absorbed in the story.

"Wow," he said when he finished.

"Yeah, it's crazy, huh? All that shady business."

"No, I meant 'wow, in your eyes I look good. I look brave and handsome.'"

I glared at him, but he just laughed. "I'm kidding. I meant it about the money and the Bettinos. That is just insane. And it's all true?"

"I think so. I mean, I obviously don't remember, but today, right before I ran into you, I was being followed by these guys and then two guys in blue jackets told me they were protecting me under orders from Uncle Manny."

"Whoa," he whispered in amazement.

"Yeah. I was actually leaving the café when they started following me. I went there to find you."

"Me? Why?"

"I was going to thank you for your help and apologize. I mean, I guess Maxine and I saw the cops on the corner and

Maxine told them about the fight, hoping that they'd help you out, but then when Archie and I went back the next day, one of the other waiters told me you'd been arrested. Which, by the way, I'm really, really sorry about that. I felt terrible."

Reece shrugged. "Don't worry about it. I wasn't charged with anything. They just took all of us in for questioning and then made me sleep in a cell that night as punishment for a public disturbance. No big deal at all. As long as you got out okay, I didn't really care if they took me to jail."

"Well, thank you for helping me. I really appreciated it."

"Any time," he laughed.

Just then, a phone rang. Neither one of us moved, and the phone rang again. Reece looked at me and said, "I think that's your phone."

"Oh," I said, rifling through my purse. "Hello?"

"Jackie? Where the hell are you? Are you okay?"

"Hi Maxine. Yes, I'm fine."

"Where are you? I came home and you weren't here, so I called Carmelina and she said she dropped you off here."

"Oh, I'm okay, Max. I'm with Reece."

"Who?"

"Reece. That waiter from the café." I looked over at him, and he motioned for me to give him the phone. "Here, Max. He wants to talk to you."

"Hello, Maxine? Hi, this is Reece. Yeah, the one who got in the fight, right. I ran into Jackie earlier and I told her I had her journals. I picked them up off the table, and had been meaning to return them, so since I saw her, I asked her if she would come with me back to my place to get them. She's okay. I'll bring her home right now. No, you don't have to come get her. I'll bring her home. Okay. Bye." He hung up my phone and handed it back to me. I put it back in my purse and then got out my map and handed it to him, showing him the mark where my apartment building was.

We walked down the street with our arms linked again, even though there weren't nearly as many people as there had been earlier. He seemed to know exactly how to get to my place, without needing the map again. As we rounded the corner, I pointed out to him our apartment window, which was framing both Maxine and Archie's faces, as they were waiting for me.

"Oh my God, Jackie, there you are!" Maxine shouted, as Reece and I walked up the stairs and down the hallway. "I was so worried," she continued. "You scared me to death. I thought you were lost. Don't do that again. You know the rule. You need to call me when you're by yourself."

"Yeah, I know. I'm sorry. I just ran into him, and he said he had my journals and I forgot about everything else. It won't happen again," I apologized.

Maxine grabbed my shoulders and pulled me inside the apartment. Reece stopped at the door, but I motioned for him to come in. "Archie, Maxine, this is Reece. I know you've seen him before, but now, I'm formally introducing you all."

Archie and Maxine both said hello, and Reece smiled and returned the greeting, all the while looking around at the amount of space in our apartment.

"Thank you so much for getting her journals for her and bringing her home. We both really appreciate it."

"Yeah, it was no problem at all," he smiled. "Okay, I guess I'll get going then. It was nice meeting you guys. Jackie, I'll see you around."

"Yeah," I replied, smiling. Maxine and Archie left us at the door and went to the couch. I stood at the doorway as he walked out.

"Oh, Jackie?" He said, turning around at the end of the hallway.

"Yes?"

"It was nice to finally meet you today."

"It was nice finally meeting you, too, Reece." I watched him walk down the stairs and I closed the door and then headed to the window and watched him stop outside the building and look up at my window and wave. I waved back and then he walked away.

I turned back to Archie and Maxine on the couch, both of whom had wide grins on their faces. "What?" I asked. Then both shook their heads smiling.

"You might as well face it, you're addicted to love."

"Shut up," I replied, turning red, as I grabbed my purse and headed to my room to write.

23

I slept peacefully that night, in spite of the plethora of Reece-related thoughts and dreams that raced through my slumber. I slept so well, Archie shook me awake, worried that I hadn't woken up and it was almost noon.

It was Saturday, and I had no intentions of doing anything, but I didn't like the sound of hanging around the apartment really either.

For a late lunch, I decided to give something in the kitchen a try. I wasn't sure if I had any cooking ability as Maxine did it all, but there was only one way to find out. I got a chunk of meat out of the freezer and stuck it in a frying pan. The meat began smoking soon and our alarm went off. Archie swatted the air with a towel until it stopped and then informed me that the meat had to thaw before I cooked it.

While the meat thawed, I found a box of mashed potato mix. I followed the directions, or so I thought, until Archie ran a spoon through the potatoes which were of curdled milk consistency.

Archie was a good sport in humoring me and ended up just suggesting we go grab a bite at the Corner Nook. I swallowed my defeat with a dash of excitement, as I was sure that Reece was working.

I immediately saw him when we walked in. He was placing dishes at someone's table, and he looked up as we entered and smiled at me. I smiled back, but was suddenly embarrassed, and turned my back and almost dragged Archie to our booth. We ordered and ate, I tried to ignore Reece, but no matter where I fixed my eyes, they found their way back to him, just wondering what he was doing every couple minutes. At the moment we decided to leave, the café just happened to be empty, one of its rare downtimes.

"Bye Archie, bye Jackie!"

We both turned around at the door to see Reece, poking his head out of the kitchen door across the room. Archie raised a hand in acknowledgment, and I saw Reece turn his eyes directly to me.

"Goodbye, Reece. See you later," I grinned. It was official: I definitely had a crush.

On Sunday, at breakfast, Maxine asked me about the doctor's appointment. I told her about Doctor Novak's advice to back up my journal and to become more involved in people's lives.

"How do you mean?" she asked.

"I don't know, exactly. She wants me to have more experiences with people, go out and do things. She said I had to stop being a spectator, and that maybe that would help me remember things."

"So, we need to do more things? Like going out? I don't know if that's a good idea, I mean, what if we lose you or you have an episode?"

"I'm just telling you what she said."

"I know! Let's have a party!"

"A party? That sounds good."

"We'll invite people over here, that way, you are safe, and we're still doing something. It'll be fun!"

Maxine settled on having our party the following Saturday. During the week, we began making plans and cleaning the apartment. I invited Chrissy, who immediately accepted, and against my better judgment, I even invited the rest of the girls, including Portia, who, unlike the other girls who politely said they were "busy", laughed in my face. Normally, I felt like I would have been angry about that, but since I didn't really want her there, I shrugged it off.

On Wednesday, Tascha finally came back from Paris. I had completely forgotten about the appointment book, but when Chrissy reminded me, I was hopeful that Wednesday would be the day that she finally cracked.

Right around lunchtime, Chrissy and I heard footsteps coming from the stairs, a rarity, as everyone but Chrissy and I seemed practically terrified of the basement. Because we were both absolutely silent, we heard the footsteps as they made their way down an aisle.

Tascha stood in front of our desks, frigid and scared. "Um, Jackie? I, I need a favor," she mumbled.

"What? What did you say? I didn't hear you," I said, mockingly.

She took a deep breath and repeated herself. "I need a favor. But you can't tell anybody, okay?"

"Go on, I'm intrigued."

"Well, I sort of misplaced my appointment book or something. I don't know, but it's completely gone. I hoped it would return while I was in Pairs, but it didn't. And I've been faking my way through the day, because luckily, I have a good enough memory with my clients, but Kat Pendleton is coming in tomorrow and Portia just told me to pencil her in, and I need help. Kat is our biggest client, as you know, and I can't screw this up. I mean, you did once, so we're on thin ice with her."

"What do you want me to do?"

"Well, since my book is gone, could you maybe get me a list of Kat's choices and things?"

"That depends."

"Depends on what?"

"If I do this for you, you have to do something for me."

"Name it. Anything at all. I can't screw this up."

"If I get you her information, you have to come to my party this Saturday."

She huffed, and rolled her eyes, but I went on. "Now, I know you don't want to go, and I certainly don't want you to come, but it would mean a lot to Archie if you would. So, if you want help, you need to give Archie a chance."

She looked around for a long moment and began tapping her foot. Finally, she said, "Ugh, alright, Jackie. I'll go. Just give me Kat's information."

"Not so fast. Here are the directions to my apartment," I said, handing her a piece of paper. "Now, I need you to give me your phone number. You know, in case you don't show." She wrote down her number, and I called it just to be sure.

"Great," I said, hanging up on the voicemail. "Now let me print off that information for you."

Friday, I woke up late again. My sleep these days was increasingly better. I made myself a bowl of cereal, even though it was nearly noon, and plopped down in front of the computer. I had asked Archie before about the internet journaling, and he set up an account for me on publicblog.com. He left a sticky note stuck to the computer screen with a screen name and password that I had to type in, and then I began.

Hello, World, I wrote. *My name is Jackie and I have amnesia. My condition is rare and results in me sporadically waking up with no recollection of the time transpired since the last time I had a "spell."*

From there, I started typing things straight from my journal, and knowing people might actually read it, I embellished just a little. I decided that I would write a couple things from my journal to my new blog every day, just like it was daily story time, only instead of telling my story to kids, I was telling my story to the whole world.

After a couple hours of doing that, then another half hour of playing a game, I decided to walk to the Corner Nook to get some food. I made it there by myself, with no help from my map, which was a small victory, especially since I was constantly looking around at every person I passed; making sure no one was following me. Even under the protection of the Bettinos, in my state of paranoia, I knew that I shouldn't be going to the café so much, because Razi and his guys knew I ate there, but I couldn't resist; Reece was making it hard for me to stay away.

Reece was there, and he smiled wide when I walked in. Since I was alone, I decided to sit at the counter. As I sat down, he rushed over to a waiter wiping the counter down. "Hey Kenny, do you want to switch spots with me for a bit? I'll wash that counter for you, and you can take the tables."

Kenny gave him a funny look, then noticed me watching them both and handed Reece the cloth and water solution and walked away. Reece smiled at his own genius and then started over to me.

"Hey Jackie! I haven't seen you in a few days. How've you been? Do you still remember me?"

"Yes, I remember you. I've been good, surprisingly."

"You look really good."

"What?"

"I, I mean, you look different, like you're healthy and well rested or something."

"Oh, okay," I smiled. "Actually, I have been sleeping a lot better lately."

He took my order and set back to washing the counter, making small talk with me while I ate. He asked me about my week, and my day so far and was intrigued when I told him about my new internet blog.

"Can I read it?"

"Well, it's accessible, but I don't want you to," I said, shyly.

"Why not?"

"Because it's a journal. Besides, you've read most of what I wrote, give or take a few embellishments."

"Embellishments, huh? Like what? Like how muscular and cut my body was when I fought off those bad guys without my shirt on?"

"Something like that," I laughed. Glancing at my watch, I noticed that I had been there for almost an hour. "I should probably get going," I said, pulling money from my purse and standing up.

"Oh, hey Jackie? I was wondering if you would maybe be interested in doing something with me this weekend." He muttered so fast, I almost didn't hear him.

"Yes, I would. I'm actually having a party tomorrow night and I want you to come. You think you'll make it?"

"Yeah, absolutely."

"Great. I'll see you tomorrow around seven. Do you remember how to get to my place?"

"It's burned into my mind," he laughed.

"That makes one of us," I smiled, and headed out the door. Outside, I picked back up with my paranoid state, altered slightly by the fact that I couldn't seem to stop smiling. I looked around for any guys in sunglasses watching me but didn't really care if one saw me or not.

Saturday couldn't come fast enough for me. Maxine spent the morning working at the supermarket, calling the apartment every ten minutes because she forgot to remind me to clean the kitchen, or make sure we had enough of this or that. Archie and I rolled our eyes every time the phone rang, but I continued to answer it.

When Maxine finally came home, she worked continuously, preparing little finger foods and dessert things. A couple girls Maxine said were from the club came over early to help, since they couldn't get the night off completely. Maxine introduced them to Archie and me as Yolanda and Robyn. They were really nice and giggled a lot when Archie spoke.

Soon after, around seven, a group of guys arrived at our door. Archie introduced us by pointing to each one individually, and when he pointed, the guy said his own name. They were friends of his from the bank. Another girl showed up that was a friend of Maxine's and soon after, Carmelina and a few others walked in, quickly followed by Chrissy.

I was thrilled to see Chrissy there, and she stuck to my side at first, but then, she got caught up talking to one of Archie's friends, and I was once again unattached.

I tried to help Maxine, but she kept shoving me out of the kitchen, insisting I get everyone drinks. Carmelina was already manning the alcohol, so I just went out into the living space. Archie had connected his stereo out into the main room and began playing some demur, but jazzy music. Carmelina danced by me, laughing, and handed me a cup. I smiled, but headed to the widow, joined by Chrissy, to wait for two people in particular.

Reece was the first one I saw. He rounded the corner, and I was so excited to see him, that after a large swig of bravery from my glass, I met him in front of the building. He smiled when he saw me, then laughed as I stood there, barefoot on the sidewalk, wiggling and waving at him.

"You made it," I said, grabbing his arm and pulling him inside.

"Of course," he was saying. "I wouldn't have missed this."

He seemed timid, coming to the door, like he was afraid to enter our apartment. I felt him lagging behind me suddenly, but I just kept pulling until he was completely inside. Carmelina immediately danced by him and then there was a glass in his hand. She stopped when she realized who it was.

"Oh my God, you're that cute guy from the Chinese restaurant. Jackie, you told me you didn't know him!"

"I didn't at the time," I answered.

"Well, he's even cuter close up."

She laughed and danced away, and I looked at Reece, who was smiling, his eyes glued to the floor. He and I walked around together, mingling with everybody. "This is so-and-so. I don't know them, they're friends of Archie's," I kept saying, and everyone would then re-introduce themselves to both of us.

I left him chatting with one of the other guys and found Chrissy again. She and I sat on the couch, watching Carmelina dancing with herself. I kept looking back every once in a while at Reece, who would catch my eye and smile, but he kept talking.

There was so much noise in the room that I almost didn't even notice the doorbell ring. At first, I thought I had imagined it, but when it rang again, I ran to answer it. It was exactly who I was expecting.

"Hello, Tascha. Thanks for coming."

"Uh, hi, Jackie," she said nervously.

I invited her in, and introduced her to Carmelina, as she handed her a drink. She took a rather large sip and then I took her around and introduced her to people. Archie saw us, and I motioned for him to come over.

"Archie, this is Tascha. Tascha, this is Archie. There, you have officially met. Now, get to know each other." I pushed her back and his back like I was trying to clang gigantic cymbals and walked away.

I went back to the couch with Chrissy, and we both continued to watch everyone else interact. "I'm socially awkward, what's your excuse?" She joked.

"I don't know. I mean, I've been introduced to all these people, but I don't know what to talk to them about. And I thought this would help, but it's not." I lifted my cup and swirled it around. Chrissy laughed and took a drink of hers.

I turned around, but my eyes didn't automatically find Reece. I didn't know where he was. Archie, however, I could see in the kitchen, talking to Tascha. She was laughing, which was a good sign.

"Archie and Tascha are hitting it off, so I guess mission accomplished." Chrissy looked back at them as I spoke and nodded.

I turned back around again, looking for Reece, but I still didn't see him in the crowd of people. I felt a touch on my shoulder, and a voice behind me.

"Who are you looking for?"

I faced him and smiled. "Nobody. Just this weird guy I invited, you know, just to be nice."

"Oh, a weird guy, huh? What does he look like, I'll help you find him." He grabbed my hand and pulled me up off the couch.

"Well, he's got this red t-shirt on, and he's got brown hair that I can only describe as windswept, and a bit of stubble on his face," I put my hand on his cheek and felt the hair.

"And he's weird? Really? He sounds like he's the coolest guy here." I laughed, and followed him to the window, where we sat.

"Are you having a good time?" he asked me.

"Yeah, I mean, I feel odd since I don't really know how to interact with people, but I got Tascha here, which was the whole point, and Chrissy's making friends, and you're here, so it's been a success, I would say."

"Who's Tascha?" I showed her to him, and told him about her standing Archie up, and me confronting her, which he remembered from my journal.

"I just want to find him someone who's good enough for him. She's definitely not, but he thinks she is, and I just want him to be happy."

"Yeah, but you can't control who he'll like, and who he won't. Maybe she will make him happy." I knew he was right, and I rested my head on his shoulder. His head leaned back on mine, and then our hands slid together, like magnets. We sat that way chatting quietly, watching the party.

Carmelina turned the music up and grabbed the first person she could and started to dance. More people joined her, and the party went from groups of conversation to a livelier event. Maxine walked in between the crowd, offering her little quiche hors d'oeuvres. A girl I didn't recognize took the plate from her hands and set it down, pulling Maxine to dance with the rest of them.

Chrissy was no longer sitting on the couch. Instead, she was hugging the wall but chatting with one of Archie's friends. I smiled, glad to see that she was coming out of her shell, even if it was only due to the drink in her hand.

Every now and then, Maxine would jump out of the crowd to offer everyone food or more drinks. She would spot me across the room and make a drinking motion with her hand and then bring me another glass. I wasn't even sure what it was, but I always took it when she brought more.

Once it was nearing midnight, people started disappearing. Chrissy thanked us for a wonderful party, and I walked her to the door and hugged her. When she left, I noticed Tascha was heading toward the door as well, with Archie behind her. She gave me a rather large smile as she passed me and whispered, "Bye, Jackie!" Then I caught Archie's face, which also smiled at me.

I found Reece again, this time, he had moved to the couch. He looked a little uncomfortable sitting on our couch, which was nowhere near as soft as his. I sat down and he looked at me and then looked around at the dying party. All that was left now were Maxine and Carmelina talking in the kitchen, and Archie talking by the door with two of his friends.

"Should I go?" Reece asked.

"No. Absolutely not," I said, looking at him like he was crazy. My head then found that resting spot on his shoulder. "Stay here. Don't move a muscle."

He laughed.

"What?"

"You're a little drunk, I think."

"No, I'm perfectly fine."

We sat there silently, every once in a while, I closed my eyes and started dozing off. Reece would lift his head and look at me, patting my face or hair, whispering, "Jackie? Do you need to go to bed?"

"No," I kept saying. "I want to stay like this."

My eyes were closed while I heard the door closing, and people saying "goodbye" to each other. Then, the music turned off, and I heard Maxine, behind me.

"Is she okay, Reece?"

"Yeah, she's just tired. She can't keep her eyes open."

"Maybe I should take her to her room," Maxine said.

"No, that's okay. I'll do it."

When I opened my eyes again, Reece had me propped up against him and I was being helped down the hall, into my bedroom. Reece set me down in my bed and was about to cover me up, when I held up a hand.

"Wait. Can I put my pajamas on first?"

"Sure," he smiled.

He helped me back up and I grabbed a pair of fleece pants from my dresser and went into the bathroom. I washed my face and brushed my teeth and when I went back to my room, he was still there, sitting on the bed, waiting for me.

"Nice pajamas," he teased. "Are those elephants?"

I stuck my tongue out at him. "Don't make fun of my elephants. I like them."

I crawled into my bed, and he pulled the sheet up over me. "You don't have much for blankets, do you?" he laughed.

"Nope. I've been meaning to get a new blanket, but I keep forgetting."

I positioned myself onto my side, and he adjusted the sheet for me. "Do you want to do something with me tomorrow? Maybe something with just the two of us, and not a party crowd."

"Of course. I would love nothing better," I smiled. He grinned back and then leaned forward and kissed my forehead.

"Goodnight, Jackie. I'll see you tomorrow. Don't forget me tonight, okay?"

24

When I opened my eyes, the sun was shining, making it impossible for me to go back to sleep, even though I tried. I curled up, then stretched out and got out of bed. My head started aching as I stood up. Perhaps I stood up too fast, but I felt a rush to my head, then volts of pain, and then my vision went fuzzy.

My fall made a loud thud against the wood floor. The thud was so loud that Archie came rushing in to see what happened.

"I just stood up too fast. I'm fine, Archie."

He helped me up and sat me on the bed. My head was hurting so badly. He watched my agonized expression and promptly brought me some aspirin and a glass of water. Once I had taken the pills, he sat with me, while I laid my head back down on a pillow. He slid my journal over to me with a tiny note in it.

It's kind of cold in here, even with the sun shining.

"I know," I replied. "I don't have any blankets. Just sheets."

When my head felt better, I got up and Archie and I went to the kitchen for some breakfast. Archie made us some eggs and toast. I sat at the counter, watching him cook, when I heard a knock at the door.

It was Reece. "Hi," I smiled, as I opened the door.

"Hi, I'm sorry I'm here so early," he said, nervously. "The café was slow, so they sent me home, and I was closer to here, so I thought I would come by, if that's okay with you."

"Absolutely. Come on in. Sorry, I'm still in my pajamas. Archie and I were just about to eat breakfast. Do you want some?"

"It's almost noon," he chuckled. "No, I'm good, but thank you."

He sat on the couch, and I poured myself a glass of orange juice and joined him. Soon, Archie joined us with two plates of food. We ate and watched cartoons, like we were five.

"So, what are we doing today?" I asked.

"Oh, I can't tell you. It's a surprise."

I left him on the couch and went to change my clothes. Then, I gave Archie a kiss on the cheek and bid him goodbye, as Reece and I left. I wasn't sure why I was surprised, but I developed a wave of goose bumps when he took my hand. I gripped it tight, and followed his lead, wondering where we were going.

He kept me talking to him, to distract me, which worked, as we walked right under a giant sign. When we were at the ticket booth, I looked around and realized where we were.

"We're at the zoo! You took me to the zoo," I smiled.

"Yeah," he said. "Unless you want to go somewhere else."

"Not at all; this is perfect."

We went to the monkeys first, and then through the arctic exhibit with the penguins and polar bears. I hardly noticed I was holding his hand the whole time, until I tightened my grip as we went through the reptile house. Next came the African safari exhibit, where we saw giraffes, lions and zebras. At the end of the exhibit was a herd of elephants. We stopped to watch them.

"They're so beautiful," I whispered, in awe of the herd.

"The elephants?"

"Yeah. Look at them. They just look so majestic to me. And they're amazing. I mean, they form tight-knit bonds, like a family, and they show affection by intertwining their trunks. And they have exceptional memories. Elephants never forget," I said, repeating the saying.

"How do you know all that stuff?"

"I don't know. It's weird, huh? How I can remember random facts about elephants, but I can't even remember who I am." I laughed, but my grin faded. "I have to rely on my stupid journal to remind me of things, which doesn't remind me at all, because I retain none of it."

He looked at me, watching the elephants. "Can I take you somewhere?"

"Okay, where?"

"I want you to meet somebody."

We left the zoo, but not before stopping at the gift shop where Reece bought me a stuffed elephant. "So you'll hopefully remember this. Always," he said.

We took a cab to a building just outside the city. The sign out front read, "THE CARNATION HOME". We walked in, and while Reece talked to the receptionist, I looked around. It was like a hospital, except there were a few homey touches here and there and elderly people everywhere, sitting on benches, slowly walking around. He took my hand again and led me down one of the corridors. I peeked into all the rooms as we walked by. Each room had someone sitting in it or laying in bed. Most of them were hooked up to machines or had all kinds of equipment allowing them to be mobile.

We stopped at the door of one room, where there was a small, frail old woman sitting in a huge high-backed chair. She was staring out the window, and from the side of her face, I saw that she was grinning. Reece knocked on the door, and she turned around and looked at us, still grinning.

"Oh, hello," she said, pleasantly, but not as though she knew us.

"Hi, grandma," Reece said. He pulled me inside the room, and we both sat down on extra chairs. "How are you doing today?"

"Oh, I'm just fine, thank you," she answered. Her voice was so soft and barely audible. She kept right on grinning, looking back and forth from him to me.

"Grandma, this is Jackie. I wanted her to meet you."

"My name is Eleanor. It's nice to meet you. You're very pretty."

I smiled and thanked her, as she started slowly turning around to where her bed was. "I have something," she kept saying. Reece stood up and walked over to the nightstand and opened the drawer, taking out a box.

"Is this what you wanted, Grandma? Your pictures?"

She nodded and smiled wider, looking at Reece in awe of his mind-reading. He set the box in her lap, and she began to dig through it.

"This is a picture of him," she said, handing me a photo of a little boy. "This is my grandson. His name is Reece. I've raised him since he was five. He's such a good, good boy. Since his grandpa died, he's been my whole world."

I looked at the picture. "He's very cute," I said, handing it back. She took it and then handed it to Reece and explained her grandson again.

"Grandma, I know. That's me. I'm Reece. Remember? It's me."

"Oh, okay," she said, politely. He leaned toward her, looking square into her eyes, saying his name again and suddenly her face lit up. "Oh, my Reece, my Reece," she cried.

They hugged for a moment, and she suddenly said, "Where have you been?"

"I've been working, Grandma, but I'm here, just like I was last weekend, and the weekend before that."

"Oh, I see. Are you being a good boy?"

"Yes, Grandma. I've been very good."

"No trouble?"

"No trouble at all."

She dug out another picture of Reece with his grandfather and began telling me about him when he was little. Picture after picture was of Reece, maybe three or four were of just his grandfather, and one was of a little white dog that was hers growing up, and each one reminded her of something to tell me. Every once in a while, she would start telling her stories to Reece too, and every time, he reminded her that it was him, and she would smile and say, "Oh, okay."

I watched his face when she would say that. He kept a fairly pleasant expression the whole time, but every time he reminded her who he was, he grimaced slightly, like he was being stabbed, but by small pins.

Our visit was interrupted by a nurse, who came in to take Eleanor to the cafeteria for her dinner. We both hugged her goodbye, she looked deep into Reece's eyes and said, "You remind me of my grandson." He introduced himself once more, but she just smiled.

"It was so nice to meet both of you," she said as we walked away.

Reece rushed us out of the room, his eyes focused on the door. We walked out and he hailed us another cab, silent the whole time. In the cab, he stared out the window, and I stared at him. When he didn't seem to notice me staring, I unhooked our hands and wrapped his whole arm around my shoulder. He finally looked, his eyes full of tears, and smiled down at me. I nestled my head on his shoulder and watched his face.

"She has Alzheimer's," he murmured. "She can't seem to remember that I'm Reece, when I'm standing there, but if she takes just one look at any one of those pictures, she can tell you anything you ever wanted to know about me, even what I got for Christmas ten years ago. She remembers me, but her brain won't let her recognize me.

"Her doctors are impressed she even remembers so much. Three years back, she had a stroke, and the doctors told me there would be no way she would remember anything when she recovered, but when she woke up, the first thing she said was my name." He was quiet for a moment, as one tear fell down his cheek.

"Those pictures are all she has, and she clings to them because she can't remember anything else. Even me when I'm standing right in front of her. Please keep those journals because even if you don't recall anything immediately, they're all you've got right now."

I wiped his face and leaned over, kissing his cheek. He tightened his arm around me and kissed me back. Then, we were silent again.

25

We exited the cab in front of a small Italian restaurant. As we walked in, Reece mentioned his name to the hostess who promptly led us through the restaurant into a courtyard strung with lights, and a stage in the corner with a handful of men tuning instruments. There were tables all around, almost completely full, except one table near the stage that was decorated differently than the others. While the others were bare wooden tables, this one had a long white tablecloth and two tall candles. I had been feeling a little underdressed for this place to begin with, and when the hostess seated us at the special table, I felt even more out of place.

"What do you think?" Reece asked.

"I think I'm not dressed up enough to be in here," I admitted, looking around at everyone else.

"No, you're fine. You're beautiful."

"Thanks," I shrugged.

"Anytime," he replied.

"How did you manage all of this?" I asked, motioning to the table and the courtyard.

"I used to work here. Most of the people here are still friends of mine, and they helped me out," he grinned.

"Why did you quit?"

"The money. This place is way too overstaffed for the amount of business it actually does, so I didn't make much. Now, at the Nook, I make tons more because we're busy all the time and there are only six guys that work there."

"Did you like this place a lot? Or were you glad to leave?"

"I certainly didn't hate it, but I'm glad I left. I like the guys at the café a lot better, I like the atmosphere there better, and I even like the customers better. One customer, especially."

I hid my blushing face in the menu. "What's good here?"

"Well, they have amazing food, but honestly, they make a killer grilled cheese sandwich."

"Really? Grilled cheese?"

"Trust me."

We ordered and talked; Reece told me all about his childhood with his grandmother. "She raised me when my mom left. I don't know where my dad went. He was gone before I was even born. When I was five, my mom took off too. She dropped me off at my grandparents' house and never came back for me. She never even called to see how I was or to tell my grandma that she was okay. My grandpa died about ten years ago and shortly thereafter, my grandma was diagnosed with Alzheimer's. I did my best to take care of her, but I was only seventeen, so I obviously couldn't keep up with bills and things. It broke my heart when they put her in that home, but I knew it was the best thing for her, because I couldn't take care of her in my tiny third floor apartment."

I slipped my hand into his, saddened at his upbringing, but secretly jealous that he actually remembered his parents and grandparents.

Our food arrived. The grilled cheese sandwiches were cut into triangles and placed around a bowl of tomato soup. There was a drizzle of balsamic vinaigrette across the bottom of the plate. Reece explained that the protocol was to dip the sandwich in the vinaigrette, then into the soup. It was heavenly!

When it grew darker, the band began to play. The gentle breeze that had been present turned cold with the darkness. Reece swung his chair around to my side and we sat cuddled, drinking wine and listening to the music. As the night went on, a few people from other tables went up to the stage area and started dancing.

"Do you want to dance?"

"No, no. That's okay."

"Aw, come on, please?"

"I can't. I don't know how to dance. It'll be terrible."

"Well, I can't dance either, so we'll be terrible together." He pulled me up out of my chair and in front of our table. He took my left hand and placed it around his neck and put my right hand in his. Then, he wrapped his arm around my waist and pulled me in close. Very slowly, we began swaying back and forth, advancing quickly to taking steps. I kept trying to look down at my feet, but I couldn't see between us, and I could feel myself stepping on his toes.

"It's okay, you're doing great. We're doing great," he said, laughing.

We regressed back to just swaying, as we began laughing at ourselves; we really were extremely out of place in our jeans and t-shirts, while everyone else around us wore formal attire. I noticed people had been staring at us as well, not just when we stood up to dance, but while we ate. I could tell they were curious about the special table set-up and were even more curious when it turned out to be a couple of kids in street clothes.

I did also notice a few of the waiters and waitresses kept stopping and watching too. I didn't want to admit it, but I knew they were watching us, wondering who this girl was with their friend. Reece saw them watching as well and it only made him grin wider.

"Those girls are jealous of you. They used to ask me out on a regular basis and I'd always hear them talking about me," he whispered.

"Did you ever date any of them?"

"No. I was never much for dating anyone. I hadn't met anyone worth my time, I guess. Plus, none of these girls are attractive to me. They belong on the arms of body builders or male models or something. I guess they didn't realize it though, because they used to hound me all the time."

"So the real reason why you quit emerges," I laughed. He kissed me, and I saw one of the girls frown and cross her arms, staring daggers into me. "Looks like they've still got some feelings for you."

He looked over at the waitresses and then looked back at me. "Too bad," he said.

"No, I think you should go for it. I'm kind of done with you already."

"Really?" he said, kissing me again. "That's a shame." He gave me another kiss. "Are you sure?" And another.

"Okay, maybe not. You've convinced me to take you back," I smiled.

We continued dancing, until almost everyone had gone, and the band was putting their instruments away. On the way out the door, Reece introduced me to some of the friends that were still there. They all seemed surprised when they got a good look at me but were polite and greeted me like they'd known me forever. I couldn't shake their stares, and even Reece asked what was wrong, as were walking down the street.

"Your friends gave me funny looks is all. Like they were disappointed at first or something."

"I'm sure it was nothing. Don't worry about it. They didn't mean anything by it."

We were silent for a moment, before I said, "I hate the way I look." I didn't think I had had that much wine to drink, but when I blurted that out, I figured it must be the wine talking.

"Don't say that."

"Why not? I'm serious. I don't like how I look at all. I'm so disappointingly plain."

Reece stopped us in the middle of the sidewalk and lightly shoved me over to a store window. He placed me in front of the window, so I could see my reflection.

"Don't say that, because it's not true. You don't look like everyone else, and I like that about you. That's what made me notice you. My whole life, I've had total tunnel vision when it came to girls. Even at work, I usually don't pay much attention to what customers look like. But you, you caught my eye the second you first walked into the Nook, and I haven't looked away since. Don't be so hard on yourself. I like you the way you are."

I turned away from the window, and we kept walking, hand in hand. Not far from where we were, I could see the street that led to my apartment. I hoped we would keep walking.

"I'm not ready to go home yet," I muttered.

"Why not? It's late, and you need to get some sleep. Don't you have to work tomorrow?"

"Yes. I don't want to go. It's going to be horrible. I'm so lousy at that job."

We were stopped right outside the apartment, and Reece wrapped his arms around me and touched his forehead to mine.

"Well, when you go in tomorrow, just think about how close you will be to me, two blocks away at my job. That will make your job seem less horrible," he smiled.

26

Brandisham's was surprisingly not as bad as I feared it would be. Reece was right: knowing he was close by made me feel better. However, knowing he was close by also made me want to leave work as soon as possible.

Tascha was all smiles when Chrissy and I walked in. She was waiting at the window as we approached, and she even waved to Archie. I had to admit that I was rather pleased with Chrissy and myself, tricking her the way we did.

"Did you enjoy the party?" I asked, walking through the door.

"Yes, I did, believe it or not. Jackie, I'm sorry about everything from before. I'm glad you forced me into getting to know Archie, because you're right: he's great. He's funny, and charming, and he's actually kinda cute."

I was shocked at her change of heart but wasn't about to question it. Maybe she really was much nicer than she had ever let on.

Chrissy was also quite smiley. She kept telling me over and over about how many people she met, which made me feel good to know that she had ventured out of her comfort zone, and was trying to be sociable. She also was dying to hear details about Reece.

I told her about the zoo and dinner and the dancing. She awed at everything, like I was telling her about a clumsy puppy, tripping over its own paws. While I was talking, I remembered that I hadn't yet written anything down in my journal since Saturday.

"Well, write, write, write, girl! You can't afford to be forgetting anything anymore. Don't even think about doing any work today. I'll take care of it."

I felt bad not doing anything, but Chrissy insisted, and luckily, we weren't at all busy. I finished every detail right up to

Reece kissing me goodnight, and not long after I had finished, it was time to go home.

Chrissy and I walked out together; Tascha was already outside, talking to Archie. I said my goodbyes to Chrissy and then began to follow him. Tascha was walking with us, or more accurately, with Archie, while I lagged behind, feeling every bit the third wheel. He seemed to be so enthralled with her, that a couple of times, I seriously doubted he even remembered he came to Brandisham's to get me.

"Hey, Arch? I'm going to go to the café. You guys go on ahead, don't worry, I'll be fine. Reece will walk me home." Archie looked at me a little concerned, but when I told him again that I wanted to go see Reece, he insisted on at least walking me to the café.

I left Archie and Tascha at the door. Reece was inside, cleaning tables when I came in. "Hey, you," he said, hugging me. "What are you doing here? Did you come here alone?"

"Yeah. Um, Archie was, uh, occupied, so I was wondering if you would take me home when you're done," I muttered.

"Of course. Everything alright?"

"Yeah," I said, unconvincingly. "I just don't feel like walking alone, especially since I haven't had one of my spells in a while. I think I'm due up any time now."

"Okay," he replied, trying to read my face. "I'll be done at eight. Are you sure you want to wait that long?"

I nodded and sat at the counter. Then I got out my journals and started to write a little bit. I didn't have much to say, since I had pretty much spent the day writing, but I needed to occupy my time for the next few hours. My head felt almost feverish. I just wanted to lie down.

I thought about Archie and how happy he was with Tascha. He had hardly noticed me. I tried to tell myself that I couldn't be envious of Tascha, because it had been my goal all along to see the two of them together. I decided that rather, I was upset at feeling like I had been replaced. Archie used to walk *me* to and from work, and today, he acted like I wasn't there. Thinking about my feelings only made my head and stomach hurt worse, so I decided to set my mind on other things. I flipped back a couple pages in my journal and read over my date with Reece, which eased my mind somewhat.

Reece was busy waiting on tables, but his friend Kenny was working at the counter. Kenny slid me a milkshake which I tried to say wasn't mine. "It's on the house," he replied. "You deserve it. I don't know what you did, but Reece has been over the moon today. I always thought he was a good waiter, but this? Today? He's in an all-new element. He's been getting the biggest tips I've ever seen. Good job." I smiled faintly and drank the shake, half expecting it to have some magical effect on my health and head, but it didn't. Even though the shake filled my stomach, there was still a pit there that I couldn't get rid of.

"I'm almost done," I heard Reece whisper in my ear, as he rushed by me to get an order for someone. I had been staring at the counter for God only knows how long, lost in my thoughts. My eyes had started drooping, every once in a while, they closed completely. Reece would swing by and whisper something else, and my eyes would open again.

"I have to grab my jacket, but I'll be right out," he said, whipping past me one last time. I looked up, and around. My whole body was aching now.

"You okay? You look sick." I heard Kenny's voice, as I started to stand up.

"I'm alright," I heard myself respond, as my vision blurred, and I hit the floor.

"Jackie? Jackie, wake up. Can you hear me?"

There was a man leaning over me, patting my face, and running his fingers through my hair. My vision adjusted, and he became clear. He put his face even closer to mine, his thick black glasses looked like they were about to touch my cheek.

"Jackie, are you okay?" he was saying. I knew he must be talking to me, but I wasn't sure who "Jackie" was. And then I realized I was on the floor.

"What happened? Where am I?" I asked, trying not to panic.

"You fell down. I think you might have hit your head. Do you remember me? Do you know who I am?"

I tried to sit up, with assistance from him, and I shook my head. I felt lousy all over, but my head was burning in pain. I opened my eyes as wide as I could and looked around. I was in a café or a restaurant, and judging by the darkness outside, it was late. The few patrons in the restaurant were up out of their seats, staring at me.

"Jackie, my name is Reece. I'm going to take you home, okay? Can you stand up?"

Reece helped me up, and then walked me outside, with his arm around my waist. I was uncomfortable with this stranger holding me so closely, and knowing where I lived, but I was embarrassed by the scene I had apparently just caused, so I was desperate to leave.

We walked slowly, I could tell he was trying to get me home as fast as possible, but I had barely stood up on my own, so we had to pace ourselves. While we walked, I calmed myself down by trying to sort out some things. I decided not to be scared of this Reece guy. I figured if he knew where I lived, he was most likely a friend. I also concluded that, although I had no idea as to how I got this way, I was absolutely sick to my core. Everything was hurting, from my burning head to my lead feet, dragging as I could barely pick them up.

"I need you to keep walking as best you can, Jackie. I can't carry you all the way home," Reece kept saying. I nodded, but every nod sent my head flopping forward and back.

Finally, we reached the landing of a building that I guessed was my home. Reece grabbed my purse, but I snatched it back quickly. "Relax, Jackie," he said, taking it out of my hands, which were starting to become limp. "I'm just getting your keys out."

He led me up a flight of stairs and using my keys again, I heard him unlock another door. The lights were on, and when we walked in, I saw another guy standing inside. Reece lightened his grip on my waist, which sent me tumbling over; he caught me as I slumped to the floor. The other guy rushed over to me and against my will, I closed my eyes.

I woke up again in a bed in a room lit only by a small lamp at my side. I reached up at my forehead and found a washcloth resting there. I started to sit up, but I was held back down. The guy who brought me home, Reece, I remembered, was leaning over me, his hands pressing down on my shoulders.

"Lay still, Jackie. Don't move, just rest."

"Am I at home now?" I said, faintly.

"Yes, you're home, in your own bed. This is Archie," he said, moving over. I could see the guy who had been inside the apartment when I fell, leaning against the wall by the door, and clutching a blanket.

"Bring it here," Reece said. "She's shivering."

The two of them spread the gray blanket over my sheets and tucked me into it. Reece sat down on the bed next to me, and wrapped his arms around me, rubbing his hands on my arms, trying to warm them up.

"What is happening to me?" I asked, feeling like I was rapidly becoming delirious.

"You're sick. But just go to sleep right now, okay? I will explain everything in the morning. You need to rest now though."

I closed my eyes, feeling my body warming up, while my face still felt hot. I thought with the conflicting temperatures coursing through my body, I wouldn't be able to sleep, but I was so physically exhausted from walking home, and from the shivering, that I quickly passed right out.

27

When I woke up again, the room was bright, and the sun was shining on my face. I inhaled deeply but felt my lungs sting and I started to cough. I tried to roll over onto my back but landed on another body next to me. I craned my head as far back as I could to see who it was. He twitched a little and then opened his eyes.

"Good morning, Jackie," he whispered, as he rubbed his eyes and sat up. "How are you feeling?"

"I still feel achy. My head hurts."

"You've got a fever," he said, pressing the back of his hand on my forehead. As he was feeling my face, a tall woman appeared at the door.

"Hi, Reece. Thank you so much for bringing her home last night, and for staying up with her. Is she feeling better?" The woman's voice was strangely deep, though familiar, but I wasn't sure why, as she didn't look like she should have such a manly tone.

"Not much. She has a fever and she's still aching."

"Okay. I better call Brandisham's and let them know she won't be in. I suppose I should call El Mercado and take the day off myself."

"Oh, you don't have to stay home. I can stay with her. I'd like to stay, if you don't mind."

"Are you sure? That would be great." She smiled and walked away. Reece got up and left the room for a minute. I heard that woman talking to him in the other room. "I'll call you later to check on her. Did you happen to hear Archie get up and leave this morning? I didn't either."

I heard a door close, and Reece came back with a new wet washcloth which he placed on my forehead, and then he sat back down next to me. I looked up at his grinning face. He returned my gaze. "That's Maxine, do you remember her?"

"Her voice sounds familiar to me, but I don't recognize her."

"She's your roommate. Like Archie."

"And what are you to me, then?"

He grinned wider and broke out into a laugh. "Jackie, I'm, um, sort of your boyfriend."

"Really?"

"Yeah. You don't remember anything at all about me?"

I searched my brain. "Nope."

He leaned down and kissed me. "Anything?"

"Um, wait, it's coming back to me, one more." He kissed me again and I smiled and said, "Nope, lost it. I got nothing."

He laughed. "Oh, wait, what about this?" He reached for the floor and pulled up a stuffed elephant. I took it in my hands and closed my eyes. I had a flash of an elephant herd. Two of the elephants had their trunks intertwined, and a little baby elephant was grasping one of the adult's tails with its trunk. My vision backed up to where I could even see my arms resting on a railing.

"Elephants," I mumbled. "At the zoo." Another image flashed of a face resting on my shoulder. I opened my eyes and Reece's face was close to mine, almost exactly like the image in my mind. "And you!" I shouted, sitting up. "You were there too, I remember! Your head on my shoulder, your arms around my waist. I remember!"

His eyes widened, and he beamed at me, like I was his honor roll student. I was pretty proud myself, and even more proud after he handed me a couple journals that he said were mine, which talked at great length about having amnesia and detailed people, places and things so that I could remember.

"You always seemed to recall *The Wizard of Oz,* also," he said, pointing to a small doll of Dorothy on my dresser. I nodded, as I caught images of her and the yellow brick road in my mind.

My excitement had been building up inside me, so much so that my breathing was shortening, and soon I was coughing again. Reece helped me to lie back down again on my side and adjusted the washcloth on my forehead. I reached for my journals, but he moved them over. "You can read them when you feel better, once your fever goes down."

I tried to sleep, but my brain was attempting to produce more memories. So far, it only had my waking up at the café and the zoo, but I was confident I could find more. The harder I thought, however, the hotter my face got. Reece looked down at me and began dabbing my face with my washcloth.

"Jackie, your fever is getting worse. Try to sleep. Don't think about anything, that'll make it worse. Close your eyes," he said in a soothing voice.

"I can't," I said, my body shivering. "I can't seem to stop thinking. My face is so hot, but I'm so cold. What do I do?"

Reece lifted the blanket, which sent a rush of chills along my back, and curled up next to me. I rolled over, facing him, and he fixed the washcloth and pressed it to his neck, under his chin. Then he wrapped his arms around me and held me close, to stop the shivering.

It took a few minutes, but eventually, I felt my body calming down, and soon my mind was at ease as well. I was only thinking about that moment, there with him. I waded in and out of consciousness and eventually, I stayed asleep.

I don't know how long I slept, but Reece was still holding me when I woke up. I moved my head so I could look at his face and saw his eyes were closed. I stretched my neck up and kissed his chin. He grinned, so I did it again.

"Feeling better, are we?" he asked, finally opening his eyes. He lifted the washcloth, which was practically dry and touched my forehead. "Your head's not quite so hot anymore. Are you still in pain?"

"I'm a bit achy but my head feels much better."

"Good. You want anything?"

"I'm kind of hungry," I said, pressing my hands to my growling stomach.

"Perfect. I'll be right back." He slipped out of the bed, and I watched him walk out of the room. I sat myself up and grabbed my journals and started reading. Out in the other room, I could hear him talking. I faintly heard "Maxine" and knew she was calling like she had said earlier.

Moments later, he came back into the room with a bowl of soup and a grilled cheese sandwich, which he told me, was his specialty. While my soup cooled, I ate a fourth of the sandwich, before I gave it to Reece to finish. We sat together, eating while I read my journal.

"How's the reading?" Reece asked.

"It's fascinating. I'm not remembering most of it, but anytime I read something Maxine said, I can hear her voice in my head, saying it," I said, my own voice sounding scratchy.

"You used to hate it because you said it seemed like you were reading about someone else."

"Well, it feels like me now. Probably because I remembered the zoo. I've re-read that part twice, already."

Reece and I spent the rest of the day sitting in my bed, reading my journal and talking. I asked him to tell me everything about our date, even though I had read through it once. I wanted to hear him tell it.

Four times I tried to get out of bed, and only once did I succeed. Every movement I made went with a flinch or a gasp in pain, which had Reece hovering over me, holding me down, begging me to just rest. The one time he let me up was when I pleaded to go to the bathroom, and even then, he helped me up and walked me down the hall.

We heard a door close, and I once again attempted to get up and see who was there, but Reece insisted I rest and he left the room. I sat very still, listening.

"Hey Archie. I was just staying with Jackie so Maxine could go to work. She's feeling better, but she's still sick. I think it's a bug. Do you want to see her? Oh, okay." His voice trailed off and I heard footsteps that I thought were headed for my room, but then I heard another door close.

Reece came back and mumbled something about Archie not wanting to catch anything, but I didn't believe him. I wondered why Archie was acting like that. It had seemed from my journal that he wasn't a moody person, and up until last night, where I read that he abandoned me for some other girl, we seemed like peas in a pod.

The door closed again shortly thereafter, and Maxine came in the room. "Hi Jackie, how are you?"

"Better."

"Do you remember me? Did you read your journals?"

"I read them. I couldn't exactly remember you, but your voice is very familiar to me. And I remembered going to the zoo with Reece."

She smiled. "Well, good! That's exciting!"

She thanked Reece again for watching me, and then told him if he wanted, he could go home, since she was there now. He didn't want to, but I talked him into it. "You need to get a good night's sleep, not worrying about me. Plus, I'm afraid you're going to catch whatever I have."

He nodded and kissed me, and then said goodnight, promising to call me when he got home. As much as I wanted him to go so he could stay healthy, it was disappointing to watch him leave.

I went to work the next day, still a bit feverish. I didn't want to go, but I figured I'd be able to handle working in a basement out of the way. I mentioned to the girl down there, whom I read was Chrissy, that I had had another spell, and that I read up on my journals, so I thought I could remember everything about the job.

"I knew that was going to happen. I called it the other day, remember? Oh, wait, of course you don't. But I did know this was going to happen," she smiled.

She asked about where it happened, and I told her what I had written in my journal about Archie and Tascha forgetting about me, and then sitting in the café, waiting for Reece. "When I woke up again, I was on the floor, people were staring and Reece was leaning over me."

Her eyes were wide, listening. "Then what happened?"

"Nothing much. He brought me home and spent the night and all day yesterday taking care of me. I mostly read my journal when I wasn't sleeping. Oh! But I did remember something!"

"What?" Her eyes bulged.

"He gave me a stuffed elephant that he had bought me, and I suddenly had these flashbacks of being at the zoo with him. I was pretty excited about that. And when Maxine was talking, I recognized her voice, for some reason."

"Well, yeah, that's wonderful to hear. That means you might be getting better, if you're able to remember bits and pieces."

I marveled at what Chrissy had said. I had been thinking of my amnesia as just needing visual reminders, but I never once suspected that my mind could actually be healing. I wondered how good it would feel to wake up every morning and remember exactly who I was, and who my friends were.

There were footsteps coming from the basement stairs and suddenly, a girl looking like my journal's description of Portia, was standing on the stairs. Her face was a little red, and she looked a little angry, which didn't seem like it was a strange occurrence at all.

"Jackie, there's some guy here to see you," she said flatly, and turning on her toes, she marched back up the steps.

I followed, a little ways behind, and when I got to the sales floor, I noticed all the salesgirls and a couple customers were crowded around the front desk area. Stepping through them, I found Reece, standing there, smiling nervously at all the girls.

"Jackie!" He grinned, as I stepped out of the crowd. He pulled me in close to him and kissed me. I turned red, with all those girls standing right there, and I even heard one or two of them gasp. Reece looked at them but then focused on me.

"How are you feeling today? Any better?"

"I've got a little cold I think now, but I'm functional," I replied, smiling back. "What are you doing here?"

"Oh yeah, um, I brought you some soup for lunch. It'll help you feel better."

"Aw, thanks. That's so nice of you. Do you want to join me for lunch?"

"I can't. I'm actually on my break right now, and I have to get back to the café. But I'll call you later, okay? Enjoy the soup." He kissed me again, and I saw him to the door. Turning around again, I suddenly became aware of the other girls standing there.

"What?" I said, annoyed, but slightly amused at their dropped jaws.

"Who was that?" One of the girls asked.

"That's my boyfriend," I grinned.

"Him?" Portia retorted. "That guy? He's with you?"

"Yes. Is there a problem with that?"

"Yeah. It's called out of your league, Jackie. How the hell did you manage that?"

"I didn't. He's the one who asked me out," I mused, walking away, nudging the girls aside. They all stared at me as I went back to the basement. I was really enjoying having what those girls wanted. I couldn't remember a time when anyone had ever been jealous of me, and I wasn't going to lie; it felt good.

28

I managed another day of work, even though this time, I didn't get to see Reece, even afterward. He called as I was getting in bed, apologizing about not coming to the store. I told him it was fine, and that we'd see each other the next day after my therapy appointment.

On Friday, Maxine woke me up early for an appointment with my therapist, Doctor Novak. She had the morning off and wanted to take me to the appointment. As we were sitting at the counter eating breakfast, there was a knock at the door. I opened the door to find a girl in sleek black dress that ended above her knees and silver platform boots beginning a few inches down. Her outfit, while seemingly inappropriate for anything that wasn't a go-go dancing dinner party, seemed pretty tame compared to what I had read of Maxine's friend Carmelina, but when I saw her hair, I knew this must be her. It was so blonde, it was almost white, and on one side, there was a patch of dark red. The actual shape itself could only be described as lumpy, as various chunks were teased up.

"Jackie, how are things?" she asked with a strange, pretend accent, pressing an unlit cigarette in her fingers to her lips.

"Carmelina?"

"Yes, indeed. What, did you forget again?" she laughed, half joking, but when I nodded slightly, she grunted. "You know, as fun as it is hanging out with you in the throes of amnesia, it's kind of a drag that every time I see you, you've forgotten me."

She let herself in, and stopped in the kitchen, at the sight of Maxine. "Are you late for work?" she asked, taking a piece of bacon off Maxine's plate.

"No, actually, I have the morning off, so I was going to go with Jackie to the doctor. Oh! I forgot to call you, I'm sorry."

"No, it's cool. I'd still like to go though, if you don't mind."

"The more the merrier," Maxine smiled.

Doctor Novak was waiting for me, so I left Carmelina to showing Maxine the best magazines in the waiting room.

"How are you doing, Jackie?" The doctor asked, motioning for me to sit down at her desk.

"I'm okay, I think," I answered.

"Have you had another episode since our last meeting?"

"Yes."

"Did you remember to journal this time?"

"Yes," I rifled through my bag and handed her the notebooks. "I had actually started a journal the last time too, but I lost it, and then had one of my spells, so I couldn't remember writing. But my boyfriend had kept them from getting lost for me."

Her eyebrows rose, while she flipped through. "Boyfriend? You never mentioned a boyfriend before. Is this a new relationship or do you just keep forgetting about him every time we meet?"

"No, I mean, yes, I mean," I started chuckling and blushing, not really sure how to describe Reece exactly. "He's someone I've seen around a lot, and I've written about him before, but our dating is new. I think, anyway; from what I've pieced together from the journals and from Reece himself."

I told her about hitting my head and the last thing I actually remembered and about how I had started retaining little things, like the zoo with Reece, and Maxine's voice. She seemed to think that was a good sign. "It's progress. It means your memory could be repairing itself. Keep focusing on familiar people and places, and hopefully, we'll see if you can find and keep anymore memories."

Our time was up and I said goodbye, heading out to the lobby, where I found Reece sitting in between Maxine and Carmelina.

"Reece! What are you doing here?" I asked, as he hugged me.

"I thought I'd meet up with you. Hello, Doctor Novak." His eyes moved from me to the doctor.

“Hello, Reece. I see you’re doing well,” she said.

I looked at both of them strangely, and was about to ask, when Reece turned his attention back to me. “Are you ready to go?”

I nodded and the four of us left the office.

“Are you guys going to go to Chen's?" Reece asked.

Carmelina smiled, lighting her cigarette. "Yeah, we thought about it. We do have a bit of a tradition going here."

"Would you care if I joined you? Or is this sort of a girl’s thing?"

"Absolutely," Carmelina said. "You are more than welcome to join us. Nothing goes better with lunch than a little eye candy."

Reece blushed and the rest of us laughed, as we headed for Chen's. Maxine and Carmelina walked right in front of us, arm in arm, Reece put his arm around my shoulders and we followed.

"Are you alright?" Reece whispered, so as not to alarm Maxine or Carmelina. "You seem a little distracted."

"No, I'm okay," I lied. "It's nothing." He stared at my face as I looked straight ahead. I knew he could tell I was lying, but he wasn't going to press the matter, and he kissed me on the forehead.

Chen's was pretty busy, but we still managed to get a table and have a good lunch. Maxine kept saying how glad she was to be out with me, since she'd been so busy lately. "I just don't want you to feel like I've been ignoring you or anything, because I haven't."

"Not at all, Max. I understand you're busy, I'm not put off at all. I mean, you're not acting like Archie or anything." I didn’t mean to mention Archie; it just slipped out. We were all silent for a moment, nobody sure of what to say.

"You've noticed Archie acting weird?" Maxine asked.

"Well, yeah, I mean, from what I've read in my journal, he and I have been pretty close, but ever since my last little episode, I haven't seen him around at all, or when he comes home, he just goes to his room. It's like he's avoiding me. Did I do something to him?"

"No, honey," Maxine sympathized. "It's not anything you did, I'm sure. His dad had been working him pretty hard at the bank. He's probably just really tired. Don't pay any attention to his behavior, okay?"

I nodded and dropped the subject, and Carmelina began asking Reece an assortment of questions, ranging from where he grew up to what his favorite food was and what he studied in college. He would grin shyly, but answered all the questions diligently, "I grew up just outside the city, my favorite food is rice, and I have a master's degree in law and business from Columbia."

"Wow!" Carmelina, Maxine and I all exclaimed, simultaneously, our mouths dropped to the table.

"Yeah, it's no big deal," Reece said, staring at the table, nonchalantly.

"Yes, it is," Carmelina said. "You graduated from Columbia. That's amazing. How old are you?"

"Twenty-seven."

"Did you just graduate?" I asked, trying to figure out if he'd ever told me this before.

"Uh, no," he looked around, nervously and took a drink. "I graduated when I was twenty. I started at Columbia when I was fifteen."

"Oh my God, you're like one of those child geniuses!" Carmelina shouted.

"Did you have any friends growing up or were people jealous of you and your smarts?" Maxine asked.

"When did you know you were that smart and how old were you when you went through high school?" Carmelina was almost three inches from Reece, leaning over the table.

"Surprisingly, I did have a lot of friends growing up, not many jealous ones, that I knew of," Reece said, looking at Maxine. Then he faced Carmelina. "And my teachers in sixth grade suggested to my grandma that I take an aptitude test which I aced and they pulled me out of sixth grade and put me in high school classes, which I completed in a year. Then I went to Columbia." His voice trailed off a bit, and I could tell he didn't really like talking about himself like that.

"So, why do you work at a café then?" Maxine said, tilting her head, staring at him.

"I just wasn't happy doing what I was doing. That's all. I made enough money at my law firm to be comfortable, so I'm fine with my minimum wage now. I don't need any special attention or treatment; I'm content to just be a waiter, blending in with the scenery."

After lunch, Reece took us to a little ice cream shop that was owned by a friend of his. "It's getting cold, so his shop is about to close soon for the winter. He makes all his ice cream himself." We went inside, and while Reece and his friend caught up, Maxine, Carmelina and I looked around at the retro shop. It had black and white tiled floors, and tall tables with silver chairs that sat high off the ground. There was a girl sitting at one of the tables. She looked at me and I smiled, just being friendly, and she hesitated a moment before smiling back.

"What can I get yas?" the guy asked, with a thick accent.

The three of us girls pressed our faces to the glass counter, gazing at all of the colorful flavors of ice cream. We all picked out a flavor, which he stacked into waffle cones for us, and then told Reece they were all on the house. We thanked him for being so gracious and we left. When we walked out, I heard the door close a second time behind us, and glancing around, I saw the other girl coming out behind us, looking at me. I turned back around, trying to ignore her. As we walked, Carmelina took the opportunity to finish Reece's interrogation.

"So, what do you like to do in your spare time?"

"I don't know. I do lots of things. I read, I watch movies, I used to do a lot of walking around, just to pass the time, but not so much anymore. I've got better things to do now."

"Like what?"

"Like hang out with Jackie. Take her out for ice cream," he smiled, squeezing my hand.

"And what are your intentions with our Jackie?" Carmelina asked, seriously.

Reece and I both stopped walking and stared at her. She and Maxine stopped and they both stared back at him.

"Um," he said, uncomfortably. "My intentions?"

"Yes, your intentions. Do you plan on marrying her?"

"Carmelina, don't ask him that. We've only just started dating," I said, embarrassed. She ignored me and kept staring.

"Right now, my intentions are to just be here when she needs me. That's it. I have no other intentions."

I was flattered at what he said, and I watched Carmelina and Maxine's faces, particularly their mouths, which both formed wide grins.

"Well then, I approve." Maxine snickered and extended a hand for him to shake and then gave him a hug. Carmelina did the same and we continued walking.

"Sophie?" I heard someone ask behind me. I didn't think anything of it, as it was probably someone on a phone. But then, I felt a tap on my shoulder.

"Sophie Gray?" I turned around and saw the girl from the ice cream shop standing there, searching my face.

29

"No. I'm sorry. You've got the wrong person." I said, turning back around to keep walking, but Reece, Maxine and Carmelina had all stopped.

"Um, no, I don't think so," she replied. "You're Sophie. I'm sure it's you. I'd recognize that face anywhere. And your scar, too. Your hair is a little different, though. I think it was black the last time I saw you." I glared at her. The perk in her voice was a bit much for me. "Sophie, it's me, Melissa Samuels. From Tallahassee? Keiser University? Remember?"

"No, I don't."

"And how do you know, uh, Sophie?" Maxine asked.

"We were in a sorority together back at school. Frances Holloway introduced us. You remember Frances, right? She got you into our chapter without even having to pledge."

I shook my head and again told her that was not me. But she wouldn't let up. "I can't believe you don't remember any of this, Sophie. It was only like a year ago. What happened to you?"

"What do you mean?" Maxine asked again. "Because, uh, Sophie's never told us about being in a sorority." She smiled and nudged me, going along with this crazy girl's scheme.

"Oh, well, I had just pledged myself, and Frances, who was a senior at the time, introduced my roommate and I to Sophie and said she was a new Alpha Gam. She was Frances' roomie, and I guess we didn't talk too much, but we hosted the Alpha Gam parties together. And then, one day, she just, like, disappeared. Frances said you got a job, but most people don't quit their senior year in the middle of the semester. So, what happened?" She was animatedly talking to Maxine, but she kept looking at me, adding me into the conversation. I opened my mouth, searching for any lie at all, but it didn't seem to matter, because she kept going. "Nobody knew what happened. Frances kept pretty quiet about you leaving. You never said goodbye."

"That sounds like Ja-Sophie," laughed Carmelina. Melissa looked at her and smiled back.

"Well, it doesn't matter where you've been for a year, because I can see that you're here now, and you're okay." She began chatting with me, telling me what everyone else was up to, and I pretended to listen, because I couldn't care less about any of the girls she mentioned. Plus, I was still convinced she had me confused with someone else. Finally, I told her we had to go, and then she awkwardly hugged me and asked for my email address. "Let me have yours," I said, "My account was hacked and I need to get a new one." She wrote hers down, and a few others' addresses as well and handed them to me, made me promise to visit if I was ever in Tallahassee again, and then skipped off.

I turned around to start walking again, and found Reece, Maxine and Carmelina smiling at me.

"What?" I asked, frustrated.

"You were in a sorority?" Reece asked.

"Oh my God! No, that wasn't me. I don't know who that was."

"That's what happened last time, when you ran into Razi. You didn't know him, but he knew you," Maxine said.

"Well, if that was me, it's not me now, so let's not talk about that."

"Jackie," Maxine continued. "This is a good thing! We know something about your past. We can send these girls an email and get more information. Perhaps a road trip, even."

I rolled my eyes at the idea of contacting these girls, especially if they were like Melissa. But this was a clue to putting my life back together, so I gave in and said, "Alright."

We continued to walk, Carmelina and Maxine laughing ahead of us. Reece was staring at me.

"What?" I whispered.

"A sorority?" he teased, still grinning. I lifted my hand that was holding his and lightly punched him in the stomach.

Maxine checked her watch and decided it was time for her to go home so she could get ready for work at the club; Carmelina had to go as well. I offered to stay with Reece, so they could be on their way, and they said goodbye and set off together. Once they were gone, Reece and I headed back to his apartment.

We didn't talk much during the walk, mostly because I was lost in my own thoughts about everything that had just happened this afternoon: Melissa recognizing me, Maxine and Carmelina interrogating Reece, my appointment with Dr. Novak.

"You've been pretty quiet. Is something bothering you?" he asked, as we walked through the door.

"It's nothing, really."

"Are you sure? You can talk to me."

"Well, it's just, how do you know Doctor Novak?"

"I had a nervous breakdown while I was in college and had to see her. It was no big deal. I mean, it was at the time, but I'm fine now."

"What happened?"

"Well, like I told you, my grandpa died about ten years ago, and shortly after that, my grandma was diagnosed with Alzheimer's. I was in college when she lost the house and I tried to work through school to help out, but it wasn't enough, because I had to pay for college. So, losing my grandpa and losing our house and my grandma's illness all sort of factored into it, as did the fact that I was in law school as a teenager, and I just couldn't deal with things. I had a nervous breakdown at school and was sent to see Doctor Novak, who worked on campus at the time, and after I graduated, I still continued to see her for a while. Does that answer your question?"

I nodded and we sat down. Reece turned on the TV and pulled me over to him so we sat curled up together. We were silent for a bit, before I said, "Why didn't you tell me about any of that stuff?"

"What? The therapy or college?"

"Both. Either."

"How do you know I didn't?"

"Did you?"

Reece read the look on my face and smiled. "No. It never came up. You never asked."

"I mean, you know so much about me because you've read my journals, but I don't know much about you at all, other than what I've learned about you today."

"To be fair, everything I know about you is from the last couple months," he reasoned. "What else do you want to know?"

"I want to know everything."

"That was pretty much everything," he laughed, but then he started to tell me stories about himself, growing up with his grandparents, his friends, school, his various jobs, all of which were waiting tables except the one at the law firm, and he even told me about his pets growing up.

"Goldfish," he said, "They were all goldfish. Grandpa was allergic to pet hair, so that's what I was stuck with. And they all died horrible deaths, because I forgot to feed them. But, in my defense, I was a child genius studying for college exams and what not; I couldn't be expected to be totally responsible."

We started watching a movie and dozed off together on the couch. The cell phone in my purse went off a couple times, indicating a text message had been sent to me. The unexpected noise had woken me, and I grabbed the phone. I had to lean over Reece, elbowing him in the stomach, waking him up as well.

"Who is it?" he asked.

"It's Archie. He wants to know if I'm coming home."

30

Reece walked me home. From the street, I could see Archie waiting by the window. "I wonder what he wants," I said. "I hope he's not going to yell at me or anything."

Reece looked at me. "Why would he do that?"

"I don't know, but he's been avoiding me, so, maybe he's mad at me."

"Well, let's find out," Reece said, squeezing my hand and leading me into the building. I unlocked the door and hesitated. In the doorway, I could see Archie standing by the couch, motioning for me to come in. Slowly, I stepped in, not letting go of Reece's hand.

As we approached the couch, Archie handed me a note. *I have something for you.* He handed me a slip of paper with my name and a long number written on it.

I opened a new bank account for you at my bank; I even put your last paycheck in it. The old account, I was able to hack into through our computer system and I changed the name and information on it. Then, I had a girl at work make an anonymous phone call to the police about a suspicious account with withdrawals from a man named Razi.

"So, what does that mean? Does that mean that the money is gone?"

"And the police will be looking for Razi," Reece said.

Archie flipped his notepad back a page, to the note that said: *I have something for you.* He grabbed me by the arm and pulled me to my bedroom. On my bed, was the blanket I recognized as the gray one I'd been using from Archie, only, as I got closer to it, I could see that it was a different color. It was a greenish blue.

I bought you a blanket because it's getting colder. I got one like mine because I know you like it. And I made sure it matched the paint for your room.

I touched the blanket and then looked at the dusty paint cans sitting on my floor. My face broke into a smile and I hugged Archie. "Thank you," I whispered.

He slid me another note that said: *I know I've been weird lately, and I'm sorry. I just had a lot on my mind, trying to get that account fixed. But I also felt so horrible about the night you got sick at the cafe, because I was with Tascha and sort of abandoned you and I feel terrible about that.*

"Archie, don't feel bad. The forgetting was bound to happen. Besides, you were with Tascha, which is what I think I wanted for you, so don't feel bad about me." I took his hand in truce, and he then hugged me.

In the morning, Maxine, Archie and I decided it was time finally to paint my bedroom. We moved all of my furniture into the center of the room and began painting. While Archie and I painted with the lighter shade of blue, Maxine was painting the trims with the darker shade. When we finished the first coat, we decided to go to the cafe for a while to let it dry.

We sat in our booth, and Reece brought us our food. "Hey, did you see those guys over there in that booth?" Reece asked us, motioning to the table. There were three of them, sitting, wearing black suits and sunglasses, staring straight ahead. "Those guys have been in here every day this week. Isn't that weird? And they're always wearing black like secret agents."

We all looked over at the men, whose sunglasses made them look like they were staring at us. They looked suspicious to me, but I couldn't place a finger on exactly why.

We went back to eating our food, and then as Archie and Maxine walked out, I gave my bill and cash to Reece. I told him we had been painting all day, and he offered to help, but he wasn't going to be off work until they closed.

"I'll come over tomorrow, okay? I'll help you with the finishing touches."

Reece didn't call that night, nor did he call in the morning. I tried to tell myself that twelve hours without a phone call was not a big deal, but wondering where he was took my interest out of painting, and leaving Archie and Maxine to work, I sat in the living area at the window, searching for him.

Finally, I couldn't take it any longer, and I called him. His phone rang and went to his voicemail, so I left a message. Then, immediately after I hung up, I called again. Still, there was no answer. I dialed the number a third time, and at last, he answered.

"Hello?" His voice was quiet, and scratchy.

"Reece? Where are you? What are you doing? You didn't call. I got worried," I blurted.

"Oh, Jackie, I'm sorry. I'm, um, I don't feel well. Uh, I think I've come down with something," he answered. His voice did sound a little hoarse.

"Do you want me to come over? I can bring you some medicine or something."

"No!" he shouted. "I mean, uh, no, that's alright. I'm really sick, and I don't want you to get it. I'm just going to stay in bed and get some rest, and hopefully, it'll go away."

"Reece, are you sure you don't want me to help you? You stayed with me when I was sick, I would think it's only fair I return the favor."

"No, please. I'm just going to stay in bed. I'll be fine, I promise. Don't worry about me, okay? I'll call you when I'm feeling better."

Despite his warning, I worried anyway. I knew that he was able to take care of himself, even in sickness, but there was nervousness in his voice that reminded me of a scared child. I wanted more than anything for him to have told me that he needed me to take care of him; I wanted to feel like I was an adult. But, if he asked me to stay away, I would, because he knew what was best for him.

To get my mind off it, I went back to help Archie and Maxine. I found Maxine creating an intricate pattern over the light blue wall with the dark blue paint. I couldn't quite make out the image, but it was certainly interesting and beautiful.

"There," Maxine said, stepping back to admire the work. "Can you tell what it is?"

Archie and I stepped back as well, studying the wall. When neither of us answered, she said, "It's a tree. It's a tree made from swirl patterns."

"It's beautiful, Max," I said, ignoring my worries. "It's really awesome, thank you."

31

On Monday, at Brandisham's I could hardly concentrate on my work, though I tried very hard not to worry about Reece. It just seemed very strange to me that he wouldn't even let me visit him. The more I began to analyze the situation I was remembering seeing him at the café, trying to recall if he had been sick then. He didn't look pale or feverish or anything and he seemed in high spirits. So then, how did he become sick so fast?

Chrissy could tell I was distracted, and took it upon herself to keep me busy, so I couldn't dwell. She even took my phone, to help me abstain from the temptation to call. I begged her for one little text message, and she held her ground, but after constant badgering, she eventually compromised, offering to send him a message herself. She asked him how he was feeling, which immediately warranted a flat response of: "I'm still sick."

"There," she said, agitated. "Are you happy now?"

"Not really, but I guess I feel slightly better that he answered. Thanks."

After work, Archie was waiting outside, and I assumed he was there for Tascha, but he insisted that he was going to walk both of us home. I appreciated his effort but still felt that it was just that –an effort. However, I walked home with them anyway. Tascha seemed just as annoyed, being very curt with me, and excessively clingy to Archie. I shuffled alongside, silently, wondering how Reece was getting along.

I refrained from picking up my phone the whole evening, and felt very proud of my self-control, but that night I tossed and turned like crazy. My subconscious couldn't stop thinking of Reece, and the last time I saw him. My mind was fashioning wild theories as to why he wouldn't let me come over. One theory suggested that he had come down with the plague or scurvy, and his body was covered with disgusting lumps and spots. Another, more probable theory suggested that he was trying to break up with me and possibly seeing someone else. I couldn't figure out why, since our relationship seemed to be going well, but I decided that must be the reason for his avoidance, and when the clock I had been staring at finally read a decent waking hour, I resolved that I needed to see him, to confirm once and for all that we were kaput.

The whole day, I was on edge, rehearsing what to say, and making back-up plans in case he wouldn't speak to me or let me in. Perhaps it was the adrenaline rush of plotting, but work went by fast and I was surprised at how efficient I was at my job. Even Margot Brandisham, who was wandering the floor, setting up a display for her new collection, took notice and complimented me at the end of the day.

I told Archie that I had something to do, and that I would be home later. At first, he refused to leave without me, but with Tascha's begging to leave and my own insistence, promising to call the minute I was on my way home, he reluctantly left me alone on the steps of the store.

I held my map in my hand, folded backward to the section where my mark at Brandisham's connected to my mark at Reece's apartment near Chinatown. I walked with vigor, anxiously wondering what I was about to find. I managed to find his apartment with no trouble and stood outside his door for what seemed like forever, just breathing, feeling the courage build in my stomach.

I lifted my fist to knock on the door, but hesitated. "Do it now, Jackie," I whispered, and knocked. I felt the door move, and I looked down to notice it was broken at the knob, like it had been pried open. My courage and adrenaline quickly changed to fear and worry.

"Reece?" My voice quivered as I slowly pushed the door. I took a step and heard a crunch under my foot. Looking down, I saw a picture frame on the ground, the glass shattered, but not from my weight; it had been broken some other way.

I pushed the door open faster to find Reece's entire apartment trashed. Every book, movie and CD was on the floor, the furniture had been upturned, the stuffing ripped out, and the TV was face-down on the ground. From the door, I could see into the kitchen. Every cupboard was open, and shards of glass were everywhere. There were holes punched in the walls; the room looked like a mob had been let loose.

"Reece? Are you here?" I asked again, almost to myself. My fear was heightening, as I called his name louder. I heard the faintest groan coming from his bedroom, and I was immediately relieved.

I found him curled up on his side, under a blanket, head and all. I turned on the light, and he lifted his head out of the blanket. I could see right away that his eyes were swollen, almost completely shut.

"Jackie?" He mumbled.

I was at his side instantly, pulling the blanket down so I could see the rest of his face. "Reece, oh my God, what happened?"

"Nothing, I'm okay. I'm so glad to see you," he whispered, pulling his hand out from underneath the blanket to touch my face. I took his arm, examining it in the light. It was covered in bruises and cuts.

"Reece, what happened? Tell me what happened!" I said, choking up. I leaned on him, trying to look straight in his face.

"Ouch," he winced. I sat back up and started to pull the blanket all the way down.

"Jackie, don't," he said, but I pulled anyway.

He cowered, wrapping the arm I examined over the other. I lifted the other arm and suddenly thought I might be sick. It was twisted and swollen, colored completely purple. I pushed at his shoulders so he lay flat on his back. His whole body was plastered in bruises and dried blood, that looked like it had dripped down from his mouth.

"Reece, your arm is broken. You need to go to the hospital," I started.

"No, I'm fine. I'll be okay."

"I'm taking you to the hospital. Let's go." My eyes began to tear up.

"Jackie, I can't move. Please, just let me stay here."

I helped him roll back over onto his side, cradling his arm, and then I crawled up beside him, stroking the bruises on his back. He lifted his hand to his back and held mine, weakly. My eyes succumbed to crying, and soon my whole body was joining in. He rolled back over to look at my face with his swollen eyes.

"Shh," he whispered. "It's alright, Jackie. I'll be fine, I just need to stay still and let my body heal." I leaned forward and kissed his bloody mouth. "You shouldn't be here," he continued. "They'll find you."

"Who? Who will find me? Reece? What's going on?"

I could see he was slipping in and out of consciousness. I gripped his limp hand tightly and watched him, crying. When I thought he was asleep, I grabbed my phone out of my purse and called 911. Next, I called Maxine in a panic. She told me she would meet me at the hospital.

While I waited, I resumed watching him. Once in a while, he would open his eyes, and attempt a smile at me, and I couldn't do anything but touch his face and cry. I begged him furiously to tell me what had happened, but he was in no shape to talk at all.

Soon enough, I heard voices at the door and found two paramedics staring at the apartment. I rushed them to Reece, and after a quick look, they ran to the ambulance for a stretcher and returned. Immediately after the stretcher, came two police officers, who started questioning me about the break in.

"I don't know anything," I repeated over and over. "I came over and the place was like this and he was injured. I don't know who did it or who could have done it." My voice started straining and I could hear myself growing more and more upset.

I heard squeaking wheels and knew the stretcher was coming out. I brushed past one officer, but he grabbed my arm. "We still have a few more questions," he said.

"I need to go with him."

"Ma'am, we are not done here."

"I have to go with him!" I shouted, prompting the paramedics to halt. The officer stared at the desperation on my face and nodded, letting me go.

As I crawled into the back of the ambulance, my gaze never left Reece's swollen eyes.

The paramedics would not let me follow them once we entered the emergency room.

"You have to stay out here," one of them said, shoving me toward the waiting area.

Maxine walked in as soon as I saw Reece's stretcher disappear from my view. Instinctively, I ran to her, hugging her and crying hard. She shushed me and petted my hair, telling me that everything was going to be fine, but I couldn't stop crying. She held me for a long while, until my body started hurting and I began to tire myself out.

When I stopped, she and I sat down in the waiting area. "I've called Doctor Viera. He's a friend of Uncle Manny's. He'll fix Reece right up. I've also called Archie, but I think he's with Tascha right now. He asked if he should come over here, but I told him not to. There's nothing he can do anyway."

I thumbed through magazine after magazine, and when I ran out, I stared at the TV. My mind was completely focused on Reece.

"They've been in there forever. What are they doing?"

"It's alright, Jackie. Viera knows what he's doing. He's a very good doctor and his assistants are equally as good. They're taking excellent care of him."

I leaned into Maxine and she pressed my head to her shoulder. I closed my eyes and before I knew it, I was asleep. I woke up to Maxine brushing my hair with her hand. I sat up and rubbed my eyes, wondering what time it was. It had to be really late.

As I yawned myself awake, Maxine stood up and rushed over to a man standing at the door. I followed after her, assuming this must be the doctor she called. They conversed in Spanish and I stared at him, frustrated that I couldn't understand.

"He will be fine," Doctor Viera said, addressing me. "We have set his arm and given him a hard cast, and his wounds have been cleaned. He is heavily sedated right now to help with the pain, but he will be able to go home in the morning."

"I need to see him," I said.

"Not now," Doctor Viera said. "You go home."

"I'm not leaving. I need to see him."

Maxine linked arms with the doctor, chatting in Spanish, turning his body away from the door. Once his back was turned, I slipped through the door and walked the corridor, looking for Reece.

Reece was lying on his back with his arm bandaged up, resting against his chest. I stood at the side of the bed for a moment then crawled into the bed, curling up next to him.

"Jackie?" he whispered, opening his eyes.

"Shh, I'm here, Reece. Close your eyes and go to sleep. I'm here."

"I love you," he said, groggily.

At first, I was caught off guard, but I responded earnestly. "I love you too. So much."

I watched him smile, with his eyes closed, as he weakly muttered my name over and over, before sleeping. "Jackie… Jackie… Jackie…"

32

Reece was still asleep when I woke. I sat up slowly, trying to slip out of the bed without disturbing him, and due to his pain relievers, I succeeded. In the corner of the room, Maxine was sitting on a chair, looking at a magazine, eating a donut.

"Want one?" She asked as I sat down next to her.

"How long have you been here?"

"I came in a little after you. I convinced the nurses to let us stay in here."

"You stayed all night?" I guessed, seeing the sun shining through the window.

"I wasn't going to let you stay here alone. Here, you should definitely eat something; you look exhausted."

I grabbed a donut and silently chewed. I wondered what time it was. Then I realized I had to go to work. I inhaled and sat up straight, searching around for a clock.

"Don't worry, I called off for you," Maxine said, reading my body language.

I exhaled and finished my donut, glad that I had someone like Maxine taking care of me. I leaned over and looked at her magazine with her before Reece began stirring from his bed. There was a knock at the doorway and Doctor Viera was standing there.

"How is he doing? Did he have trouble sleeping at all?"

"He was fine," I answered. "He just started moving."

Doctor Viera tapped Reece's shoulder gently and called his name. He opened his eyes, a little wider today than before, and asked for me.

"I'm right here, Reece," I said, faking a smile.

The doctor examined him and gave him a pill, telling him it would help with the pain. "Everything seems to be in order," he said. "He will need time to heal and plenty of rest, but he should be fine to go home."

"He can't go back to his apartment. It's trashed," Maxine said. "It's too dangerous."

"Is there any way we might be able to get him to our apartment?" I asked, looking at Maxine, who nodded in agreement.

"No. I can't go there. They'll go there," Reece said, in between breaths.

"Who? Who will?" I asked, but Doctor Viera silenced me.

"I will see what I can do."

Half an hour passed before the doctor returned carrying a folder of papers for Reece to sign. "I have a car waiting out front for you," he explained. "The Bettinos will take you to Maxine and Jackie's apartment. I have also sent a couple boys to your apartment to get some clothes and any personal belongings that you need."

Soon, we were on our way, hidden in the backseat of an SUV with black windows. Reece had been quiet and drowsy the whole time, and barely seemed to notice I was there, holding his wilted hand.

The two Bettinos who occupied the front seats carried Reece between them up to our apartment when we arrived. Maxine and I followed, as she conversed with one of them in Spanish. I kept my eyes on Maxine, trying to read her expression, before thankfully, she elaborated. "He's going to get some of the boys to station themselves out here and maybe one or two to stay at Reece's old place to see if whoever did this will come back there or come here looking for him."

"Who would know he was here?"

"Anybody could have seen us leave there. We don't know who to look out for; we have to be careful, Jackie."

The boys put Reece in my bed. His eyes were open a bit, but he didn't speak. I asked how he felt and he just nodded, so I patted his forehead until he closed his eyes. I sat there, watching him, occasionally gazing around at the walls, trying to push the worrying to the back of my mind. The paint looked wonderful, and much better than the plain white. On the dresser, I noticed someone had set up my Dorothy doll and my stuffed elephant.

There was a knock at our door, and shortly after, Maxine moved two suitcases brought from Reece's into my closet and then left for work. Archie came home moments later, rushing to my room to see if he was okay. He then went to the kitchen and made some sandwiches for us and brought everything into my room. He handed me a plate and then joined me on the bed also.

Reece groaned groggily and I offered him some food. We managed to lift him a bit, enough that he could sit up to eat. He didn't take much, but I was just thrilled enough that he ate anything at all. I had been wondering how long he had been stuck in that bed, bleeding and bruising, his arm broken; he seemed too weak to move a muscle, let alone eat.

He slept the rest of the afternoon and night, and in the morning, Archie woke me up with a note that said he'd taken the day off work to stay with Reece so I could go to Brandisham's. *You need to get out of the house for a bit. This is stressing you out. Don't worry, we'll be fine.*

I resisted heavily, to the point where Archie was practically pushing me out the door. I felt safe to go only after one of the Bettinos out front walked with me. I had never walked to work without Archie that I could remember, but he was confident I could do it, which I did, if only to get the day over with so I could get back to Reece. Portia was at the desk, eyeing me funny when I walked in.

"Skipping work yesterday?" Her tone was mocking.

"I had an emergency. My roommate told you that over the phone," I answered, aggravated.

"What was the emergency?"

"None of your damn business," I replied, heading to the basement.

"Jackie?"

I turned around. Margot Brandisham was standing by a rack of clothes. "Yes ma'am?" I asked, stepping toward her.

"Is everything alright at home? I heard there was an emergency."

"Everything is fine, thanks."

"I was thinking that I would like you to stay upstairs today. I want you to shadow Victoria. I think it's time for you to move up to sales. Are you up for it?"

"Not really today, ma'am. I'm sorry. My head is a bit of a mess right now. Maybe another day? A better day?"

"Of course. You let me know when you're ready," she smiled. I was glad that she didn't press the matter and hurried down to the basement.

I told Chrissy about Reece. Even a day later, I was still choking back tears, just thinking about him in bed for days, unable to move. Chrissy was really sympathetic and let me take care of all of the clients at my insistence to keep my mind off it.

Mrs. Brandisham spent the day observing the sales floor. I could tell she watched me closely every time I came upstairs. I didn't know what she wanted from me, but I knew it wasn't what *I* wanted. I didn't want to be a salesgirl. I wanted to stay in the basement with Chrissy; I felt safe there.

The day couldn't have ended sooner. Chrissy offered to walk home with me, even though she lived in the other direction, but I declined. I wanted to get home as soon as possible, no distractions. The same boy who had walked with me earlier was waiting outside. I was practically sprinting home, and he was right there, sprinting with me.

Archie was sitting on the couch. Reece was awake, he wrote, but pretty delirious from the medication Doctor Viera had given him. I went in to check on him and found that he was staring at his cast, poking it with one finger, giggling.

"Reece? How are you feeling?" I asked, sitting on the edge of the bed.

"Hello, Jackie. I'm not feeling at all. I'm perfectly numb. Watch this," he prodded his cast again. "My skin is rock solid."

I wanted to explain, but I just laughed and moved to the other side of him. While he poked his cast, I got out my journals and started writing. Within minutes, he started snoring. I smiled and then adjusted his head on the pillow.

It was well into the night when I felt my shoulder being shaken.

"Jackie," Reece was whispering. "Jackie, wake up."

I reached for the light and then rolled over. "What's the matter?"

"Jackie, we have to get out of here."

"What? Why?"

"Because they'll find you if we stay."

"Reece, it's two o'clock in the morning. Can't this wait?"

"No, no it can't."

"Who's going to find me?"

"Razi."

I knew the name well, from my journal, but I couldn't picture his face. Even still, the thought of "Razi" sent a chill through me. I knew he was after me, and I knew he wanted money; the money that Archie had turned over to the police. The money I no longer had. I wondered if Razi knew that I didn't have it. I wondered if he knew the police were after him.

"Will you please tell me what this is about? You sound crazy," I yawned.

"Do you remember last Saturday when you guys came to the café? Remember when I pointed out those guys in the suits? Well, they stayed in the café all day, and when I went home, they followed me, broke the lock and attacked me, asking for 'Mara'. I told them I didn't know who that was, and then one of them told the other that they were looking for 'Jackie'. I refused to tell them anything, obviously, and while they trashed the place, the one guy said, 'Tell Jackie that Razi said she may have Manny's protection now, but if she wants to keep her friends alive, she knows what she has to do.' And then they left.

"I didn't want you coming over to my place because I knew they'd be hanging around for awhile, thinking you'd show up, and I didn't want to leave, because I knew they'd follow me, and somehow, they'd find you."

He was trying to get out of the bed but seemed to be having difficulty. I could tell by his awareness that his medication had worn off, and the pain was setting in again. Before he got too carried away, I hopped up, tugging him back down. I offered him more pills if he would stay in bed and go back to sleep. I accidently pressed a bruise on his shoulder and he winced a little but then complied.

Once he had taken the pills, I knew it wouldn't take too long for them to kick in, but I could still tell he was ready to go at any moment. "You don't have to worry. Razi won't come here. Doctor Viera's got some of the Bettinos hanging around the building to keep an eye on things. I'm sure if he was really looking that hard, he would have found me already. Besides, he'd be stupid to show his face now, with the money in police custody and his name on it."

"Jackie, he's got guys too. Look what they did to me. I can't believe you're not afraid of him coming after you."

I shrugged nonchalantly, but in the back of my mind, I too was concerned that I wasn't scared enough. "I guess you can't be scared of something you don't remember." I turned the light off, laid back down and gently rested my head on the same pillow as Reece. "I'm not thinking about that anyway. I'm focused on you healing."

"Well, you should be thinking about yourself. You shouldn't have come to get me; that was extremely dangerous," he scolded, then sighed. "All the same, I'm glad you did. If you hadn't, this arm would probably have been damaged beyond repair, as would the rest of me."

"I was actually going there to confront you," I muttered.

"About what?"

"About not calling me or letting me see you. I got so paranoid that I assumed you were trying to break up with me, so I was going over there to find out for sure so I wouldn't be torturing myself wondering."

"You thought I was giving you the slip?" I could hear the smile in his voice. "Why would you think that?"

"Oh, I don't know, maybe the fact that I can't remember a damn thing and you got the crap beat out of you because of me."

I felt a kiss on my forehead. "I'd let it happen again if I had to. I love you, and I want to be with you, and nothing will change that, unless *you* don't want to be with me."

"Consider us unchangeable then."

33

I felt like I hadn't even had a chance to blink, and already, it was Monday, and I was getting ready to go to work. Reece was finally going back to work too. None of us were sure how he'd fair waiting on and bussing tables with his cast, but after thirty calls from various other waiters from the café, he decided he should probably go back.

Portia shot me a dirty look when I walked through the door, which was typical, and I paid her no mind, but when I moved on past the front desk, Mrs. Brandisham was standing there, waiting for me. For the second time, she asked if I would shadow Victoria. I didn't want to, but I said yes, for fear that she would fire me if I declined. As I agreed, she handed me a black blazer jacket that I had to put on. The jacket was ridiculously small, and I had the hardest time buttoning it, so I gave up. I looked around at the other salesgirls, who had their blazers neatly buttoned over their non-existent stomachs. They seemed offended by not only me being on the sales floor, but my ill-fitting jacket as well.

Victoria glowered at me, but I did as I was told and followed her, watching her deal with customers. She didn't seem friendly at all to anyone, but her clients were regulars of hers and I could tell they weren't very friendly either, so I guess it was a winning combination. I made a mental note to just be the exact opposite of her. Chrissy would appear out of the depths of the basement from time to time and would pass by and whisper to me a thing or two about the customers Victoria was attending to.

"That woman favors things that are pink, but she looks much better in darker colors," she'd say, or "That woman always tries on the baggiest clothes she can, even though she has a slim figure under all that fabric." I'd listen to her whispers, and whenever I felt brave enough, I would chime in during Victoria's consultation and make Chrissy's suggestions. I could tell it was frustrating Victoria, but when her customers listened to me, buying the dark rouge dress or the correct size pant suit, she could do nothing but keep her mouth shut and take care of the sale.

Mrs. Brandisham was lurking around, watching me, and as Victoria was checking her appointment book, she insisted I take the lead on the next one. "What!" Victoria and I both exclaimed at the same time.

"I want to see if Jackie can do this," she said, smiling.

I wanted nothing more than to be back downstairs with Chrissy. Victoria, I'm sure, wanted the same thing. However, once she glanced at her appointment book, a grin streaked across her face. "Of course," she said. "Jackie should have all the practice she can get." I scrunched up my face and looked at her.

The front door opened, and I heard Portia. "Oh, *hello,* Miss Pendleton. How *are* you? It's wonderful to see you!" I rolled my eyes and snorted.

The name sounded familiar, but I couldn't exactly remember until she walked in. The big sunglasses, the messy, teased hair, the leather jacket, and leggings were a dead giveaway. I recalled from my journal that she had caused a scene the last time she was there. My fault, apparently.

"Hello, Miss Pendleton," Victoria said. "This is Jackie. She's going to help you today."

This Miss Pendleton, Kat, if I remembered correctly, didn't show any sort of sign that she was listening, or even cared for that matter. She kept her head tilted down at her phone, texting away. Everyone was silent for a moment, watching her use her phone.

"What can I do for you?" I finally asked. She looked up from her phone.

"Uh, I'm here for clothes, what do you think?"

"Well, what are you interested in seeing?"

"Whatever."

I heard a whisper behind me. "Suggest our winter line. She likes red." I didn't have to turn around to know it was Chrissy.

"I can get a few pieces of our winter collection, if you'd like. I'm sure I could find something red for you."

Her eyebrows rose, and she nodded slightly. I turned around to look for Chrissy, who was standing at the steps. She acknowledged me and went downstairs. I turned back to Kat and stood there, looking at her, smiling. Everyone else around me had gone on with their work, but I could tell they were still trying to be attentive over my way.

Kat snorted and made a face at me. "Aren't you going to offer me some coffee while I'm waiting?"

"No," I said flatly. "Why would I do that?"

"Because that's what you people do here."

"Actually, that's what people at Starbucks do. We sell clothes." I heard three gasps from various parts of the room, and I noticed Victoria's eyes popping out of her head.

"I'll get you something, Miss Pendleton," she said, and took off for the break room upstairs.

"See? That's how things are done," Kat said, pointing to Victoria.

"Well, I've never once seen anyone offer any other customers coffee while they waited. Why do you think you're so special?"

Her mouth dropped. "How dare you!"

"What? knock you down a peg? Give you a reality check? Oh, I'm sorry. Is that not what you want to hear?" I was suddenly furious. She had no right to think she was any better than anyone else. I figured my job was now over, or at least, that was an end to my career as a salesgirl, so I turned around and headed for the basement.

"You did what?" Chrissy asked at the stairs. She sprinted over to Victoria, who was handing a still shocked Kat a cup of coffee, and then immediately sprinted back after me down the stairs. I told her what had just happened, and her mouth fell open too, only she was smiling.

"That is priceless," she laughed. "Somebody needed to do that. I'm glad it was you."

"Yeah, well, not everyone is going to be glad. When I get fired, I just want you to know that it was great to work with you."

Just then, the radio went off. "Jackie, you're needed up here, please."

I took a deep breath and then slowly marched up the stairs to face my punishment. Everyone on the floor was still working, to my surprise, which I thought for sure that there would be a crowd. Victoria and Mrs. Brandisham were standing by the dressing rooms, staring at me. Kat was nowhere in sight.

"Yes?" I said quietly.

"Where did you go?" Mrs. Brandisham asked.

"I just went back to the basement. I'm afraid I'm not very good at this job," I muttered, apologetically.

Victoria suddenly cleared her throat. "Miss Pendleton requested that you come back up here and help her pick an outfit. She's trying one on right now."

"What?"

"She specifically asked me to call you back up here."

I could see Mrs. Brandisham smiling out of the corner of my eye. Victoria, on the other hand, had a look of defeat about her. I was just in shock that I was being requested back to help Kat, who, at that moment, stepped out of the dressing room in a short, bright red dress covered in beads.

"Jackie. There you are. What do you think of this outfit?" she demanded.

"What?"

"Tell me what you think. Does it look good?"

"Honestly? It looks alright." I heard gasps again. Kat turned around and looked at me, her sunglasses finally off so I could see her surprised eyes.

"Oh, really? What do you think would look better?"

I thought for a long time, trying to decide if I should tell her what I really think or if I should lie. I was on a roll with this honesty thing. "I think you should wear something that is longer, and maybe not so bright."

"What did you have in mind?"

I ran down the stairs and had Chrissy help me find a different dress. She grabbed a long, deep brown dress with folds, and absolutely no beads. Kat glared at me when I showed it to her, but I insisted, so she tried it on. By this time, everyone in the store had stopped working and was watching me, flabbergasted that I suggested something out of Kat's comfort zone.

She came out of the dressing room and stood in front of the mirror. She looked stunning; the fit was sleek, and the folds looked interesting on her slender frame. She looked like a vintage movie star.

"Okay, now tell me what you think."

"I think you look amazing," I said.

"I don't look old?"

"Not at all. You look glamorous."

She stared for a long moment. "That's what I want. I want to look glamorous. That's exactly it. What else you got?"

I left her at the mirror, drowning in compliments from Mrs. Brandisham and the various other salesgirls and went back to the basement, asking Chrissy to help me collect five more pieces. Kat tried them all on, and each one looked even better than the last. Every time she stepped out of the dressing room, she radiated an elegance that was not present when she first walked in the store.

When she was finished, she changed back into her street clothes and decided that she was going to buy all six of the dresses she had tried on. The girls in the store gasped again, but this time, not because of anything I said. I walked her dresses over to the register and she followed behind me.

"Thank you for your help," she said, putting her sunglasses on.

"You're welcome. I guess I'm sorry for what I said." It was a horrible apology.

"Don't be. You were honest. I get so used to people catering to me and kissing my ass all day long. I tire of it. I really do. Just once, I wish people could stop being so fake to me. It was extremely refreshing. I want to be your client." I tried to decline the offer, but she wasn't hearing it.

When she left, Mrs. Brandisham approached me and congratulated me on the sale. "She had requested to see you next time. You did a fine job, even if your tactics seemed a little strange to me. I want you on the sales floor all the time."

I sighed. Even though it was flattering that Kat liked me, I didn't want to do this. I wanted to be in the basement. I had no desire for advancement. The other girls stared at me, impressed with my sale, but upset that I had been offered a sales position.

"Oh my gawd! What happened to you? You poor thing!"

I turned around and saw Reece coming through the door. Portia was out from behind the desk, touching his arm, smiling at him. He was looking away, visibly uncomfortable. "It's nothing. I fell. Can I see Jackie?"

The other girls began to flock in his direction as well, each one taking turns touching his arms and shooting him a flirty glance. He craned his neck over their heads, looking at me. "HELP," he mouthed.

I interrupted the crowd, sending all the girls away, angry. Reece gave me a kiss and then looked me up and down, touching the tiny jacket.

"Your jacket's kind of small," he laughed.

"Yes, it is. You've no idea what I've been up to today."

"I brought you some lunch." He handed me a bag with two sandwiches in it. "One's for me," he said as I looked through the bag. "Mr. Thestas let me take a long lunch break, since I can't really do much. The tables can only be washed so many times."

I asked Mrs. Brandisham if Reece could eat lunch with me, and she nodded. I took him upstairs to the break room and told him all about my day; everything, from the small jacket to Kat

Pendleton. He smiled the whole time and when I finished, he kissed me again and congratulated me.

"I'm so proud of you! This is exciting!" he said, still smiling.

"Yeah, I guess," I said.

"What's wrong?"

"Well, it's not that I didn't mind Kat, because in all honesty, I liked telling her what to wear, but I don't want to be a salesgirl. I'm perfectly content in the basement, away from customers."

"I'm sorry. But you know, you apparently sound like you're good at being a salesgirl."

"I'm only good at being mean to people. It's just weird that Kat actually appreciated it. Most people would want me fired for how I talked to her."

"So? Let those people be helped by girls who are going to lie to them and tell them they look great in orange leather pants when they don't. You can handle the people like Kat, who need to hear the truth once in a while."

I shrugged and continued eating, trying to change the subject by asking about how his day was going. "It's going," he said. "I can clean tables, and I can work the register, and counter because that only requires I deliver one plate at a time. Luckily, my boss and the other guys are being very accommodating to me."

I walked Reece to the door and hugged him goodbye. He looked around at all the staring girls and smiled, then gave me an embarrassingly big kiss and then bid me adieu until five o'clock.

My phone went off right before five, and I found a text message from Archie saying that he wouldn't be able to walk home with me, but Reece would, so not to worry. I didn't think much of it; I plainly assumed he was stuck at work.

"Hey, Jackie." I heard behind me as I was waiting for Chrissy upstairs. I turned around; it was Tascha.

"Oh, hi, Tascha."

"Um, so, how are you? Congratulations on the sale, by the way."

"Uh, thanks. I'm fine, how about yourself?" I gave her a weird look.

"Oh, I'm okay, I guess." There was a long pause. "So, can I ask you a question?"

"Shoot."

"Um, how's Archie doing?"

"What? You'd know better than I would, I think."

"I haven't seen him in days. It's been almost a week. He hasn't called and he won't answer my calls. Has he said anything about me?"

I shook my head. This was all news to me. As far as I knew, he'd been going out with her all the time. As I thought about it, I realized he had been home a lot, since that day he apologized for ignoring me. Suddenly, I realized the reason he wasn't coming by after work. He was avoiding her. Exactly why, I didn't know.

"No, huh? Nothing at all? He didn't say why he wasn't calling me?"

I shook my head again, and thankfully, Chrissy appeared. We started to walk away, and Tascha called behind me, "You'll let me know if he says anything, right?"

"Sure," I said, flatly, rolling my eyes.

"What was that all about?" Chrissy asked when we were outside.

"Ugh. Now Archie's avoiding her and she's paranoid." We started walking toward the café. It was out of Chrissy's way, but she said she didn't mind.

The café was fairly busy when we went in. Reece spotted us from the counter and motioned for us to take a seat, until he was done. An hour rolled by, before business slowed down at all. Finally, Reece came out from behind the counter, taking off his apron and leaving it in the kitchen.

"Alright, ready? Hey, Chrissy," he said, smiling at me, and then nodding at Chrissy. He grabbed my hand and we started for the door.

"Oi, Reece!" We all turned to look. The man who spoke was older, with a little accent, peeking his head out of the kitchen door. "Is dat Jackie?"

"Yes, sir."

"Che is beautiful. Is nice to meet you, Jackie."

"Nice to meet you too," I said, blushing. The other waiters were looking at me too, which embarrassed me even more. I hid my face in Reece's shoulder, like a shy toddler.

We exited the café, and parted ways with Chrissy. As Reece and I walked home, I began telling him about Tascha's strange questioning. "I mean, I had no idea that he was avoiding her. I assumed this whole time he was still meeting up with her after work and stuff."

"You should ask him what the deal is."

"I want to, but at the same time, I really don't care. I guess I sort of feel like he's better off without her. Is that mean of me?"

"No, it's okay," he grinned, squeezing my hand.

"How long do you think the Bettinos will keep watch over us?" Reece asked, seemingly out of nowhere, as we were about to go to sleep.

"I don't know," I replied, hopping onto the mattress and scooting over to one side, while simultaneously worming myself under the blanket. "Why?"

"I'm just wondering. Actually, I was thinking about my apartment and wondering how long they would stick around there."

"Are you missing something? I'm sure they could bring it to you."

"Well, I don't know. I'm just thinking about how long is too long to crash here. I definitely don't want to overstay my welcome."

I pulled his face in for a peck on his lips. "You're always welcome here, Reece. You don't ever have to go back. I want you to stay."

"I know you do, and I would, but I don't want to intrude on Archie and Maxine. I mean, this is their apartment too."

"Archie and Maxine are more than happy to let you stay, and you know that I don't mind."

"I don't know. I don't-"

"I see absolutely no reason why you can't move in permanently," I interrupted, with a much longer kiss.

"Okay, okay. You've convinced me to stay," he laughed, wrapping his broken arm around me, grazing his lips over mine.

34

Archie and Maxine were thrilled to have Reece move in. Adding him alleviated what we were paying for rent, plus, Maxine felt safer having another person to look after me. Archie was just happy to have another guy in the apartment.

Reece spent the next few days calling various companies with his change of address. He hired a company to fix the damages, and the landlord was satisfied enough to let him out of his lease early but kept his security deposit. He also called Uncle Manny, asking if his guys could help him get rid of his stuff. I insisted that he not go over there, even with the protection of the Bettinos. Uncle Manny was very understanding, insisting that his boys would do all the work, and would send him anything left behind.

Every day, when he and I returned home from work, there would be another box at the door, full of books or various things. Reece continually apologized for having so much stuff, but it didn't bother me at all. Our apartment had been so bare, that having more things in it made it feel homier.

Archie, it seemed, was still avoiding Tascha. Every morning when I walked through the doors at Brandisham's, she would say hello to me with desperation in her voice, like she was waiting for some good news. News which I didn't have, because I didn't bother asking Archie about her. She would always check out the window, hoping to catch a glimpse of him walking away, I suspected.

By the end of the week, I could tell my inability to answer her was beginning to show in her appearance. Her clothes didn't seem quite so pristine, and her face looked sleepless. I finally gave in and promised her that I'd find out what was going on with Archie, and I'd let her know on Monday. That seemed to cheer her up a bit.

Archie was already home when Reece and I arrived. His door was slightly open, enough that I could see him sitting on his bed reading, and he could see me standing at the doorway, but I knocked anyway, and heard him respond, "Come closer, honey that's better."

"Hey, Arch. Can I talk to you?"

"Hit me with your best shot."

"So, listen, um, I talked to Tascha today." I watched his body stiffen, and his eyes enlarge. "Actually, I've been talking to her a lot this past week, and uh, she seems pretty upset. She mentioned something about you not returning any of her calls or anything. She's been bugging me about it, so I thought I'd ask, so I have something to tell her. What's going on?"

He sighed and then began scribbling a note. *We just don't have the connection I was hoping for. Unfortunately, she doesn't seem to see that. She's beautiful and she's smart, but she's always making rude comments to or about other people. And then she started asking me when I wanted to move in with her, and she was planning these vacations that we were supposed to take, and it freaked me out. She moves way too fast; I'm not ready for any of that. It's not that I'm not grateful to you for hooking us up because I am. I'm just disappointed that she and I aren't that similar.*

"Archie, you need to tell her this. You can't just avoid her; it's driving her crazy. She looks like she hasn't slept in days. You owe her some closure at the least. She needs to know you're finished, so she can start over."

He sighed again but nodded. "I promise you I will."

Friday morning, I woke up and Reece was gone. Instead, I found a bleach blonde mop of hair and a zebra coat resting on his pillow.

"Hello, Carmelina," I said, yawning. Her eye widened.

"You remembered? You haven't forgotten since last week?"

"Nope. Sorry. I remember."

"Whoa, this is like some sort of record," She stared straight ahead for a moment. "Well, come on then. Let's get you to your appointment."

I came out of my room dressed to go, and noticed Carmelina rifling through her purse, her hands a bit shaky. "Everything okay?" I asked.

"What? Yeah. I just, I can't find my cigarette. I had one left, and I seem to have misplaced it. I need it badly, too. Look." She held up her hand so I could see the shakiness clearer.

"Um, I think it's tucked behind your ear," I said, pointing.

She stared at me, and patted the side of her head, finding the cigarette. "Oh my God, thank you!" she shouted.

"You know, you should probably think about quitting," I scolded.

"I tried once. The shaking got too bad for me. I need this nicotine."

"You don't need it. You want it. There's a difference. I think you should quit. There will be some shaking, yes, but that will subside in time. You just have to tough it out. I'll help you if you want."

"I'll think about it," she smiled, lighting the cigarette before we'd even left the apartment.

"So, it's been about three weeks? That's impressive," Doctor Novak said.

"I feel like a timebomb. I have no idea when I'm going to forget, and now that it's been this long, I feel like it's going to happen any day now."

"Jackie, you've been a timebomb since you started seeing me, and probably before that. You know you're liable to forget, and yes, because it hasn't happened for some time does suggest that it might happen soon, but it certainly could also mean that it won't happen. You're on the right path to getting better. You're keeping up the journals; your relationships are flourishing. You seem really happy. Hopefully, the next time you do have an episode, you'll be able to pick back up faster, now that you have your life together."

"My life isn't completely together, though," I admitted. "I still wonder from time to time about my past, my life before I met Archie and Maxine."

"Well, maybe that's something you should start thinking about: exploring your past. That could bring back memories too. Keep it in mind, and maybe we'll talk about that next time."

When I left the office, Carmelina was quick to slip what she was reading into her purse.

"What's that?" I asked.

"Nothing," she said. I folded my arms and looked at her.

"Fine," she grumbled, handing me the reading material. It was a pamphlet with tips on how to quit smoking. I smiled and looked at her. She rolled her eyes.

"I'm not quitting yet. I'm just thinking about it," she proclaimed.

I was in a hurry to get to Chen's, as I had forgotten to eat breakfast. Carmelina was being oddly sluggish, always slowing down behind me, to the point that I was practically pulling her along. Once we sat down, I was looking for a waitress, already sure of my order.

"Eat as much as you want. Are you sure you don't want anything else? We don't need to rush home," Carmelina said, looking over at my dish of rice.

As we left the restaurant, she kept making little detours, wanting us to stop at this store and that one. I couldn't remember her ever being so sidetracked before but reminded myself that I also didn't remember her other than what I had read up until three weeks ago.

"Let's go in here," she would say, guiding me by the arm. "Maybe we'll find something for you." I tried resisting; I wasn't interested in shopping at all. I just wanted to go home.

Every shop was something different. In one, Carmelina was picking out dresses that she wanted me to try on. They were mostly short and strapless, and they looked about ten sizes too small for me, but before I knew it, I had a pile of clothes in my arms.

"This one's nice. Oh, how about this one?"

"No, Carmelina. I don't want a dress. I don't need one." She completely ignored me, and pushed me into a dressing room, threatening to come in after me and dress me up herself. When I came out of the dressing room with the first dress on, she stood up and clapped.

"This is perfect. This is the one," she cheered. Thankfully, I went to change back into my jeans. Unfortunately, she stopped me and demanded that I keep the dress on. She pulled the tag off and I grabbed my stuff, throwing my hooded jacket on, and she paid for the dress. I tried to tell her I didn't want it, but she insisted.

"I don't want to waste my money on some dress I don't need," I reasoned.

"We're not wasting your money," she answered, flashing a wad of cash at me.

"Whose money is that? Carmenlina? Where did you get that money?"

"Don't worry. It's not stolen or anything. It was given to me to spend on you."

I wondered who the anonymous donor was, figuring it was probably Maxine, who was sick of my lackluster wardrobe.

In another shop, she squirted me with various samples of perfume; each one stunk worse than the one before. I did my best to keep from sneezing, which worked most of the time. She eventually settled on a fragrance that she then covered my whole dress with.

"It's got a peach scent to it. It smells great," she said, putting the bottle on the counter, and handing the woman some money. Again, I refused. Again, she ignored me.

"Why are you doing this to me? What did I do?" I asked, tortured.

"Come on, Jackie. Can't I be nice to you? I just wanted to buy you a new outfit as a token of friendship. Chill out," she laughed.

I drew the line at the lingerie store. She hustled me in, picking up lacy bras and thongs, and I couldn't take anymore. "Carmelina, I don't want to be here. Why are we in here?"

"You need some sexy underwear to go with that new dress," she smiled.

"No, I don't. I don't want to shop, and I definitely don't want to shop *here*. I want to go home, please," I said sternly, my face turning beet red at the mention of anything "sexy".

Carmelina rolled her eyes. "You're no fun," she pouted.

We left the store empty handed, and headed for the apartment, slower than we had originally set out. I was trying to keep a steady pace, unlike Carmelina, who was constantly stopping, or checking her phone. I asked her why she was being so slow.

"It's my shoes. They're hurting my feet. Oh, damn, we forgot to get you new shoes! Jackie, can we go back, please?"

I looked down at my sneakers. They seemed like the perfect accessory along with my hooded sweatshirt for the dress.

"No. We're going home," I said, curious as to her behavior. I knew she was lying about the shoes, as they were tame compared to the ones I had seen her wearing last time.

She followed behind me, sulking, and defeated. Every once in a while, she would come up with one more thing, like jewelry, or the salon, all of which, I adamantly refused.

"I do have to stop at the Quick-Stop. I need to get a pack –" She stopped mid-sentence and read the stare I was giving her. "Come on, Jackie. My last pack, I swear."

I rolled my eyes and followed her inside.

"Oh, but Jackie, you know what sounds good? Ice cream. Remember that place Reece took us? What do you say, want to go?"

"Carmelina. It's October, almost November. It's far too cold for ice cream. I want to go home." She stared at me for a moment, taking a few long drags of her cigarette, never letting it leave her mouth. Then suddenly, her phone rang.

"Hello? Yes. Yes. Ready? Okay." She closed the phone and put it in her purse. "There," she said, with a grin. "Now, let's quit dawdling and get you home."

The sky was beginning to darken, as we approached the building. Carmelina brought us to a halt at the door. She turned me around, facing her. Then, she touched my face and brushed my hair around with her hands. She dug through her purse and pulled out some lipstick.

"Hold still," she demanded.

I swatted her hand away and walked inside. Something was up, so when I walked into the apartment, I was ready for anything; anything except nothing. The apartment was desolate. The lights were off, and nobody was home. I checked all the rooms, thinking they must be hiding, but they weren't.

"What are you looking for?" Carmelina asked, coming in behind me.

"Huh? Oh, nothing. I was just being suspicious, I guess," I said, a little embarrassed.

"Suspicious of what?" she asked, turning on the light and sitting on the couch.

"I don't know." I joined her.

We sat for a few minutes, before I looked at my watch and realized it was almost five. "Hey, Carmelina, you don't have to stay, if you don't want to. I think I'm going to walk over to the cafe and wait for Reece."

"Okay. Actually, is it cool if I join you? I should get something to eat for Maxine for work tonight. She's not here, so she's probably going to be late to the club and have no food."

Carmelina and I walked in silence, except for a few minutes when she insisted I take my jacket off, and I refused, because I was freezing. Eventually, we compromised, and I left the jacket on, but unzipped.

The café appeared to be closed when we got there, which was unusual, as it normally was open until late. I peeked in the window, but there was a curtain down. A sign taped to the window read *Closed For Maintenance.* Through the curtain, I could see a little bit of light, so I peered closer.

"What the –" I rushed to the door.

Inside, the café was dimly lit with strands of Christmas lights everywhere. In the center of the room, all of the tables were gone, except one little table and two chairs. There were lit candles strewn about and one large one on the single table. I could hear music, and I noticed that there were two guys sitting off to the side playing mandolins.

Carmelina stepped up next to me and linked our arms. "Right this way, ma'am." She led me to the table and helped me sit. She then pulled on my jacket until I took it off. "There," she said, leaving the jacket on the back of my chair and walking into the kitchen. I continued to look around, lost in the beauty of the lights and the music.

"I'm so glad you could make it," I heard Reece whisper in my ear.

I turned around and stood up, taking his hands. He stepped back and looked me up and down. "You look absolutely gorgeous," he smiled, and then looked at my sneakers. "Nice shoes, by the way."

I giggled and detailed him as well. He was wearing pleated black pants and a white collared shirt under a dark sweater. "You look absolutely handsome," I laughed noticing he, too, was wearing sneakers. "Also, nice shoes to you too."

He helped me sit back down and joined me. Maxine and Archie came out of the kitchen with two glasses and a bottle of wine. Archie placed the glasses and Maxine poured the wine and then wished us a pleasant evening. As they went back to the kitchen, Reece's boss, Mr. Thestas, came out with a tray.

"For de two of you, at de request of Mr. Reece, we ave grilled cheese sand-wishes and tomato soup," he said, putting down plates in front of us. I laughed, looking at Reece, who was staring at me. "Enjoy." He left us to join the others in the kitchen, all of whom were watching us through the window. Reece instructed me on dipping the sandwiches into the soup, which I vaguely remembered reading about in my journal, and we listened to the mandolin players. When we were finished, he asked me to dance.

Once we stood up, and he wrapped his arms around my waist, I had a sudden mental image of him and me dancing in a courtyard. "We've done this before, yes?" I asked.

"You remembered?"

"Yeah, I think I do."

We danced for a moment, silently staring at each other. Finally, I wondered, "May I ask what the occasion is?"

"No occasion," he shrugged.

"Reece, come on. I'm an amnesiac, I'm not stupid. There's an occasion. You're dressed up, I'm dressed up. This wasn't just a romantic dinner of grilled cheese sandwiches, served by our friends."

He took a deep breath and looked to the kitchen window. Suddenly, Archie, Maxine, Carmelina and Mr. Thestas came out of the kitchen. Reece then looked back at me and mumbled, "No time like the present." He reached into his pocket and bent down on one knee.

"Jackie Dawes? I know this seems sudden, but will you marry me?" His cast posed a slight problem opening the box in his hand, so I bent down to the floor and took the box myself and opened it. The ring inside was silver and shiny with little diamonds encrusted in it.

I gazed at the ring for a long moment. "Right now?" I asked. He seemed taken aback, but he laughed.

"Anytime you want to. *If* you want to, that is. I'm aware that we haven't been together that long, but-" he paused before looking deep into my eyes. "I just *know* I want to spend my life with you." He took the ring out of the box and put it on my finger.

I looked at his face and kissed his smiling lips. "Yes. Of course I will." His smile widened and he hugged me and kissed me again. The others started clapping, and I felt my face redden. Reece held my embarrassed cheeks in his hands.

"Now that that's out of the way, let's continue dancing, shall we?" He said, helping me back to my feet. We continued to dance. I motioned for the others to come out and join us.

"Jackie, you're being quiet," he whispered after a long moment of nothing but music. "What are you thinking about?"

"I'm thinking about you. I'm thinking about being Mrs. Jackie-"

"Howard," he grinned.

"Mrs. Jackie Howard," I replied, resting my head on his shoulder.

"And how does that suit you?"

"It suits me just fine," I laughed. "I'm really happy right now."

Too soon, the night came to an end, as the wine was gone, and the mandolin players had tired. I tried to help Mr. Thestas take down the lights and put the tables back, but he refused my help or anyone else's and begged us to go home. I thanked him for doing all this.

"It was not-ting. Reece's idea," he said.

Carmelina went her separate way to her place, and the rest of us walked tipsily to ours. When we were home, I climbed onto the bed, lying on my side; I hugged a pillow between my hands and my head.

I felt Reece sit down, and as he took off his shoes, I rolled over and sat up, wrapping my arms around his shoulders. He smiled wide as I started kissing his cheek and then his neck. Reece dropped his shoe and turned toward me, lying down and pulling me on top of him. A hand reached for the back of my dress, unzipping halfway before I tipped over back onto my side of the bed.

"I'm sorry, I feel really dizzy all of a sudden," I said.

"Hey, it' perfectly fine, Jackie. Are you alright though?" He placed his hand on my shoulder, then my face.

"Yeah," I sighed. "I think I just drank too much. I'll be okay."

"You want to put on your pajamas? Or at least take your shoes off?" he asked, a tone of laughter in his voice.

"Not right now," I murmured, as he leaned over and slipped my shoes off my feet. "In a minute. I just need to rest for a second." He kissed my cheek and I looked at him.

"I just want you to know how much I love you."

"I know. And I love you."

35

The bed trembled. Startled, I opened my eyes and gazed around in the dim light of early morning outside the window. The trembling stopped and then I heard footsteps. Someone had just gotten out of this bed. I shot up, feeling panic course through my body. I looked to the door, plotting to make a run for it, until I saw a light on just outside the room. Whoever had been in this bed with me was now out there, blocking my escape.

But whose bed was it? Was this my bed, or did it belong to the stranger I was sharing it with? I leaned over and felt the spot where the other person had been. Then, I looked around the room. It was difficult to clearly see, but I was able to make out the outlines of some furniture, and the walls seemed to have a bluish color to them.

My first instinct was that I was in some kind of trouble. I contemplated yelling for help but wondered if anyone would even hear me. As far as I could tell, it was only the stranger and me, trapped in this room.

I heard water running from another room, and footsteps again, heading back in my direction. Quickly, I thrust myself back down on the bed and I froze.

It appeared to be a man, in a tight t-shirt and boxer shorts. He walked toward the bed, and, seeing me lying on my back, he crawled back into the bed and wrapped an arm with a cast on it around me. "Good morning," he whispered. "Did I wake you?"

I was afraid to answer, and the only thing I produced was a little grunt. He kissed my cheek and then went back to sleep. I lay there, still frozen, and now trapped under his broken arm.

Wide awake, I stared at the ceiling, wondering who this was next to me. Although the immediate fear I was in trouble vanished, my mind still searched for any memory of him at all. I did a self-assessment, and realized that I was wearing a nice, black cocktail dress, partially unzipped, then wiggled my toes and found that I was not wearing any shoes. Could I have possibly gone out somewhere and went home with a stranger?

My mind raced, trying to recall what I had done last night, but produced nothing. In fact, I couldn't produce memories of the day before, or the day before. I scrunched up my face and tried to concentrate as hard as I could; my head was even shaking. But still, I had nothing.

The shaking sent a rush of blood to my head, and I started to get a headache. I let out a tiny moan, rolling my head back and forth on the pillow, trying to sit up. The guy next to me jumped and then lifted his head, looking at me.

"Something wrong?"

"I need to sit up, please," I managed to say.

"Oh, sure, sure," he said, removing his hand and sitting up himself. I propped myself up and slid so I was leaning against the headboard. I kept my eyes closed, trying to make the pain go away.

"Jackie," he said. I kept still, unaware that he was talking to me, but then he touched my face. I opened my eyes and looked at him. "Jackie, your nose is bleeding. I'll be right back."

He left the room and returned with some paper towels. He handed them to me and I put them to my nose. Then, he placed his hand on my neck and told me to tilt my head forward.

"Thanks," I said, trying to look at him out of the corner of my eye.

"No problem. What happened? Did you hit your face on something? Oh my God, did I hit you with my cast?"

"No, no. I was just lying here, trying to think," I replied casually.

"Trying to think? Oh. Uh-oh. Did you have another spell?"

"Another spell?"

He took a deep breath and looked down. "Okay, your name is Jackie. You have amnesia. You've been keeping a journal. I'll get it for you later; it'll explain everything. First, let's stop this nosebleed and then you should probably get more sleep."

I sat still, my chin on my chest. He sat next to me, just watching. "So," I said, offhandedly. "Who are you?"

"I'm Reece. I'm your boyfriend. Actually, I'm your fiancée," he said with a smile in his voice. I straightened my head and looked at him. My neck ached.

"My what? Really?"

"Yeah. You agreed to marry me just last night. Do you remember any of it? The dinner? The dancing? Anything?"

"No, sorry."

"And I don't think you wrote it down either," he said, glumly.

I felt bad that I didn't recognize him, or that I didn't remember last night. I was relieved that his account explained the dress I was wearing. "Did we, um, I mean, have we –" My voice trailed off, not sure of how to ask what I was trying to ask.

"Huh?"

I looked around, trying to think of what to say, but I didn't have to.

"Oh," he said. "Uh, no. No, we've never–" he trailed off himself. I watched his face turn red, and I was sorry I asked.

"I didn't mean anything by it. It's just that, you know, I don't remember, and we're in the same bed and all," I was making myself uncomfortable and wished I could stop talking. I slapped a hand to my forehead, trying to hide some of my mortification. I felt something hard hit my head, and I looked at my hand. There was the most beautiful ring on my finger.

"No, it's okay. I understand," he laughed sheepishly. "We were about to last night, but you weren't feeling well." Then, he noticed me looking at my hand. "That's the ring I gave you."

"It's beautiful." I smiled, wishing I could have remembered last night.

The sun was beginning to glow in through the windows, and Reece got up to get ready for work. He brought me a bag and said my journals were inside, so I got them out and started to read them. I read the names Archie and Maxine, and I suddenly had a mental image of a guy wearing sunglasses and a woman covered in make-up. My hand felt the back cover of the first journal. I flipped to it to find some pictures stapled in. One picture was of the guy in sunglasses and the woman in make-up, with arrows indicating them as Archie and Maxine. My mind had been right; they looked exactly the way I had seen them.

Excited, I flipped back and continued reading, hoping that more images would come to me. I found myself so engaged in what I was reading; I almost didn't even notice Reece come back into the room. "How's the reading?" he asked. "You remember anything?"

"I got a little mental picture of Archie and Maxine, but so far, that's it."

"Wait until you get to the stuff about me," he smiled, cheekily, running his hands through his wet hair. I gazed at him, wondering how I could possibly not remember him. He was funny and charming and handsome and apparently, he was mine.

I smirked and looked down at the journal. "You know, you're being awfully calm about this. Have I done this that many times?"

"You've had a few spells since we've met, not many since we've been dating. But my grandmother has Alzheimer's -you'll get to that later- so I'm used to her not recognizing me. You're also being strangely calm as well."

"Yeah, I suppose I am," I replied, thinking about waking up and just staying frozen, not bothering to make a run for the door or panicking. My body must have trained itself to stay calm during my "spells," as Reece called them.

"Well, I have to go to work, and unfortunately, I have to work double shifts, so I won't be back until later; it's the price I'm paying for last night. Anyway, when I get home, I'll tell you all about everything, okay?" He leaned over me and kissed me on the forehead and again on my lips. "In the meantime, maybe these will jog your memory a little bit." He tossed a stuffed animal and a doll at me. I examined them. The doll was Dorothy, from *The Wizard of Oz,* which immediately came to me, and the stuffed animal was an elephant. I suddenly found a mental image of live elephants, and of Reece's face next to mine, watching them.

I heard him leave, before changing out of my dress into actual pajamas. After that, I returned to my reading. An hour or so later, I heard movement from the other room. I got up to investigate and found Maxine walking toward the bathroom. "Good morning, honey!" she said, pleasantly. "How does it feel to be engaged?"

"Don't know. I can't remember."

"Aw, again?" She sighed and left her path to the bathroom and hugged me. "I'm sorry, honey. I'm Maxine."

"I know. I've been reading these," I said, holding up the journals. "When I read about you, I got a mental picture before I had seen this one here." I flipped to the back again, showing her the photograph I had of her and Archie.

"Oh! That's wonderful! You're starting to keep some things!" She squeezed my shoulders and then excused herself to get ready for work.

Since I was already awake, I decided to go out into the kitchen and get some food. I searched through all of the cupboards, before finding a bowl and cereal. Once I had assembled my breakfast, I went to sit on the couch and read. Moments later, Maxine, dressed in business attire, said goodbye and when she left, I heard noise again, and saw Archie come out of his room and join me on the couch.

"Good Heavens, Miss Sakamoto -you're beautiful!" he said, grinning. He took one look at me reading my journals and got out a notepad and scribbled something.

Did you forget again? The note said. I looked at him and nodded.

It took me another hour or so to completely finish reading. The last entry I made was the day before yesterday. I wished I had taken the time to capture the events of last night, as everyone seemed excited about them. Reece had promised to tell me about it when he came home, so I didn't dwell much on the matter. Instead, I asked Archie if he would show me how to get onto the internet journal I read that I had started a while ago. I figured, if I had nothing else to do, I might as well record more of my journal, maybe seeing if anything else would come back with repetition.

He logged me in to my site, and I was shocked to find that my last entry that I posted had been commented on twenty-five times. I clicked the link that took me to the comments and began to read them.

I'm sorry to hear about your condition, but your story sounds fascinating.

Wow, this is a crazy story! Do you have anything else to post?

Are you going to keep us updated on things?

I had to admit that I was rather pleased that so many people had read the entry I posted and were actually interested in hearing about my condition. And they wanted *more.* I decided not to keep them waiting, so I created another entry, picking up where I had left off the last time.

As I finished my internet entry, I wrote a little note to myself on the cover of my latest journal to keep updating my internet blog more often. Then, I hit the "Post" button and turned the computer off.

I spent the majority of the day watching TV and being utterly lazy with Archie, waiting for Reece to come back. It felt like I was a high school girl, the way my stomach tightened thinking about him. Everything, from how I first met him this morning, to how I had officially met him in my journal, made my heartbeat faster. Even though I wasn't showing any of this outwardly, I worried Archie would notice, so to hide my infatuation, I set my concentration on the ring on my finger.

"Hey, Archie? I'm curious, could you tell me anything about this Razi guy? I've read the newspaper article, and I know that he's after me, but I'm just wondering if you know anything about him. I want to know him if I see him."

"Some people can be bad, the things they do, the things they say," Archie answered, then scribbled another note. *The police are looking for him, and we're under the protection of the Bettinos, so he's not likely to come after you himself these days. His men might, though, and you'll usually recognize them by their suits and sunglasses. They're the guys that went after Reece.*

"Yeah, I read about that in my journal. That's entirely my fault, isn't it?" He paused, but I urged him to be honest, and he sighed and nodded. "I feel awful about that. I certainly don't want anyone to get mixed up in anything because of me. I can't believe he's still hanging around me after something like that. Why would he want to marry me now?"

He held up his finger and started to write again. *If I may say so, when those guys attacked him, Reece refused to give them any information on you, which is what caused the beating. So technically, he brought that on himself. He very easily could have escaped that, but chose not to. Now, in my eyes, if someone is willing to go to such lengths for someone he cares about, then he's definitely worth keeping.*

What he wrote was nothing short of the truth; Reece could have walked away any time he wanted to and saved himself the agony he went through, and he didn't. I knew at that moment that my crush on him was more than that. I didn't have to remember anything about him to know that I truly did love him.

Finally, when I didn't think my heart could take it anymore, the door unlocked, and he walked in. I wanted to jump up from the couch and run to him and give him the biggest kiss I could possibly muster. But I also wanted to not seem like a crazy, obsessive teenager either, so despite my racing heart, I sat perfectly still on the couch.

"Hello," he said, joining Archie and myself. "How was your day? Did you get yourself all caught up on your reading?"

"I did. And, I updated the journal I had started on the internet. Did you know that I had comments on the last one I left? People actually read it."

"Cool," he smiled. "I brought you something." He handed me an envelope of pictures. "They're from last night."

I flipped through the photos, only recognizing myself by the dress I had woken up wearing. I found Archie and Maxine in a few pictures, and remembering my descriptions from my journal, I was able to pick out Chrissy and Carmelina as well. The last picture was of Reece and I dancing, our foreheads touching and our eyes lost in each other's. We looked so happy.

He put his broken arm around my shoulders, resting it on the back of the couch. I felt my stomach leap a tiny bit, and I became rigid. He glanced at me funny, then took his other hand and held mine. "You alright?" he asked, a smile in his voice.

"Yep. Fine," I said, taking a deep breath, trying to slow my racing heart.

He was still watching me and put his hand on my chest. "I can feel your heart beating. Are you sure you're okay? Am I making you nervous?"

"Nope, I'm fine. Totally fine," I lied.

He kept his hand there and looked into my eyes. "It's just me."

"I know, that's the problem."

"You're acting like you have a crush on me," He laughed, kissing me.

"Shut up," I said, stifling a giggle. "I can't help it. I'm trying to be cool, but it's not working."

"Look at me," he instructed. "Focus on me and take deep breaths." I did as I was told, and immediately I felt slightly relaxed. He recounted the events of the night before so I could write them down. He mentioned dancing and I had an image of us in a room decorated with Christmas lights. I was thrilled to remember something about the night before. Archie slid me a note about Carmelina, who had spent the morning with me and told him and Maxine later about our aggravating shopping spree, where I complained and refused everything she tried to buy me. I wrote that down as well, even though it sounded a little mortifying.

As we curled up together in bed, Reece said, "I was thinking about going to visit my grandmother tomorrow. Would you like to come? I don't know if you remembered meeting her once before or not."

"I'd love to come with you."

"Great!" He turned out the light, holding me close, meeting my lips with his.

36

The next morning, I wasn't sure what to wear; should I just wear my t-shirt and jeans, or should I look a little more polished? I stood at the foot of my bed, staring back and forth between two outfits, not sure of either one. I didn't want to look like a bum, but I didn't want to look too uptight.

"Just wear what's comfortable," Reece said, entering the room, and noticing that I still hadn't picked an outfit. I looked at what he was wearing: a striped sweater and jeans. The idea struck me then to follow suit and combine the clothes. "She's not going to care what you're wearing. Besides, you were wearing jeans and a t-shirt the last time."

I settled on the semi-formal shirt to wear with my jeans. However, I ended up counteracting the formality with my hooded jacket. Reece was relieved when I was finally ready to go. He couldn't understand what the big deal was about picking out what to wear.

"She's important to you, so I'm nervous to meet her," I explained, tacking on, "Again."

"Don't worry about making an impression. She's not going to remember you anyway. She can't even remember me sometimes," he said, lightheartedly, but a sinking feeling came over me; I related to that all too well.

We were both quiet the whole cab ride to the Carnation Home. The nurses inside greeted both of us warmly as we entered. "Good morning, Reece, good morning, ma'am," they all said almost continuously one right after another. The head nurse stepped out from behind the desk and led us down the corridor, telling Reece about various things his grandmother had been doing the past few weeks.

"We haven't seen you in a long time. She's been doing better on this new medication; more aware of things, although she still has her moments. She's been asking about you," she said. Reece held up his cast. The nurse made a little gasp and asked if he was alright.

"Yeah, it's no big deal. I tripped and fell down the stairs in my apartment building," he said, nonchalantly. I knew he was lying so as not to reveal to her that he had been beaten up by some thugs who were after his girlfriend.

We found his grandmother sitting on her bed, looking back and forth between the tree outside dropping its browning leaves, and her feet, which were swinging in circles. Reece walked over and sat on the bed next to her. She looked at his face, deeply. Then, to his surprise, she smiled and touched her forehead to his.

"Reece. My Reece. Where have you been? You haven't visited me in months," she whispered in a weak voice.

"I have visited, Grandma. It's been a couple weeks now, but I have visited."

"What happened?"

"I was unable to visit because I fell in my apartment building, and I broke my arm. I've been in too much pain. I'm sorry," he answered, keeping their foreheads touching.

She placed one of her tiny, frail hands on his and kissed his cheek. "I'm so happy to see you," she said, sweetly.

Their heads moved apart, and Reece turned around and motioned for me to come over. I did so, and he unhooked his good hand from hers and held one of mine. "Grandma, this is Jackie. Do you remember meeting Jackie?"

She looked up at me, with large, round eyes, like those of a small child's, and a huge grin appeared on her face. "Jackie. Lovely Jackie. Still so pretty. I remember Jackie. I showed her pictures of my grandson," she said, looking around for her box of pictures.

"Yes, Grandma, that's her. And your grandson is me. Reece, remember?"

"Of course, I always remember my Reece."

"Grandma, I want to tell you something. Jackie and I are going to get married."

"Today?"

Reece looked at me, grinning, and I smiled. "No, no. Not today, because I've only just proposed to her two days ago. But I wanted you to be the first person to know. And I wanted you to meet her, because she's extremely important to me."

"I've already met her. She's very pretty. I hope you two get married."

"Grandma, we are going to get married. She's going to be your new granddaughter."

"Good. I like her."

Reece stood up and said to the both of us, "I'll be right back. I need to go talk to the nurse for a second."

I turned to watch him leave the room, while his grandmother looked back out the window. When he was gone, I faced the window as well. We were silent for a moment, when suddenly, she faced me and stared intensely into my eyes.

"Do you remember me?" she asked.

"What? Yes, of course I do," I answered.

"I don't think you do. I remember you, though," then she giggled. "Isn't that strange? How you don't remember me, but I remember you?"

"Yeah, that is strange."

"Why don't you remember me?"

"Because I have amnesia. Every so often, I wake up, and I can't remember anything at all." I knew I probably shouldn't be telling her all of this, but since she called me out on it, I felt like I had to.

"Oh, see? We're very much alike, you and I. I forget things too. You should meet my grandson, Reece. You'd like him."

"I have. That's who I came here with. We're engaged, see?" I lifted my hand to show her the ring. She took a hold of my hand and gazed at the ring.

"That is so beautiful. I was married once." She gripped my hand and stared into the diamond like it was a crystal ball. "He was the love of my life," she whispered. "I have a picture." She motioned for me to hand her the box of photos and began to dig, before handing me one of her, much younger, in a bridal gown with a very handsome man.

"He was my world." Eleanor's faint smile quickly fell, and I watched tears well up in her eyes. "My world," she repeated. "But I can't seem to remember his name."

I could tell forgetting Reece's grandfather's name broke her heart and I felt as though mine were breaking too, watching her stare at his picture.

Reece came back shortly after, and the three of us sat on the bed, while his grandmother showed us pictures. "I need a picture of Jackie to put in my box, please," she said two or three times while passing out the photographs.

When the head nurse came back to take his grandmother for her medication, Eleanor asked her for a camera. "I want a picture of Jackie for my box. She's my granddaughter," she explained. The nurse nodded and led Eleanor out, Reece and I following behind her. She then stopped us all at the front desk and rifled through a drawer, producing a small camera. Reece put his arm around me and we both posed, and the nurse snapped the picture.

"There, Eleanor," she said. "We'll print that out for you, okay? Now let's get your meds."

Reece hugged her goodbye, and they pressed their foreheads together again. Then, she reached out for me, and I embraced her. "Goodbye, Jackie. Don't forget me," she whispered. I laughed and said I wouldn't. As we left, I heard her tell the nurse, "That Jackie is very pretty, isn't she? She should meet my grandson."

"Should we get some dinner?" Reece asked when we got in the cab.

"Mmhmm," I mumbled, distractedly.

"I'll text Archie and Maxine to meet up with us."

"Mmhmm."

"What's wrong?" he asked, closing his phone.

"Huh? Oh, nothing," I said, fixing my eyes on the ring on my finger.

"Are you not feeling well? I can call Maxine and cancel dinner."

"No, I'm fine." For assurance, I leaned over and kissed him. The truth was I didn't feel so fine. I kept thinking about Eleanor and the heartbreak she felt, not remembering her husband's name. I was inevitably going to end up the same way someday and I wasn't sure I could handle it.

My conversation with Eleanor looped in my mind and I hadn't even noticed that we had arrived at the restaurant and even sat down. I listened to Maxine and Reece talk, while I pretended to read the menu, wishing I could shake my feeling.

"What do you think, Jackie?" Maxine asked.

"What?"

"About that date? March fifth."

"What about it?"

"Haven't you been listening?" she lightly scolded. "For your wedding. It's a ways away, but spring weddings are always beautiful."

"I don't really want to talk about wedding stuff right now," I murmured.

I felt Reece's hand rub my back, as Maxine's eye became concerned. "What's wrong?"

"It's nothing," I lied. "Spring is just far away. I don't need to plan too much now. I mean, I'll probably forget before then." I hoped she'd accept that answer.

"Alright," she shrugged.

37

The cab pulled up in front of our building. The four of us got out and headed inside. The apartment was dark, the setting sun outlined objects around the room.

"The power's out," Maxine said, flipping the switch.

"I'll find the circuit breaker," Reece said.

"Great. I'm going to take these shoes off." I heard high heels on the wood floor and surmised that Maxine had walked to her room.

There was enough light that I could see a path to my room, so I followed it. I felt the wall of my room for my dresser, and then I felt inside the dresser for my pajamas. I stepped toward the closet, kicking Reece's suitcase on the way. Once I felt around the closet, I changed my clothes, finishing as soon as I heard Reece yell that the power was fixed. I felt my way back out of the closet to the light switch and flipped it.

I heard a groan behind me and my body went rigid. Slowly, I turned around. There was a man in a red shirt laying on my bed, curled up in a fetal position. My eyes then were drawn up to the wall above my bed, where I found some words in red paint over the beautiful picture Maxine had painted for me.

You can't hide from me anymore. I've found you. -R

The paint was still wet, and I stood on the bed to examine it. The man on the bed groaned again. The paint dripped onto the pillows and made a little trail that led all the way to the groaning man. I followed the path to him and noticed the back of his shirt was white. I crouched down and touched him. He groaned a third time, and I rolled him over. His stomach was bleeding profusely all over the bed.

"Oh my God!" I screamed. Reece was at the doorway in a second, and Archie and Maxine followed. I watched all of their faces as their mouths dropped in horror. My stomach sank and I felt sick. I began to dry heave, and Reece hurried over to me, helping me off the bed. Maxine picked up a blue jacket on the floor and then rushed to the man, speaking in Spanish to him and Archie ran to get some towels. I hid my face in Reece's chest as he called an ambulance.

"Uncle Manny said to stay put. He needs to make a few phone calls and he's going to call right back," Maxine said, dropping the phone back on the hook. The paramedics had just wheeled the man out of our apartment while three of us sat crunched together on the couch. Maxine was up and about, talking with the man, talking on the phone and talking to the police, who had arrived shortly after the ambulance.

They attempted to question us, but it was difficult, as we didn't know the man or anything. Maxine tried to tell them she knew where he was from, mentioning Uncle Manny, which made the police back off, suddenly.

"You just tell us who this "R" guy is, and we'll be on our way," One of them said.

"His name is Razi. He's after me. He seems to think I'm someone else," I answered, and they left.

My entire body had been shaking the whole time. I wasn't at all cold, so I assumed it was fear. The problem was I only knew Razi through what I had read in my journals, so I thought I should be more scared than I actually was. I really shuddered when the paramedics rolled the man away on the stretcher, and I knew in reality I was scared of what Razi was capable of. Reece held me close, but the shivering never stopped. I thought for sure that I would start crying any second, but I didn't.

When the phone rang moments later, I jumped. Maxine answered and "okay"ed a few things, then hung up. "Uncle Manny is sending a car for us, and we're going to get out of New York."

"Like go into hiding?" I asked.

"Yes."

"Where?"

"I don't know. He said to pack some clothes, and that there will be a car around the back to take us to the airport. At the airport, we'll decide where to go. We can't stay here with Razi on the loose, especially if he knows where we live. We just need to go away for a while and lay low."

For the first time in hours, the shivering stopped as we got up from the couch and entered our respective rooms to pack. Walking into my room, I jumped again at the sight of the blood on the bed and the wall, like I had forgotten it was there. Reece put a hand on my shoulder.

"Why don't you go help Archie and Maxine? I'll pack your stuff." I nodded and went into Archie's room.

"You need any help?"

He nodded.

He had a suitcase out on his bed and the closet open, taking trips back and forth, hauling out all sorts of clothes. I sat on the bed, waving my hands over his soft, fuzzy blanket, thinking about my own, which was now covered in blood. I began to fold things into his suitcase, and when I finished, I left him going through his music collection and went to check on Maxine. She, too, was packing everything she could get her hands on.

"Geeze, Max. How long do you plan on being gone?" I joked, unintentionally. She shot me a serious glance.

"I don't know," she said. "I don't know how quickly the police or the Bettinos will find Razi."

"But, if the Bettinos and all the police are after him, it shouldn't be too much longer, right?"

"Jackie, the police have been on Razi's trail for a couple weeks now, and Uncle Manny's been looking for him for longer than that, and no one has seen him since that altercation in the café, and even with a face to go with the name, he's well-connected enough that he's still impossible to track. They might never find him."

"So, what happens then? Do we just keep running?"

"I'm afraid so. I don't know what else we can do."

I helped her pack in silence, before I asked, "Max, where are we going to go?"

"I don't know," she answered again, which was not what I was hoping for. I sat on her bed and buried my face in my hands. Now, I really felt like crying, but still, I had no tears.

"I am so sorry about all of this," I whimpered. "This is all my fault."

"Jackie, don't apologize. It's not like you have any control over any of this."

"I know," I replied. "I just wish I had never run into him."

"Hey!"

"What?"

"What was that girl's name?"

"What girl?"

"That girl that we ran into when we were getting ice cream? Oh, forget it."

"I did," I said, cheekily.

She began digging through her purse and pulled out a paper and read out loud, "Melissa Samuels, Keiser University. Tallahassee. We should go there. If we find this Melissa girl or even that Frances Holloway she mentioned, they would hide us out for a bit, right?"

"I don't know."

"Come on, Jackie, we could dig up information on your past while we're there, and it would keep us out of New York."

"I guess."

38

It was nearly midnight and the airport was pretty empty. I was wide awake and well aware of every person who walked by or grabbed a seat at our gate. I was convinced they were all personnel of Razi's, or even Razi himself, as I didn't remember what he looked like.

Even though I was on the lookout, my mind was wandering. I was thinking about leaving the apartment, how we slipped out the back, and into the sleek, black car waiting for us.

"Here is a credit card," the driver said, as we pulled up to the airport. "Maxine, use this card for any and all expenses and remember to sign absolutely everything as Maria Vuelo. The rest of you, nobody use their real name." Maxine was told that Manny would send her a blank text message when he had any news, at which point she needed to call someone else to get the information. The whole explanation was complicated enough, that I doubted the follow through would be at all smooth.

The others looked restless. Their eyes were drooping and they yawned incessantly, refusing to fall asleep. I watched Reece's head slowly sinking down to his chest, and back up again, suddenly. Then, he drifted to the side, almost clanging his head against mine and waking up again.

Watching out the window, I saw the plane pull into its designated area. The expandable walkway reached out like an arm to the plane. After a few minutes, the flight attendants came out of the walkway and began calling for the passengers to board.

Once we were situated in our seats, the others kept themselves awake, scanning the oncoming passengers, as I was. The minute the captain announced they were closing the door, I suddenly noticed that Archie and Maxine were out completely, like the flip of a switch. Reece waited until the plane had taken off, before he nestled in his seat and rested his head on my shoulder. I dozed off myself, waking up every so often and lifting the shade to find us still above the clouds, but a little bit closer to our destination.

The plane landed, and I lifted the window shade completely, to a light ray of sun that hit Reece's face and didn't even wake him. I gazed out; it was early in the morning, and the sun had yet to reach its full potential. I could see palm trees, which excited me, because I had no memory of actually seeing a real one. I told myself that I had, in fact, seen them, as I had apparently lived here, but it was exciting, nonetheless.

We exited the plane, and rushed to find a hotel, at the insistence of Maxine, who claimed we all needed to get some rest, and change clothes. We hailed a cab, which took us somewhere with a vacancy. Maxine made our arrangements and we followed her down the hall to the room, where we plopped down onto the beds and just slept.

I woke up to the sound of multiple phones ringing in various bags on the floor. I got up and scrounged around for mine. I had four missed calls, each one from Chrissy. As I was checking, it rang again.

"Chrissy?"

"Jackie! Oh my God, finally! Portia has been trying to call you for ages. You're supposed to be at work."

"Shit," I answered, looking at the beds, where Maxine and Reece's eyes were just opening. "Okay, well, Chrissy, something's come up, and I can't exactly tell you anything except that I'm not in New York right now."

"What? Jackie, is everything alright?"

"No, it's not, Chrissy, but I'm not at liberty to tell you right now."

"Okay, well, just do me a favor. Update your internet journal when you get a chance, just so I know you're okay."

"Surely will, Chrissy. Bye." I hung up and promptly called Brandisham's. Portia answered and yelled at me, but I calmly explained to her that I had a family emergency and that I had to fly home. Luckily, she didn't ask me where home was.

Maxine and Reece used the same excuse of family emergency, but Archie had to come up with something different, as his father was his boss.

"I'm alright, nobody worry 'bout me." Surprisingly, he didn't need to say anything more; his father somehow understood that and asked no questions.

Once we had all cleaned up a bit, Maxine decided we should go to the college campus and get some information on Sophie Gray. "I know you think this is stupid, Jackie, but could you please pretend to be Sophie? I mean, these people are convinced it's you, so just go with it." I agreed reluctantly, as the four of us piled into another cab and headed for the university.

Immediately outside the cab, Maxine grabbed the first student in close proximity. "Hi, my name is Maria. My cousin Melissa goes to school here and I wanted to surprise her with a little visit. Is it possible for you to direct me to her sorority house? I think she said she's an Alpha Gam?" Maxine smiled, as the woman directed us toward the block of sorority houses down the street.

As we neared the house, I wondered just what kind of information we were going to find. Had I really been a part of a sorority? Was this Sophie Gray person really me? What if Melissa had just been confused? Or was it possible that she worked for Razi? Did he lure me here on purpose? My stomach tightened as we drew closer, fearing that we wouldn't find out anything about me, fearing that Razi would be there.

"I think we should stop," I blurted.

"What? Why?" Maxine asked.

"I don't know, I just don't feel right about this."

"Come on, Jackie, it'll be fine."

I opened my mouth to protest, when I heard a voice coming from the steps of the house across the street.

"Oh my God, Sophie! You're here! I didn't think you'd come for a visit!" Melissa had been about to leave the Alpha Gam house when we arrived. She threw her arms around me, and I did my best to keep from backing away. I scowled, and looked at Maxine, Archie and Reece, who all looked at me, their eyes telling me to get pretending. I rolled my eyes and then plastered on a fake smile.

"Yeah, I didn't realize how much I missed everyone down here until I saw you in New York," I said, utterly ashamed at my attempt to act excited. Thankfully, she didn't notice how bad I was at acting.

"Well, welcome back. Please, come on in, all of you." She stepped back and invited us inside. We sat down on the couches in the common room, looking around at everything. There was a fireplace against one wall that looked untouched, as I assumed it would be, in Florida. Surrounding the fireplace were various pictures all over the wall. I got up to look at them, as did the others. It looked like we were in a race, each of us scanning the pictures furiously for one of me. Melissa, meanwhile, stood at the doorway, watching us, and continuing to talk at me about people I didn't know, who I supposedly did.

"Did you hear me, Sophie?"

"Hmm?" I turned around.

"Found one!" Archie, Reece and I congregated around Maxine, who had her finger on a frame. "She's right here, in this one."

The picture was of five girls, three of them blonde, all in matching pink shirts with Greek letters on them. They also had black lines painted under their eyes and pink ribbons in their ponytails. Off to the side, under the arm of the only girl in pink with dark brown hair, was a girl in a black shirt and shorts. Her hair was jet black, and off to the side in a braid. I had to admit that she looked an awful lot like me, but I was still in denial. I closed my eyes, trying to conjure a memory from that picture.

"That's definitely you, Ja-Sophie. Who's that girl next to you?" Maxine asked.

"Frances Holloway," I said, as the image of her face appeared in my head. I turned around to Melissa, who said the same name at the same time. Archie, Maxine and Reece all looked at me, surprised.

39

The shock of my friends made the room silent, as we all concluded that I was actually Sophie Gray, and that I had lived this life before. Melissa was oblivious to the realization and didn't uphold the silence for too long.

"She's not here anymore, but she doesn't live too far away, if you want to visit her sometime," Melissa said.

"Do you have any more pictures of Sophie around here? I'm curious to see them," Reece said. I nudged him gently with my elbow and he made a silent laugh and put his arm around my shoulder.

Melissa motioned for us to follow her to her room, where she got out her photo album, and thumbed through it. "I don't have many. Sophie was always so opposed to having her picture taken, but I might have a few."

She showed us a photo of that same dark brown-haired girl, the one I identified as Frances, and that same black-haired girl, who I was being forced to admit was me. "This was the first time we'd met you," she said, handing me the photo. "It was Rush Week, and Frances brought you to pledge with the rest of us."

Melissa begged us to stay until the other girls came back from class at six, because she claimed they would be thrilled to see me. Maxine poked me in the back before I could refuse, and I smiled wide and accepted. We waited around, listening to her gab on about this girl and that girl, and looking at more pictures. Finally, a crowd of girls came in the door, and we peeked around the corner as they walked in. Melissa pointed them into the common room, where a couple of them looked at me, then screamed and jumped up and down, pulling me up and hugging me. I caught a glimpse of Reece out of the corner of my eye who was hysterically laughing about all of this.

These two girls, who were now seniors, Shelly and April, chatted at me until I couldn't stand it anymore, and then demanded that they get some pictures of me before I left. I obliged so as to get out of there faster. I hugged them all goodbye, as we left, and Melissa handed me Frances' information.

Reece and Archie both laughed uncontrollably once we were in the cab, heading back to the hotel. "Don't laugh, you guys," Maxine scolded, holding back a smile of her own. "These were Jackie's friends."

"No, they weren't. I don't know what that was all about," I tried to explain, my face reddening.

At the hotel, Maxine reminded me to call Frances. I picked up the phone in our room, but feeling everyone's eyes upon me, I put it down. "I, uh, I think I'll go call her from the pay phone downstairs," I muttered. The three of them stared at me, concerned, but let me go. When I left the room, however, I saw that Archie was following behind me, but far enough to give me some distance.

I sat in the chair in front of the phone, pulling my knees into my chest. I sat there for a moment, watching my hands shake, knowing why I was so nervous. I remembered Frances Holloway. When I saw her picture, I remembered her. I couldn't recall anything we did, but I knew who she was. I peeked around the booth, and saw Archie at the end of the hall, and then I turned around and started dialing. I called the number on the paper, which went to Frances' voicemail. I left her a message, asking to meet up with her in the morning if she was available. Then, I spent the rest of the night within inches of our room's phone.

Early in the morning, the hotel phone rang, and I woke up and answered. "Hello?"

"Is this Sophie?"

"Uh, yeah, it is. Frances?"

"Yes, it's me. Is this really you, Sophie?"

"Yeah. Listen, Frances, are you free to meet with me today? I, um, was in the neighborhood, and I was hoping to see you." I was impressed with myself at suddenly being able to keep up with the façade so well, I wondered if that had always been a talent of mine. We made a little plan to meet at a coffee shop called Marino's; apparently, it was somewhere that I was supposed to be familiar with.

Around noon, the four of us headed out, looking for Marino's to meet Frances. She was sitting at an outside table. I knew it was her, as when she came into view, the mental picture flashed in my mind again. She smiled when she saw me, obviously recognizing me as well. She stood up, and opened her arms, which I received, and we hugged briefly.

"Sophie," she said, in a soothing sounding voice. "It's so good to see you. I thought I'd never see you again."

"It's nice to see you as well," I answered slowly, being careful not to tell Frances exactly why I was in Florida. I introduced her to the others, and we all sat down at the table. Surprisingly, I felt relaxed and comfortable around her, not at all the way I felt around the other girls. "I stopped for a visit at Alpha Gam and Melissa gave me your information."

She rolled her eyes. "Oh, God. If I never see one of those stupid girls again, it'll be too soon. Especially that Melissa."

I laughed and suddenly knew that she wasn't like the rest of those girls; I could definitely trust her with at least part of my secret. As I was thinking of what to say, she asked, "So, where did you go? What happened? I was afraid you got caught."

"Got caught?" I asked. She tilted her head at me, so I began to explain. I told her about my amnesia and the journals I had to keep to remember things. "I have no recollection of anything up until about two months ago, and even most of those details I've only read about, so I'm sort of trying to figure things out."

Frances bobbed her head, listening, and didn't seem terribly surprised. "That makes a lot of sense," she said. "When I met you, we were on a bus, and you didn't know where you were going or where you had been. I thought it was weird at first, but when I saw the stuff in your bag, I assumed you were running away from home. I tried that a couple times when I was younger, and when you started crying, I took pity on you. We got to talking and you didn't seem to have much of a plan, so I suggested that you enroll at Keiser."

"What bag?"

"You had a leather bag; it was embossed with a tree design. Anyway, once you had stopped crying, I asked you where you were headed, and you said you didn't know, and then you opened the bag and pulled out some pamphlets about New York City. I told you the bus was headed for Tallahassee, and that you weren't going toward New York, but you just shrugged and put the pamphlets back. That's when I sort of peeked and saw you had a huge wad of cash and a handful of little gold trinkets. They were animal shaped figurines; I think one of them was an elephant. I didn't mean to pry, but I tried to make small talk and when you didn't know how long you'd lived in Texas, I thought maybe something terrible had happened to you at home, which was why you were running away. And since you weren't headed to New York, I thought I'd try to look after you, help you out a little."

"Texas?"

"Yeah. San Antonio. My parents live there, and I had been visiting and was on my way back to school for the fall semester and you were on the same bus. Actually, it was funny, I saw you in the station, and you were in the bathroom with an empty box of dye, drying your hair under the air dryer. The only time I'd ever seen anyone dying their hair in a public bathroom was in a movie once, where this girl was on the run and needed to be incognito, which set in motion my little suspicions that something was wrong. Do you have any idea what you were running from?"

I shook my head.

"Well, it's a thirteen-hour trip, which you and I both slept for part of it. Eventually, when we were awake, we got to talking; you told me your name was Sophie, which I figured was a fake name, but I really don't know. But I trusted you, God knows why, and you stayed with us for six months or so. You pawned the gold in your bag and enrolled in the same classes as I did. Then, one day, you were supposed to meet me here, and you never showed up. You never had a phone, so I called the house and nobody had seen you all day, and I knew that you had split. I didn't need to go searching for you; I just knew that you were gone for good. I tried to tell myself that someone had caught up with you, which still could have been the case, but I guess from what you've told me, you probably suddenly forgot and panicked and ran."

"What did you tell the girls?" I asked.

"Not much. I just told them you had an incredible job offer that you couldn't pass up. I didn't want to tell them anything else, because you can imagine how a house of girls would react to learning one of their roommates was on the run." She took a drink of water and cleared her throat. "You know, I've never told anyone about this, but when you didn't show up, in the back of my mind, I was convinced that stupid Zack Rodney had done something to you. Even though I didn't want you to leave, I hoped it was that over the alternative."

"Zack who?"

"Oh, I forgot. Zack Rodney. He was in our Spanish class. He was dumb as a box of rocks, and couldn't get the language to save his life, so he asked our prize student here to tutor him," she smiled, nodding at me. Maxine and I both burst out laughing, trying to imagine me speaking fluent Spanish. It seemed impossible. "Anyway, he had the biggest crush on you, which was probably due to the fact that you wouldn't even give him the time of day. I mean, he was there on scholarship to play football, which he was amazing at, and most girls just threw themselves at him -but not you. He seemed all hot and bothered by that. And he begged you to tutor him, and finally you got sick of him asking, so you agreed. You were supposed to be tutoring him that day and meet me here after, but, well, you know.

"I was so mad at him, thinking he had done something that I planned on going after him. But he was actually waiting on the porch when I got to the house. He had been waiting for you for two hours, and then thankfully, I confirmed you had left. And that's everything. That's all I know. You left your bag in our room, but your pamphlets were gone, as was any cash you had, and I never told anybody anything." We were all silent for a brief minute, absorbing the information.

"Why did you offer to help me? I mean, especially if you knew I was hiding something? I could have been a killer," I asked out of curiosity.

"Come on, Sophie. You're not a killer. I could never believe that in a hundred years. When we were on that bus, you wouldn't even swat a fly off your arm. You had this look in your eyes, like you were terrified. Even if you had killed someone before, that wasn't who you were on that bus."

"What happened to the bag?" Maxine asked, out of nowhere. We all looked at her strangely.

Frances shifted in her seat and produced the bag. "I kept it. I thought maybe you'd come back for it, because it was a really nice bag. It was a nice reminder of you." Maxine grabbed it off the table and examined it. "You can have it back now," she said, watching Maxine's face.

"Did Jack, I mean, Sophie mention any names from Texas?" She asked, still investigating.

Frances shook her head.

"Maxine, what's your deal?" I asked.

"My sister makes these bags. And she sells gold trinkets. I think you might have met her. She lives in Catarina, which isn't far from San Antonio."

40

I thanked Frances for the information, and after hugging her goodbye and exchanging email addresses, we left the café. We went back to the hotel; Maxine busied herself making us arrangements to leave for Texas in the morning. Archie flipped on the TV while I settled next to Reece and wrote in my journal about everything Frances had told me.

When I had written about Zack Rodney, I giggled. Reece looked down at me. "What?" he asked.

"Nothing. I'm just trying to picture this Zack guy. In my mind, his head is disproportionately small compared to his body, and he has a piggy face. For some reason, I keep picturing him trying to do keg stands and failing miserably," I said, detailing this little scenario I had made up.

"Sophie! Hey, Sophie," Reece said, in a jocular voice. "I need you to help me with my Spanish! I was thinking we could have our study session over some food on the Quad!"

Archie and Maxine snickered. I pursed my lips, but my smile broke through, and I started to laugh too. I elbowed Reece in the side and he pulled me closer and kissed my forehead.

Much later, when it was still dark, I had woken. I rolled over and reached out for Reece. He took my hand and I knew he was awake as well. "Are you asleep?" I whispered.

"No."

"What's the matter?"

"I'm just thinking. Go back to sleep," he whispered, adjusting his body to accommodate for mine.

"I can't. Tell me what you're thinking about."

"I was just wondering what would have happened if you hadn't forgotten that day. You know, like, if you had actually met up with that guy for tutoring."

"Huh. I don't know. I suppose I would have forgotten at some other point. But if I didn't, I could have finished a year of college and pretended to graduate."

"That's not what I meant," he whispered, with a hint of a chuckle in his voice. "Never mind, it's stupid."

I propped myself up on my arm and leaned close to his face. "What are you talking about?"

"I just meant that I wondered if you had tutored him, maybe you guys would have hit it off or something and you could have started dating."

"Reece, you heard Frances. I wasn't interested. If he's anything like the picture in my mind, I would never in a million years be interested in that."

"I'm just thinking, Jackie. I'm lucky that you are the way you are, because otherwise, I might never have met you, or if I did, you could have been attached to someone else."

"Ugh, I don't even want to think about that. If that's the case, my amnesia is a blessing," I whispered, settling back down next to him.

"Everything happens for a reason," he whispered quietly, almost to himself.

"I guess it does," I answered.

Early in the morning, Maxine checked us out of the hotel, and we headed to the bus station. It was across the street from a library, and we had an hour or so to kill before our bus left, so Archie and I ran over there for a bit. I immediately grabbed a computer and logged in to my journal. I had forty comments on my last entry. I read them all; one was a message from Chrissy identifying herself, and the rest were messages of support, or a couple people shared their own stories about having amnesia after some accident, but they all were better now. *"You'll pull through and get your memory back,"* they said, but I knew it wasn't necessarily like that for me. My condition was rare, and I had no way of knowing if I'd be alright.

I remembered Chrissy asked me to keep her updated, so I opened my journal and picked up where I left off. At the end of the blog, I decided to leave Chrissy a personal message, without giving too much information away, to be safe.

C. - Everything is alright. That's all I can say. –J.

When I had finished, I found Archie again and we got back to the bus as it was flaring the engine, ready to take off. Reece was sitting by the window, already watching the scenery of the bus station. I sat down, and we were quiet. As the bus started to move, I too found myself watching out the window, instead of burying my face in my journal like I had planned. I lost my thoughts a number of times, as the world outside the bus captured my attention. Then, suddenly, I would blink and realize that I was so absorbed, I almost forgot to breathe. Eventually, I gave up trying to write and laid my head on Reece's chest so I could see the view. He put his broken arm around me and leaned his head so it rested on top of mine.

The bus ride went long into the day. It was around dinner time when we finally crossed the state border of Texas. I could see Maxine in her seat in front of me getting her compact out and checking her make-up, which told me it wouldn't be too much longer. After the bus stopped in San Antonio, we got out, walked around for a bit to stretch out, before grabbing another bus. The bus rolled by a sign reading "CATARINA" and shortly thereafter, we pulled into a station.

"Now what?"

We stood in front of the bus station, looking around the Podunk town. The road wasn't even paved anymore. I could see the dust whirling up into little clouds with the slightest breeze.

"We walk," Maxine replied, picking up her suitcase and starting to march, her heels kicking up more dirt. Archie, Reece and I exchanged glances, and then followed. We followed her off the main road, and down a few side streets, if they could be called streets at all. Alleyways seemed too modern a word.

Once we ran out of alleys, and buildings, we found ourselves staring into the desert. Maxine somehow found a trail that we followed, leaving the town behind. It was beginning to get dark, and I was worried that we were about to get lost. I started thinking that perhaps Maxine had suddenly lost her mind, maybe her heels were too tight, and she was leading us to our deaths.

But, to my surprise, a huge rock formation attached to a little tiny mud hut appeared in the distance. There was a tiny hole cut out of the side of the hut, exposing a faint glow. As we neared, the hut seemed bigger, but still not efficient to hold extra people. There was no door, but rather, a curtain made of an animal hide draped over a rectangular cut-out in the wall.

"Penny?" Maxine called. No answer. She lifted the drape and peered inside, calling for Penny again.

I looked to my side and saw a figure a few yards away, coming out from behind a group of cacti, holding a large bowl. I could tell it was a girl, dressed in a long, flowing skirt, and a tank top. Her hair was a rich brown and it was braided on the side of her head. She saw us, and smiled, but kept her steady walking pace.

"Maxine. My Maxine. How are you, brother?" She set down her bowl and embraced Maxine's face, pressing it close to hers.

"I'm great, Penny. How have you been? It's been a couple years, hasn't it? I was afraid you wouldn't be here anymore."

"I'm still here," she motioned to the hut. "I don't feel the need to leave just yet."

Still smiling, Penny looked around at all of us, making a double take at me, but continuing to gaze at Reece and Archie. "You must be Archie. I can tell by your energy," she said. "And who are these other two?"

"This is our third roommate Jackie, and her fiancé Reece," Maxine said. Penny looked at me a third time, straining her face slightly.

"It's a pleasure," she said, before inviting us inside.

The hut was surprisingly roomier than it looked from outside. We set our bags down in a corner and found seats on a tiny couch in the center of the floor. I perused the hut. It was primarily one room, with the exception of a bathroom off to the side that looked like it had actual working plumbing. There was a little kitchen area, and then the couch, with a tiny TV against the wall. In the other corner, was a decent sized bed and next to it was a desk with a computer. I was shocked at how contemporary it was inside.

"Now, what brings you all the way out here? Especially with no phone call," Penny asked.

Maxine shuffled in her purse and pulled out the leather bag. Penny's eyes grew large, as she stared at the etching. "My bag!" she cried. Then, her head rotated my direction. "You! I knew you looked familiar to me! What did you do with my stuff?"

41

"Penny, it's okay. Let us explain what happened," Maxine said, trying to calm her down. She took a deep, heavy breath and glared at me, so I started talking. It was rather rehearsed, explaining my condition, but I told it the way I had been telling it, and reading it.

"So, I have no recollection of being anywhere besides our apartment in New York, but we were able to trace me back to Tallahassee, where I was told I was found on a bus leaving San Antonio, and here we are. I left the bag with a friend in Florida, but the gold trinkets, I apparently sold."

Penny's mood calmed significantly, and soon, she was smiling again. "Well," she said. "This is all I can tell you: I was walking through town, picking up some food, and a truck pulled up to the grocery store, and you popped out of the back, all by your lonesome. You stood around in front of the grocery store, like you were looking for something, and there I left you. However, in the morning, when I came back into town to get my mail and send a letter to my brother, you were still outside the grocery store. I asked you what you were doing, and you just answered that you were looking for work. I offered you a place to stay, in exchange for your help selling my gold pieces. I made a leather bag, like the one I use, and we went to the flea market outside town, where we walked around, selling the pieces. You weren't here long, a little over two weeks, and then, one day, at the flea market, you disappeared."

"That explains your bag of gold and cash," Reece said to me.

"Her friend in Florida said something about pamphlets. Do you know about those?" Maxine asked.

Penny closed her eyes. "Yes. I asked you where you were going, and you said you didn't know for sure. Once, when I went to the post office, I noticed a stand of brochures by the bus station. I grabbed a couple for you to look at, and you seemed very interested in New York. I told you all about Max who lived there, and I even wrote a number on there for you to get in touch with him. Guess it worked."

"Did I ever mention where I came from?"

"You never mentioned it, but I figured it was somewhere in Arizona, as that was the license plate on the truck that dropped you off. I know that's not terribly helpful, but that's all I know. I suppose I should have inquired since you lived with me, but I just didn't think it mattered. I mean, wherever you were from, you seemed like you certainly weren't going back."

Even though she had given me a state to trace myself back to, it still felt like I was at square one. There were enough cities in Arizona that it was going to be impossible, and insanely time consuming to find information, especially with no identity.

"What did I tell you my name was?"

"You didn't at first, but after a couple days, I asked again, and you were very thoughtful, before you said, 'Just call me June.' I think it was because it was June when I took you in. I knew it wasn't your real name, but I'm not one to press issues. If you wanted me to call you June, I called you June."

Her watch beeped and she got up and walked to the kitchen area to take something out of the oven. Maxine went to help, and I offered, but both of them declined it, and then laughed.

"She tried to cook with you too?" Penny asked Maxine. Reddening, I sat back down next to Reece and Archie, who had turned on the tiny TV.

Penny had a small table, and the five of us couldn't fit around it. "No problem," she smiled. "We'll sit on the floor." She produced a blanket and tons of pillows out of nowhere, and spread them out, like it was an outdoor picnic. We sat in a circle, distributing portions of rice and various vegetables to one another. Penny wanted to hear all about what we had been up to, particularly me. We told her all about my various episodes, from the subway to the café. Reece told her about how he and I became acquainted and the night we became engaged. Then, we talked about Razi, and Uncle Manny's protection over us until we found the man on my bed.

"How is Uncle Manny?" she asked.

"Wait, you know Uncle Manny?" I asked.

"Of course. He's my uncle. *Mi tio*," she answered.

"Jackie, Manny is my mother's brother. He took care of me when I left home for New York. Why did you think I called him Uncle Manny?"

"I don't know. I guess I assumed it was some mafia nickname or something," I replied, embarrassed. Maxine and Penny laughed.

When it was nearing midnight, Penny produced more blankets, again, out of nowhere, and handed them out. Each of us found a place on the floor and made a little bed.

In the morning, Penny took us out into the desert to show us where she panned for gold. Then, we walked with her into town so she could buy groceries. Maxine, Archie, Reece and I walked around, investigating what there was to see in the town, which wasn't much. We looked at antiques in a couple different shops and then went to the grocery store to find Penny and buy a few things.

"How long are you planning on staying here?" Penny asked, as we walked back to her hut.

"I don't know; not too long," Maxine replied.

"You're certainly welcome. I'm not kicking you out or anything. I just wondered."

"We should see about going to Arizona to find some information, but I don't know where to even begin, with that," Maxine answered. "I need some time, maybe look at a map or something to plan."

"Maybe you should visit Mama while you're here," Penny mumbled.

"What?"

"She'd be glad to see you, I'm sure."

"Penny, you know Mama hates me and what I've become. She won't want to see me."

"You're her son," Penny reasoned. "She still loves you, no matter what you do to your body. She always asks about you, you know. On the occasion when I see her or if she's well enough to call."

"Really? She asks about me?"

Penny nodded.

"Well," Maxine said, heavily considering Penny's suggestion. "I suppose I could check up on her or something."

The next day, the five of us borrowed a van from a friend of Penny's and drove to Carrizo Springs, where Mama Perlita lived.

The city wasn't very big, but it was vast in comparison to Catarina. Archie, Reece and I were staring out the windows, trying to take in the views. Maxine, however, sat staring at her hands, while Penny drove.

We turned onto a side street of houses that were all the same shape, with different color siding. Penny stopped in front of a yellow house with huge patches of grass growing up the side of the porch and spilling out onto the sidewalk. The paint on the siding was bubbled and scratched off in some places.

"Mama?" Penny called. We followed her inside, Maxine in the back of the line, being pulled by me. Our line moved to a room in the back, where I could hear a TV blaring. "Mama. It's Penny. Where are you?"

There was a little groan coming from the basement of the house. Penny left us to the living room to make ourselves comfortable, which we did, except Maxine, who sat absolutely rigid. Then, Penny went downstairs, and we could hear a muffled Spanish conversation below. Soon, there were footsteps coming up the stairs slowly, and Penny was lifting a large, but old woman up the steps.

The woman was very tan, and her face was wrinkled around her eyes, which didn't open very wide. Her hair was pulled back into a small ponytail, and a handkerchief rested on top. She had the same brown hair as Maxine and Penny, only it was peppered with gray strands. She glanced at us, emotionless, and then moved to a rocking chair in the corner and sat herself down.

"Mama, aren't you going to welcome my guests?" Penny asked, impatiently.

"*Si,*" she said. "Welcome."

"Mama, don't you have anything to say to Max?"

"Hello, Max. How are you?"

"I'm fine, Mama. How are you doing?" Maxine asked, her voice sounding deeper than usual.

"I not good," she said in broken English. "I not feel well, and I cannot clean my house. It falling apart outside. I cannot ask Penny to fix it. My son would have."

There was an air of insult when she spoke. Maxine clasped her hands and I could tell she was very uncomfortable, as were the rest of us. "Should we go?" I asked, looking from Maxine to Penny.

"No. You don't have to leave. I have nothing to say that can't be said in front of everyone," Maxine said, quickly wiping her eye. "Mama, I'm sorry. I am not your son anymore. You know that. I haven't been your son for ten years. Why can't you accept that?"

"Because it not right. It not the order of things. You were born my boy, you are supposed to stay my boy and you are supposed to be here when I need you."

"I'm here now, if you need me, Mama. I will always come visit you if you need me, but you need to understand that I can never be what you wanted. I've never felt like a man my whole life. I was meant to be a girl."

"I need no more girls. I have Penny," she muttered, gruffly. "You need to honor your father. He is in Heaven frowning on you now."

"Mama, you have to stop treating Papa like he was some kind of hero. He wasn't. Who came home drunk every night? Who spent his paychecks on booze so that the rest of us had to get jobs to pay for our house? Mama, he beat you incessantly, and Penny and me too. You know that." Mama Perlita closed her eyes, scrunching her whole face and shrank into her hands, crying. Maxine's composed voice crumbled and she too began to weep. "Papa wasn't a hero, and he wasn't a good man, and he's not looking down on us in Heaven."

Her mother's wailing grew louder, and she started muttering something in Spanish and steered her eyes toward the ceiling. Whatever she was saying seemed to make Maxine and Penny both uneasy.

"Excuse me," I interrupted unintentionally. "Maxine is a wonderful person. She's a kind and caring human being with a lot of talent. She's perfectly fine the way she is."

The old woman turned her face to me, looking me up and down. "Who are you?" she asked, like she was suddenly aware there were other people in the room.

"My name is Jackie. And your son, Max is my best friend. She took me in when I needed help and she's taken great care of me. I always know I'm safe around her because she never lets anything bad happen. She's like a mother to me."

"Where your real mother?"

"I don't know. We're actually trying to find out where I came from right now. But I do know that if I ever find my mother, I can only hope she's as wonderful as Maxine."

Mama Perlita sat back in her chair and looked at the ground, rocking back and forth, slowly. Penny suggested that we leave the room for a moment so Maxine and her mother could talk in private. I didn't see a reason, as they had been so outwardly open with their conversation thus far, but as awkward as the whole situation was, I couldn't get out of there fast enough.

Archie and Reece both offered to fix the outside of the house, which Penny thought was a great idea. She sent them into town to get some paint, and while they were gone, she took me on a tour of the little house. She brought me up the stairs, which creaked enough that I feared we would collapse right into the basement. There were three bedrooms; one belonged to her mother, one belonging to Penny and one for Maxine.

Penny's room was the smallest and didn't have anything in it except cardboard boxes. "Those are full of things that belonged to my father," she explained. "Mama couldn't stand to look at it anymore after he died, but she didn't have the heart to throw it away either."

After seeing her room, she showed me what used to be Maxine's. I never would have guessed that Maxine used to be a man, judging by her bedroom, which was a lavender color, not that dissimilar to her room in New York, and there were wigs and lady's clothes hanging in the closet. "It's funny," Penny said, pulling out one of the flower-printed dresses, holding it up to herself. "Most of these dresses are old ones of my mother's. Max used to wear this stuff all the time around the house growing up. Never out in public though, because of course that kind of stuff was frowned upon around here."

"Is that why she went to New York?"

Penny nodded. "My uncle Manny let her stay with him for a while, and he was surprisingly supportive of her wanting to change. So, he put up the money for her operations, and when my mother found out, she stopped speaking to him, she was so angry."

"Uncle Manny hated my father," Maxine said, suddenly. Penny looked, as I jumped, startled. I didn't even hear her come up the stairs. "He was so angry at my mother for marrying him, because he knew my father was no good. But my mother was convinced that she would be able to turn his life around, or God only knows what, so she stuck by him, which was a mistake. Then, thankfully, he died. Cirrhosis. Once he was gone, it was like something released me and I could finally be the woman I wanted to be. Papa would have beaten me until I bled if he had ever seen me dressing in those."

I walked over to where she stood and hugged her with all of my might. I knew that it didn't matter to me what Mama Perlita, or her father, or God himself said; she was an amazing woman and better than most.

We went back downstairs and found Mama Perlita standing halfway out the front door, watching Archie and Reece chipping paint off the siding. She was trying to hide her smile, but it escaped when she looked at Maxine and said, "They paint my house."

"Yes, Mama. They'll paint the house for you."

"Who are they?"

"The one on the ladder is my best friend Archie, my roommate. And the one with the broken arm is our Jackie's fiancé, Reece."

"So, you do have a family," she said.

"Yes, Mama. This is my family. They can be your family too, if you'll forgive me."

She was silent for a moment. "They paint my house first. Then we see."

42

The four of us ended up staying with Penny for three more days. In that time, Reece and Archie stripped and repainted Mama Perlita's entire house and even cut the grass. Penny and I bought some flower boxes and filled them with colorful marigolds, and by the time we were finished, Mama Perlita's house was the prettiest on the block.

Maxine had stayed indoors and cleaned every surface inside the house. She had convinced her mother that it was time to get rid of her father's belongings and one night, we set up a small fire in the backyard for them to burn his possessions. It gave the three of them much needed closure and release to burn his memory, especially Mama Perlita, who had held onto her false admiration of him for so long.

Whenever we came back to Penny's hut, Maxine would work on a plan for attacking Arizona that would help us gather any information about me. Eventually, she had compiled a little list of towns in Arizona for us to check that she thought would cover the state.

I wrote another entry in my online blog and read more comments. This time, I had seventy. I was surprised at how many people seemed interested in what I was writing about. And again, I read more stories about other people who had amnesia. Chrissy even left me a comment or two, telling me about work. She said the rumors were swirling, only because Mrs. Brandisham was concerned about her newest salesgirl.

While I didn't necessarily feel like leaving, because I had been enjoying the peacefulness of the desert and the hut, I knew eventually, we'd have to. Penny, as welcoming as she was, was not equipped to accommodate four extra people in her tiny hut. Plus, we had started our journey with the intent of finding my past, and if we were to get to the end, we had to press on.

Maxine made the arrangements for us to take a bus out of town to the airport in San Antonio. Mama Perlita insisted on seeing us off at the bus station with Penny, which we took to mean that Maxine was back in her good graces. She gave us all large, heartfelt hugs nicknaming us in Spanish, which Maxine later said were family titles. Then, we hugged Penny goodbye, thanking her for her hospitality and promising to stay in touch. She and her mother continued waving at us once we sat in our seats and kept waving until we couldn't see them anymore.

The bus rolled into a station in San Antonio and from there, we took a cab to the airport. At the airport, Maxine made some arrangements and got us a flight to Tucson.

I sat by the window, which I hogged all to myself for a few minutes, but then tired of seeing nothing but runway tarmac, I straightened up, turning my head forward. Reece looked at me and then put his arm around me and kissed my cheek.

"You alright?" he asked.

"Yeah. I'm fine. I'm just wondering how we're going to get anywhere in Arizona," I replied.

"Well, you know, we could always rent a car, or take a bus, or a cab, even." I looked at his grinning face. I couldn't help but giggle and nudge him.

"You know what I meant," I said, trying to stop smiling.

"Don't worry, Jackie. We'll find your past, even if it takes a long time. This is important to us too," he said, then laughed, "I mean, I'd like to know what kind of girl I'm going to marry."

The flight finally took off, and in a matter of hours, we landed in Tucson. Maxine decided the bottom of the state might be the best place to start, so she checked us into a hotel, and then found directions to the police station. The police did a check on my fingerprints but didn't find anything. We asked for any missing person's reports, which they checked also, but no one was missing who matched my description.

I felt a little discouraged, but Maxine did not. She simply crossed Tucson off her list, and back at our hotel, she made some arrangements for getting us to the next town in the morning. We left early in the morning and headed to Casa Grande. Again, we went through the standard procedure: fingerprints and missing person's reports, but again, we found nothing. The Casa Grande police had a list of picture-less reports that they let us sort through, but the descriptions didn't sound like they matched. Another cross on her list and after a night in a Casa Grande hotel, we left in the morning and headed to Phoenix.

The Phoenix police were less accommodating to our predicament. The officer we talked to refused to let us see the reports, instead, he looked them over and compared them to me. He claimed he didn't have one of me in there, but I grew secretly paranoid that he was intentionally hiding something from me, like every report had my picture on it.

I knew this endeavor would be tough, but it was beginning to wear on me, thinking we'd never find where I came from. The last two stops on our journey, we had a specific place and specific people we were looking for, and now, we had nothing. I was quickly losing hope.

Reece could see that I was increasingly down and tired from constantly being on the go. He decided to cheer me up a little by finding us a nice restaurant. Archie and Maxine came along but decided they would go somewhere else to eat just down the street, so we could have a nice, private dinner.

"It's nice to be alone," he said as we sipped wine in the candlelight. "You know, since we've been engaged, we've hardly spent any time together just the two of us."

He was right; since our engagement, or what I could remember of it, we'd been visiting Eleanor, or in reaching distance of Maxine or Archie, and now that we were on this journey, we'd been crammed in the same room every night as well. I wondered if things were always going to be like this: on the run, sharing a hotel room, never even getting to kiss Reece without someone seeing. Our relationship seemed to be on the back burner for now, and it didn't seem fair. Reece didn't deserve this. For all I knew, he'd endure this with me, only to find one day that I wouldn't be able to remember him or want him anymore. Like Eleanor, I'd just forget his name.

Once our dinner was over, we found Archie and Maxine, who were in some tiny little bar, having drinks and dancing with the locals. Reece and I sat and watched them, laughing hysterically at these two complete misfits, intermixed with people dressed in plaids and cowboy boots. They did their two-steps and their electric slide and Archie and Maxine struggled to keep up.

Eventually, we wandered out and found our way back to our hotel. Maxine caught her reflection in a window as we walked inside and suddenly focused on the pool in the courtyard. "Oh my God, you guys, let's go swimming!" She screamed and ran out of the nearest door. We chased after her, but it was too late; she was already in the pool.

"I can't swim very well in this skirt," she laughed, beckoning us to join her. Archie sat down in a lawn chair and took off his jacket, shoes and pants, and he too jumped in.

Reece squeezed my hand. "You want to?" he asked, smiling.

"But your arm is broken," I said, searching for an excuse not to go in.

"Come on, I'll keep it up. It'll be fine." He frowned and stuck out his lower lip, like a sad puppy.

I rolled my eyes. "Ugh. Fine." He took off his shirt and jeans, while I extremely reluctantly took off my jacket and slid off my jeans. I looked back at Reece, who was staring at me, grinning.

"What?" I asked, slightly annoyed.

"Nothing," he smirked.

We stepped up to the edge of the pool. "How are we doing this? Are we jumping, or are we going to just step in?" I asked.

"I guess I'll just step in," Reece answered. "You can jump."

"No way," I answered, as he gave me a hard nudge that sent me falling into the water. The cold hit me, and my body shivered. I felt my lungs expand, and soon, water seeped into my nose, burning as it ran through me. I threw my arms out, wading around, reaching for something, but found nothing. I reached up, hoping to feel air, but I only felt more water. My lungs were aching, and I started to choke. Bubbles forced their way out of my mouth, but fewer and fewer came out every time. I continued to flail until finally, I caught something. It was a leg. I grabbed it tightly and in seconds, two hands grabbed my shoulders and lifted me up.

As soon as I felt air on my face, I began to cough. I gagged a few times, and tried to catch my breath, while Archie held onto me. My eyes burned, the more I opened them, so I tried to keep them closed while I choked. Archie moved one hand to my back and the other under my legs and I hugged him as he carried me to the side of the pool.

When we reached the edge, I grabbed hold of the side and rested my head on my hands, taking deep breaths. As I rested, I felt a dry hand on my back and heard Reece in my ear.

"Jackie, are you okay?"

I coughed a couple times but nodded. I caught my breath and looked up. Reece had his broken arm holding the side of the pool, while his other hand moved itself up and down on my face. "I am so sorry," he said, then whispered a couple more times.

"It's alright," I answered. "You didn't know I couldn't swim. I didn't even know."

He put his arm around my waist. "Well, I guess you'll be sticking with me on the side then, huh?"

I let one hand go from the side and placed it on Reece's shoulder. Then, I saw his kicking feet and started to kick mine.

"Good. That's good," he said. I let go with my other hand and placed it on his other shoulder and I let my body bob up and down in the water.

He continued to cheer me on, and I couldn't help but smile. I was learning how to swim; even Reece was beaming with pride. I heard a cheer from Maxine and realized she and Archie were watching me too.

Eventually, I let go of Reece and started paddling my hands. At first, I immediately began to sink, but the second time, I stayed afloat. Then, paddling my hands and kicking my feet, I started to move. I swam away from Reece to Archie, gripping his arm, and then away from him to Maxine's arms. As I was making my way back over to Reece, a young man came strolling over to us.

"The pool's closed for the night. You have to get out," he commanded.

We swam to the ladder and one by one, we climbed out. The man's eyebrows rose when he saw Maxine get out, wearing her tiny skirt. He overtly checked her out as she walked away. When I climbed out, I could see him out of the corner of my eye looking me up and down also. Bothered, I turned to say something, but Reece beat me to it.

"Excuse me," he said. The man quickly looked down. I turned my face back away and smiled, turning a little red.

We took turns taking showers to wash the chlorine off our bodies and our clothes. Then, Maxine draped our wet clothes over the railing of our small balcony.

In the morning, we went to the dining area for some breakfast, while Maxine told us what was on the agenda for the day.

"We're going to Flagstaff; I've got a good feeling about Flagstaff."

The first bus we were on was hot. The minute I stepped inside, I was covered in sweat. The driver made no apologies for the temperature, which I took to mean that his bus was always like this. The drive was short, but it seemed like forever in the sweltering heat. Finally, when I didn't think I would be able to take anymore, he pulled off the main road and into a bus station. We rushed out, anxious to cool ourselves.

"I'm dying of thirst," I reported. Maxine paid me no mind, reading the bus schedule. Archie and Reece were of the same mind as me, and we told Maxine we were off to find a store.

"The bus will leave in thirty minutes," she called after us.

The nearest store was a tiny little shack a couple buildings away. The lady inside was reading a magazine, chewing on a piece of licorice.

"Hey," she said, without even looking up.

We looked around at her selection of food, which was bigger than I thought would fit in a shack. Archie grabbed four bottles of water and brought them up to the counter.

"Is that going to be it?" she asked, again, eyes glued to the paper.

"Yes," I said. She looked up to the register and pounded a couple keys. Then, looking at me, she said, "That'll be four dollars- Whoa! You're that girl!"

"Excuse me? What girl?"

"That girl." She pointed her finger at my head, and I turned around. Directly behind me, on a bulletin board was a piece of paper with a picture on it. It looked just like the pictures Melissa had showed us in Florida; it looked just like me.

"That's not me," I said, laughing nervously.

"It is too. You got that same scar by your ear and everything. Jesus, they've been looking for you for well over a year. Almost two, now."

"Who has?"

"I don't know 'em personally, but their names are on that flyer."

I stepped up to the flyer and ripped it from its staple. "Is it okay if I take this?" I asked.

The woman stared at me. "Well, it's you, ain't it? If you're found, I don't need a missing person poster cluttering up my board."

Archie slid her four dollars and we left. Maxine stood outside the bus station, tapping her stiletto on the sidewalk. "There you are," she said. "We've got to hurry and get on the bus."

"We need to go to Prescott," I said.

"Why?"

I held up the poster. Maxine grabbed it and looked back and forth between the face on the paper and mine. "She has the same scar and everything," I repeated.

Maxine went back to the bus route map. There was a bus that had just pulled in that was heading in the direction of Prescott. We rushed to get on the bus before it took off.

My heart started to leap as I read the poster over and over. Above the picture in big black letters was the heading "MISSING" and below the picture it said:

Name: Amy Bennett   Age: early 20's
Hair: Blonde   Eyes: Green
Please Contact: Lyle and Janet Bennett

I stared at the words, absorbing them. Was this the end of my searching? Were these my parents? Am I Amy Bennett?

43

The bus ride was long; I was anxious to get to Prescott and find my parents. To my knowledge, I had not given my parents much thought, until Mama Perlita brought up my mother, so this was unexpected. I never thought I'd want to see them this much.

I lay back in my seat and closed my eyes. I tried to picture my house, in the middle of the desert, like Penny's, only it was a regular house, with bricks and wide windows. I also tried to picture what Lyle and Janet looked like. Were they relatively young, or were they an older couple? Did I have any brothers or sisters? I squeezed my eyes shut, trying to search for any memories at all. I felt my body tense up a bit, exerting all my energy into finding a memory.

Reece put his head on my chest, under my chin. "Whoa," he whispered.

"What?" I asked, keeping my eyes clenched.

"Your heart is beating really fast," he snorted. Then he rubbed my arm. "You're really tense. Are you okay?" He lifted his head to look at me.

"Yeah, I'm just thinking," I said.

"Jackie, why don't you relax a little? Take some deep breaths. Stop thinking so hard. I'm sure your memories will come back when you see them," he advised, putting his head back on my chest. I obeyed and took three large breaths, clearing my thoughts.

Prescott seemed like a little metropolis in the middle of nowhere. Unlike the last town we'd stopped in, there were cars and people everywhere, and a multitude of stores. We walked down the street, looking for a police station, when we happened upon a post office. "That'll do," Maxine said, and she and I went inside.

"Excuse me, sir," Maxine said to the man sorting envelopes behind the counter. "I was wondering if you could tell me an address. I'm looking for someone."

"Name?"

"Lyle and Janet Bennett."

The postman looked up and stared at her. "Who are you?"

"My name is Maria Vuelo. My friend and I are looking for them." She motioned to me, peeking around from behind her. His eyes grew large.

"Is that Amy?"

I smiled and waved.

"Well, you know the way, don't you?"

"Actually, I don't, and it's really complicated to explain," I said.

"Oh, did your memory handicap come back?"

"My what? How did you –" I started to say, but he spoke.

"Everyone who knows the Bennetts knows about you and your condition. I can't recall how many times I introduced myself to you," he chuckled.

"Do you know what happened to me?" I asked.

"No. I don't remember ever hearing how you got that handicap. Always had it since I've known you."

I closed my eyes trying to absorb this information. He said I had always been like this. Had I gone my entire life not remembering a single thing?

"Could we have the address please?" I asked. He wrote down the address quickly and handed it to Maxine.

"Aaron finally came home this week. He'll be shocked to see you, after so long."

"Aaron?"

"You don't remember Aaron either? Well, hopefully, it'll all come back when you see him."

We left the post office, and Maxine explained to Archie and Reece what happened while I quietly wondered who Aaron was.

We caught a cab, which took us just outside the city to a suburb that led to a big house in the back, different from all the others.

It wasn't quite what I had pictured; there was a white stable fence surrounding the yard, which was full of fake green grass. The pavement was various shades of red that made a swirl pattern all the way up to the front door.

I felt my heart again and tensed up completely. Reece gripped my hand. "Calm down, Jackie. It's okay. Everything is fine. Breathe. Deep breaths." Again, I took a few breaths and finally, I was calm enough to step up to the door. I raised my hand to knock, when the door opened.

"Amy? Oh, my goodness, is that you, Amy?" the woman's voice was soft and delicate, just like her features. She stepped out onto the porch, examining me in the sunlight.

"I don't know," I said. "I think so."

She pressed her hand to her chest and started to cry. "We had given up hope. We thought you were gone forever. But here you are. You're back." She hugged me tightly.

"Can we come inside?" I asked.

"We?" She suddenly detected that there were other people standing at the bottom of the porch. "Oh! Yes of course, bring your friends right on in." She stepped to the side, guiding us in.

The house was absolutely immaculate. Not a thing out of place. The living room was all neutral tones, with sparkling white carpet. From the door, I could see into the kitchen, which also looked spectacular.

"Please, sit down. Oh, shoes off, please." She motioned to the furniture and then pointed at our feet.

The four of us all sat on the couch, and she sat in the chair adjacent to us, smiling. "Oh, where are my manners?" she gasped. "Would anyone like anything to drink?"

We all shook our heads simultaneously, and she continued smiling. The room was quiet for a moment, before she said, "My goodness, Amy. I'm so glad you've come back. You haven't changed a bit. Well, your hair might be a bit darker."

"Well, I came here because I found this." I pulled out the paper and set it on the glass table in front of me. She leaned forward, glanced at it, and leaned back up.

"See? I knew those posters were a good idea. I mean, it certainly took quite a while, but I knew it would work. So, where have you been?"

"All kinds of places," I answered. "I've been in New York for the past few months."

"Ooh, New York. That sounds exciting. May I ask what you're doing there?"

"I work at a boutique-"

"I'm sorry, I meant, why are you in New York? Why didn't you come back here?"

"See, that's the thing. I had no idea I was even from here. I woke up in my apartment with absolutely no memory at all, and I've been trying to trace myself back home. Back here."

"So, you're still experiencing your lapses in memory?"

"Yes. I need you to tell me everything you can about me, because I'm hoping I'll remember."

"Of course, honey. Now, let me see," she sat back in her chair and looked at the ceiling.

I felt a nudge from Archie, who pointed to a photograph by the couch. It was Janet, and the man next to her I guessed was Lyle. Below them was a young boy, around fourteen or fifteen, who I guessed was Aaron.

"How come you're not in that picture?" Reece asked.

Janet sat up and looked at us. "That was taken years and years ago. Before we found you."

"Found me? You mean I'm not your daughter?" My heart sank slowly.

"You're not our real daughter, almost, though. Oh! That reminds me: Aaron came back! He came back home! He's been gone ever since you disappeared. He and Lyle are out to the hardware store right now. They'll be back soon."

I wanted to explode with questions, but I was so flabbergasted at the information that I couldn't find any voice to speak. I stared at the floor, focusing on my aching heart, trying to forget what I had just heard. Reece put his hand on my knee, and Maxine rubbed my back.

Outside, there was a loud truck roar. "Wonderful! They're back!" Janet shouted, jumping up from her chair, and standing by the door, like a stage actor, waiting for her cue. I could hear two men's voices growing closer and the door opened. Both men stopped in their tracks and stared at us.

"Honey, isn't it wonderful? Amy's come home!"

44

"Well, I'll be," Lyle said. He dropped his bag and stepped to me, bear hugging me to the point where I had to catch my breath. Over his shoulder, I could see Aaron standing close to the door, staring at me with a strange look on his face.

"Aaron, aren't you going to give Amy a hug? You've missed her so terribly, haven't you?" Janet said softly. Aaron stood frozen, his eyes piercing into me. Lyle had let go finally and I averted Aaron's gaze by looking at the floor.

"Come on, Aaron. You can't be mad still. She's come home," Lyle said. Aaron sulked for a moment, but at last, stepped forward and slowly put his arms around me. I hugged back, to be polite, and suddenly it was like I had melted an iceberg. His body relaxed and his grip tightened. "I can't believe it's you. I thought you were dead, that I had lost you forever," he whispered, his voice choking up. He moved his hands to my shoulders and held me out, getting a good look at me. "As beautiful as I remember."

"Well," Janet interjected. "Shall we get some dinner started?" Archie, Maxine and Reece stood up from the couch.

"Hey, who are your friends?" Aaron asked, taking his eyes off me, and noticing the others. Janet behind him was muttering to herself, "Oh my, what a terrible hostess. I didn't even ask, myself."

"This is Archie, and Maxine, my roommates. And this is Reece, my f –"

"Friend. I'm her best friend," Reece interrupted. I gave him a confused look and he winked at me. I couldn't understand why he said that but decided he must have some motive. I looked at Janet and Lyle, who just smiled and acknowledged everybody. Aaron's eyes stuck on Reece, who smiled and stuck out his hand for a shake. Aaron received the hand, never looking down, and they shook hands hard, neither looking away from each other. I could tell Aaron seemed suspicious.

"Well, let's move to the other room, and I'll get dinner started," Janet said, showing us to the hallway. We formed a single-file line, marching to the other room. I felt Reece's hand grab mine and then my ring slid off my finger. I turned my head to protest, but he whispered in my ear, "Just go with it, okay? Trust me."

We moved to the den, where there was a large TV and softer, lived-on couches. Maxine offered her assistance in the kitchen, which Janet accepted. Archie got comfortable in a reclining chair, as did Lyle. I sat next to Reece on the couch, and then Aaron sat on my other side, wedging me between them.

"Aaron, honey, Amy was telling me before you got here that she's been in New York City for the past few months," Janet called from the kitchen, making conversation.

"How'd you get there?" Aaron asked.

"I don't know. I just woke up there one day, and now we're trying to retrace my past."

"So, you're still having your amnesic episodes? Did you remember us at all?"

I shook my head. "Yes, I'm still having episodes, and no I don't remember you. May I ask how everyone knows about that, though? The postman who gave us this address knew too."

Aaron looked down at his hands, trying to figure out what he wanted to say. "It was an accident. You bumped your head and at the hospital when you woke up, you had forgotten. We tried helping you and you would get better, but after a while you would just forget again."

"Yeah, that sounds like me," I grumbled. "Do you have any pictures or anything that I could look at? I'd like to see if that could bring something back." Asking about the pictures reminded me of what Janet had said not five minutes earlier. My heart still felt very heavy, but I knew that I needed to set that pain aside so I could learn what happened.

Aaron bounded up off the couch and sprinted upstairs, quickly returning with a small album, which he set on my lap. The first picture was of Janet, Lyle, Aaron and the girl I confirmed was me. They had been right: with the exception of my darker shade of blonde, nothing else had changed.

"This is the family portrait we had taken professionally," he pointed, then turned the page. "And here is when we went to my Cousin Jeff's party, and this one is from our first official date. We went to dinner –"

"Date?"

"Well yeah. That's what couples do, right?"

"*Couple*?"

"Yes, Amy. What did you think?"

"I thought this was more of a platonic relationship. Like a brother and sister sort of thing. I mean, it says my last name is Bennett on this poster and your mom said I was almost her daughter."

He turned the page to a picture of the two of us, sitting in front of the den fireplace, holding out my hand, exposing a huge diamond ring. "You were almost her daughter because you were almost my wife."

45

I felt like fainting; I felt like vomiting. I even felt like abruptly making a run for the door. Now, I was starting to understand why Reece had denied our relationship; he saw this coming. The Bennetts had adopted me as a wife for their son, Aaron. They had found me God knows where, and took me in, harvesting me for Aaron. He even said I'd forgotten a few times, and I could only imagine what kinds of things they filled my head with, instead of telling me the truth.

I was growing frustrated. "Okay, somebody please tell me exactly what's going on. Start from the beginning," I demanded.

The noise in the kitchen stopped; everything went silent. "Go ahead," Lyle nodded to Aaron.

"Well, I was just leaving church, after my study with Father Kent, and I was rushing to get to the store before they closed. As I turned a corner, you were coming at me and we smacked into each other. You fell backwards and bumped your head on the side of a streetlamp and passed out. We weren't very far from the hospital, just a few blocks, so I carried you. I called my parents and waited while you were being examined by the doctors. They brought you to a room and I stayed there, hoping you would wake up so I could apologize.

"I watched you sleeping on the bed, and I couldn't stop thinking how beautiful you were, like an angel. I knew that there was a reason for us meeting like this. Everything happens for a reason. Right before my parents came, you woke up and had no idea where you were or who you were, but you didn't seem remotely scared one bit, and you smiled at me, and I knew I was in love with you. It was fate. My parents offered to let you stay with us, until you could get back on your feet, but they began to grow to love you too. Mom called you Amy, and that's how it began.

"I proposed to you, and then you forgot a couple of times, but you seemed to be getting better and then, one day, you were supposed to meet me at the church for our couples counseling and you never showed up. I searched for you desperately, as everyone figured you had forgotten and run off, unknowingly. I refused to accept that, I didn't want to think that after all we had shared, you could forget enough to leave. I feared that you had been kidnapped and killed or something. The point was, you were suddenly gone, and I lost my mind. The next thing I knew, I was pushing myself deep into my ministry, and I found myself on a plane to Costa Rica to do mission work, which is where I've been for a year."

Janet appeared at his side and whispered, "Why don't you show her the room?"

He nodded and helped me off the couch and took me upstairs. At the end of the hallway was a closed door, which he opened and I stepped inside. There was a small bed and a dresser in the corner. On top of the dresser was a pile of papers that I picked up and scanned: wedding plans. Aaron's voice came up behind me, so close, his breath heated my neck. I jumped.

"We left the room exactly the way it was when you left, hoping you'd come back to it." He moved to a drawer in the dresser and opened it. "This is all you had on you when I found you." He lifted up a hooded jacket and a small purse. "I know I shouldn't have, but in the hospital, I peeked in your purse for some sort of identification, but all I found was this airplane ticket. It says MT on it, and you didn't know where you were from, and I was afraid you'd go back, so I pretended not to know, and I hid it in this pocket here. I'm sorry." He pulled the ticket out of a hidden pocket and handed it to me.

I sat on the bed, perusing the various papers, the ticket and the jacket. I was trying to find something that would send me a memory, but I wasn't finding anything. I picked up a picture of a church, the very one I assumed the Bennetts frequented, and an image flashed in my head. I closed my eyes, looking for it again. I was standing on the lawn in front of the church for a long moment; the sky was darkening in the background. Then, I watched myself walk away.

"Amy? Are you alright?"

"Yes, I'm fine. I just zoned out for a minute." I blinked a few times and pretended to get back to sorting through the papers.

"So, that friend of yours, what's his name?" Aaron asked casually.

"Reece?"

"Yeah. Um, how long have you guys been friends?"

"I don't know. You know, I forget," I replied, knocking on the side of my head.

"Right, so, he might not even be a friend of yours then. He could be some stranger that's playing up your handicap. He could be using you."

"What could he possibly want from me? I don't have money, I don't have model looks, I'm not famous, and I'm not promiscuous. Reece isn't using me. He's not like that."

"How do you know? You've said you don't even remember how you became friends, so how can you be absolutely sure?"

"I'm absolutely sure because I trust him. I trust him with my life. Most people wouldn't stick around too long when you forget everything about them from week to week, but he stays."

"Are you really just good friends, or is there something else going on between you?"

I hesitated, unsure of whether to just tell him the truth or not. He took my silence as an answer and made a sulky face. I rolled my eyes, remembering I had been instructed to play along.

"No, nothing. We're just good friends. Best friends," I said. "Can we please go now?"

We headed back down the stairs, to the den; where it appeared nothing had gone on, save for a staring contest between Lyle, Reece and Archie. I plopped down next to Reece, flanked by Aaron. I stared straight ahead at the fireplace. Reece watched my face and then looked at his hands as Aaron snapped his head in Reece's direction.

"So, what was up there? What did you find?" he asked quietly. I opened my mouth to speak but was interrupted.

"All of her stuff. Clothes, her purse, *our* wedding plans," Aaron said to Reece's irritated expression.

His mention of our wedding plans made my stomach turn. I couldn't describe how I was feeling. My heart had dropped, learning that Janet was not my real mother, and then it sank low into the bowels of my body learning that Aaron had actually been my fiancé and not, as I hoped, my brother. And now, I had conjured a clear memory of myself intentionally walking away from the church, from Aaron. I knew now that everyone assumed I had forgotten and skipped town, which seemed to be a normal response from me, but my memory proved otherwise. That time, I left on purpose.

The guilty feeling and churning stomach were intensified by the food smell in the kitchen. I was physically sick now and desperately wanted to leave. I wished we had never come here.

"Dinner's ready," Janet called. Relieved, if only from the tension in the den, I promptly stood up and went to the table. Janet and Maxine had prepared a lovely chicken dinner. We all sat down; again, I was wedged between my former fiancé and my new one.

Aaron asked that we bow our heads in prayer. "Gracious Lord, thank you for the meal we are about to receive, and thank you for the blessing you have bestowed on us with the return of my love, Amy..." I opened my eyes and looked around. I couldn't believe that I hadn't noticed before, but these people were anticipating on keeping me, again. And why wouldn't they? I escaped once, but I came back. That was their sign, right?

"Amen," everyone said, digging in.

"So," Janet began after a few minutes of silence. "What's in store for you all? Are you planning on going back to New York?"

"Um, we haven't decided," Maxine said. "Right now, our priority is finding Jackie's past."

"Who?"

"Oh, um, well, we've been calling her Jackie since we met her. You know how she forgets her own name," she recovered. Janet nodded slowly, apparently disapproving of the new name.

"Well, I hate to tell you that we don't know where Amy came from. I'm afraid that should make your plans difficult. But, hopefully you all could stay here. You seem so nice, and it would be great for Amy to have companions in the area."

"What?" Maxine and I both said at the same time. Archie coughed, choking on a piece of chicken. Janet ignored us and kept talking.

"Of course, you absolutely must stay in touch. I want to contact you when we have a new wedding date."

"What?" I said, this time, in unison with Reece. Again, Archie swallowed a large piece of chicken and coughed loudly.

Unexpectedly, I felt Aaron slip a ring on my finger and hold my hand. "What are you doing?" I asked, lifting our hands, showing the rest of the table.

"Come on, Amy. I'm just putting this ring back where it belongs. It's been practically burning a hole in my pocket since I showed you the photo album. I just couldn't wait to give it back to you."

That was it. I had had enough. Standing up, I slid the ring off. "I don't have room for anyone else's ring on my finger."

Aaron grabbed my hand. "Amy, I don't understand what's going on. I still love you."

"I'm not marrying you, Aaron," I said harshly.

He pursed his lips and then looked at Reece. "It's him, isn't it?"

I sighed, tired of pretending, just wanting to leave. "Yes. It's Reece. He's my fiancé."

The whole room went dead. Lyle and Janet's eyes bulged from their heads. "Excuse me?" asked Janet, trying to blink her eyes back into their sockets.

"Now Janet, let's be understanding," Lyle said, unexpectedly. "She does have amnesia. We couldn't expect her to be gone for so long and still remember about Aaron."

"It's my fault," Aaron said, his eyes locked on me. "If only I hadn't knocked her down so hard, none of this would have happened."

"I don't know about that Aaron. I honestly don't think we would have gotten married even if I did remember," I said, angrily. "Now, I'm extremely sorry to have ruined your wonderful dinner, really, I'm sorry, but I have to go." I moved around the table and walked toward the door. Archie, Maxine and Reece stood also, and followed, as did Aaron.

At the door, I heard, "Hey, what the –"I turned around and found Aaron grabbing Reece's shoulders, pushing him off the porch into the grass. Reece fell on his back and winced, as Aaron was suddenly on top of him, punching him in the head.

"Aaron? Aaron dear!" Janet called. She and Lyle stood watching from the porch.

"Aaron, stop it!" I yelled, with such ferocity that the rest of the onlookers turned to my reddened face. Aaron lightened his last punch, about to stop, when Reece's cast smashed the side of his face. Janet screamed as Aaron went rigid and slid off Reece, who immediately sat up and leaned over him, asking if he was alright.

"Get some ice," I shouted to Janet, who obeyed. Then, I squatted down over him and touched Reece's chest. "Are you okay?" I asked.

"Yes, I'm fine," he answered, dabbing his bleeding lip. I put my other hand on Aaron's face. He opened his eyes and looked around. Janet came rushing out with a towel full of ice and placed it on the wound. He laid there for a moment, then sat up and sent her and Lyle back to the house. Reece and I stayed at his side, to see if he was okay.

He took a series of large breaths. "How bad is it?" he asked me.

I touched his hand and moved the towel away. "Well, it's pretty red. I imagine it'll bruise soon, but it's not bleeding," I answered.

Aaron looked at Reece. "Could you give us a minute, please?" Reece stood up and joined Archie and Maxine, who was calling us a cab, in the driveway.

"You know," he panted. "Everyone assumed you had left town that night. They kept telling me, 'perhaps she had another episode. She'll remember and come back, hopefully.' But I refused to accept that you could forget me, as in love as we were. That's why I reasoned that you had to be dead. Seeing you here today, alive, I'm ashamed to admit made me angry, because it proved that they were right. I've been working a lot during my ministry studies on acceptance and letting things go, so, it's been quite a while since I've been angry about anything; it's not helpful to anyone, especially someone serving the Lord. I've had no trouble giving up things for God, but you were the hardest thing to give up and my poor behavior proves that I guess I haven't yet. I'm sorry. Forgive me."

"I'm sorry myself," I answered. "I shouldn't have led you to believe that I was here to stay. You remember when you said it was fate that brought me to you? Well, I'm sure our meeting did happen for a reason, but maybe not the reason you thought. I can't say for sure because I can't remember you, but that's how I know it wasn't right. See, I remember Reece. Every time I wake up and he's there, I remember something about him, which is how I know he was meant to be with me. And he takes exceptional care of me." Aaron looked at the grass, downtrodden. "Don't worry," I continued. "You will find what you need someday."

"If God wills it," he said.

"He will. You deserve to be happy."

"Thanks," he smiled. I stood up and helped him stand. "Can you do me a favor? Will you please keep in contact with me? I should like to know what becomes of my Amy."

"It's Jackie, now. Jackie Dawes."

"Oh, okay. I should like to know what becomes of you, Jackie."

I gave him a big hug as our taxi pulled up. Aaron said goodbye to Archie and Maxine, then shook Reece's hand. "I'm sorry for the way I acted. I see now that you're the better fit for Am -I mean, Jackie. Please continue to take care of her. She's a very special girl."

"That she is," Reece smiled. "I'll take excellent care of her."

"Well, that was interesting," Maxine said, as the taxi drove away. "Too bad we didn't get any information."

"No, actually, we did," I said, staring out the window. I reached into my pocket and pulled out the airplane ticket.

Maxine took the ticket for safety, and we made our bus route back to Phoenix. Perhaps it was out of embarrassment, but I waited until we were on the bus, where Archie and Maxine were sitting in front of Reece and me, before I started crying. It had been welling up inside me the whole day at the Bennett's house, and even as we left, I tried to keep my cool, until I finally couldn't anymore.

Reece hugged me, pressing my head to his chest, so I could cry in silence. He rested his head on top of mine and whispered over and over, "It's okay, everything's okay."

Eventually, I cried myself out, just in time for the switch to a new bus. Continuing the journey, I curled up in his lap, and we sat silently. Reece was kind enough to let me gather my thoughts before he asked me how I was feeling.

"I feel horrible. The last places we went, I felt like there was closure, like those people had moved on with their lives, but not here. I got my hopes up, thinking this was my real family, and they turned out not to be. They led me on. Of course, I guess I should feel bad for leading them on as well. I didn't mean to make them think I planned to stay."

"Jackie, you didn't lead them on. You told Janet that you were searching for your past, and they wouldn't listen. Sometimes, people think everything will go back to the way it was. They forget that people change," he said, kissing my cheek. He then reached into his pocket and pulled out my ring, putting it back on my finger. The phrase "people change" played over and over in my mind as I looked at it. I wondered if at the time, I had loved the ring Aaron gave me as much as I loved Reece's ring. *People do change, but not as much as I do,* I thought. *Could Reece handle me being a different person? Would Aaron have been able to?* I remembered Eleanor forgetting her own husband's name. Was this what I wanted? To be with someone even though I eventually won't remember them?

I slipped the ring off and handed it to Reece. My head on his chest could hear his heart beating faster. "I'm sorry about everything. I just don't think I can handle this right now."

He took a few deep breaths, before he put the ring back in his pocket, forced a small smile and said, "I love you Jackie, and always will. So if you change your mind, I'll be right here."

I faked a smile back, noticing that giving Reece his ring back didn't exactly make me feel better like I hoped it would. As the pain welled in my chest, I rolled away from him and closed my eyes.

46

It was late when we returned to our hotel. I slept most of the bus ride. The four of us shuffled like zombies to our room and crawled into our beds.

In the morning, unlike his usual kiss, Reece woke me up with a nudge. "Archie and I are going to breakfast. You coming? Maxine's down there already, talking to the concierge." I nodded and stretched my body out, feeling my pain worsen. I kept telling myself, it was the overall trip that was hurting my heart, not Reece. I was going to have to force myself to be happy.

"What's the plan for today?" I asked in between bites of pancakes.

"Well, I guess we're going to Montana. I've booked us a flight, that doesn't leave until late tonight, so we can do whatever you want today."

"Like what?"

"Anything."

"Something touristy?" I smiled.

"That would be preferred, yes," Maxine smiled back.

"Fine. The Grand Canyon, please," I said, with my mouth full.

It was another long bus ride, but it gave me the chance to catch up in my journal. Remembering yesterday and the Bennetts only depressed me, even though I knew it had to be written down. "I hope this works out," I muttered, mostly to myself.

"What?" Reece asked.

"Well, it's just that I was so let down by the Bennetts that I really hope when we do find out who I am; that it's not in vain."

The "oohs" and "ahhs" as we approached sent my journals back into my purse, and my face to the window. We got out of the bus and I froze, struck at how vast and beautiful the canyon was.

"What do you think?" Maxine asked beside me, staring at it too.

"It's big," I said. "I feel so small right now. It's nice to feel small once in a while. I'd like to see Razi try to find me here."

We walked across the glass bottom bridge, watching the abyss of canyon below our feet. It sent a chill through me; looking down, feeling like I was walking on air. The farther we walked out into the canyon, the higher up I felt. The realization sunk in, and my stomach knotted. I squeezed Reece's hand anxiously, no longer wanting to be over the canyon, but on safe ground again.

After walking the bridge and stretching our legs a little, we hopped on a guided bus tour that went all around the canyon, stopping at various points that the tour guide called the "most spectacular views". Indeed, all of the points were exceptional, and after three or four hours, when our bus returned to our starting point, the four of us found our own spectacular view with a bench, overlooking the whole canyon.

"Do you guys think I'm a bad person for walking away from the Bennetts like I did? I mean, the other times I ran, it was out of fear because I didn't recognize my surroundings. But, walking out on them was intentional. That memory is clear in my head," I asked out loud, perusing my thoughts.

"Jackie, of course not. You left because you didn't feel right. You should never go through with anything you don't feel right about," Maxine said reassuringly.

"Yeah," I said, staring down at my ringless hand. My mind was so clouded, I was desperate for a single clear thought to help me figure out what I wanted. "I think I need to take a walk."

Maxine stood up, but I halted her. "Alone, if you don't mind. Don't worry, I won't go far. I just need to think."

The path sloped, and soon, I found a new bench. Looking back, the others were no longer visible beyond the hill. I sat down, crossing my legs, hoping I could process something, anything.

An older couple stopped near the bench, standing at a rail, looking over the canyon. I watched them, as the man, put his arm around the woman and hugged her close. They stood there, staring into the canyon, and I smiled as the man leaned over and kissed the woman's cheek. I couldn't see their faces, but I knew they were happy. When they finally did turn around to move along, I noticed just how old they were. The woman looked as frail as Eleanor, the man did too, and they both had wide, honest smiles on their faces that made my stomach crave their happiness. I wanted to be able to go walking on a beautiful day holding hands and sharing kisses, filled with the joy of being alive and with someone I couldn't live without, and I wanted to be able to do that every day of my life, even when I became old and fragile. And instantly, like fire igniting my heart for the first time, I positively knew exactly who I wanted to spend my days with.

"Hey. You mind if I sit here?" I took my eyes off the disappearing couple. Reece was standing behind me, his hands in his pockets, his face a little downcast. I shook my head and he sat down.

He looked straight ahead at the canyon, silently, with his lips pursed. I suddenly felt horribly guilty to the point where my insides were shriveling. Without saying a word, I buried my face in my hands and started bawling.

"Shh, it's okay, Jackie. Everything is okay." I felt his broken arm around my back and his other arm wrap itself around my head. "It's okay. Don't cry," he chanted, resting his head on my back also.

I couldn't help it; my body felt like all the weight it had been building since we left New York was rushing out of me in the form of salt water and wailing. Reece didn't move; he just held me, which I realized was much needed. After a few minutes, my body began to tire and soon, my eyes stopped producing tears. I rubbed my face with my hands, as Reece slid me a tissue from his pocket.

"I'm sorry," I muttered, sitting up straight. I looked at his face, staring at me. The corner of his mouth lifted in a crooked grin.

"It's alright. What's the matter?" he asked.

"I don't know. I was so sure about everything, you know, with us, and then I wasn't."

"You got a little scared."

"I'm terrified."

"Terrified of what?"

I sighed, and looked down at Reece's hand, holding my shaking ones. Suddenly, the clouds in my mind parted and I was able to say what I had been trying to reason out. "I'm afraid of what's going to happen to me. Like, what if I have some sort of tumor developing and I just die suddenly. I don't want to put you through that."

"Okay," he replied, shooting me a funny glance. "But Jackie, that could happen to anybody. Don't think that it's more likely to happen just because you have amnesia. Nobody would want to put their spouse through that, but that's not really something you have any control over. What else you got?"

"Well, I started thinking about how we'd only just met, and I wondered if this was rushing things too much. What if you got tired of me and my forgetfulness, or worse, what if I woke up one day and didn't want to be with you?"

"I know that we haven't known each other that long, but honestly, we're going to have just met after every one of your episodes, and I know that; I'm aware of the challenges of being with you. But I also know that I'm in love with you and have never felt the same about anyone else in my life, and I've known that you were something special the first time I ever saw you walk into the café. It was confirmed the day I fought off Razi for you, a girl I hardly knew, I didn't even know your name, and yet, there I was, fish hooking that guy's mouth, trying to save you. I spent that whole night in jail thinking about you, reading your journals, trying to figure you out, and when I saw you on the street, looking for me, I just knew that I shouldn't let you get away if I could help it. The night I proposed, it wasn't my intention to marry you immediately; I just wanted a formal way of keeping a hold of you.

"I would never tire of you, either. I understand that you can't help it. Besides, it's kind of cute when you don't remember things; you act all weird around me, like you're falling for me all over again," he laughed, and I couldn't keep a smile off my own face because I knew it was true. I had to admit; maybe re-falling in love with him every time wouldn't be so bad.

"But my tastes can change, without me even realizing it. I don't want to wake up one day and not be in love with you."

"If that ever happened, I would do everything I possibly could to change your mind. I wouldn't give up. I don't want you to be afraid of marrying me. You couldn't possibly hurt me, unless you left."

"I'm sorry I've treated you so badly. You've been nothing but wonderful to me."

Reece cupped my face with his hands and pulled me in for a long kiss. Our foreheads touched and we both smiled at each other before he grabbed my hand and slipped my ring back onto my finger.

As we walked back to Archie and Maxine, I told him about that older couple. "I realized that's what I want. I don't care if I never remember you ever again. I want to grow old with you and be that happy even in old age."

"We will," he said. "I'll make sure of that."

We sat back down for at least another hour, watching the sun go down. "I want to stay here forever," I said.

"Well, we can't. The place closes in a few minutes," Maxine laughed.

"No, I mean, I want to stay in the desert like this. I don't want to search. I don't want to run. I'm tired of it."

"Are you sure that's what you want?" Reece asked.

"It's what I want right now. But I know that I might regret it later. If I didn't have something to find, or someone to hide from, I think I would like to disappear here."

I made sure we took as many photographs as possible before heading back to the bus for yet another long ride. Back at our hotel we had just enough time to pack our things and get to the airport. I hated to leave the beautiful desert; I had fallen in love with it over the past couple days, but I knew it was time to press on. If I didn't go now, I might never leave, and as tired as I was of running, I was deeply curious and anxious to find my real family.

I had been thinking of the possibilities since my disappointment with the Bennetts. I imagined that if they were not intended to be my real family, then my parents must be so much better. If I felt that strongly about seeing my actual parents, there was no way I could be let down.

47

Again, we had no starting point when we arrived in Montana, simply the airplane ticket, and nothing more. I had no new alias, or any new memories off the bat, so again, we checked into a hotel and Maxine got out a map and plotted.

The weather was much colder than Arizona, as it was nearly December. Archie, Maxine, and Reece dug out coats from their suitcases. I realized I didn't have one myself, so, despite Maxine's offer to go buy me a new coat, I just threw on a second jacket.

We decided to head out for a little food and maybe some drinks, and just down the street from the hotel, we found a little dive of a bar called The Lasso Saloon. We went in, sticking out like an entire sore hand, as we still hadn't seemed to have mastered the concept of dressing like locals.

"This way, it might be easier for us to find information," Maxine reasoned, laughing slightly. "If we blended in, we might not get anywhere."

The locals, of course, stared at us, holding still, but watching our movements like we were rattlesnakes entering a nest of prey. The saloon had been fairly empty, as we entered, but soon, it began to fill with younger and noisier crowds, all drinking and dancing endlessly.

Archie and Maxine left Reece and I standing at the bar, while they went out to attempt line dancing among the mob, who at first reacted to them as if they were aliens, but soon were drunk enough to just be happy to have two more people on the dance floor.

"I'll be right back," Reece yelled, and made his way across the floor to the bathroom. I took another little sip of my drink and continued to watch the dancing crowd, in which I had lost Archie and Maxine. A couple of guys dressed in skintight jeans and cowboy hats stepped up to the bar on either side of me to order some drinks. I pretended not to notice them staring at me as I continued searching for my friends.

"Howdy," The one to my left said, winking at me as I turned to look. I smiled, and took another sip, then looked away. "You don't look like you're from around here," he continued.

"I'm not," I said flatly, hoping he'd leave me alone.

"Well, what brings you to Helena?"

"Uh, I'm, um, I'm looking for somebody."

"Well, I sure know lots of people, maybe I could help ya. What's their name?"

"Uh, I don't know," I said, growing nervous, and peeking up over the crowd, hoping Reece would come back soon.

"How are you gonna find somebody if you don't know who you're looking for?"

"Story of my life," I muttered.

He took a large swig of his drink then leaned around me and nodded to the guy on my right. "Well, ma'am, my friend and I would be more than glad to help you find what you're lookin' for. Maybe we should go outside, where we can talk better."

"No, that's okay, really."

"I'm just trying to help ya," he smiled, touching my face. I winced and took a step away from the bar. His friend stepped up with me, grabbing hold of my arm. "Now, you can scream if you want to, but no one's gonna hear you in this noise." As he spoke, I heard a piercing scream from the corner and saw that it was a girl sitting on a railing, being lifted over the edge, and now was laughing. I looked to the dance floor where not one person acknowledged the scream. I dropped my drink, as he grabbed the other side of me, and the two of them hoisted me out of the bar. I prayed that Archie and Maxine had seen me leave, and that someone would come after me.

Outside, it was completely dark, except for one light hanging off the side of the building over the parking lot. The two men carried me to the wall and held me there.

"I think we should have a little fun first, ya know, before we get to talkin'." He pressed himself against me, squishing me to the wall. Then, slowly, his head touched my neck, his breath tickled as he stopped there for a moment. I wriggled as much as my body would allow, but nothing happened. I even moved my head back and forth, only to have it held down by the friend. In a last-ditch effort of panic, I did scream as well as I could having no breathing capacity.

"There ain't nobody out here," the friend laughed, and the man proceeded onward, moving his hand from my arm across my chest and down, pulling my shirt up, exposing my bra. I started to tense up, tears streaming down my face. The friend just stood there, hand on my forehead, laughing. Soon, I felt his hand slide from my breasts down my body, into my jeans and I went rigid.

I suddenly got an image of myself in a similar situation. I was against a wall, being held up like I was, by someone wearing a cowboy hat. In this image, he was doing the same things, only it was just one man, and when he moved his hand, I had a free arm clutching a towel, which I wrapped around his neck, choking him until he was down on the ground. But I started hitting him, with two hands, until I found blood on my hands. Then, shaking and crying, I rifled through his wallet, taking a wad of cash and I ran.

I opened my eyes again, trying to decipher if what I had been thinking was real. I tried to move my hand to hit him, but the friend's arm was blocking the way. The man's hand suddenly unbuttoned my pants and tugged at the side, trying to pull them down. I screamed again, crying harder, and wishing to God that someone would hear me.

My tears clouded my vision as I heard a loud thump. I looked up and the cowboy's face slid off my neck and down to the ground. Behind him, I found Reece, yielding his cast like a weapon. The friend let go of me and went after Reece. I fell to the ground, and hid my face in my arms, crying hysterically. I heard a shout that sounded like Maxine and when I looked up, I saw Archie going after him from behind, so Reece could get up. Maxine's body was now around me, blocking my vision, which I accepted warmly and held her close. I heard another thump, and I knew that he was down.

I heard some shuffling and felt a few more hands on my back and head, but I kept my face buried. Maxine shushed me like a baby, rocking me in her arms. "You're safe now, Jackie. We're here and you're safe. Let's get you back to the hotel. Can you stand up?"

I moved my face away and tried standing. Archie grabbed my hand and arm, holding me up, and then, we started walking back to the hotel in the dark. Archie had my arm around his shoulder to prop me up, while Maxine held my other arm, rubbing it comfortingly. Reece walked behind us. I tried to turn around to see his face, but with my own soaked in tears that were continually filling my eyes, I was finding it difficult to see and walk straight, let alone look behind me.

Once we got into the hotel room, Maxine took me to the bathroom so I could take a shower and calm down. I asked to be alone for a minute, and once she left, I wailed silently, while the hot water poured over me. I didn't stop myself, because the more I cried, the lighter I seemed to feel, like I was releasing an enormous weight from my shoulders. After a few minutes of intense sobbing, I heard a knock on the door, and I stood up and beckoned Maxine back in.

"The front desk lady wasn't going to give this to me, because she said they only offer them to people in the suites, but as I was coming back, the door to the laundry room was open, so I peeked my head in, and talked to the maid a little bit and she let me have this one. It's fresh from the dryer, so it's warm." She wrapped the robe around me, and then wiped my face with a regular towel, and then tapped my hair dry.

"Are you okay now?" she asked.

"Maxine, that's happened before," I whispered.

48

"What happened before?"

"That. What just happened outside that bar. As that guy was putting his hands on me, the memory flashed in my mind. It was almost exactly the same." I told her of the memory, and how I had stolen the man's money and ran.

She waited with me while I put my pajamas on under the robe, before stepping out. It was really late, nearly two in the morning. Archie was in bed with the TV on, and Reece lay in the other bed, watching too. Both of them had serious looks on their faces, Reece's had a hint of sadness to it. They turned their attentions from the TV to the bathroom door, as Maxine and I stepped out. Reece sat up and threw the blankets off his legs, about to stand. I tiptoed over to the bed, slipping the robe off and crawled in on the other side. He put the blankets back over himself and then threw them over me. His hand brushed over my stomach and I jumped. It hovered over my arm, like it was polarized, and drew it back. Then, he watched my face carefully. I could tell he wanted to kiss me, but he again withdrew.

I hated this. I didn't mean to jump, but after what happened, I was on edge. It wasn't fair that it was now affecting my relationship. My eyes started to water again, looking at him watching me, as the lights turned off. I lifted my hand to wipe my tears, when his hand touched my face first.

"Please don't cry, Jackie. Please," he whispered, pressing his face up to mine. I wrapped my arms around him and he held me. My tears quickly dried, and I felt great relief, as I yawned and closed my eyes.

In the morning, I lifted my head off Reece's chest and found him awake, staring at the ceiling, that serious expression still on his face. I looked over at the empty bed across the room. Archie and Maxine must have gone down to breakfast. Reece didn't look at me, which I found surprising. I shifted myself up so that my head was parallel with his and kissed his cheek. He turned his head to me and smiled weakly. "Hey," he said.

"Hey," I answered.

"How are you feeling?"

"I feel good, surprisingly. How do you feel?"

"Lousy," he replied. "Maxine told me about your memory. I'm sorry I left you alone. I shouldn't have taken so long to find you. I'm so sorry."

"It's okay," I sighed, with a slight smile. "You saved me."

"But I should have been there faster. When I came back and you were gone, I assumed you were out dancing, so I stood at the bar for a minute, before I saw Archie and Maxine without you. Then, I looked at the bar and found your drink next to two others, and I knew something was wrong. I should have known right away, and then, you wouldn't have had to go through that."

"Reece, it's fine. I'm okay. I'm okay because you were there. You were right to assume I was with Archie and Maxine, so I don't blame you at all. You just need to know that you came to my rescue and I'm wonderful now. You're my hero," I smiled.

He smiled back, a bit stronger, gazing at my face. "You know that I love you more than anything in the world."

"Absolutely. If you didn't, you wouldn't be saving me all the time. And I love you most." His smile widened, like he was coming back to life, and finally, he kissed me.

We walked down to the breakfast room hand in hand. Archie was at the bar making himself a cup of coffee. Maxine was sitting at a table, absorbed in a map.

"Are you ready to do this today? Or do you want a little more time?" she asked. I knew the agenda. It was the same as always. First, we would go to a police station and ask for any missing persons reports and from there, it was a bus trip out to somewhere, hoping to find what we were looking for.

"I don't need any more time," I said. "I want to find out who I was. Who I am."

At the police station, Reece and Archie waited outside. Reece was afraid that news from the brawl outside the saloon would have no doubt travelled, and the police might be more apt to question strangers in town, particularly casted ones. The police were friendly to Maxine and me, politely taking my fingerprints, and checking their computers. The fingerprints came back clean, and the sheriff handed me a stack of papers of missing women throughout most cities in Montana. Maxine held each picture up to my face making comparisons. "Too thin, too fat, too dark," she would repeat after each one. A couple of the reports had no picture to go by, only a description. Maxine read the descriptions out loud, but again, we decided that none of them were a match. The pile got smaller, but hadn't yet ended, when we were approached by a younger cop, who I noticed had been staring at me from his desk outside the sheriff's office. He knocked politely and the sheriff let him in.

"I'm sorry to interrupt, sir," he said, politely.

"It's fine, Cody. What can I help you with?" The sheriff asked.

"I noticed these ladies were looking through missing persons reports."

"Yes, Cody, now what do you want?"

"It's just that," he looked over to me, "you look very familiar to me."

"Do I?" I asked. "Do you know how you know me?"

"I'm sorry, I can't place it. I've been over at my desk for the past twenty minutes trying to figure it out."

"Well, think, Cody. Think hard," the sheriff prodded.

He was quiet for a moment. "How long have you been a cop?" Maxine asked.

"Uh, just about four years now, ma'am. I started out in Geraldine and then about a year and a half ago, I was transferred here to Helena. I got hurt, so I ended up here doing paperwork."

"Is is possible that you remember her from Geraldine?" Maxine continued.

"Why, I might have to say yes." I stood up and walked over to him, looking closely at his face, hoping he was doing the same to me.

"Think," I said. "Do you remember me?"

He stared into my eyes, and suddenly muttered, "Lisa." He blinked his eyes hard, and then tipped his head, looking at the side of my face. "The scar."

"Cody?" The sheriff asked.

"You are from Geraldine. Your name is Lisa. You were a bartender. I used to visit the bar a lot right before I was transferred. Couldn't do much else when I was injured."

"What else? What else can you tell me?"

"Nothing much. I remembered you being new to town, and then about six or seven months later, I was here, doing some paperwork when I received a missing person report from Geraldine." He grabbed the pile from Maxine and began rifling through it. "Here it is; the bottom of the pile." The flyer had a black and white picture on it. The girl had my round face and a lighter shade of hair. I knew it was me when I saw the white towel in her hand. It was just like in my memory. We took the paper and thanked the sheriff and Deputy Cody. Outside, we showed Archie and Reece the paper and quickly headed to a bus station.

"He said I used to be a bartender," I said to Reece on the bus, "Which would explain my memory. I had a towel in my hand that I was using to choke the man. It obviously happened outside of the bar where I worked."

As we exited the bus in Geraldine, there was an older gentleman standing in the station, waiting. He watched us walk through the station, and then I noticed him following us out. We stopped at a bench outside, unsure of where to go next. There was a wispy cough behind us and I turned around to find the old man standing there. I was immediately suspicious, so I glared at him. He looked down, and then took a step forward to us, facing me to talk.

"Lisa?" he whispered almost inaudibly.

I raised my eyebrows in acknowledgment.

"You, uh, you coming from Helena?" he asked, quietly.

"Yes," I said, growing reserved.

"You come from the police department?"

"Yes," I answered again, squinting my eyes.

"Good, good. Come on, then." He started walking to a busted old truck, possibly older than he was. Maxine and I climbed into the cab with him, while Archie, Reece and our bags sat in the bed.

"Deputy Cody contacted me a few hours ago. Said there was couple of gals headed this way, and one of 'em was Lisa. Asked me if I would kindly take ya to the bar. I sure didn't believe it til I seen ya, but I still remember yer face. Good to have you back." I didn't want to ask him who he was, because I felt like it would be rude, so I kept quiet.

The rickety truck pulled up to a miniature barn-shaped building with a faded sign just reading "BAR" on top. The sun shone on the slats of wood, each single board a different darker shade of rust than the next. The man walked in first, holding the door for us while we followed. The bartender, an older woman with hair like the rusty boards, looked up from the glass she was cleaning.

"How's it, Barney?" she asked in a deep smoky voice that rivaled Maxine's or Carmelina's.

"Jes fine, Tess. Jes fine. Get me a shot of whiskey, will ya?"

"Whiskey? What's this? An occasion?"

"It sure is," he said sitting at a stool, flanked by the four of us. "Look what ol' Barney's found." He motioned at me as Tess set down his shot and picked up another glass. She gazed at me and her eyes grew large and there was suddenly a loud ting, as the glass fell and shattered on the floor.

"Oh my God, oh my God!" She completely disregarded the shards on the floor and ran around the bar area to our stools. She grabbed my face tightly and swung it back and forth, scanning every inch of my face, saying "oh my God." I smiled politely, even though I had no memory of her. She seemed very attached to me, as I watched her eyes flood with tears. "I've missed you so terribly, Lisa. Where have you been?"

"It's a long story," I said.

She looked around the empty bar. "I've got all the time in the world."

She sat at a stool and listened to my story, starting with my life in New York, and working my way backwards, to the most recent events. By this time, I knew it was best to not go into any details involving Razi, citing a mere "run in with an old acquaintance" as my reason for hightailing it out of New York. "So now I'm here, trying to find out who I am and where I came from," I concluded.

She stared. "That's fascinating! Well, dear, here's what I know: you came into my bar here one night. Didn't talk to anybody, and when I started closing up shop at two, you were still sitting here. I told you that you had to leave and I walked out with you, and noticed you had no car. I offered a ride and asked where to, but you didn't know. 'A hotel, I guess,' you said. I asked where you came from, but again, you didn't know. You seemed harmless enough, so I offered you a place to stay if you were just passin' through, and eight months later, you suddenly left." She sighed loudly as she finished.

"So I stayed with you the whole time?"

"Yes. After I took you home, I fed ya some, even though it was late. I don't know if it was the hot soup in your belly or what, but you relaxed a little and started giving me more than short answers. You said that you had planned on passing through, but you didn't know where you were going to go, or what you were going to do, so I offered my home and a job at the bar to earn a little cash and make up your mind about where you were going.

You ended up liking the bar, and we became real close. You were like the daughter I never got to have."

I cringed as she spoke the last part, thinking hardheartedly of the Bennetts. She laughed at my face. "You used to enjoy hearing that from people."

"It's just that I had a bad experience with my last mother figure."

"Oh, that lady. Well, I was nothing like that. I suppose we were more like good friends, but I liked to think of us as being closer than that," she chuckled.

Tess called in another bar maid to take over so she could take us to her house. She was excited, hoping that I would have any memories, like I had in my other stops. I remembered the image of the molestation outside the bar, debated whether or not to tell Tess about that, and hoped that I would produce better memories.

Her house was small, but quaint, hidden in a patch of trees, all by its lonesome. There was a swing chained to the porch ceiling, and little empty pots on the steps. I imagined in the summer, when it was hot, the pots would be full of flowers, and the swing would be in continuous use.

Inside, we were hit with a brick of heat. "Ooh, it's toasty. I forgot to turn off the heat while I was gone. Guess it's a good thing I came home," Tess said, throwing off her coat. "Please, please make yourselves at home. Take off your coats, sit down." I stared at everything in the kitchen. The whole home was nothing short of cozy. Cookbooks filled the shelves, pictures filled the walls, and every corner had something to look at. Tess got out a kettle and warmed up some water to make some tea.

"Cocoa for you, dear. You never were a tea person." Then, she went into the other room and got out a photo album. "I don't have many pictures of you, but there are a few, I suppose."

I opened the book to the first page, where I found a picture of a much younger Tess, with a man and a little red headed baby. "Is this your family?" I asked.

Tess closed her eyes and sighed. It was clear something about the mention of her family hurt her, and I immediately regretted asking. "Yes. That was my husband Charlie, and daughter Olivia. They, they're gone now."

"May I ask what happened?"

"She was four years old the first time I noticed she was sick. The doctors said it was brain cancer, and where it was meant it was impossible to operate on. He gave her six months to live. She died three weeks later. Charlie and I were absolutely insane with grief. We left our house in the city and holed up in our cabin here. I poured myself into the bar, working night and day, trying not to think about her. Charlie poured himself glass after glass of whiskey. Then, one night, a little over a year later, I came home one night and found him gone. His things were missing. I heard he moved to Helena. Probably drank himself to death for all I know."

"Didn't you ever want to find him?" Maxine asked.

"No. I didn't see a point in tracking him down. He wasn't going to come home. He didn't want to be here. Nothing I could do would change his mind, so why even try." There was a choke in her voice now that hadn't been there before.

"I'm sorry I asked," I apologized.

"It's fine. You didn't remember," she smiled, pressing a finger to the edge of her eye.

I continued flipping through the book silently. Each page had picture after picture of Olivia. "She would have been twenty-six," Tess murmured. "I guess that's especially why I took such a liking to you. You were the daughter I was missing all this time."

Finally, I stopped at a page with some pictures of people at the bar. There was a sign reading "HAPPY BIRTHDAY TESS" in the background. I found me, huddled in with the group of women, possibly other bartenders. I actually looked genuinely happy. "You planned that party for me."

We continued to flip through the album, Tess looking over my shoulder. There weren't many pictures of me at all: a couple more at the bar, and then two or three at the house. The very last page was a photograph of Tess and me, at the bar, for her birthday. "That was the last picture I had of you, and the only one of you and me. I thought about putting it in a frame, but after you left, I was sort of too upset to get it out. I knew you were planning to leave, but I guess I had hoped you would stay. I've been abandoned too many times in my life." She sat down in an empty chair and took a deep breath, watching her hands in her lap. "If you don't mind me asking, why did you leave? Were you planning to run that whole time? Or don't you remember?"

"No, actually, I do remember. It's the only thing I've remembered since I got here," I said, detailing my vision of the incident. I choked up thinking about it over and over, and Tess raised her hand to her mouth in horror.

"Oh my God," she whispered. "Randall West."

49

"Who?"

"Randall West. That's who it was. I remember that night- I remember it so clearly now. I was at the bar, wondering where you had run off to, when Barney came running in, yelling for me to call an ambulance. I did and went outside, and Randall West was laying there, his face covered in blood. He was in the hospital for two whole days. Never told anybody what happened to him. Now I know why."

"Is he still around?"

"Yeah, he is."

"I want to see him."

"You *want* to see him?"

I thought for a moment. "I think I do."

"Okay," she hesitated. "I'll take you to him tomorrow." Tess was quiet for a moment, before she looked at the clock and said, "Oh, I better get some dinner started. Why don't you go take a tour of the house?"

Maxine offered her help, and Archie, Reece and I got up and strolled through the house. The next room off the kitchen was a living room, just as cozy: lots of shelves full of books, lots of pictures hanging on the walls. The front windows were decorated with various hanging shapes of colored glass, leaving spots of color around the room. We moved around the corner to the stairs, which creaked as we went up, each step had its own pitch. At the top of the stairs was a bathroom, then to the left there were two bedrooms. The one at the end of the hall looked lived in, while the one closest to the bathroom was closed. I guessed that probably had been my room, so we opened the door.

The room was stale, with cobwebs in the corners. The walls were a dull shade of blue, but as I looked closer, I realized it was the same color as my room in New York. The room wasn't terribly large, but there was room enough for a bed, a small dresser and a little table. I opened a dresser drawer that had some shirts, then another drawer with some pants. I opened two more drawers of clothes, and then the bottom drawer, where I found an empty knapsack. I pulled it out and examined it. It was dingy, and in black letters on the side, it read: "Vida Traveling Circus, Wichita, KS". Below that, in felt marker was the name "Lisa". I closed my eyes and envisioned myself walking into this same blue room, in almost the same condition as now, pulling the knapsack off my back and sitting on the bed looking around. I blinked a couple times and told Archie and Reece that I remembered the room.

The bag felt heavy, so I opened an inside pocket, and produced a heavy mirrored compact and a couple metal jars that held face paint. The compact had an amazingly intricate pattern on the front which I ran my fingers over, feeling all of the curves. The nearly dried jars of paint, I dabbed a finger in, examining their colors and consistencies.

"Is that yours?" Reece asked over my shoulder. I shrugged.

"It must be," I said, "It says 'Lisa' on it, so it must be, but what on earth did I have to do with the circus?"

Archie chuckled, obviously trying to picture me as some sort of circus performer. I guessed by the intensity of his laugh that he was probably imagining me as something ridiculous, like a trapeze artist or human cannonball. I started laughing about that myself.

I brought the bag with me when we went back down the stairs to the kitchen and showed it to Maxine and Tess. "That was the only thing you had on you when I found you at the bar, and I noticed it said "Lisa" so I called you that. At first, you didn't respond, and I said it again.

"I said, 'Your name is Lisa, right? Like it says on the bag?' Then you looked at the letters, smiled and said, 'Oh yeah, that's it. Lisa.'"

"So, our next stop is going to be Wichita, then?" Maxine asked, setting plates down to the table.

"I guess so," I answered.

"Oh, but you don't have to go right away, do you? Can't you stay a few days?" Tess asked impatiently.

"Of course," I replied. "We don't have to get there right away."

After dinner, it began to snow. I couldn't remember the snow, and I went outside to watch it. I took a step off the porch, letting the flakes fall on my hands, and my face and eyelashes. I laughed, twirling like a child. I heard some laughter from inside, and realized the others were watching me. I stopped, embarrassed, and bent down, cupping a handful of snow. The door squeaked, but I didn't turn around. Then, a mass of wet snow hit my back. I looked to see Reece standing out in the snow with me, and Archie, Maxine and Tess on the porch. I smiled, and balled up my handful of snow, throwing it at him.

Soon, Archie was joining in, and the three of us ran around, laughing hysterically, chucking snow at one another while Maxine and Tess looked on from the porch. When we finished, we trudged back inside, cold and wet, but laughing still.

Maxine and I took some rags to dust my old bedroom, wiping the cobwebs out, and putting clean sheets on the bed. Tess dug out as many sleeping bags and blankets as she could find for all of us. Maxine took the couch downstairs, and Archie claimed a sleeping bag on the floor. The bed in my room was a tiny twin, so Reece made up a sleeping bag on the floor beside it.

The house was old and made various creaking noises. Despite the creaks, I fell asleep quickly, and I slept well. The amazing scents of coffee and bacon woke me in the morning, and I hopped up, almost stepping on Reece, who was still sleeping. I crept on my tip toes, trying not to make any noise, but even on tip toe, the floors squeaked. Downstairs, the scents were more potent. Archie was still lying in his sleeping bag on the floor, but I found Maxine and Tess in the kitchen, cooking something that smelled amazing, and chatting, like old friends.

“My mother will never completely understand, but she’s talking to me again. I’ve been trying to forget who I used to be these last few years, but going on this journey with Jackie, helping her find herself, it’s really helping me realize not to forget who I was, because that’s part of who I am today.”

“I’m really happy you feel that way, Max,” I interrupted.

"Good morning," Tess smiled. "How did you sleep?"

"I slept extremely well. I was so comfortable," I said, stretching out a bit as I sat down at the table.

"Where's your other half?" asked Tess.

"He's still sleeping. I didn't want to wake him. He hasn't slept very well lately."

"Neither have you, for that matter," Maxine scolded.

Maxine handed me a cup of hot cocoa and a plate of eggs and bacon. I all but devoured the plate. I didn't realize how hungry I was. I heard some shuffling upstairs, and soon Reece came into the kitchen, scratching his unkempt hair and yawning.

"Good morning," I said. He muttered incoherently and then kissed me. Before he had even sat down, Maxine had a plate and a cup of coffee on the table for him.

Archie followed suit, and then Maxine and Tess finally sat down to eat as well. After breakfast, we dressed, and then piled into Tess' car, and she drove us through Geraldine to Randall West's house.

Randall's house was held together by two planks of wood. The foundation was shifted, and the house was on an angle. The shutters were broken; a few were missing completely. It didn't look livable, let alone able to hold five more people.

Tess didn't even knock; she opened the door and yelled his name. A murmur came from another room, and the rest of us followed Tess in, hesitantly. Randall's floors creaked, but it was a different sound than Tess' house. These creaks were scary, and dangerous. The house looked trashed, like no one had lived there in years. And it smelled awful, like a thousand dead things had rotted there in the house. Tess yelled Randall's name again, like we were playing a game of Marco Polo. We found him in the back of the house in an overstuffed chair, with slashes in the fabric, and stuffing falling out. There was a familiar cowboy hat resting over his face, and an empty bottle in his hand.

Tess lifted the hat off his face, and he jumped as the sun hit his skin. "What?" he grumbled.

"I got someone who wants to talk to you, Randall. You've got some explaining to do, and not just to her," Tess said sternly.

Randall sat up and adjusted the hat onto his head. "Who?"

"Me," I answered quietly.

Randall's eyes squinted, his vision slowly focusing, and then enlarged. "You," he said, clearly. "What do you want?"

"I need to know what happened the last time you saw me."

"I'll tell ya. You beat me half to death, course, I was too drunk to fight back, is all, then you stole my money."

"I know all that," I explained. "But you tried to take advantage of me. I need to know what led up to that."

"I forget," he grumbled, sucking at the empty bottle.

"Why don't you sober up before she beats you again?" Tess threatened, holding out a thermos of coffee. Randall eyed her suspiciously, then grabbed the thermos, and took a couple swigs.

"I need to think a moment. I'm a little out of sorts these days," he said. He then closed his eyes and started to talk, as if in a trance. "It was the night of Tess' birthday party. We were all celebratin' and havin' a good time, me, maybe a better time than I should have been havin'. I was hittin' on ya, I don't deny that. I tended to do that from time to time. You was bartenderin' and suddenly you got a headache. You thought maybe the loud music was getting to ya, so you took a couple aspirins and rested your head on the bar.

"Then, you fell over. One of the other girls, Sarah, I think, came running over to you and helped you up, asking ya questions, but you weren't responding. She said you needed to get some air, so I volunteered to take you outside. I can't even believe she agreed to that, to be honest with ya. Well, I led you out, and you kept looking around mumbling, like you didn't know where you were. Then you asked me who I was, and I got to thinkin' if you didn't know who I was, ya probably wouldn't remember nothin' about that night, and I was kinda particular about ya, so I went for it, and the next thing I know, I was on the ground, and you was punching me in the face. Then I woke up in the hospital a few days later, with my face all swollen, and they were saying you disappeared."

We were silent for a moment. Reece put his hand on my shoulder, and I felt his grip tightening as Randall went on with his story. To calm him, I put my hand on his. After he gave his testimonial, the rest of us huddled to converse.

"It sounds like you had your episode at the bar," Maxine surmised. "Then Randall scared you and the way you beat him probably frightened you too. I'm guessing you ran because you thought he was dead or something."

We separated and I looked at Randall fiercely, as the image ran in my mind. "Now I do apologize for stealing your money, but you had no right to take advantage of me like that and there's no reason why I shouldn't hurt you right now," I said, standing up suddenly with my fists clenched. Everyone reacted: Archie and Reece were up behind me, ready to hold me back, Maxine was leaning in front of me, blocking my path, Tess froze in fear, and Randall pulled his hat down to his chest and shivered, staring at my fists. "But now I see you're just nothing but a drunk, and I'm a better person, so I'm just going to walk away and let you destroy yourself." I unclenched my hands and I headed for the door, feeling the anger leave my body little by little as I left the house. I climbed back into Tess' car, focusing my eyes on my white hands, which were shaking slightly. I felt a tear roll down my cheek and I pushed it away. I was not going to let myself dwell on Randall West. I was going to forget about him and forget what he tried to do to me.

I wasn't sitting in the car long before the others came out and we left.

"That went well," Tess said. I snorted, thinking she was being sarcastic, but she shot me a look that told me she was perfectly serious. "He deserved that. He deserved another beating. I can't believe that bastard did that, taking advantage of you, especially with you being in a fragile mental state and all."

We were silent all the way back to the house. When we got there, Maxine was quickly at the phone, talking to anyone and everyone she could about the Vida Traveling Circus. Tess showed me to her computer, which I used to make a new journal entry for Chrissy to read. I had over a hundred comments on my last entry, which I sat and read through. Chrissy's was rather sad, telling me about how lonely she was down in the basement of Brandisham's all by herself.

"Well, the circus is still traveling down south, until next week, but then after that, they'll be back to Wichita for the rest of the winter," Maxine said, hanging up the phone.

"So, can we stay here?" I asked, looking at Tess.

"Absolutely. I would like nothing more," she smiled.

We bided our time over the next week; we went with Tess to the bar, and Maxine and Reece went right to waiting on and cleaning the tables. Archie set himself to reworking Tess' finances. I tagged along, hoping to conjure any memories. I didn't come up with any distinct visuals, but I did find that I had a familiarity with the bar. I instinctively grabbed an apron from the shelf under the cash register and walked right over to the cupboard of glasses and began to clean them without even thinking.

Her usual customers were also glad to see me. I figured their happiness was more directed toward the fact that with me in town, Tess' spirits were much higher. I couldn't count the number of times one of the old men told me how great a woman Tess was, and how she had such an amazing spark when she was happy. "It's nice to see that spark again," they would say.

Even though she knew I wasn't planning on staying, Tess really wanted to have a "Welcome Back" party for me.

"I just want to celebrate seeing you again, and hopefully, we'll be celebrating return visits in the future," she said.

The other bartenders decorated the place with streamers and balloons, making the inside look strikingly similar to the birthday party photo. Maxine baked and decorated a cake and there was a surprisingly big turnout. All the regulars wanted to come see how I was doing and give me well wishes.

50

Seven days flew by at Tess' place, and it was time to move on. We had to get to Wichita. Tess hated to see us go but understood completely. She drove us all the way to the airport and cried as she hugged us all. Maxine and I shed a few tears as well. Tess was one of the best people I'd ever met in my life, and I hated to leave her behind. "You are all absolutely welcome back to see me any time, and please do come back. Now, go. Go before you change your minds," she said, wiping her eyes.

On the plane, I planted my head on the window and watched outside solemnly. Reece put his chin on my shoulder. "Sad to leave?"

I nodded. "I wish that had been the end of the journey. I wish she had been my real mother, so I could have stopped searching."

"Well, you can stop searching at anytime, but I know you really don't want to." I looked at his face and kissed his nose, knowing that he was absolutely right. I could stop if I wanted, but I wasn't going to. I needed to know who I was.

We touched down in Wichita and wasted no time getting ourselves a hotel room and hopping in a cab to our destination.

"This guy's name is Ted Heckler. He's the owner of the circus," Maxine said, reading a piece of paper with the address on it. Our taxi pulled up to a giant cinderblock gate that extended forever. I suspected it was the length of two, maybe three football fields. There was a sign painted on the cinderblocks at the entrance with the "Vida Traveling Circus" logo that mimicked the one on my bag. The cab dropped us off by a security booth outside the gate.

Maxine asked the guard where to find Mr. Heckler. The guard refused to let us see him at first, but then I stepped forward, thinking he would recognize me. He didn't, but he saw the knapsack.

"You ain't Lisa," he said.

I'm not? I thought. I became confused, but what else was new? I ignored my confusion and played along.

"I'm trying to give this back to her. We need to see Mr. Heckler."

"Mr. Heckler don't like to be seen," he answered. I put my head down, feeling defeated. "But I suppose if I just happened to be testing the button here, and that gate opened, and if perhaps you snuck in and headed left, and maybe stopped at the biggest trailer in the corner, you might possibly catch a glimpse." He gave me a wink and leaned on the button and the gate opened. I smiled back and we went inside.

It was like a miniature suburb, with rows of cookie cutter trailers set the same way. Each trailer had a square patch of green grass perfectly tailored in front, and a little mailbox with a nameplate on top. I read each name and contemplated what kind of performer each one was. I imagined "J. Martin", the amazing contortionist, or "R. Smith", the lion tamer. It was difficult, trying to guess each person's act, based on their normal names and their normal houses. It occurred to me that these were normal people just trying to fit in, trying to live normal lives, and thanks to Ted Heckler, they were able to do so in the confines of the suburb.

Following the guard's instructions, we headed to the left, walking down the road. As quaint and beautiful as the whole park was, it was absolutely dead; there didn't seem to be a soul around.

Ted Heckler's trailer was at the curve of the street, butting up to a corner of the cinderblock wall. It was a trailer that had been built upon, various rooms added, at various times. It, too, looked desolate, but I went up to the door and knocked anyway. After several unanswered knocks, I turned around to the others to leave, when the door opened.

"Mr. Heckler?" I asked, looking at the tall, lanky man at the door.

"What?"

"Hello, I don't know if you remember me, my name is Jackie-"

"No, it isn't," he interrupted. "I don't remember exactly what it was, but it wasn't Jackie. She's one of my lion tamers."

"But you do remember me? You remember my face?"

"Yeah. You have one of those faces. I think it's that scar. You were an assistant for a tour. It was a while ago, but I believe you might have been in charge of trapeze costumes. That was for Boris and Ana, and Peter and Lisa."

"Lisa!" I exclaimed. I moved the knapsack around to show him. "Where's Lisa? I need to see Lisa and give this back."

"So, you're the one who took it? She was pretty upset that her stuff went missing. Gimme a minute and I'll take you to her."

We waited in the front lawn, while Ted got out his extended golf cart. We sped off, down one street and another, all identical to the last one. Finally, he braked in front of a trailer that had Christmas lights hanging from the roof.

"Most of the performers go on vacation for the month, spend time with their families for the holidays and what not, but not Lisa. She doesn't ever leave."

"Doesn't she have family to visit?"

"She has a family, but she doesn't care to ever see them. They write to her a lot, but I'm certain I've never seen her send any letters to them."

The nameplate on the mailbox read: "L. Penn". As the four of us jumped out of the cart, Ted took his merry little time, ducking his head low, and curling up one leg to stretch out onto the pavement, then the other. Then he shuffled up to Lisa's door and knocked. The door opened just a hair, and I could hear a voice coming from inside. Ted mumbled something, and then the voice spoke again, followed by another mumble from Ted. The door shut momentarily and opened again, wider this time, and Ted motioned for us to come in.

The inside of Lisa's trailer was an ode to herself. There were pictures on the wall, every one of which was of her in action on the trapeze. Some frames contained newspaper articles, with headings like, "Child Prodigy Joins Circus". There was almost no furniture in the living room: one tiny couch and table and a TV. Next to the couch was a huge bag full of letters, and some open ones lay on the floor. Lisa had disappeared into the kitchen upon inviting us in and was now returning dressed in a bathrobe with a coffee mug in her hand. She was tall and thin, just like Ted, only she had an essence of beauty attached to her frame. Her hair was loose around her face, bright blonde and frizzy. It reminded me of Carmelina, and I missed her. Lisa smiled at us, but it seemed forced, like her performance face.

She sat down on her couch. "I don't have many chairs, forgive me. Would you mind sitting on the floor?" Everyone sat except Maxine, whose skirt prevented her from doing so, so she leaned against the wall. "Now, what can I do for you?"

I put the bag on the floor in front of me. "I found this and I wanted to return it."

"You! You're that little thief who stole my stuff! Where is it? Where's all the stuff? I want it back!"

"I, I don't know where all of your stuff is. There are a few things in there, but I don't even know how I got this. Please, let me explain," I reasoned. Lisa folded her arms, and took in a large breath, never exhaling. I started to explain that I had amnesia, and that I was tracing my past and I had discovered her knapsack in a drawer of a house I had occupied.

She stayed quiet, listening to my story, then said, "Well, what do you want from me?"

"All I need is any information you remember about me. Like, what my name was, or how I came to be in the circus."

She bent her steel rod-like back and thought for a moment. "I think you told me your name was Josephine. Yes, that was it. Josephine Muldoon. I remember laughing at the way it sounded, like it was totally made up, but then you shot me an evil glance, and I stopped teasing you out loud. Most of the time, I didn't call your name, I would just talk to your face. You were hired as the wardrobe assistant, so your job was basically just keeping track of our costumes and fixing them if they ripped. You were supposed to make sure we dressed at the right time, and when we were finished with a performance, you took the costumes back and washed them. You really were quite a diligent worker, I do recall. Better than the past few we've had, and the few before. I don't know why, but for some reason, we keep having to get new assistants. You people don't last very long, although, I suppose for you, it was different circumstances which caused you to leave."

"Do you remember me ever saying where I came from?"

"Well, we picked you up in Minneapolis, I think. We did a performance, and afterward, I found you wandering around behind the tents, you were by yourself. We had just had our last assistant quit on us, and I was carrying all of the costumes to our trailer, and I kept dropping them, so you stopped to help me. I mentioned we were without an assistant and without any hesitation, you volunteered, and you left with us that night. Then, the last night of our summer tour, after the performance, you were nowhere to be found, and my bag with some of my costumes and my mother's compact was missing. I was so upset, because I had never pegged you for a thief, but I supposed I never really talked to you much or got to know you at any great length."

Lisa thanked me for returning her bag and compact and invited us to stay for dinner, which we accepted. I felt bad for Lisa not wanting to communicate with her family and thought she would like a bit of company for once. She seemed glad to have guests, but I could tell she felt awkward with so many people in her house.

After our dinner, Ted drove us back to the front gate. "You interested in coming back this summer and maybe sticking around for more than a summer tour?" he asked, as we poured out of the golf cart.

"No, thanks," I replied. "I appreciate the offer, but I've got a similar job back in New York."

"Okay. Well, you're always welcome back."

We holed up in our hotel and crashed. Maxine made some arrangements to leave for Minneapolis in the morning. "Unless you wanted to stay here for a while," she said.

“No, there’s no reason to stay,” I reasoned. “Lisa and Mr. Heckler both said they found me and lost me while on the road. So, onward.”

51

Once we landed in Minneapolis, we were feeling optimistic about this city; we had a name to help with our tracking. Unfortunately, over the next two days, our optimism began to diminish. The police had no information on Josephine Muldoon, and they actually snickered at the name. My face wasn't in the missing person's archives either. It was discouraging, but so were our other ventures until crossing the path of someone who used to know me, so I tried not to get disheartened. In almost desperation, Reece and Archie had been reduced to dragging me into random businesses and asking people if they recognized me. We were continuously met with dead ends, and an exhausted Maxine suggested that we do something relaxing, or fun to take our minds off of searching.

"Think about it," she reasoned. "We tend to find people when we're not technically looking for anyone." What she said did make a little sense, and I agreed that I needed a break myself. We were in the downtown area and found an art museum. It was so soothing to just walk slowly and absentmindedly peruse the paintings and sculptures. We stayed until the museum closed and grabbed a bite to eat in a tiny hole-in-the-wall Coney Island. We passed the Mall of America getting back to our hotel, and I could see the light in Maxine's eyes flicker as she watched the monolithic mall go by. I told her that if she wanted, we could go there in the morning, and she beamed at me, clapping her hands.

We boarded a hotel shuttle and headed for the mall. Every single store I could ever think of had at least one installation, a few even had three, and in the center of the mall was a roller coaster. Maxine and Archie both seemed to be having aneurisms about which store to go to first, so after reading the illuminated map, Maxine turned to the rest of us and said, "Okay, let's meet back here at this map at three." Then, she took off in one direction and Archie in the other. Reece and I stood still for a moment, watching them run off.

"Where do you want to go?" Reece asked, taking my hand and starting to wander.

I shrugged. "I don't know. What do I need to shop for?"

"I don't know," he repeated. "What *do* you need to shop for?"

"Nothing I can think of that I need. I don't even have any money."

"Jackie, I'm your fiancé. I'll buy you anything you want."

"I don't want anything," I said, catching a breeze from a nearby door and shivering.

"At least let me buy you a coat."

I caved, as I still didn't have one, and the weather was cold and snowy, even worse than it had been in Montana. I tried on a few, having difficulty finding one that didn't make me look paunchy. Eventually, I settled on a plain pea coat, and we resumed our walk of the mall.

As we continued to stroll, popping in one store after another, my stomach started growling, so Reece pulled me through the food court. "Take your pick," he said. I looked around, salivating at every kiosk. I pointed to the hot dog stand and ordered a dish of miniature corn dogs. We slid down the counter to the register to pay.

The girl at the register had her paper hat pulled down almost over her eyes and was fiercely chewing a piece of gum. "That will be five dollars and sixteen cents," she said in between chews. Reece handed her a bill, and she looked up, and froze, completely enamored at him. She took the bill, smiling, and then did a double take and said, "Oh, hi."

"Hi," I said back, giving her a weird look.

"Wow, what a surprise seeing you here again."

"What? Do you know me?"

"Uh, yeah, of course I do, Josephine. We used to work together, like, years ago."

"Oh, well, do you mind if we catch up?"

"Sure, let me get someone to cover me."

Reece and I went to a table and sat down. The girl came out from behind the counter with a tray of corn dogs and our drinks. She sat adjacent to Reece, and stared at him, while he and I ate.

"Do you mind if I ask you what your name is?"

"You don't remember me?" she said, a little insulted.

"It's a long story, but basically, I have developed amnesia, and I can't remember certain things," I said, moving my head to capture her attention away from Reece's face.

"Oh. That's strange. Well, my name is Sam."

"Okay, Sam, now what can you tell me about Josephine? About me?"

"Um, you used to work here at the Hot Dog Hut with me. We were new together. Gosh, that was like, what, almost three years ago. We started out dipping and cooking the corn dogs, but we kept burning the dogs or not dipping them in enough batter. We were so bad at that, so they sent us to the front to work the registers."

"Then what happened? Did I just disappear?"

"Well, sort of. Actually, you got fired first. Then, after that, I never saw you again."

"Fired?"

"Yeah, you came in one day, and you had no idea what you were doing, it was like you'd never been there before, when you'd actually been working for like, three or four months. Hey, was that your amnesia?"

"Probably. But what exactly happened?"

"Well, you came in, a little late, and I kept saying your name but you weren't responding, and then, the boss came out and asked you why you weren't at the register, so you joined me, and people were telling you their orders, but you just looked at them, or you stared at the register, like it was in Japanese or something. A couple of people complained, and I asked you what was up, but you just said that you weren't feeling good. You asked the manager if you could just go home and sleep it off, but he said no because it was a Saturday, and we were really busy. Well, needless to say, you screwed something up, I think you gave someone back a fifty instead of a twenty or something, and the boss was furious, and he fired you. You took it pretty well, though. I mean, you looked a bit upset, but you didn't cry or anything. I think I would cry if I ever got fired." She reached over while talking and grabbed one of the little corn dogs and chewed on it.

"Then what?"

"Huh? Oh, nothing. Then you left the mall, and I never saw you again. I hoped I would, like we could still hang out and stuff, but you never gave me your phone number."

"Did I ever say where I was from?"

"Um, no. Not that I know of. You didn't talk about yourself much at all. I thought that was weird, until I found out that you were sleeping in a homeless shelter. Then, I figured you were probably just too embarrassed to give me any details."

"How did you find out I was staying in a shelter?"

"The manager mentioned it one time; you had to state a place of residency on the application for the job. So, where are you from, anyway?"

"I don't know. That's what I'm trying to find out."

"Sam!" She turned around to an older man, standing at the counter pointing to his watch.

"Well, I gotta go. My break's over," she said, mostly to Reece, who was completely disinterested in anything that wasn't a mini corn dog.

"It was nice to see you," I lied, standing up as she did. "Thank you for the information. I truly appreciate it." We faked a hug, and she walked backwards back to the Hot Dog Hut, staring at Reece.

"That was informative," I said, sitting back down.

"Now we know that you were staying in a shelter, so we can go to the shelter and ask if anyone remembers seeing you."

We met back at the map at three, and surprise, surprise, Archie and Maxine weren't there yet. Ten minutes passed before I caught them in the distance. I told them about Sam at the Hot Dog Hut, and all about the information she had given me.

Archie and Reece helped carry some of Maxine's bags and we hopped on the bus that carried us back to our hotel. Reece and Archie went up to the room with all of our bags, and Maxine and I stayed in the lobby, while she asked the concierge where the closest homeless shelter was. He gave her the strangest look for asking but did his job and pointed it out to us on the map. It wasn't terribly far, he said, just a short bus ride.

The shelter was inside a building that took up an entire block. There were a number of businesses inside that building, all of them pertaining to homeless or less fortunate people. There was a soup kitchen, a thrift store, a job center, and the shelter. Inside, it was fancy, like a corporate office.

"May I help you?" asked the secretary behind the front desk.

"Yes, I would like to see whoever is in charge of the homeless shelter," I asked, thinking how silly I sounded asking a corporate secretary for the shelter.

"Mmkay, now, are you looking for employment, a volunteer position or something?"

"No. Actually, I used to stay here, and I was wondering if someone could maybe give me some information."

Her eyes tightened, but she picked up her phone and talked to someone. "Mrs. Spicolli will be with you shortly."

We sat in the chairs, and a few minutes later, a short woman with a messy black ponytail came in. She made a look at the secretary, who made some sort of eye motion in our direction.

"Hello, I'm Rita Spicolli. I'm the operating manager of the United Mission House. Please come with me to my office." We stood and followed, through a slew of office rooms, stopping at hers on the end. She offered us chairs, but as there were only two, Archie and Reece stood behind them.

"Now, what can I do for you?" She asked, swiveling in her chair.

"Well, Mrs. Spicolli, my name is Jackie-"

"Josephine," Maxine interrupted quietly.

"I mean, my name is Josephine Muldoon, and according to a friend I used to work with, I used to stay here at the shelter."

"Hmm, your name sounds familiar." She put her fingers to her mouth, in a pensive pose.

"Well, I was wondering, first of all, if you had any record of me being here, or anything, or if you could tell me where I came here from."

She typed on her computer quickly. "We have that name on record as having stayed here for approximately four months, three years ago. I don't see any background information."

My stomach sank. I feared that this was a dead end, that we would not be able to trace my past anymore. I figured I probably came to the city, before having an episode, and had no way of knowing where I had come from.

"Wait a minute," Mrs. Spicolli said, leaning close to her computer screen. "Wait just a minute. I have a special file attached here. You left behind a bag of items, clothes mostly, which we gave away, but we did recover some personal items, which we locked up. A handful of pictures and a Bible, it says. Alright, let's go get it."

We followed her again, through the building past a loading dock, and by a kitchen door. She stopped at a fence door which she unlocked. Then, she stepped in and unlocked another gate and led us into a room full of drawers. "This is where we keep things that are left behind that we can't sell. Most of the stuff is pictures or notebooks, even mail. We've had the occasional passport, and once or twice, we had people leave behind boxes of letters."

"Why keep them?" Reece asked. "I mean, if you're going to get rid of their clothes or trinkets, why keep the pictures and mail?"

"Because sometimes, people come back for their stuff. Half the time, they don't realize they've left it, or they know they lost it, and can't remember where. Plus, we like to keep things for funerary purposes. Once in a while, we'll read about one of our former patrons passing away, and it's always nice to be able to give their stuff back to their families, or even to just put in the casket, with them." She ran her fingers down the drawers until she came to one marked 207. She unlocked it and produced a large Bible, and a stack of photographs.

"These were in the drawer by your bed when we cleaned out your space." She handed me the stuff, and I flipped through the photographs.

"Well? What are they?" Maxine asked.

"They're pictures of nuns."

52

We stood on the lawn of a massive and old building that looked like it could have been a boarding school somewhere in the Swiss mountains, but was here, in flat Middle America. There was a sign set in the stone that read: "Sister Alfreda Mission". Directly below that stone sign, was another carved stone that read: "Chicago, 1857". The building looked cold, which was amplified by the overcast sky, and frigid weather. I didn't want to say it out loud, but I was frightened of the place.

I looked at the picture, hoping we were at the wrong place, but we weren't. The picture looked exactly the same, overcast and all. Even the stone signs were the same. I must have taken a thousand nervous breaths, before finally, Reece put his hand to my back and urged me forward.

The door opened before we reached it. There was an old, frail man standing in the doorway. "I've been watching you on the lawn," he said, with a raspy voice. "I was wondering when you were going to come inside."

He invited us into a grand hall made of stone and marble, our steps echoed as we walked. The old man led us into a room off the hall path decorated in dull red leather couches and chairs.

"Please, have a seat," he rasped. "I will go fetch Mother Gertrude for you." I listened to his footsteps echoing as he walked away and then sat down.

The room was unsettlingly plain. There were no pictures, no color to the walls, or even a rug on the floor. I wondered if all of the rooms were similar. I remembered reading in my journal about how much it bothered me that the walls in my bedroom in New York were so white and plain. I wondered if the plainness here ever bothered me.

Suddenly, a small woman, who could have passed for a child, stepped into the room. I jumped, as I didn't hear her feet coming down the hallway. She looked at all of us, one by one, smiling. Then, her eyes moved to me, and she gasped.

"My goodness. Is it? Are you? Could it be, Jane?"

I didn't exactly know how I was to answer her questions, so I started to introduce myself. "Hi," I smiled. "My name is Jackie, and I have amnesia. I found these pictures in my belongings." I handed her the photographs.

"I remember your amnesia. We have had a lot of girls come through our halls, and only one stood out as having amnesia. It was you, Jane."

"Uh, I go by Jackie."

"Oh, I see. Well, in truth, we never knew your real name. You came to us from the hospital as Jane Doe, and we left it that way. Nevertheless, Jackie, welcome back."

"Thank you," I said politely. "Did you just say that I came here from the hospital?"

"Yes. You had been in the hospital, recuperating from a coma, and when you were healthy enough, they brought you here to stay with us." She invited us back to her kitchen, where she was preparing some hot coffee, so we followed and gathered around the table.

"How long ago was I here?"

"Oh, I don't exactly remember, it must have been almost four years ago, now."

"And how long did I stay?"

"About four months. We hoped you would stay longer, because I didn't think you had enough time to get well, but you were desperate to leave. You really wanted to try living on your own, without constant supervision. I know that can seem bothersome at times, but we had to, because of your episodes."

"Did I have them a lot?"

"Oh yes. Almost every week or every two weeks. It was strange, like clockwork. Do you have them that often still?"

"I had been up until very recently. In fact, I haven't had one in about five weeks." I took a sip of my coffee, trying to think of something else to ask her. "Do you remember what kind of person I was?" She looked at me strangely, so I tried to elaborate. "What I mean is, was I a good person or did I cause trouble? Was I really quiet and reserved or loud and out of control?"

"Other than your first couple days here, I didn't see much of you, but I seem to remember you being very quiet whenever I made my rounds. I'm sure we still have your file available, but if you want details, you should talk to Sister Edith. She was your caretaker."

Mother Gertrude left us in the kitchen and returned quickly with another woman who was younger, and much taller. She introduced the woman to us as Sister Edith. Sister Edith looked at me, and grinned wide. She walked over to me, and held out her hands to my face, but then she pulled back. "I'm sorry," she said.

"It's okay. You can touch my face if you want. I get it a lot lately."

She pushed her hands out again and lightly grazed my face. "You look the same as I remember. Your face is unforgettable."

"I would like you to tell me about myself, when I was here," I said, after a moment of silence. Sister Edith sat down in a chair next to me and folded her hands.

"You were very hostile at first. The hospital told us your health had returned and sent you here as a sort of halfway house to get you back on your feet. I believe that they wanted you out of their hands. Maybe they thought if anyone could help your behavior, it would be the Lord's servants," She laughed at this, and I noticed Mother Gertrude scowled. I frowned a bit too, disappointed to hear that I was hostile. "It was very hard to get you under control. You looked angry, sitting on one of those red couches out front, in between two orderlies. When I went to escort you to your room, you folded your arms and refused to go. One of the orderlies lifted you by the arm and you spat on him. He became angry and picked you up over his shoulder. That was when you started screaming. I don't recall ever having a young lady in our Mission that had ever acted like that before or since, which is why I remember it so clearly.

"The orderlies had to give you a shot to sedate you. Once you stopped screaming and fell asleep, they carried you to a bedroom. After your fi Mother Angelica suggested one of our hospital rooms, rather than a regular room. The hospital rooms have bars on the windows and arm straps on the beds." I closed my eyes, trying to picture this, but I couldn't imagine myself acting like that. I felt so embarrassed to hear that I was such a nightmare.

"You slept the rest of the day and night, and in the morning, I heard screams from the other side of the mission. That was how I knew you were awake. I brought you some breakfast, but you wouldn't eat. You were so concerned with your hands in the straps; you kept pulling on them, and wiggling. I told you over and over that you weren't going to do anything but tire yourself out, and eventually you did, and you broke out into a fever and a bloody nose. I cleaned your face and you started to calm down. You did ask me where you were and what your name was and why you were strapped to the bed. But, when I told you it was because you were violent, you didn't believe me and the screaming started again. Still, I think you were starting to warm up to me at that point, but it did take a good week or so before you actually stopped all the spitting and yelling."

My face completely reddened, and I sank in my seat, my eyes welling. I wanted to disappear. Reece grabbed my hand and touched his cold fingers to my cheek.

"I'm so sorry. I had no idea I acted like that. I'm terribly embarrassed."

"It's okay, Jane. I'm sorry, Jackie. You were only like that at first."

"Well, what happened to snap me out of that?"

"You had an episode. I went to your room early that day while you were still sleeping, and when you woke up, you didn't know how you got there or why you were in straps. I was expecting you to scream, but this time you didn't. You just cried. I calmly told you who I was and where you were and explained that I would take the straps off if you didn't scream or fight me.

"You asked, 'Why would I fight you?'

"I wasn't sure if I should tell you about your previous behavior, so I changed the subject, and unstrapped you, and suddenly, you were completely tame. You asked me a lot of questions, but mostly you were silent, touching your scar. You touched your scar a lot."

"So, I was fine after that? I was good and quiet?"

"Yes. For the most part. Every once in a while, I would see a flicker in your eyes, like you were a lion about to pounce on your prey. That mostly occurred when you were interacting with the other girls that stayed here. You liked to be alone, in your room. We encourage the girls to interact with each other, to form sisterly bonds, but I could tell right away that wasn't for you. Other than your attitude toward the other girls, you always did as I asked."

"Would you like to see your room?" Mother Gertrude asked.

I nodded.

The room was down in the basement. The window was a small rectangle at the top of the wall, and just like Sister Edith had said, there were bars across it. The walls were plain and white, just like the rooms upstairs. In the middle of the room was a small hospital bed with silver rails. Under the mattress, were two brown leather straps hanging like nooses.

"You were the last person to stay in here. It's virtually untouched since you left," Sister Edith said.

"How did I leave? Did I tell you I was leaving, or did I just disappear?"

"You told me you wished to leave. We had to clear it with Mother Gertrude, but once we did, I gave you some pictures to remember us by, and a Bible. I bought you a nice outfit and a bus ticket to Minnesota, because that's where you said you wanted to go. I even drove you to the bus station."

After more touring of the building, our visit was cut short. I didn't feel comfortable in the mission, especially thinking about how bad I was when I first arrived, so I was very quick to want to leave. Sister Edith was sad to see me go. "You seem to have become a wonderful young woman," she said, holding my face again. "I wish you the best, and I hope you can find what you're looking for. God bless you."

"Now what?" I asked, as we stood back on the mission's front lawn again.

"Well, you came here from the hospital, but I don't know if they'd still have records of you there, especially after four years," Maxine said. "You want to try the police station?"

I shrugged. "I guess we don't have much else to go by, do we? And I don't have any other ideas."

"To the police station," Archie said suddenly.

Maxine, Reece and I stopped and stared at him.

"What song is that from?" I asked.

"It's not from a song," he replied, walking ahead of us as we stared at him.

53

We almost couldn't remember what we were doing at the police station; we were so surprised at Archie. He seemed nonchalant about what he said, like he hadn't been talking in Eighties song lyrics for the past God only knows how long.

"Can I help you?" asked the secretary, for the third time.

"Uh, sorry. Yes. We would like to speak to someone about a missing person," Maxine said.

"Are you reporting a missing person?" she asked.

"Um, no. We found one."

She dialed an extension, before pointing us to a big office on her left. Inside, there was a man waiting for us, sitting at his desk, rummaging through papers. "What can I do for you?" he asked.

"We were wondering if you had any missing people that matched this description," Maxine said, pointing at my face. The man scanned my face a moment and then opened a filing cabinet.

"How long ago were you missing?" He asked.

"I don't know. Maybe four years. I was at Sister Alfreda Mission, and before that, I was in the hospital, I guess in a coma," I answered.

"Jane Doe," he said, rifling through the cabinet, pulling out a file. "We found you out by the pier, with the side of your head smashed up. A blow like that to the head, we figured you were dead, but you were still breathing, so we shipped you to the hospital. No identification on you, so you were labeled a Jane Doe."

I took the file and opened it. The first item was a picture of the pier and a body lying on its side. I had an instant image in my mind of myself, lying on the ground, staring out over the water, and I felt an excruciating jolt of pain on the side of my head, by my scar. I flipped the picture over and found another picture, a close up of the wound on my head. The brightness of the blood didn't even look real. I quickly flipped to the next picture, which was of my face, although it was difficult to tell, because my blood-soaked hair covered half of it.

I closed the file and set it back down on the desk. The man was watching my face, half grinning at my disgust. "Is that you?" he asked.

I closed my eyes and nodded.

"Well, to be honest, you're not exactly a Jane Doe. I mean, you were at the time, but we had one of our investigators identify you. The timing was bad, though. He had been out in California for some training when we found you. He went looking for you when he came back, but you had already left the hospital. He tracked you to Sister Alfreda but lost you after that."

"Did he give you a name?" I asked, feeling my heart starting to pump.

"Yeah, but I think, maybe he better tell you himself," he said, still grinning. He pushed a button on his phone. "Dee, send Robertson in here, please."

There was a knock at the door and it opened. "You wanted to see me, sir?"

I turned around. Over Maxine's shoulder, I could see the face of a younger man, easily Reece's age. He looked around at the crowd of people in his boss' office but didn't make eye contact with me.

"I've got some information on Valerie's case."

"What?" Robertson exclaimed, pushing through us to his boss' desk. At the desk, he looked at me, and his eyes almost fell out of his head. "Oh my God! Valerie!" He grabbed me and pulled me in. I stayed motionless, wondering why the cop was hugging me, and I grew even more suspicious, when he pulled away and looked at me, with tears running down his face.

He was smiling, every time he looked at my face, but my reaction seemed to pull his smile down at the corners, until he stopped. "What's the matter?"

"I'm sorry," I said, "But who are you?"

"Val, are you serious?"

The look on my face confirmed my seriousness, so he continued.

"I'm Eric. I'm your brother."

54

I stared at him, absolutely convinced that I was being tricked. This was all I ever wanted, and now it was here, so I couldn't help but wonder if it wasn't real. I could tell by the look in his eyes, and the smile on his face that there must be some morsel of truth here, but I also was reminded of the way the Bennetts received me.

"Don't you remember me at all?" he asked.

"No. Not yet anyway. I might be able to if I can get some information or see pictures."

"I'll do you one better," he said. "I'll take you to the source."

"The source?"

"Mom and Dad. I'll take you there tomorrow. It's kind of late now. Who are your friends?" He eyed the others curiously as he spoke.

"Maxine and Archie are my roommates. Reece is my fiancé."

He nodded in acknowledgment of the first two, but when I introduced Reece, he puffed up, glaring at him, so Reece offered his hand to shake.

"Nice to meet you," Reece said.

Eric looked leery. "What happened to your arm?"

"I broke it, protecting your sister," Reece answered without hesitation.

He broke into a smile and clasped the extended hand. "Nice to meet you, too."

Eric offered us all a place to stay in his apartment downtown, which we accepted. We never got a hotel room when we arrived, we had simply been lugging our bags all over Chicago. His apartment was small, as he lived by himself, but there was plenty of room to accommodate the rest of us.

He pulled out a shoebox that had some pictures of me. "These are what I had been using when I first started looking for you. I had to admit, I gave up when I lost you in Minnesota, but I held on to these in case anything ever came up again." Two of the pictures were just me by myself, and I was smiling, but then the other two were pictures of me and "friends" as Eric said. I looked sour and angry. I flipped through the photos again and noticed that my scar was gone.

Twice, I had asked Eric about growing up, and how I was as a person, and twice he changed the subject.

"So, tell me, Val," he said. "Where have you been all this time?" I detailed my story to him: the amnesia, all of the various places I've been and the different names I'd had, making sure I emphasized that my name now was Jackie, which I preferred.

"Wow, that sounds exciting," he said.

"It could have been, I suppose, but I don't remember any of it."

"Well, what brought on the need to find out?"

I hesitated. "Um, it was just an acquaintance I met in New York who recognized me," I answered, casually.

"Well, I'm glad for that," Eric said.

I thought about the acquaintance and shuddered a bit. I too, was happy to finally have found my roots, I just wished it had been under different circumstances; not on the run, not fearing for my life, not involving Razi.

55

"You know, I've been looking for you for almost four years now. When the chief found you on the pier, I was away at training, and when I came back, I came across the file, and I instantly knew it was you. They said you were in the hospital, and when I went after you, you were already gone. The hospital told me they'd shipped you to Sister Alfreda, and when I got there, you had left. Minnesota, I was told. Well, I did some research, but couldn't find you anywhere there," Eric said. It was early the next morning, and we were headed out of Chicago to Aurora, where he said we had grown up.

During the night, I had dreamed about a large, white house with green shutters, which didn't make any sense until Eric pulled into a driveway. "Here we are," he said, getting out of the car. We piled out and I stared at the house.

"This is the house I dreamed about last night," I whispered.

"So, you do remember it?" Eric asked.

"Well, I guess. I mean, it was just a dream."

"Okay, well, let's go see Mom and Dad," he replied. "Are you ready?"

I shook my head, and Eric took my hand, leading me up to the house. I suddenly grew frightened, and reached my other hand out for Reece, who was right behind me. Eric didn't knock, he walked right in.

"Mom? Dad?" he called at the entryway.

"In the kitchen, dear."

The voice was sweet. It reminded me of Glenda, the Good Witch. I followed Eric around the staircase, through a living room, to the kitchen, where I saw my mother and father.

I stared at them both, absolutely sure that they were my parents. My mother's face was similar to mine, and my father's hair was the same shade of sandy blonde. My mother's black hair reminded me of the pictures I found of myself in Florida, when I had dyed my hair. She and I could have been twins.

She looked up from the newspaper she was reading and seemed overwhelmed by the five people that had entered her home. "Eric, who are all these people? You didn't tell us you were bringing friends." She sounded upset.

"Mom, look who I found," Eric said, beaming with pride, and stepping sideways, showing me off like I was a game show prize.

My father looked up from his paper, and stared, as did my mother. They were both silent. I smiled weakly, but still, they said nothing.

"It's Valerie," Eric finally said.

"Oh, it *is* you! My Valerie!" My father stood up and rushed over to me, hugging me. I hugged back, excited to know that I had found them. My mother stood up behind him, and when he stopped hugging me, it was her turn.

"Good to see you," she said, sounding lackluster. I didn't dwell, believing that she was just a woman of few words, and even fewer emotions. "Well, come in, sit down. Let me get more chairs." She pulled a couple of stools out from under the kitchen island. "Who are your friends?"

I opened my mouth to speak, but Eric, in his excitement interrupted me. "These two are her roommates, and this guy here is her fiancé." My parents stared at the others and rested their eyes on me.

"Archie, Maxine, Reece," I said, pointing them out.

"Your fiancé? How exciting!" my mother said with an odd tone to her voice. "So, what brings you here to see us?"

"Well, I wanted to meet you –or see you, I mean. I'm here because I was trying to find out where I came from. I was trying to find you, my family."

"What are you talking about?" My father's voice was stern this time, and I noticed he was eying Reece.

I started to tell them about my amnesia, and the places I'd been. They listened, but my mother especially looked disinterested. "So here I am," I finished. "I've found you guys, and now I can learn about my childhood, and what kind of person I used to be."

"So, wait," my mother said. "You don't remember anything at all? Nothing?"

"Nothing about my childhood. Actually, nothing up until the past five months, which I've been journaling."

The two of them looked at each other, talking with their eyes. Then, my mother looked at me, and said, "Well, Val, you were a good kid."

I watched her face as she nervously looked away. I knew something was up. "That's it? That's all you can tell me?"

"Mom, what's going on? Why are you acting like that?" Eric asked.

"Like what? I don't know what you're talking about."

"Valerie asked you a question."

"It's Jackie, now," I muttered.

"Right. Sorry. Jackie asked you a question."

"You go by Jackie now?" my mother asked. "Well, that's kind of pretty. I liked Valerie better. You should go back to Valerie."

"Mom!" Eric yelled, startling everyone. "Jackie has been all over the country, trying to find out where she came from and who she is, and I suggest you start telling her the truth."

My mother was startled that Eric had raised his voice to her. Then, she looked down at her hands, and then at my father. "Okay. Well, what do you want to know?"

"How old am I?"

"Oh, let me see. You're twenty-three. Your birthday is December sixteenth."

"That's today," Archie said, pointing to a calendar on the wall.

"Oh, well, happy birthday," my mother replied.

"You didn't know it was my birthday?" I asked.

"Well, you've been gone, so we didn't see a point in celebrating it."

"How long have I been gone?"

"Well, you took off right after high school. You barely graduated, you know, but once you did, you just left."

"And you never bothered to check on me, or see what I was up to?"

"No. You've always been an independent person, and we thought you needed some space." Her answers were gapped, like she was searching for the appropriate words, without divulging too much information.

"Some space? How did you know I wasn't dead?"

"Oh, because I figured you were in Chicago. You used to go there all the time, when you'd run away."

"Run away?" My mouth dropped off my face entirely. This wasn't what I was hoping to hear.

"Yes. You used to run away a lot when you were in high school. It got worse when you turned eighteen, because then you were an adult. But I assumed that you were off with that drug dealer you used to hang out with."

"You thought I was living in Chicago with a drug dealer? You think that was where I've been this whole time? Why didn't you ever come looking for me? Aurora isn't that far away from Chicago." I could hear my voice growing angry. My mother could sense it too, because I watched her tense up her body, like she was afraid.

"N-no," she stuttered. "I knew you were in Chicago, because I saw you there a number of times that first summer. I just assumed you were still in the hospital."

"Wait, how did you know she was in the hospital?" Eric asked.

"She just told me."

"She *just* told you. So, four years ago, you wouldn't have known that. How could you have assumed it then?" He stared at her, intensely, putting his investigatory skills to use.

My father put his arm around my mother's shoulder, and whispered, "Just tell her, please." She burst into tears.

"The truth is," she wailed. "We knew you were at the hospital. You left after graduating, that's true, but then, after a few months, we got a call from one of your friends asking about you; it was one of those hoodlums you used to bring around. Jeff, I think. I told him we hadn't seen you, and he said you were missing, so we went to the police to file a report, and the chief asked us if you were involved in any gang or drug related things. I said it wouldn't surprise me, and he said there was an unidentified girl at the hospital if we wanted to make sure it wasn't you." She couldn't finish talking because she was crying too hard, so my father continued.

"We got there, and sure enough, it was you. You had a bandage wrapped around your head, and they said you were in a coma. The doctor said they suspected you would never remember anything, so your mother–" he took a large breath and paused. "No, your mother and *I* decided to leave you there, unidentified."

My heart sank instantly. I was certain I even heard it shatter a few times. No sluggish descent into the abyss, caused by a slow leak. This time, it was a total capsize, one colossal wave and my heart lay on the floor. I couldn't believe what I was hearing. My eyes were dampening. "What the hell," was all I could muster.

"Are you kidding me?" Eric exclaimed. I knew that he was also receiving this information for the first time. His face paled. "I didn't know, I swear," he whispered, turning to me.

"Now, Valerie, please understand," my father said.

"You were such a bad child," my mother explained, in between her sobs. "I don't know how it happened, but once you got to high school, you just turned into a completely different person. You were hanging around losers like Jeff, sneaking out, and running away, and yelling and screaming at me all the time. We even sent you to one of those camps when you were fifteen. You did well, and graduated early from the camp, but when we brought you back home, you disappeared for three days. It never ended, Val. You had been an alright kid, up until your brother left for the police academy. Then, you just turned into a monster."

"We decided that if you were going to wake up from your coma with no memory that it was probably for the best. That way, you could go on with your own life, and we could live ours without having to worry about you. So, we told the doctor that you weren't our daughter, and we told the police that you had come back home." My father stared at my mother's face the whole time he talked, like he was repeating lines from a script. He never moved his eyes off her, not even to look at me.

"I-I," my voice was cracking and I started to feel anger rising inside me. "I can't believe you did that to me. I could have died there in the hospital or out on the streets when I woke up."

"We didn't think of it that way. You've always been tough. Obviously, you survived that blow to the head. We never worried that you wouldn't be able to take care of yourself. And see? You've done a good job. You've got nice friends and a nice fiancé," my mother reasoned.

"Every time I go to sleep at night, I wonder if I'll remember anything in the morning. I can't even go to the store down the street alone without three calls to Maxine because of my condition. All that bouncing from one place to another happened because I would wake up with no memory of where I was, so I would run, because I was scared."

My mother pursed her lips, having no comeback for what I said. "What do you want, Valerie? Do you want me to say that I'm sorry? I'm sorry. I feel terrible that I did that to you, but if you had seen yourself, you would have understood my motives, I think. That being said, I am sorry."

"You disgust me. I can't believe this. You're absolutely putrid!" I shouted. She winced as I stood up, but instead of lunging at her, like she thought I would, I ran out of the room.

"Valerie," I heard her call.

"It's Jackie! My name is Jackie!" I shouted, as I opened the front door and leaped out into the snow. I started walking, and I slipped on a patch of ice, falling onto my back. It didn't hurt; my adrenaline was pumping too much to feel anything except sick. I lay there, staring at the sky, watching the snow fall around me. I closed my eyes and started crying. I heard Reece call my name from inside the house, and then I heard my father say something. There was a fumbling noise at the front door, before Reece said, "Let me get her."

I opened my eyes and Reece was knelt down beside me. He slipped his hand into mine and just watched my face. "Did you fall? Are you hurt?" he asked.

"Yes and no. I'm fine." I tried to sit up but was having trouble in the snow. Reece slid his broken arm behind my neck and helped lift me up. Once I was sitting, I started to cry again. He moved his arms to put them around me, but I grabbed hold of his waist and hid my face.

I could feel him shivering, as he didn't have his coat on. "Jackie, I know you don't want to, but could we go back inside? It's freezing out here." I looked at him, and he wiped a tear off my face. "You don't have to talk to them if you don't want to."

"I don't even want to look at them. I think I just want to be alone right now."

"Are you sure? You're going to stay out here?"

"Yes," I lied. "Now, please go back inside, and leave me alone for a bit."

He looked at my face for a long moment, before he rose slowly and walked into the house. I heard the door close, but I could still feel someone watching me. Sure enough, I turned around and found the lot of them peeking out the windows at me. I definitely didn't feel alone, so I stood up, brushing the snow off my pants, and then I started walking down the street. I heard the door open again, and without even thinking, I broke out into a sprint.

I didn't know where I was going at all, but I ran for blocks. My lungs burned, and I figured I was far away enough that I could slow down. I bent over, clutching my knees to catch my breath, and when I stood back up, I looked at my surroundings. I had ended up in a part of town where there were no longer houses, but businesses instead. I squinted my eyes a bit, noticing a library across the street. I hurried over there, thinking it was the quietest place to be alone, and probably the best place for me to hide if they came looking for me.

Inside, I made my way down the marble hallway, my wet shoes squeaking, disturbing the people at tables. I found the private desks with walls and slid into a seat. I looked ahead at the blank computer screen in front of me. I suddenly remembered about my journals, reaching for them so I could record what had just happened, and hopefully sort my thoughts. But my fingers couldn't find my purse. I looked down and realized that I had left my purse back at the house. I had nothing. No money, no journals. I felt my pocket vibrate, and sighed, relieved that I did happen to have my phone.

I pulled out the phone and read on the screen that Maxine was calling me, so I answered the phone as quietly as I could. "What," I whispered.

"Jackie! Where are you? Why did you take off?"

"I'm not telling you. I need to be alone right now."

"Come on, you can't do this. You're in no condition to be alone, especially with your purse still here. Tell me where you are."

"I can't."

"Jackie, you're going to forget, and then you'll be in serious trouble, and we'll never find you."

"I'll be fine. I'm always fine. Haven't you paid any attention these past few weeks? I always land on my feet."

"No, you run off, and forget everything, but you don't have to do that anymore. You need us, and we need you. Reece needs you. We all do."

Her mention of "we" pushed my thought of Reece aside, and I was struck paranoid. She was in alliance with my parents. "No. I don't need them," I said, thinking strictly of my parents. "I want to be alone."

"It's not safe for you. You'll either have a spell, or you'll be found by you know…" I imagined Maxine talking to me on the phone, surrounded by the others, trying not to say the name I knew she was thinking.

"Razi can come and find me, I don't care anymore," I said, loud enough that my voice echoed.

"Razi?" I heard a faint voice say on the line. It was Eric's voice, and I knew I had been on speakerphone the whole time.

"I'm hanging up now," I said.

"No! Jackie, wait! What are we supposed to do?"

"Go home. Just go home," I said, closing my phone.

56

I left the phone sitting on the table, constantly buzzing, as Maxine kept calling my phone. I didn't answer, and eventually, it stopped. I really wanted to write, now, and staring at the computer, I remembered my online journal.

I had over two hundred comments on my last entry, but I ignored them. I made a new journal entry that detailed everything I'd just been through with my parents. I made it perfectly clear in my journal where I was now. I was done being secretive.

"I'm in Chicago. If you're looking for me, come and find me. I don't care. I'm over this whole thing. Come out of hiding and find me." I wrote, particularly to Razi, even though I knew he wasn't reading my blog. After detailing the rest of my excursion in Illinois, including the nuns, I submitted the entry, and I sat, motionless, staring at my newly published post.

As I stared, my computer screen changed, and I could see that there was already a comment on my entry. I clicked on it. *"I'm out of hiding, and now I've found you."*

My eyes bulged at the comment. My heart felt like it stopped beating entirely. I started breathing quickly now, completely frightened. I wished that Reece was here, to protect me. I kicked myself for running away.

My phone vibrated again, and without even looking at the screen, I picked it up. "Max?"

"No. Jackie? It's me."

"Chrissy?"

"Hi," she said. I could hear something strange in her voice, a nervous sob or a choke. "Hi, Jackie. How are you doing?"

"I've been better, Chrissy. How about you? Is something wrong?"

"Yea- um, I mean, no, I'm okay. But um, listen, Jackie, I, um, someone wants to talk to you." I heard a shuffling sound, then a voice.

"Hello, Jackie. Or should I say Mara? Or perhaps, Valerie?" My brain flashed an image of a man; I had no doubt it was Razi.

"What do you want? What did you do with Chrissy?" I said in an angry whisper.

"Oh, she's fine. Where are you?"

"You know damn well where I am," I growled.

"That's right. What did your journal say? You're in Chicago? Hmm, what a surprise. So am I."

I almost dropped the phone. I looked around, and then promptly hopped up, out of my chair, heading down a neglected aisle of books. "What do you want me to do?" I sighed, holding back a sob.

"I want you to meet me at the pier. I want you to be alone. Don't tell anybody, otherwise, I'll shoot Chrissy in the head." I heard a bit of shuffling in the background and then heard a faint whimper and a nearly silent sob from Chrissy. "Now, can you be a good girl and follow directions?"

"Yes," I said, bursting into tears. I heard a click on the other end and knew he had hung up. I tried to take a breath, and wiping my eyes, I walked swiftly out of the building. I held out my hand and stopped a cab.

"I need you to take me downtown toward the pier," I said.

The driver did as instructed and took off, heading into the city. I watched the sky darkening out the window. I worried about Chrissy, and if she was okay. I knew I was going to kill him if he hurt her.

My phone vibrated again, and I looked at the screen. It was Maxine. I put it back in my pocket. I couldn't answer her; she couldn't know where I was going, otherwise, Chrissy would be killed.

When I could see the pier in the distance, I waited until the cab stopped at the light, then jumped out, yelling "thanks" as I ran through the snow. I could hear him shouting behind me, and eventually, it faded.

The pier was desolate. It was the best place to commit a murder or two, I thought. The lights were illuminated now, with the sun almost gone. They exposed massive garage doors with descending numbers painted on them.

I called Razi's name, as I followed the doors almost to the end. I heard no response, so I screamed his name. Then, Chrissy's. There was a clanging noise, and I could see a door ahead open and two shadows come out. One was tall and confident, the other hunched and hardly able to stand.

"You came alone," Razi said.

"You told me to."

"I didn't think you would listen to me. You never did."

"What do you want from me? I don't have your money."

"Oh, I'm aware of that. You know who does have my money? The police. Someone wired the cash to some faulty account, then, the police were notified. You wouldn't have any idea who could have done that, now, would you?"

"It wasn't me."

"I'm sure one of your little pals did it. Don't worry, I'll find them too."

"Well, if you know I don't have the money, then what do you want?"

"I want you dead. The police are wise to me now, and you know too much about me, whether you remember it or not. You will eventually, and I just can't have that."

"I don't know anything."

"But you do. You see, we have a history, you and I." He stepped toward me, lugging Chrissy behind him. He stepped close enough that he and I were under the same light. He looked over my face, even tilted his head to see the scar under my ear. "This place looks familiar, doesn't it? Do you remember the pier? Do you remember that?" He lifted a finger, pointing to my scar, but I winced and moved back. He laughed.

"What do you know about my scar?"

"I know that I gave it to you. And you decided to return the favor by giving me one, too. Yes, Valerie, that's right. You and I go way back. We didn't just meet in New York like you think. You were one of my protégés here in this very city. I first met you seven years ago, when you accompanied a friend of yours to buy some stuff from me. Then, you were around all the time, and I put you to work. You did well, too; always the money man. You were the perfect third party I needed to facilitate my deals.

"Eventually, I decided that you were far more valuable than what I had been using you for. I never would have noticed it if you hadn't come to see me after a fight with your parents. There was this intensity about you that was bone-chilling, I'll be honest. And I knew you'd be better off being my debt collector. But you couldn't stomach the job, and I should have known, especially with you being a teenager, and when the debts went unpaid, well, we just couldn't have that, could we? So, I drove you out here, under the pretense that we were dealing, and I took a baseball bat to your head. I thought you were dead, and I should have made sure. The next thing I know, I find you getting off a bus in New York City, years later, healthy as a horse. Except, you had no memory of me or Chicago, which was the best thing that could have ever happened to me, because here, I had one of my best workers, who I could use again, without her remembering any of it.

"But then you had to go and ruin it by running off with my money and putting Kane behind bars."

I started up again with my sobbing. Razi watched me, rolling his eyes. I couldn't believe it had been him, this whole time. He was the bastard who cursed me with this incurable amnesia. I was never going to be the same again because of him. My weeping turned into angry wailing, and before I knew it, I had lunged at his throat, clasping my hands as tight as I could.

He laughed, and grabbed my shoulders with both of his hands, slamming me against the wall. I hit my head and heard glass shatter behind me. I let go of him and fell to the ground. I glanced behind him, watching Chrissy, her limbs tied, slowly fumbling backward, into darkness. Thankfully, Razi didn't notice. He was too focused on me.

"You can't beat me," he said. "You don't have any paint cans this time." He reached in his jacket, and pulled out his gun, pointing it at my head. In a panic, I reached my hand out, for the first thing I could find, which happened to be a large shard of glass. Unthinking, I thrust the shard into the side of his knee cap. He shouted and flung his hands in the air, firing the gun. I froze for a minute but realized he hadn't hit me.

In a burst of adrenaline, I was up on my feet, running as fast as I could. I heard another shot, and I slowed, thinking he had shot at Chrissy. As I slowed, I felt instant, sharp pain in my thigh. I looked down and could see a bloodstain forming on the front side of my jeans, right above my knee. My leg suddenly felt like Jell-O and I could no longer hold my weight, and I fell. No longer moving, the pain was excruciating.

With my head to the ground, I looked out at the water, reliving the memory of looking out over the water after being hit. I looked down the pier at the light, where Razi was standing up, limping his way over to me, his gun pointed. I closed my eyes, still writhing in pain, but trying to prepare myself for another blow to the head.

I heard another gunshot, and I stopped wiggling, trying to determine where the pain was now, where I had been shot. I felt nothing but the bullet in my thigh. I opened my eyes and lifted my head. Razi had stopped walking and was clutching his arm.

"Freeze!"

I looked into the dark, searching for the body attached to that voice, and soon, Eric's face appeared. Despite my pain, I sighed with relief that he had found me, and I even felt my lips curl into a smile, and my eyes well up with tears.

"Eric," I whispered, out of breath.

Then, out of the darkness, I saw two more policemen appear, flanking Eric, with their guns at the ready. They inched forward, passing by me, headed for Razi.

"I told you to come alone!" Razi yelled.

"Shut up, dirt bag. Don't move!" Eric shouted.

"I did," I responded to Razi.

The pain in my leg was beginning to make its way through my entire body. My tears began to fall, and I could feel myself going in and out of consciousness. My mind wandered, and I heard myself whispering Reece's name.

"I'm here, Jackie. Don't worry. I'm here. There's an ambulance on its way, okay?"

I opened my eyes, looking for Chrissy and found her a few feet away, with Eric's arm around her, comforting her as she sobbed. I moved my head the other direction and Reece was sitting next to me, holding my hand with his cast and brushing my face and hair with the other hand. He bent down and kissed my forehead at least a dozen times, and I couldn't help but cry.

"I need you," I cried, nonsensically. "Don't leave. I need you to stay with me."

"I know. I won't leave. You need to stay with me too, okay? Stay awake, stay with me." I heard what he said, but my eyes fell shut, heavy, like I hadn't slept in years.

57

I woke up to the sound of machines beeping. I opened my eyes and found that I was in a hospital. My eyes fell to my leg, which had thick bandaging wrapped around it. I flexed a muscle, which was a bad idea, as my whole leg seared with pain.

What happened?

My scanning eyes rested on a man's upper body that was lying face down on the bed. I wondered who it was, and if I knew him. I tried to shift my body into a more comfortable position, which proved unsuccessful, as my whole body was screaming. I made a tiny groan, and the body on my bed jumped. He lifted his head and looked at me.

"Jackie!" He stood up and leaned close to my face and he kissed me. I felt my stomach turn into butterflies, as this strange, yet very attractive man kissed me and petted my hair.

"Um, hi." I hoped the hoarseness in my voice would overshadow the nervousness.

He looked into my eyes, and his smile faded. "Do you remember me?"

I put my head down and shook it. He sat down on the edge of the bed and clasped my hand, pressing it to his chest, to his heart. "One more time," he smiled. "Think really hard, okay?" With that, he leaned forward and kissed me again.

A flurry of images assailed my brain. One of him staring at me across a café, one of him watching elephants at a zoo with me, one of him simply smiling, and one of him sleeping next to me.

"Reece?" I whispered.

His smile widened. "You remember."

"What happened?" I asked.

He told me everything he could, about meeting my parents, and how I ran away. "Maxine called you, but you wouldn't come back, and then you mentioned Razi's name on the phone and your brother recognized the name. We found your description of him in your journal, and Eric remembered that he was wanted for some misdemeanors and had been under suspicion of dealing drugs in Chicago years ago. Your parents mentioned that he was the guy you hung around when you were younger, and so Eric, Archie and I headed downtown to the police station, and when we got there, there was a call from an angry cab driver who said that a blonde girl that he picked up in Aurora hopped out of his cab without paying, and we tracked you to the pier. The police got Razi, Eric and Archie found Chrissy, and I stayed with you all the way here."

"I don't know who any of those people are," I said, bashfully.

"Oh, right. You need your journals. I'll be right back." He rushed out of the room, and in moments, he was back with a huge crowd of people. He introduced them to me and then, seeing that I was overwhelmed, sent them out to get some rest or clean up so I could read my journals. I sent him to go along with them, as he looked like he hadn't slept well in awhile.

The journals were fascinating. I absorbed every detail of every page, and found myself growing excited, as every once in a while I could picture the images, like a movie about me, playing in my mind. I remembered Archie and Maxine's faces and how well they had taken care of me. I remembered Chrissy at work, and how she could read me like a book every time I showed up with no memory. I even remembered Carmelina, the chain smoker who intrigued me, and was intrigued by me, every other Friday, as she walked me to therapy. When I got to the last written page in the third notebook, I found two folded pieces of paper stuck inside. I unfolded them and read an apparent online journal entry that I had made the day before. I had written about meeting my parents and how they left me to be unidentified in the hospital after I had been put in a coma. I suddenly remembered laying on the ground at a pier, staring ahead at the water, my head sweltering with pain. Then, I saw an image of a man swinging a baseball bat at me, and I shivered.

I finished reading the folded papers, and, like a light bulb turning itself on, I suddenly remembered being in my parents' house, listening to them tell me these things I read. I felt my stomach knot and my face redden with anger. I couldn't believe that they had chosen to leave me comatose in a hospital for over a year. I couldn't believe how incredibly unloved I felt in that moment.

A few hours later, there was a knock, and I saw Chrissy standing in the hallway. I beckoned for her to come closer, and when she was close enough to the bed, I reached out and hugged her, glad that she was alive.

"Are you okay?" I asked.

"Yeah, I'm fine," she smiled, rolling up her sleeve so I could see her little injuries.

"What happened? I mean, how did he get you?"

"I was leaving work a few days ago, and I stopped at the Corner Nook, to grab some food on my way home. Ever since you left, I'd been going there a lot, talking to the guys there. They were really concerned about you and Reece, so I'd fill them in every time I read a new entry from you. The last time, I went in there, and the boss, with the accent, I can't remember his name -"

"Mr. Thestas," I replied, unthinking.

"Yeah, well, he overheard me talking to someone and then started asking me questions about you guys and he kept saying your names loudly. When I left, these two guys followed me, and caught me in an alley. They tied me up and slapped me around a bit and then threatened to kill me if I didn't tell them where you were. All I said was that you weren't in New York anymore, and he somehow pieced together that you might end up back here. He covered my mouth with a rag, I passed out, and the next thing I knew, I was in an abandoned building, all tied up with that Razi monster. He forced me to tell him about your internet journal. I'm so sorry, Jackie, he put a gun to my head, I panicked. I'm sorry," her voice trailed off, and she started to cry. I touched her hand.

"It's alright. Your life was in danger."

"He pulled up your journal on a laptop and he sat at it for hours, waiting for you to post something, and then when you did, he made me call you."

"Oh my God, Chrissy. I'm so sorry. I didn't mean to get you involved in all of this. I feel terrible."

"I'm alright. Besides, if he hadn't kidnapped me, you wouldn't have gone to the pier, and he wouldn't be in jail now. I'm not glad that it happened, but at least now, you don't have to be afraid to come back to New York."

We continued talking; Chrissy told me she was going to leave for New York that night. "I've been gone for three days, and they're probably flipping out wondering where both of their stock girls ran off to. Plus, I really need to be home, resting in my own bed. I've had a strange couple of days that I need to recover from. I honestly don't know how you do it."

"Neither do I," I joked.

She hugged me goodbye and hoped to see me home soon. Eric stepped in, checked on me, and then escorted Chrissy to the airport.

Reece peered his head in a few minutes later. I smiled and held out my arms, waiting for him to receive them. "Did you finish reading?" he asked.

"Yes, I did. And I found this one here," I said, pulling out the typed entry.

"I had it printed out for you in case you forgot," he said. "So, I guess you're pretty mad at your parents again?"

"Of course, I am. And you can tell them that if you want, because I don't want them to come near me."

"Okay," he said. "I'll tell them. But they really want to see you, so could you let them? You don't have to talk to them if you don't want to, okay? I promise."

I rolled my eyes and surrendered. He went out into the waiting room and came back with them behind him. My father had a smug look on his face, coming close to the bed, while my mother stood two feet away, looking on.

"I'm glad to see that you're alright," she said, stagnantly. "You gave us all quite a scare."

"Oh good," I replied sarcastically. "I'm glad that I produced some sort of concern out of you for the first time ever."

"Valerie, that's not nice," she said.

"My name is Jackie. Please don't call me Valerie."

"Okay. That's something I will have to get used to, while you're here."

"Well, you won't have to for too long, because I'm not staying."

She tilted her head in annoyance and looked at Reece. "You didn't tell her?"

Reece took a large gulp of air and looked at me. "Jackie, um, we have to stay here for a few days because of your surgery, and the police would like to question you. But the doctor said you need at least two weeks of recovery time, and checkups, so we need to stay somewhere close by."

"Okay," I replied. "Well, we're staying with Eric, aren't we?" I flipped to the printed journal and pointed to a sentence I had read.

"Well, we were, but Eric's apartment is on the fourth floor of his building, and your room at your parents' house is only up one flight of stairs, so-"

"So, your father and I offered to let you stay at our house until you were free to go." My mother made her statement, trying to be the good guy, the heroine of the situation.

I was angry, but I couldn't do much about it, so I rolled my eyes and threw my head back against my pillow. "Fine."

58

"Easy, easy," Eric instructed. He and Archie were carrying me up the stairs, to my bedroom in my parents' house. Eric tried to carry me all by himself, but my bandaged leg was an issue. I told them I could probably walk, but they wouldn't hear of it. "Third door on the right."

He and Archie led me to a bedroom and opened the door. The room wasn't as stale as I had expected it would be. It was large and had a good deal of furniture in it. There was a small bed against the wall and a nightstand. Then, there was a desk, a dresser and even a couch lining the walls. A dark curtain hung over the one window, so the room was fairly dim. Reece, behind us, hit the light, and the room came into color. The walls were a soft, light pink color, with little pin holes everywhere. I reached my hand out from around Eric's neck and touched the walls at the pin holes.

"Mom and Dad took your stuff down," Eric said, as he and Archie put me down on my bed. "It's all still here; it's just packed up in those boxes." I followed the direction of his pointing. Spilling out of the closet were multiple stacks of boxes. I leaned over to the nightstand and opened the drawer. It was empty.

"You weren't kidding," I said to Eric. "They cleaned it out. What was on the walls?"

"Some posters. A couple were of bands I got you into. I sent you a few mixes while I was in California, and you ended up liking most of it. Then, I think there were movie posters too. Gangster movies, like *Scarface* and *Goodfellas,*" he chuckled a bit. "Then, you had another poster over here next to the bed." He pointed to the space, then turned around and looked at the pile of boxes, digging through one on the top of the pile. "Here it is," he said, leaning over my bed, tacking the poster back up.

When he moved his body, I saw a certain familiar yellow brick road, and a pair of ruby slippers. "No way," I said, mouth agape. Even Archie and Reece looked surprised.

"Yeah, you've had that poster since you were really little. That was your favorite movie growing up. I always thought it was funny that even when you were older, and rebellious, you still kept that picture up." He sat down on the couch, still gazing at the picture. "You know, Mom and Dad used to call me at the academy all the time and beg me to talk to you or do something to calm you down. They were really quick to give up on you, and I always knew that. But whenever I thought of you being here, and all the trouble you were in, I would always remember that poster hanging there, and I knew not to write you off as a lost cause. It sounds strange, but I knew that as long as you kept a special place in your heart for Dorothy and Toto, that you could still be the good little girl you were."

I heard Maxine's voice in the hall, and I watched my door, as her face leaned in the doorway, followed by my parents. I felt overwhelmed suddenly and pushed my head down onto my pillow, hoping to suffocate.

"Could you give us just a minute?" Reece asked. I heard some feet shuffle away, and I rolled over, to find Reece, Archie and Maxine still in my room. Archie sat on the couch, and Maxine joined him, while Reece curled up next to me. I was glad he was here, distracting me from the disgust I was feeling about being in my parents' house. I put my arms around him and lay there, breathing heavily.

"Are you okay?" he asked.

"Not really," I answered. "It's bad enough that I have to be questioned by the police when I don't know anything, but to be stuck here, in this house, with *them*. I keep remembering what they said to me. It's a vivid memory. I can't believe what kind of people I came from. I mean, they abandoned me while I was in a coma. That's horrible. And they never cared about me; they never wondered if I was alright." As I spoke, I began to choke up. "I know I should let this go, but I can't. I'm completely disappointed. This was all I've wanted since we started this journey: to find my parents and live happily ever after. And now, I've met them, and they're just horrible people, so now I feel entirely let down."

"I know, it's terrible, and I'm sorry that it happened to you," he whispered. "And I know how you feel."

"You do?"

"My mom left me when I was five. She took me to my grandparents' house and never came back. I know exactly what it feels like to be abandoned. The only difference is that my grandparents did everything in their power to make me feel wanted, but despite all the love and attention they gave me, I still felt that pain deep inside. I can't say I know what it's like to be left fending for myself, but trust me, I know that abandonment."

"I'm sorry that it happened to you too," I whispered.

"Don't be. I mean, sure, it hurt me, and it still hurts, but I've learned to be the bigger person. I've learned to move on. I didn't care about her, just like she didn't care about me, and I know that I wouldn't be the same person I am today if she had stuck around."

"Hey, Jackie, do you want to look through your stuff?" Maxine asked, eyeing the boxes in the closet.

"You can. I don't want to right now. Tell me if there's anything good in there."

Archie and Maxine started to dig through a box, while I rested my head on a pillow, my forehead touching Reece's cheek. I closed my eyes, trying to calm my nerves.

There was a knock at the door, flaring my nerves again and I heard my father's voice. "May I come in?" he asked.

"No." I said, flatly.

"Val, I'm sorry, Jackie, I would like to talk to you, please."

"Too bad."

"I understand that you're mad at me, but I want to talk, so I'll just be standing out here in the hallway until you're ready."

I took a deep breath. I was still angry, that was true, and I didn't want to talk to him, but the tiniest fragment of a part of me was saying that I should let him in. I sighed; my eyes still closed, and waved a hand, motioning for him to come in. I heard his feet move and then stop and I could feel him looming over me.

He was silent, and I was losing patience, so with one eye opened, I watched him. "What do you want?"

"I was hoping to talk to you privately," he said, wringing a newspaper in his hands.

"Anything you have to say to me, you can say in front of my friends."

"Well, no, actually, I can't. I'm uncomfortable enough as it is. Jackie, I just want to talk to you, nobody else. Please."

I opened my mouth to refuse, but Reece wiggled away from me and got up off the bed. I watched as he and my father looked at each other as Reece walked by him. He nodded once, and then my father nodded in return. Then, Archie picked up a box, and he and Maxine followed Reece out of the room. I listened to them settle themselves in the hallway, keeping the door open so they could eavesdrop.

"May I sit down?"

I rolled my eyes, and huffed, then scooted over to the wall, painfully rolling onto my side. He gently set himself on the edge, so as not to touch me.

"Can I show you something?" he said, rolling up his sleeve, not waiting for an answer. He showed me his arm, exposing a large scar that ran the course of his forearm.

"What happened?" I asked unsympathetically.

"You threw a kitchen knife at me," he said, in the same flat, indifferent tone.

"I did that?"

"Yes. It was the first time you had run away from home. We were so concerned; we had the police out looking for you everywhere. Eventually, they found you, defacing a building with a couple friends, and they brought you home in handcuffs.

"Your face was completely red, and you had tears streaming down your cheeks. I guessed you had been screaming too, because your voice was pretty hoarse when they brought you back. Anyway, the police carried you inside to the kitchen, where they left you cuffed as they explained where they found you. The whole time they talked, I couldn't help but notice that you had been staring at me, unblinking, and I tried to think why on Earth you would be looking at me like that. As soon as the cop took the handcuffs off, I suddenly realized that you weren't just staring at me; you were staring at your mother and me both. I knew you were angry that we tracked you down, but I didn't know how angry until you grabbed the knife and flung it at my head. I raised my arm to protect my face, and the knife sliced me. The cop tackled you, but I made him get up and leave, and I flung you over my shoulder and carried you up here. And that was the last time we called the cops whenever you went missing." He stared at the scar, like he was reading his words from it.

"Sorry," I said, aghast at what I'd done.

"I know that you don't have any memory of how you used to be, but I want you to know that I tried as hard as I could to be a good dad, but you just made it so difficult. We took you to therapy, got you some medication, and nothing worked. But you need to know we always loved you. Now, I know I spent more time with Eric than you, and I don't wonder if that was what made you resent me so much, but after Eric left, I tried. I suppose it was far too late at that point, though."

"Was I always like that? Even when I was little?"

"You weren't that bad when you were little, but you certainly had your fair share of fits and tantrums. You always wanted to do what Eric and I were doing, and you never could, so you would scream and cry. Your mother and I thought you would grow out of it when you were older, and you almost did. When you were about ten, you suddenly were quiet all the time. You never screamed or yelled, but you never talked at all either. It was awkward enough that I once begged you to yell at me, because that would be better than the silence. But you didn't.

"I had no idea what to do. I tried giving you all of my attention, and when that didn't work, I tried to ignore you."

"Did that work?" I asked.

"Not exactly. You threw a knife at me." We were both silent for a long moment; he was searching for his words, while I absorbed what he had said. "Your mother doesn't know this, but after that one time she and I saw you in the hospital in your coma, I came back to visit. Mostly, I would stop and see you on my way home from work or something, but I would visit once a week or so. I never told your mother because I knew she would lecture me about trying to let you go. It was her idea not to claim you in the first place. For some reason, it was a lot easier for her, but I just struggled. I didn't want to never see you again, but with the way you treated us, I suspected that if you ever woke up, you would never want anything to do with us anyway. I always thought you hated us, and I knew that even if I couldn't let go, you already had, and this way, you could start over, find some people you didn't hate so much. So, finally, I stopped visiting, but not before I asked one of your nurses for a favor."

"What favor?"

"I told her that if you ever did wake up, when you were healthy again, to send you to the Sister Alfreda Mission. I wanted to be sure that if you were going to start over again, that you were going to start over right, and in my mind, there was no one who could turn your life around like the ladies there. You're a better person for not staying here, in my opinion."

"Thanks, I guess." I was reminded of what Reece had just told me about being a different person. He was right; they both were. I seemed like I was a good person now, and I can't say I wouldn't have ended up in jail or dead if I had stayed with my parents.

He looked around the room and then stood up. "I'll leave you alone now," he said, walking to the door.

"I didn't hate you, you know," I called after him. "At least, I don't think I did. But I do see how you could have thought that."

"I know you don't want to think of yourself that way, but trust me, you did," he said, nonchalantly. "I've never seen fire like that in anyone's eyes."

He walked out, and I continued to lie there, staring ahead, thinking about what he said. I was starting to see his point, but I didn't want to let either of them off the hook that quickly. Reece slipped back in and sat right where my father had.

"Did you hear him?" I asked.

Reece nodded. "I saw that scar too."

"I feel bad, for what I put them through, but I'm still a little angry, I think. I mean, yes, I get it, I was a bad child, but I was still their child, you know? And you don't ever just abandon somebody. You don't do that. It's not right. They should have fought to help me. Families take work, and it's like they just gave up."

"Jackie?"

I lifted my head off the bed to see Maxine peering inside the room. She stepped in, followed by Archie, who had the box in his hand, and then by Eric.

"You want to see what's in these boxes?" she asked.

I shrugged, and then sat up, as she set the box on the bed. She pulled out a framed picture of Eric and I, which Eric said I used to keep on my desk. Then, she pulled out a shoebox of letters from Eric, telling me all about the police academy and all of his training. The next item was a baby photo album, cataloging my development all the way up until I was a teenager. We flipped through the album, marveling at how cute I looked in my first snowsuit, or Eric and I swimming in a mini pool in the front yard.

"Why didn't you tell me I was so bad?" I asked Eric.

He shrugged. "Mostly because I didn't know. You weren't like that until I left for the academy, and Mom and Dad never filled me in on any of that, unless it was a phone call, which they always made sound like you were just having a tantrum, like they had everything under control. I had no idea how things actually were.

"But when we were growing up, you were completely fine around me. It seemed like any time Mom got involved in anything, which was rare, or when Dad wanted to do stuff with me that you would throw a fit, but it was never as extreme as it was when I left."

The next week was rough. I spent my time re-reading my journals over and over, trying to familiarize myself with my life. Often, I would find myself zoning out, staring at my *Wizard of Oz* poster.

A visiting nurse came to check up on me every other day, and because she insisted I rest, I hardly left my bedroom, except to eat meals or use the bathroom. I could walk, but required assistance, so I spent most of my time in my bed, so as not to bother anyone for help. My father offered help, but I refused. My mother never did. She kept out of my way, which was what I wanted. Reece was constantly calming me down, but I couldn't seem to let my anger subside.

The police came to the house to conduct their questioning. They seemed rather disappointed when I couldn't answer most of their questions, but I showed them bits of my journal, to give them any information that they needed. I told them that I had apparently been involved with Razi years ago, but they didn't report me as being involved. I wondered if Eric may have had a hand in that, even though one officer told me that it was my cooperation that kept my record clean.

After two weeks of being cooped up in the house, I had to go back to the hospital for a check-up on my leg. The doctor said my thigh was starting to heal, and that I should make sure I visit a doctor when I went back to New York. As soon as that doctor gave me the go-ahead, I had Maxine on the phone making arrangements for us to go back home.

"We're gonna get going," Eric said, the next afternoon. My parents were in the living room. The TV was on, but they were both reading books. Eric's car was packed with all of our luggage and he was taking us to the airport.

My father stood up and walked us to the door. My mother then followed suit. "Are you sure you don't want us to come along and see you off?" she asked, making conversation. "It would be no trouble at all. I mean, we'd like to."

"No," I said gruffly. "There's not enough space in the car, and it would be pointless for you to drive by yourselves. It's alright."

"Well, would you like me to make you something to eat before you leave?"

"No." I watched her face sink with disappointment, but I didn't care. I may have lightened up on my anger of my father, but I couldn't let go of my hatred for her. It was, after all, her idea to leave me unconscious in the hospital, severing ties with me completely in a matter of seconds. Dad, at least, took a few months.

We piled into the car and headed for the airport. My mother yelled for us to call her when we made it home. I nodded, but I knew that I wasn't going to.

"Are you ready to go home?" Reece asked.

I looked out the window, staring at the house I had grown up in, realizing that the whole time I had been there, it never felt like it was truly my home; I wondered if it ever did. I looked at my parents, watching us drive away, and realizing that they may have the genetic distinction of being my parents, but I had a different set of parents, who loved me more and took better care of me, who took me in to their wonderful apartment and never gave up on me when I woke up without my memory. I glanced over at Archie, on the other side of Reece, and Maxine in the front seat. I couldn't see myself having any better parents than them. As for Reece, he was the goodness in my life. I needed him to keep me balanced. When he was near me, I could feel my aggression melting away. It was all those times when he wasn't around that I really scared myself. Now, there was no way I could ever be without him. And why would I want to? I remembered Tess calling him my other half, and he was.

He caught my glance and smiled, looking in my eyes. "Well? Can we go? Any other pit stops you'd like to make? Want to go to Canada for anything?"

I looked down at the cover of the journal I held, on which, during my captivity in my room, staring at my poster, I had scribbled, *There's no place like home.*

"No," I said, smiling back at him. "Let's go home."

EPILOGUE

"Are you ready for this?"

I opened my eyes, lifting my head from my chest, where it had been resting. My face looked directly into a mirror. I couldn't help but smile, looking at myself; I looked beautiful. Maxine had worked all kinds of magic on my make-up and hair.

I remembered how difficult I was earlier when she began making me up.

"Are you excited?" she had asked.

"Do you even have to ask? I think you know the answer to that."

"Everyone is going to be watching you. And everyone is here."

"I hope not everyone," I had replied, picturing the two people in particular that I wished not to be present.

"Well, not everyone. Your parents won't be here, because you didn't invite them," she said sternly.

"I don't want to share important events in my life with them, because they didn't want me in their lives. I'm giving them a taste of their own medicine," I retorted. My face started to redden.

"Ugh! Come on, Jackie, calm down. You're going to ruin your make-up."

"Okay, okay. I'm sorry."

I took a breath, and blinking back into the present, noticing Archie standing behind me, looking handsome in his crisp tuxedo. He rested his hands on the back of my chair and was also looking at me in the mirror.

"You look beautiful," he said. "Now are you ready for this?"

I attempted a laugh that I couldn't complete, as my lungs were being stifled in my corseted dress. "Ninties songs now?" I asked.

"One decade at a time," he said, winking.

It seemed like these days Archie was a completely different person. He seemed to have shaken that lyric compulsion. We never asked him why, but since he had never told anyone how it started, I had a feeling that he wouldn't have told us why he stopped. I even found his little note pad in the trash. Every once in a while, I would recognize a song, but I gave him credit, because sometimes, one can't help but quote Milli Vanilli.

I stood up from my chair and checked for wrinkles in my dress. Maxine was going to kill me if she saw any wrinkles, especially since she told me I wasn't allowed to sit down. She had been more starry-eyed at my dress than I was. She insisted that I keep it in her closet so that she could keep it safe. "It's not every day I get to put my hands on a Margot Brandisham couture wedding gown," she said.

The gown was a gift. Maxine practically lost her mind when I told her that because Margot Brandisham's pieces were highly sought after, and it was rare to find a couture piece that wasn't going to cost someone thousands of dollars, and here I had received one for free.

But it wasn't entirely free. I was still wanted at the boutique four days a week. Mrs. Brandisham was all too happy to have me back at the store, and she couldn't thank me enough for giving up my position and instead recommending Chrissy as a far superior salesgirl. "She's absolutely perfect," Mrs. Brandisham told me. "She can read the customers so well, and I'm really pleased with the success she's been having."

The dress came to me shortly thereafter as a thank-you, and also as an "I'm sorry I gave her your job." I wasn't upset; I was glad that Chrissy had the sales job, because she deserved it. Luckily, my healing leg kept me out of the basement, and Mrs. Brandisham put me at the front desk to greet customers and answer phones. She then summoned Portia to the basement to take over the inventory job. It just so happened that once my leg healed, however, Mrs. Brandisham kept me at the desk, citing that I was much friendlier than the previous receptionist.

I did a quick spin for Archie, and he smiled, giving me a thumbs up. Then, he held out his arm for me to take. "Your husband waits," he said. I took his arm, and slowly, he and I walked out of the dressing room.

At the end of the hallway, I could see the chapel. The stained-glass windows glowed, and the yellow lighting added warmth to the room. Archie and I stopped short of entering, waiting for our cue in the music. The grand piano in the front of the church quieted, as Maxine and Eric walked down the aisle and separated. Then, the piano went into the wedding march, and Archie and I began to walk.

One step at a time, trying to remember my pacing, I looked around at the decorations, trying to calm my nerves. Everyone was staring at me, and even though it was a small affair, I could only think that made it worse. Reece's boss, Mr. Thestas, and the guys from the Corner Nook sat in the very back, each one of them giving me a nod of respect, like I had earned their blessing to marry their Reece. Mr. Thestas even offered the café to us for a reception.

Carmelina was the next person I saw. Her hair was now a modest brown color, long and curly, and her clothes seemed entirely appropriate for the occasion. She had a healthy glow about her that I could only attribute to her recent renouncement of cigarettes. Next to her was Doctor Novak, who had the same smug look on her face as she did in all of our sessions. "It never changes," Reece told me. She was so proud of the progress I seemed to be making. Since returning home, I had only had two spells, and recently, I had been completely fine for the last four months. She reminded me that I could still forget at any time, but she also considered that I could finally be snapping out of it.

Then, I saw them. Sitting farthest away in the next to last pew, trying to seem unnoticed, were my parents. The constriction of my corset held in my sudden rush of anger at seeing them. I knew I didn't invite them, so someone else must have. I quickly shot Maxine a death stare that she blocked by pretending to itch her eye, so I sent it over to Eric, who looked down at his feet.

I looked over at the other side of the church. A couple girls from Brandisham's showed up: Tascha and Victoria. Tascha's eyes bulged when she saw Archie, and she promptly looked away. Mrs. Brandisham was there, proudly watching my dress, more so than me, which lightened my anxiety slightly. Chrissy sat next to her beaming at me. Kat Pendleton, who now relied on Chrissy for every clothing decision she ever made sat next to her, which surprised me that she would even come.

The next pew had Frances Holloway and Maxine's sister Penny, holding the hand of Mama Perlita, the three of whom had traveled to New York for the wedding, as did Tess. I sought her out back on the opposite side, sitting next to Reece's grandmother, who watched with a large smile across her face. I wondered if Eleanor knew what was going on, but then I heard her whisper to Tess, "That's my new granddaughter. She's marrying my grandson," and I couldn't help but grin.

I turned my attention to the front of the chapel, locking eyes with Reece, who pursed his lips to contain his smile. He blushed shyly, like he was seeing me for the very first time, but he never looked away. It was clear to see that his smile wasn't going to contain itself, and it canvassed his face.

Finally, Archie and I reached the altar where Reece stood, next to my former fiancé and newly ordained minister Aaron Bennett, who had a rivaling massive smile, waiting to conduct our ceremony. Archie hugged me, and then passed me over to Reece, who extended his freshly healed arm and took both of my hands tightly.

Aaron opened his Bible and began to speak, "Everything happens for a reason," he announced. "We don't always understand why things turn out the way they do, but eventually, it becomes abundantly clear what was and wasn't meant to be, and I know that the chance of Jackie and Reece finding each other happened for a reason. They were both two souls in need of something that was missing in their lives, and fortunately, they found it in each other: their missing pieces. And now, they are complete." He went through his Bible, reading a few scriptures before leading us into the traditional wedding vows. Reece repeated the words Aaron said, and even though I knew the vows by heart, as did everyone in the world, just hearing Reece say them gave me goose bumps, as I knew he really meant them. I hoped mine would sound the same to him.

"Reece, do you take Jackie to be your lawfully wedded wife?"

"I do," he replied, squeezing my hands, grinning.

"Jackie, do you take Reece to be your lawfully wedded husband?"

"I do," I answered, and for the first time since I could remember, there was no hesitation or confusion behind my voice. I meant every word I said.

"I now pronounce you husband and wife," Aaron announced, and before he could finish, Reece wrapped his arms around me and kissed me, to the clapping of our audience, and the cheering from his coworkers.

The café had been decorated again, in a scene that looked familiar to me. "It's the same as the night I proposed to you," Reece whispered, reading my mind. I closed my eyes, able to recall the images of that night, with the dancing and music. Now, it was exactly the same, with the addition of more people, and a cake.

The guys from the café served everyone grilled cheese sandwiches, at my request. Everybody laughed, at the meal, saying, "That's Jackie, for ya." We all ate, and then Reece and I went to cut the cake. As we stood there, holding the knife, a slight movement off to the side caught my eye, and I realized that my parents were here, too. Reece noticed my distraction, so he wrapped one hand around my waist and kissed my neck. The cake was cut, and everyone cheered.

The band playing in the corner had been, up until this point, playing festive, faster paced songs, but then, once the cake was cut, they slowed down.

"Dance with me," Reece said, with a sort of confidence that I didn't remember ever seeing in him before.

"What's with you?" I asked, amused.

"What?"

"You're swaggering."

"I know. I just feel amazing. You're officially my wife." I laughed and kissed him. He twirled me around a couple times and even dipped me. The room was watching the two of us, lost in each other. Normally, I would have felt uncomfortable with their stares, but Reece's coolness was wearing off on me.

I looked to Carmelina, who was sitting with Maxine, and motioned for them to join us on the floor. Slowly, our guests rose in couples and began to dance.

"Who invited my parents?" I asked, off topic.

"What?"

"Who invited them? Was it Maxine? Or Eric, was it Eric?"

"Jackie, why does it matter? Just be happy today, okay?"

"I am happy. I'm just curious."

"I did."

I could feel myself growing tense, and out of fear that I would raise my voice, in front of our friends, I whispered as quietly as possible, "Are you serious?"

Reece seemed unbothered in his newfound confidence. "Yes, because I wanted to make sure that our day was perfect, and I knew that if they weren't here, you would regret it someday."

"Why on Earth would I regret not having them here? I don't want them to be part of our lives."

"But they do. They honestly do. You can't deny that they are trying really hard to be involved in your life. I can tell they're truly sorry. Your dad, especially. He called me specifically and asked if he could come, if it was okay with you. He wants to be here. I'm not asking you to talk to them, I'm not asking you to look at them, I'm just asking that you allow them to be here and allow them to be happy for you, for us."

I looked away, at the corner table, where my parents sat, my father watching Reece and I with a look of pride on his face. "I don't mind that he's here, I suppose."

"I knew you wouldn't mind him, but you see, your parents are like a packaged deal, like you and I, so I couldn't say yes to your father and not your mother. For now, how about you set your feelings aside, and just be happy? This is our day, just you and me. Focus on me, and nobody else, alright?" He looked deep into my eyes and smiled. I took a moment, then returned a smile, and kissed him.

"Okay. You're right; it's just you and me. And I'm happy. I'm so happy." I rested my head on his shoulder, as our guests closed in around us. Focusing on us in this moment made me flutter with amazement. I thought of our life together with great hope, and how I was determined to never forget a single moment of that future.

www.ingramcontent.com/pod-product-compliance
Lightning Source LLC
LaVergne TN
LVHW041102080826
845145LV00007B/1660

* 9 7 8 0 9 8 9 0 1 5 3 0 1 *